I0397791

CHEAP LIVES

'Antony Sher's powerful third novel . . . A haunting examination of loneliness and isolation . . . The dark beauty of *Cheap Lives* stems not from its call to remember those who died in the struggle, but rather its reminder that there will always be people whose struggle is internal, lonely – and unwinnable' *Sunday Times*

'Forceful and inventive . . . Sher conducts a scalpel-sharp inquiry into the nature of fantasy, amorality and revenge' *The Times*

'Mesmerising . . . the writing is impressive, often alarming and always compassionate' *Daily Telegraph*

THE INDOOR BOY

'*The Indoor Boy* is an unqualified success. Antony Sher must now count as another of South Africa's splendid writers . . . His is a rude, original voice' *New York Times*

'Fresh, funny and memorable' *Independent*

'A tour de force' *The Times*

MIDDLEPOST

'A remarkable début . . . Clearly as much a born writer as a born actor' Francis King, *Spectator*

'Fearfully accomplished . . . peeling away skeins of history with blinding imaginative certainty' Adam Sweeting, *Guardian*

'Original and rumbustious . . . his depiction of the great grim comedy of South Africa then and now is brave and memorable' Christopher Hope, *Evening Standard*

Also by Antony Sher

FICTION
MIDDLEPOST
THE INDOOR BOY
CHEAP LIVES

NON-FICTION
YEAR OF THE KING:
An Actor's Diary and Sketchbook
CHARACTERS:
Paintings, Drawings and Sketches
WOZA SHAKESPEARE!
Titus Andronicus in South Africa
(Co-author Gregory Doran)

ANTONY SHER

the Feast

With six drawings by the author

LITTLE, BROWN AND COMPANY

A *Little, Brown* Book

First published in Great Britain in 1998 by
Little, Brown and Company

Copyright © text and drawings Antony Sher 1998

The moral right of the author has been asserted.

The author gratefully acknowledges permission to quote from
Let's Call The Whole Thing Off
Music and lyrics by George Gershwin and Ira Gershwin © 1936, 1937
(renewed 1963, 1964) George Gershwin Music and Ira Gershwin Music.
All rights administered by WB Music Corp.
All rights reserved. Reproduced by permission of IMP Ltd.

A CIP catalogue record for this book is
available from the British Library.

ISBN 0 316 64764 0

Typeset in Times by M Rules
Printed and bound in Great Britain by
Clays Ltd, St Ives plc

Little, Brown and Company (UK)
Brettenham House
Lancaster Place
London WC2E 7EN

For Mic

Acknowledgements

My special thanks to Alan Samson, who has been an inspiring editor, to Peter Cotton, the art director at Little, Brown, and to my research assistant, Sue Powell. Thanks also to Apollo Angugo, Peter Blake, Dr Kathy Powell, Victoria Willing, and the two people who read the early drafts of the book and helped shape its progress: my partner Greg Doran and my literary agent Mic Cheetham.

prologue

It begins. Darkness, then light, then the flesh of people. Just an ear at first, some scalp, a flat nose, the eyes still in shadow. Another head, a pair of shoulders, breasts bulging into the gleam, the curl of body hair, the fat of a thigh. Dozens of figures, scores, hundreds; as the light grows so does the crowd, as deep as it is wide, and as tall; the air is stacked with human beings, a wall of them, standing on each other's shoulders, on ladders and platforms, others lying on hammocks, some wound onto ropes, one or two upside down.

Her nostrils are taut. The smell of all their nakedness is spilling down towards her along with the smoke, which has started to travel along the floor, between legs, up over buttocks and backs, draping across one arm like a scarf.

Nothing in the child's life has prepared her for this. She checks briefly with the adults alongside, then twists to look behind. Her view is of steep steps, rolled-up sun umbrellas, sandalled feet, boulder knees and fists, big guts and busts, and, topping these, inquisitive faces all pointed the same way, line upon line of them. There are even more people here than in front! They're on gigantic slopes, each mass perched at a giddy angle, each like an avalanche waiting to happen.

A sound brings her round. Among the naked crowd, someone is playing a drum, softly, just using the heel of their hand on the skin. A few people shuffle their feet in rhythm, rustling with anklets of sea shells, others cut across it with gently clapping hands or clicking fingers. Some kneel in small circles, interlocking bare arms and necks, folding into shapes that remind the child of roses, pies and octopuses, and these groups add to the music with purrings and pantings, or weeping together. One gathering of children performs a tribal song about harvest time, while elsewhere a husky-voiced dame croons a popular tune, sweetly.

The picture is growing complete, a colossal square whose bottom edge is level with the child's eyes and whose other perimeters make her turn her head completely from left to right, or up, up, up; all of this space filling to the brim with music and light and bodies and smoke . . . The smoke is most mysterious, most lovely . . . It softens the people, turning a solid torso into nothingness, leaving a head floating on its own; it holds the light in tunnels, full of small clouds and ghosts; it carves the air into different planes and windows; it makes the girl think of shutters being opened in a dusty room, and of a painting she was once shown of heaven.

She's frowning now; the look comes from deep inside, the centre of her innocence, and it's a deadly serious. She doesn't understand how the whole thing can be so beautiful and yet frighten her (it's passing so quickly!), and she can't work out whether – despite the human smell, the heat of the lights, the draughts of air shifting the smoke – whether any of it is *real*.

A figure in the crowd whistles. Instantly, fifty drums join in, the humming voices burst into song, the shuffling feet kick and stamp as one, *bang!*, and the smoke turns red. The whole tremendous square turns red.

The child can't bear any more. Her frown vanishes, all resistance vanishes, she lurches to the edge of her seat and stretches out her arms, trying to touch, trying to work it out, trying at least to put the silhouette of her own hands into the picture.

The man next to her suddenly tenses. 'Oh shit,' he mutters.

It comes again. A particular sensation. He was hoping to avoid this, but no. After a little signal to the other adult in their party, the child's father, he slips from his seat and hurries, ducking, along the front row to a pass door on the right.

Beyond is a nocturnal labyrinth of passages and waiting areas, of cloth-and-plywood compartments for dressing or storage; a shadowy limbo-land of makeshift tunnels and tents. Its curtains, brickwork, air-ducts and pipes are all coloured black, its surfaces never swept or dusted, its gloomy routes defined by arrows on the floor, in white masking-tape, which also delineates sharp edges and steps. Sitting or standing around in the near-darkness, like figures hanging round a red-light district, is a team of bored but efficient workers: serious women with headphones and lists, hefty blokes waiting to carry, shift and hoist. As their boss hurries through, each makes room demon-stratively, flattening themselves against walls, pushing aside drapes for him, their own bodies held away, almost flinching from contact, giving him more space than he needs. Their fear, although routine, never fails to surprise him; to please and disgust in equal measures.

Through another door – thick and heavy as a bank vault – and into a narrow, half-lit stairwell. He climbs to the top with an angry puff and a suspicious upward squint; the numbers of floors seem to change with his temper these days. On each small landing, a wedge of sunlight hits him in the face. Despite the volumes of darkness downstairs, it's just gone ten in the morning.

Reaching his office, he lunges for the whisky in a way that he wouldn't want anyone to see. Except for a trickle, the bottle is empty. 'You cunt, you useless fuck!' he snarls, unsure whom he's abusing, yet unable to stop. He fetches a fresh bottle from the case under his sofa. The imported blend – his only luxury – comes with a cork, not a screw-top, wrapped in a red metallic seal that can't be torn without a blade, a coin, or fingernails less squeamish than his. He finds a fork under some papers and uses this.

At last he sucks on his bottle, shivering with a kind of rage. Pleasure burns through him at the same time. His mood flips over like a well-trained pet. He beams, his eyes brighten.

Bringing the child here today – her first-ever visit – was bound to delight him as much as her, but he wasn't expecting it to be so touch-ing. If he allowed himself tears, this could be the occasion. The way she held out her arms!

'. . . And the Lord God planted a garden eastward in Eden; and there He put the man whom He had formed'

– he hears over the tannoy, and winces. That's something which needs work: the narration. It's too bald, the phrases are too familiar.

He must instruct the KiSwahili speakers to half drown the English ones; that'll muddy it a little. The best works of art always have a few blurred edges, even a flaw or two. These make it more realistic. But when will he find the time to make all the necessary changes and improvements? The days are getting shorter and shorter, he muses, gazing at the bottle. He masturbates its neck slowly, thoughtfully, then slides it between his forearms and elbows, pinioning it, and drinks like this, imagining his hands are missing, enjoying the feeling.

'. . . and to the fowl of the air, and to every beast of the field.'

He stands, twirls the dial to *Off*, goes into the toilet adjoining his office and stands above the bowl, one arm against the wall. Closing his eyes, he tries not to inhale. There's no fascination left in the thick, dark, fitful stream. It's just hard to believe that anything from your-self can offend so fiercely. He finishes and pulls the flush, but it doesn't work. Again he tries and again it gives a dull splutter – as if in disgust, refusing to swallow. Growling with annoyance, he reaches for the lid of the cistern. He misses, sways. A pen slips out of his pocket and into the bowl beneath him, the unflushed bowl. He steadies him-self, mouth open in surprise. The pen is only a Bic ballpoint, but difficult to obtain in this part of the world. Can he bear to reach in and retrieve it? Unable to decide, he screams, 'You cunt!' and punches his face. The blow is shockingly hard. His fist is spotted with blood. He hates it when things like this happen – small accidents and violent rages – and they happen more and more. The thought of it makes him even angrier. 'Cunt, cunt, cunt!' he shrieks, flailing around in the air, reeling back into the office. He stops, eyes popping, teeth bared. It's a grimace of ultimate terror. Yet no one's here; there's no one to intimidate or subdue. Only himself. The stupidness of it overwhelms him, and he instantly calms, almost laughing.

The only sound in the room comes from a little plastic radio tuned to the Overseas Service. Always on, providing companionship, it never holds his attention. So he is back at the table and sucking on his bottle again before anything registers:

'. . . in a helicopter from one of the palaces, after his generals con-firmed they would not fight to protect him. It therefore appears that a bloodless takeover has been successfully achieved, and that the regime of the Emperor Duma has finally ended.'

The bottle slips from his grasp and hits the table with a bang that would shatter a lesser brand. He sits still. Several minutes pass. Then he leans forward, licks the little puddle of spilled whisky. He sits back. He puts his hand over his mouth.

It's over. We're rid of Duma. This is what it feels like.

He washes the blood off his face and knuckles, gargles with mouthwash, chews a clove as an added precaution, and then returns downstairs. Re-entering the blacked-out limbo-land of tents and tunnels, he heads for the light, among the naked crowd.

People at the back notice him and step aside. The word spreads, silence spreads.

Passing among them, thinking how to phrase the opening of his announcement, he catches their view, their performer's-eye view, of the great space ahead: a darkness full of faces, thousands upon thousands of foreheads and cheeks just catching a reflection of the stage light, which makes them gleam with a fleshy, secret eagerness. In the middle of the front row, he can just detect the small figure of the girl, still on the edge of her seat. He wonders how he strikes her. Is it the fact that he's clothed – in his customary, threadbare black suit – among all these naked people? Or is it his other darkness – his scowling gloom – is that still most distinctive?

He is sweating – the stuff is as pungent as his piss – the beads creep over him like insects.

Now he hears an extraordinary noise. It's coming from the onlookers. Cheering, whistling, ululating, heels hammering on wooden boards, all growing into a kind of thunder. They've just seen him. He blinks at them. He hasn't opened his mouth yet, hasn't started to tell them the news. This is for him – a roar of recognition, of welcome, of thanks.

He stands amazed. Behind the scenes, there is so much fear and hatred of him, yet here there is so much love. The people love him. He half bows, pleased that the girl is witnessing this, and lets it continue for a long time. Then he requests silence by raising his arms, and takes a deep breath.

The stance is heroic, but when he hears his voice it's tiny:

'Free. We're free.'

PART I

home

one

Home had a colour.

You expected it to have smells and noises of its own, a unique taste to the air, particular patterns of afternoon shade, all infused with that tender familiarity, but not a *colour* somehow. Grey-green. Fluid, intriguing, the colour of dreams and fevers, of humidity, of equatorial soft-land, it was full of light and moisture, so that instead of things looking dull, flattened by the half-tones, this part of Africa was possessed by a curious luminosity. You saw it everywhere, this radiant, wet green-greyness: in most skies, where the grey would burn to white, and the green hovered round the edge, freakish and stormy; in the jungle, where both colours rotted gloriously, rotted and ran and seeped into the leafy floor; in the monstrous heaps of bananas carried on people's heads or stacked in the markets – those distinctive grey-green bananas, black-bruised here, lime-bright there; on local television, whose poor equipment could only produce this peculiar hue, trapped somewhere between monochrome and colour; and on the surface of the land, its mud and dust, grasses and reeds, the cheap concrete of the pavements, the erupting, lava-like tarmac of the roads, or of the airport runway, where Felix's face was presently squashed.

His return was not meant to have started like this, with a stumble down the aircraft steps and home rushing up to hit him in the face. He had something altogether nobler planned. But, never mind, it had happened, he must accept it, he was powerless to do anything else.

'Sozzled,' a voice above him said. 'I know this fellow. He's sozzled. You're sozzled, aren't you?'

A glimpse of open sandals, mustard brown feet, red toe-varnish, and then the hem of a turquoise wraparound swept over his shoulder and disappeared.

Other legs wanted to get past. Attempting to rise, Felix realised that the hot runway was slightly pliant, slightly melted – *already, at this hour of the morning?* – and it held on to his nose for an instant, like a sloppy kiss. Welcome home, home was saying in its own way, welcome home. Smiling mawkishly, Felix struggled to his feet, and slowly, swayingly, trailed after the line of passengers who looked faraway and tiny.

He made it into the Customs area – a low, hot room – and to the back of the Domicile queue, before his balance gave way again. He was forced to perch on his hand-luggage: an old leather briefcase solidified with books and belts.

At first, as the queue inched forward, he rose and sat each time, rose and sat, but eventually gave up and just dragged himself and the briefcase along in a squatting waddle. He was aware that he must look like an infant playing on its potty, and that he was crashing into people's ankles and calves, but when they glared down at him, he could only grin back woozily.

The woman in the turquoise wraparound was staring at him. That face . . . that lemur face, the wide eyes behind flyaway specs, the small mouth under a light moustache . . . where did he know it from?

His gaze drifted to the Customs desks where the procedure was exceptionally slow. It wasn't the examination of passports, visas and health certificates which was so time-consuming but the payment system: the slipping of ready cash, preferably American dollars or German marks, to your Customs official; a little sleight-of-hand, an Open Sesame, without which you couldn't enter the country. Newcomers were confused, regular visitors were incredulous at how much the rate had escalated under the new regime, and nationals always saw it as a matter of pride to barter.

Hypnotised by the chaos, Felix nodded off, and when he woke

the Customs area was empty, except for a cluster of three faces peering down at him.

'Hey, ol' buddy, look at you,' said one of them. 'Just take a look at you!'

It was Charlie . . . Charlie, having found his way from the other side of Customs where he'd been waiting to meet him . . . Charlie with his driver-bodyguard Noah, who was armed with a polished black AK47. The third man was an airport official.

'Oh, sorry,' Felix mumbled, as he was helped to his feet. 'Sorry, I must've . . .'

'It's OK, OK,' said Charlie, hugging and kissing him. 'How're you doing, buddy?'

Felix tried to formulate an answer. This was difficult, so he just sobbed happily on Charlie's shoulder.

The other men looked away, but Charlie was unembarrassed, and held Felix's hand as they went through Customs (Noah palming dollar bills in every direction), and to the baggage carousel, which was only now disgorging the luggage from the New York flight. Collecting his, they proceeded into the arrivals hall, where the rest of the passengers were being greeted by family, friends and bodyguards, while beggars, pickpockets, kidnappers, and other predators milled around the half-constructed building known as the New International Airport.

Outside, the mass of beggars thickened and heaved, stew-like, with loose bones, popping eyes, flies, babble. Noah was normally an affable man, short and round, but now he raised his AK47 and aimed its butt at the starving figures, using it as prodder, then club – at one point even releasing the safety-catch – while expertly moving his charges forward all the time.

As they struggled to weave through not only crowds but clusters of makeshift shelters, Felix realised that, during the five months of his absence, a new *mki-mbizi* camp had sprung up right there, in the air-port car-park: refugees from neighbouring states that were war-torn, famine-racked, dictator-ruled, or all three.

Early-morning mist from the marsh-lands surrounding Lake Tidhamulala still trailed along the ground, mixing all the surround-ing images – the smoky, plasticky zones of tents and cooking fires, the gleaming rows of glamorous jeeps and German limousines – softening, beautifying everything, and adding to Felix's sense that home, with its grey-green colour, its complexion of dreams, fevers and swamps . . . home was a place of shifting wonders.

He went on all fours to kiss it again – without quite meaning to – his ankles giving way as they reached Charlie's silver Land Cruiser.

'Sozzled – it's disgusting!'

That voice. Lifting his nose from the dust, Felix saw painted toe-nails in open sandals. The woman in the turquoise wraparound. Charlie's jeep was next to her Mercedes.

'It's a disgrace,' she said to Charlie, whom she seemed to know. 'The fact is, he's sozzled. Isn't he?'

'No,' said Felix, summoning all his strength to stand and face her. 'The fact is more shocking. He's *sober*!'

Apart from the growing refugee problem, the *mki-mbizis*, Liberation had been a great success – right from its spectacular and bloodless start, almost a year ago now. Emperor Duma had been caught off-guard by a host of surprises: rebel forces were pouring into the country over the border and from the sea, and his own generals were refusing to fight and protect him. They'd had enough. Their allegiance had been transferred to the rebel leader, John C. Guwedekko, 'Africa's Guevara', as the overseas papers dubbed him, 'Charismatic, bright, and remarkably young.' Guwedekko had abandoned his training in African Studies at a British university to return home and liberate it.

Felix remembered the day itself well – it halted a preview perfor-mance of his new show at the theatre, one of his biblical epics – but little beyond.

As he'd found before at times of licensed abandonment, at Christmas and New Year, for instance, it was difficult to accelerate his drinking to join in with public festivities. He tried though, gamely, valiantly, and the next few months went missing. The solid world ceased to be. Time itself became a liquid thing, sodden, pissed, wet through. And then suddenly it cleared, and steadied itself again. He woke up, not on a strange floor, roadside or beach but in a police station, surrounded by an emergency medical team, and Charlie . . . Charlie leaning forward to gently break the news: 'Buddy, we're gonna have to do something about this.'

Felix just managed to say, '*We?*' and see Charlie laugh, before passing out again.

Kept buoyant by Charlie's humour and encouragement, and especially his credit cards, Felix boarded a plane, flew to New York, and checked himself into a private psychiatric hospital. A discreet building in the Hamptons, Long Island, the Horace Spencer Clinic specialised in three illnesses, dividing them floor by floor: eating disorders on the first, depressive illnesses on the second, and substance abuse on the third. Felix occupied Suite 318. To everyone's surprise, his own included, he took to the recovery programme with the same pleasure, commitment and inventiveness that he had lavished on his drinking. He spent twenty-one weeks there and was so enchanted by the safety of the place he would have stayed for ever if Charlie hadn't suddenly phoned two days ago, summoning him home.

An emergency . . . wasn't that it? Some emergency at the theatre? He couldn't recall. Never mind, it would be revealed in time.

'So!' Charlie exclaimed now, his fingers still intertwined with Felix's, as Noah steered the Land Cruiser out of the airport compound and across a wasteland of shrub-lined soda pans.

'So!' Felix echoed vaguely. He felt drowsy again. He was sleepwalking through life these days. His vision, his balance, everything swayed soothingly. Was it the anti-depressants, or just the strange, exhausting clarity of his new existence, in what he called 'the dry world'? And now he had jet-lag too. Resting his head on the window, he watched pedestrians float out of the mist, each with a burden on their head, firewood or plastic jerry-cans of water, the tendons tight in their strong necks.

'So,' Charlie said. 'How does it feel, ol' bud?'

'Hmn?' went Felix. As before, he felt flummoxed by the question. 'Alys . . . how's Alys?'

'Great, she's great, can't wait to see you, talks about nothing else, if the airport wasn't so, y'know, *dangerous*, these days, I'd've brought . . .'

'Yes, yes, 'f course,' mumbled Felix, trying to sound indifferent.

He'd passionately wanted Charlie's five-year-old daughter to be there, waiting for him . . . Alys, his godchild, the dearest thing in his life . . . never mind, he'd see her soon.

'But what about *you*?' Charlie persisted. 'How does it feel ol' bud?'

'Precisely that,' Felix answered slowly.

'What?'

'It *feels*.'

'Huhn?' Charlie laughed. 'What does?'

Felix opened his mouth, closed it, wet his lips, then sighed. He wanted to say: *It's like I've lost a layer of skin. Everything is very tender. In both senses of the word. Sweet and sore. That's how it feels. Everything is sweet, everything is sore.* But it was so, so difficult to translate that into spoken words. He heard himself too clearly. It was like listening to a recording of his voice. And what a bizarre instrument this was! Plummy and clipped, haw-hawing and tut-tut-ting, *received pronunciation* wasn't the phrase for it. He had received pronunciations from Pathé newsreels and Ealing comedy films, from Overseas Service transmissions of *The Goon Show* and *Round the Horne*. He said golly and gosh, spiffing and top-hole. And then there were the elocution lessons when he was a child, with the for-midable Miss Rosewood, who encouraged him to lose all trace of Jewishness in his voice – the see-sawing, maybe-schmaybe signature tune of his ancestors – and instead taught him to say *ek-tu-welly* for actually, and other tongue-twisting frills. And finally there was the drama training in London, sprinkling his speech with words like 'tis and anon. All of which went unnoticed in this part of Africa where Felix's group expressed themselves in an elaborate variety of foreign accents and languages: British, Asian, Portuguese, German, French. Known originally as the expats or non-blacks, the tiny community had officially been dubbed non-Africans by Duma, and this was shortened to *non-Afs*. Like others, Felix resented the word at first. It had a negative, impermanent ring, and was frankly inaccurate, for he had been born here, he was one hundred per cent kosher African. Nevertheless the term had stuck.

Now, however, hearing himself as if for the first time, Felix was shocked. A colonial ape is what he sounded like, and non-Af seemed a fair description. It was a jolting revelation – yet these were occurring daily now. The dry world was full of echoes and mirrors. You couldn't escape yourself. You were there, crystal clear and in close-up. Every tic and gesture, the way you ate, the way you sat, the way you moved. The feeling wasn't always unpleasant; it just made talking and walking difficult.

Charlie pressed on: 'I've spoken to your specialist at the clinic, and your counsellor, and they were a little stressed about you missing out on their – what do they call it? – *aftercare* service. They wanted to know if we had the AA here.' He grinned. 'I said, not even for motor-cars. So they asked where the nearest meeting might be. I said, "Half a continent away, north to Cairo, south to Johannesburg. Dunno, maybe there's something closer, maybe Nairobi . . ."'

Felix cut in, 'Listen, old boy, I'm going to get through this!' He spoke with such intensity that it silenced them both. Staring ahead, Felix noticed a pair of pedestrians on the road, distinctive because they were white-skinned and completely naked: a boy on crutches and an old legless man, travelling on his fists with a fast, ape-like swagger. Felix swivelled round to see the pair more clearly. But they were gone, engulfed in a mixture of mist and dust from the road.

Charlie was grinning at him again. 'Anyway, your people were relieved to hear that, y'know, at least I'll be here for you.'

Felix smiled drowsily, but with politeness, as he might to a *Charlie* kindly stranger. The man sitting next to him was exceptionally handsome, a Jew with white-blond hair; looks that someone in his circle once described as having been blessed by both God and the sun. Another said in that case God was Marilyn Monroe – for the blessing had been left on Charlie's neck in the shape of a pouting, lipstick-coloured birthmark; a divine lovebite. Despite his forty-six years, and despite his cynicism about gyms and jogging, and despite indulging in every excess known to man and medicine, Charlie's body was in perfect shape. He was also fabulously rich, the family having made their fortune decades earlier in the copper mines of the Belgian Congo. Charlie was so opposite to Felix – *Felix* with his frayed, dark clothes, his heavy-browed, black-bearded look – and so symbolic of everything Felix envied and despised,

that he would have dropped him as a friend years ago if it wasn't
for a dominant and charming oddity in Charlie's character. A
touch of the hippie. An aura of the sixties hung round him like his
glowing shoulder-length locks; actually worn with flowers while he
was a medical student at UCLA, the American university. Charlie
retained a shy laugh from those days, a Californian drawl – intro-
ducing a new accent to the non-Af community – and the way in
which he made himself *available* to you, to your changing moods
and needs, always keeping his own out of the picture. He showered
friends with everything he had: his wealth, his love, his professional
services.

The latter were, in fact, only accessible to his circle, and he made
no charges for them. He was the most private of doctors. He only
continued to work at all, he explained, because of a flaw in his personality – perhaps the only one – boredom. His own life bored him.
And despite his popularity, his looks, his wealth, his famous wild
parties, the physician couldn't find a way of curing himself, of
easing this small, constant pain, of filling the emptiness.

'. . . Everyone's been hooked on it. It's been like watching the
Roman Games.'

Felix blinked. Charlie was talking. Describing the major event
during his absence – the Hakika. Like others before them, in Chile,
Argentina, Uganda, South Africa, the new regime had invited the
old one to confess its sins and be pardoned at a public forum, tele-
vised nightly. This national catharsis was known by the KiSwahili
word for fact or truth – *hakika*.

'. . . But the amnesty finishes tomorrow, at midnight,' Charlie
continued. 'So then the fun ends. Or starts. Those who haven't come
forward will be rounded up, arrested, tried, God knows what.
Lynch mobs, public stonings? There's even talk of *crucifixions*!' He
laughed grimly. 'So anyway, buddy – welcome home!'

The jeep was circling Lake Tidhamulala. Giraffe, pelicans and
flamingo had gathered along the shoreline to feed and drink. With
their assortment of mismatched body parts – necks too long or too
short, a giant beak on one, a tiny face on another – they struck Felix
as very odd indeed, wonderland-creatures. What joking genius had
made them up? What planet were they from? The white of the birds

showed against a vast hole of blue sky, where the mist was burning
away, swirling outwards in great pale hoops. It would go soon, the
blueness, giving way to a more familiar greenish-grey sheen, that
bucket of moisture always hanging over the land.

Like an infant in its cradle or an old man in a rocking-chair,
Felix felt lulled by the motion of the jeep as Noah skilfully negotiated the broken roads of home . . . up and down they went, up and
down . . . and now sleep was coming . . . the moment of starting to
talk gibberish to yourself, of dwelling on beautiful nonsense, of
becoming easy in a world of giraffes, pelicans and flamingos . . .

Charlie was talking again: 'Anything you want, buddy? Anything
you need? For home.'

Felix opened one eye. The darkness of buildings, their shoulders
against the sky; sweaty concrete blocks and flaky colonial fronts, the
pavements collapsed into tracts of rubble, everything varnished by
an oily brew from exhaust fumes and kerosene smoke, the roadsides
boiling with dust-clouds, the silhouettes of traders and street-
dwellers, dogs and chickens, a goat on a string. Struggling to wake
fully, he answered Charlie: 'Ice-cream. Eat quite a lot of ice-cream
now.'

Charlie registered surprise, and then said, 'Any favourite brand?'

'Ben and Jerry's. American make. Served it at the clinic. But . . .
doubt if we'll find any here.'

'Ben and Jerry's,' Charlie repeated to Noah, who began to look
worried. 'And what about the flavour, buddy, any particular
flavour?'

'Oh, rather!' replied Felix, with the finickity tone of one who
had few remaining pleasures. 'Chocolate Chip Cookie Dough.'

'One tub of Ben and Jerry's Chocolate Chip Cookie Dough ice-
cream, please,' Charlie said to Noah, who swore quietly, before
turning down a side-street.

The daylight dimmed. They were near the harbour. Dark
awnings, rusting iron balconies, rickety bridges above the road,
blue-painted mud walls crumbling in the salt air. Noah stopped the
Land Cruiser at a corner and, shifting his rifle closer, lowered the
window. The car filled with the smells from a fish smokery nearby,
and from the ocean, the Indian Ocean, somewhere beyond, just out

of view, its presence invisible yet huge, like a god's. Felix gasped
with pleasure.

A figure darted from the doorway of an abandoned shop. Small,
dirty, wearing only Adidas shorts and a pair of Ray-Ban shades, it
was a boy, aged about ten.

He was one of a new breed of street children, who arrived with
the army of liberation. John C. Guwedekko had enlisted soldiers as
young as five; puffy-eyed dwarfs struggling under the weight of
automatic weapons, carrying them on their small shoulders like
crosses. These young saviours had at first been welcomed by the city,
but now it afforded them a more fearful respect. They ruled over a
complicated and powerful sub-culture – the *magendo* – the contraband market, never called black in this part of the world.

Noah reached through the window, directing one open palm
towards the little dealer, slapped five with him, and then placed an
order, speaking in patois. Felix couldn't understand a word, but he
saw the expression change behind the Ray-Ban shades – a fly crawling under the lens sprang away – and then the boy scurried back to
a group in the doorway. A fatter ten-year-old, wearing curiously
dated clothes, floral shirt and loons, and smoking *bangi* from a
carved pipe, did most of the speaking. He was probably the head-
man, the local baron, a pimp too, perhaps; he was surrounded by
child prostitutes of both sexes who wiggled and waved at the Land
Cruiser, tongues and fingers flickering. One older girl, aged about
twelve, was suckling a newborn infant.

'You're testing their ingenuity,' said Charlie with a chuckle, as he
observed the animated discussion in the doorway. 'I mean, if you'd
asked for Häagen Dazs it would've been tough enough, but . . .' He
hesitated as the first boy left the group and sped off down an alley.
'But we'll see, we'll see.'

They waited. A new customer arrived in the doorway, a middle-
aged Asian woman in a purple-and-white sari. A deal was
negotiated in the most precious of underground commodities:
drugs. Not the recreational kind – these had been decriminalised by
John C. Guwedekko and were freely available – but antibiotics,
quinine, dysentery tablets. The boy-baron produced a long foil strip
of red capsules and cut off a piece. Although the woman seemed to

part with a fortune, she looked pleased with the deal.

'They're ripping her off,' observed Charlie, his tone compassionate but weary. 'Bet there's just palm-oil in those capsules –' He interrupted himself to give a cheer, for the boy in Ray-Ban shades was racing back to the Land Cruiser, a newly chopped block of ice held high in one hand. As it came closer, Felix could see that trapped inside the block – its dark and sinful colours blurred frostily, attractively, as in an advert – was a Ben and Jerry's quart tub of ice-cream, Chocolate Chip Cookie Dough flavour.

'Attaboy!' laughed Charlie.

A quick bartering joust now took place between the boy and Noah, then a roll of bills changed hands, and the block of ice was passed back to Felix. He was careful how he handled it. Having made a mental note of where the boy's grip had been, he allowed that section to melt first, dripping into the rubber mats at his feet. He feared that his immunity to the everyday germs of home might have been weakened by his five-month absence.

The block of ice was still relatively intact by the time they reached their destination: a side-street with a long, high wall. Here, set among governmental fly-posters, police 'Wanted' notices, graffiti in different languages, patches of mud and mould, was a small box sign, its iron letters caging a long-dead bulb: *Stage Door*.

In previous centuries, Felix's homeland had been ruled by many masters: Arab and Indian traders, Portuguese seafarers and the German East Africa Company. Whilst a German Protectorate, it gained an opera house – Der Hatzfeldt Oper – erected by a rich Nuremberg family as a massive and ornate monument to themselves. Following the First World War, when the country was divided like a cake between Portugal, Belgium and Britain, with the latter securing the prize slice, then Der Hatzfeldt Oper became the Alexandra Theatre. And even after independence, and Duma's takeover, when the building was officially renamed the State Theatre, everyone still called it the Alex. In apricot and cream colours, with high-flying gables, stained-glass windows, and a marble frieze of the Muses, the playhouse towered above its neighbours – a church, a mosque, a tin-roofed school – looking both magnificent and battered, defiant and lonely; a spaceship that had got lost.

Felix was artistic director of the Alex, and it was his sole address these days. Earlier in the year, during the <u>new government's Wealth Redistribution Campaign,</u> he had moved into the theatre, along with all his actors and technical staff, everyone converting their dressing-rooms, workshops and offices into little apartments.

As Felix collected his belongings, Charlie said, 'Woah, woah, we'll take all this up for you. You just take it easy, sonny boy . . .'

'No,' said Felix. 'I'd like to go up solus. Be fine, be fine.'

Charlie surrendered without argument. 'OK, cool, we'll leave you be, give you some space. See you at the board meeting tomorrow.'

'At the wha'?'

'The board meeting.' Charlie stared at his friend, frowning. 'The reason you've come back.'

'Board meeting?' Felix repeated sluggishly. 'Oh, gosh, did I know 'bout tha'?'

Charlie laughed. 'We talked about it on the phone several times – even yesterday – before you left Long Island.'

That was it – the emergency Felix couldn't remember: Charlie ringing, as one of the theatre trustees, a day or two ago, saying there was a problem, saying that there were ominous noises coming from some of the board members, concerning the future of the place, and that the chairman had called an urgent meeting.

''f course,' Felix mumbled now. 'Tomorrow, see you then, thanks awfully for the . . .' Aware of Charlie and Noah watching anxiously, he tottered away from the jeep, laden with belongings, the dripping ice chunk held in one outstretched hand.

Unlocking the stage door, and then closing himself into the huge, cool shadow of the interior, the sensation was of entering a tenement block. He could hear distant noises – a row, chickens, someone practising the drums – and smelled cooking, garbage, urine. The mixture was sweetish. Home.

No one was visible though. No welcoming party.

Chuckling to himself – that he should even imagine such a thing! – he let himself through the special door, thick as a bank vault, and into his own private stairwell. Now began the long, slow ascent. He rested between every step, and sometimes climbed in a sitting position, lifting himself and his luggage along.

It's like I'm injured, he thought happily. It reminded him of childhood illnesses and accidents; those peaceful times when you were excused from duty, let off, absolved, freed.

Some kind of vine or weed had taken root on the stairs during his absence, and seemed to mock him, having progressed so much faster and more effortlessly than he could manage. Perhaps it was a variety of the pyjama lily, which you saw growing wild in ditches, for here and there it sprouted similar pink-striped flowers. It gave off a hot, mildewy scent. Midges clustered over the moister twists, and on one landing, where the window-pane was broken, a pale butterfly or moth was perched, slantingly, on a new shoot.

The ice chunk had melted completely by the time Felix finally reached his room. Dropping all his luggage, he cleaned the Ben and Jerry's tub with a traveller's wipe from the airline toilet bag, and then tucked into the ice-cream. Breathing noisily, greedily – '*Mng, mng!*' – he gorged on the taste. Oh, that thick wet sweetness, lingering after every swallow, tickling and tempting, *more*, it said, *more, more*. In under a minute the container was empty. Panting, he looked round.

Here he was. At home. In the room, his room. It wasn't as bad as he feared. He expected it to be packed with ghosts, mad ghosts – calling themselves cunt, cunt, cunt, punching their own faces – a weekend's worth of them, weekend after weekend, grown into an asylum-full. But they were nowhere to be seen, these ghosts; not yet anyway. Even so, there was, in the airless, sealed, shadowy room, with its closed shutters and untouched collection of possessions, a sense of death, his death.

But he wasn't dead. The battle to conquer what at the clinic they called his disease, this had left him enfeebled, certainly, but very much alive. More than alive. Smiling, he spoke aloud that curious Christian word: 'Resurrection.'

There had been much quasi-religious talk in the clinic, talk about surrendering to a Greater Power. When challenged by atheists, the experts said you could make the Greater Power whatever you liked, God, Nature, Art, anything that helped you shift the universe off your shoulders and embrace your powerlessness. In frisky mood – this was in the early days of his stay – Felix had declared, 'I'm a non-practising, non-believing Jew, a non-Jew in a way, like back at home I'm a non-African, but as I recall there's an old Yiddish saying about this powerlessness-lark – "Man plans and God laughs" – and, all right, even if true, isn't it a trifle dangerous to make that the rule of thumb? To open one's arms to it? I mean, what if it turns out to be a dark force, *my* Greater Power? What if, now that I'm open for colonisation, an unholy ruler comes visiting? What if you're setting me up for an appointment with Old Nick himself?'

Nobody knew what he was talking about. That night they increased his medication.

Felix laughed aloud now. Such stupid thoughts he'd had in Long Island. Here he was in his room, his ghost-free room, utterly safe.

He moved to the windows, shuffling like an old man, and released the catches on the wooden jalousie shutters. With their slatted wings fluttering and clicking, they had a looseness, parting almost like cloth, like curtains. He caught his first glimpse of a familiar view – the tall palm tree and sky beyond – and then his trembling fingers opened the windows. The light and air touched his face, and he breathed so deeply, so giddily, he almost toppled over.

Without removing his clothes or even shoes, he crept into bed. This was a raffia mat spread under his big table, his work desk, with a mosquito net hanging from the rim, creating a sort of tent, a childhood hiding-place, a sleep-haven.

He sensed it coming . . . the delicious sensation . . . the smooth, light slippiness, the front of his face turning to milk . . . He saw an infant suckling the breast of a child-mother, a lake with flamingos, pelicans and giraffes, and a crippled couple on the road, a boy and an old man, travelling together through a greenish-grey mist . . . the colour of home, of dreams.

two

The devil was here. In the room. In a small cage.   *Duma*

Felix watched, drowsy but transfixed.

With weird slowness – so slow that its flesh juddered with each exertion – the devil stormed to the front of the cage, which was curved glass, and pressed into it, threatening to break through, snarling and roaring, all soundlessly.

The head was dominated by brows and muzzle, a mass of hardness, of bone – bunched bone, toothed bone – the large, discoloured eyes bulging to the sides.

It was a cow-like shape, a bull, a buffalo . . .

The Buffalo; this had been one of the devil's official titles, Felix now remembered.

His Most Excellent and Revered Presence, the Strong One, the Buffalo, the Big Man, the Life President, the Supreme Commander of Land, Air and Sea Forces, the Might of the Nation, the Scourge of All Africa, His Royal Highness the Emperor Duma.

As though giving a salute, Felix's trembling hand stretched towards Duma's face behind the glass, and then, rearranging his fingers around the remote control, he restored the picture to normal speed and volume.

The video was a collection of documentary material covering Duma's regime, a kind of scrapbook that Felix had assembled over the years. It was mostly news bulletins, both local and CNN, including some offcuts (material too gruesome to broadcast) which he'd bought on the _magendo_ market. It also featured his own home movies . . . like this sequence now, a young woman being tied to the traffic lights in front of the theatre and executed. Damaged by the bullets, the lights show green, orange and red simultaneously, a go-wait-stop signal congealing above her head, which is in a white sack. Her body, restrained by the ropes, bows forward gracefully, concealing the wounds; the only visible spillage being three almost pretty rivulets of urine down one bare leg.

Watching between his fingers, Felix shivered with shame. Shame that he had videoed the execution, shame that he was watching it now – he often ran this sequence – and shame that he wasn't doing what he should be doing: preparing for the board meeting in half an hour's time.

Yet this _was_ preparation, in a way.

During the twenty-four hours since his return, in between bouts of euphoric sleep and strange wakefulness, when things were so clear they loomed at him madly, in between all this, he had convinced himself that there was no reason to worry about the board meeting. It was just to map out the next season – presumably. The theatre had been dark for months now. The trustees were fully entitled to ask, What next?

So – was Dictatorship the answer? As a theme for a new show.

'_You_,' Duma said suddenly from the television screen, 'I am hereby, herewith, in person, informing _you_ of an important new development affecting national security . . .'

The video was showing examples of Duma's surprise appearances on the airwaves. Inspired by a saying in his village of birth, where they called the wireless _the one who can roam where he likes_, Duma had built radio transmitters and television studios into all his residences, even some of his vehicles, and was able to interrupt scheduled programmes whenever he chose. This might be to announce that it was now illegal to touch a soldier, or to support the rival side when the army football team was playing, or to mention the ruler without using his full ten-part title. For a few months, after one of Duma's senior wives fled the country, it was even illegal to _laugh_ in public. During some periods – whenever there was unrest among students or the intelligentsia – it was forbidden to wear spectacles. And then there were the laws aimed at those tribes which were the traditional enemies of Duma's own. Or people of mixed race, whom he called 'mongrels'. Or the witch-hunt of twins – only animals bred in duplicate! – and so on and so forth, they were never-ending, the Commandments of Emperor Duma. Bodies filled the television screen now; bodies dumped on road-sides, bodies in rivers, flowing over a waterfall, one stuck like a log.

Only one group was safe from persecution. The non-Afs. When he seized power in the early sixties, Duma – then Sub-lieutenant Cecil Mshangama Duma of the King's African Rifles – amazed everyone by encouraging the small community of non-Africans to stay, those of Asian or European origin; the owners of the country's rich cobalt mines, the barons of the cotton and sisal plantations, the fishing and shipping magnates, the merchants, medical specialists and uni-versity lecturers. Overcoming his contempt for the group (in private he called them 'our tourists'), the dictator achieved one of his mas-terstrokes: great stores of wealth and expertise remained within the country. In return, the non-Afs were offered one of the most privi-leged lifestyles in Africa, as well as the security of a police state.

Those with pricking consciences had two choices: either to pack up and leave or to devise ways of fighting the system.

Felix's way was to transform the Alex into a venue for popular culture, for film shows, jazz nights, storytelling marathons, the song theatre of the Tege people, Kangi drumming, educational shows using Humhum puppets. And once or twice a year he mounted stage versions of the Old and New Testaments, the *Ramayana*, Homer's duo, and mankind's other great stories. Choosing these enabled Felix to keep one step ahead of Duma's censor. Known as the Public Information Office, it was there to supervise the newspa-pers, radio and television, to select school, university and library books. Nobody took plays seriously – they were done so rarely – but Felix was nevertheless required to submit the material personally each time he wanted to do a show. Being able to plonk down a copy of the Bible or *The Iliad* always allayed suspicion, and Felix was then free to do his own semi-improvised adaptations, incorpo-rating local legends about creation and catastrophe, and using local music, rituals and citizens – hundreds of citizens – making up a

mighty Chorus alongside a handful of professional actors. Within
the Alex the feeling was exhilarating; people felt they were participating in a small act of subversion, of protest against Duma's
regime. Despite a reputation for tyranny himself, terrorising all
those who worked for him, Felix was given the street-title, *sungura*:
the rabbit, the true king of the jungle, in Swahili mythology, the
king of wit and slyness, the one who builds his house with two exits.

But now, with Duma gone, fled into exile (no one knew where),
Felix could be less oblique. Now he could do a show about what
had really happened in this country. Now he could put the great dictator himself on stage.

From the television screen, Duma smiled at Felix.

Aware of a peculiar flutter going through him, Felix smiled back.
His old instincts were returning. He had feared that his creative
juices might dry up along with his liver. Analytical and cautious by
nature, he'd always wondered if alcohol provided the danger and
spontaneity in his work. But no, his imagination was still in working order. Images were coming to mind – you could stage the
traffic-island execution, you could have a waterfall of corpses, like
the wall of naked bodies in the Creation – and there was the perfect
actor to play Duma.

On the screen, Duma stopped smiling, and lifted his chin, suspiciously.

Elated, blushing slightly, as if they really were together in the same
room, Felix reached across to a sweet box. It was giant-sized, with a
torn seal, *J.F.K. Duty-Free Gifts*. Slipping his fingers under the lid, he
helped himself to three chocolate-covered peanuts, then five more,
then just another two, and then, with a little whispered cry of 'Stop
it!', he withdrew his hand and sucked his thumb instead.

Better get ready for the meeting, he thought. He started to rise.
But the video was like the peanuts: you wanted just a little more.

'I dream the truth!' Duma bellowed in the film. 'I dream, I know!'

This was it, the famous speech. Circled by the thin moustache
and beard, Duma's great mouth was angled to one side, as if seeking a greater chomp at the words. 'I dreamed I would be an Army
commander and it was so. I dreamed I would be head of state and
this came to be. I have dreamed I will be the first Leader of the

United States of Africa, and this will surely come to pass. Nothing can alter my path. For I have dreamed when people are planning to kill me and thus all attempts have failed. I know how I will die, where and when, what time exactly, all this I have dreamed and I know. I dream the truth, I know everything . . .'

'Oh, really?' Felix scoffed at the screen. 'Did you know you were going to be deposed then, and flee?'

'I know everything,' Duma said, as though in reply. 'What will happen to this land and to me. For we are as one. I am Africa and Africa is me!'

Reaching for the remote control, Felix was aware of a little flutter in his depths again, a feeling of mystery, sinister mystery; a kind of dread, a kind of eagerness.

He glanced over his shoulder. This was silly. No one was there. Yet his heart was thudding. There was a palpable sense of some presence in the room . . . No, not *some* presence . . . His Majesty's.

Felix turned back to the screen.

Duma's face was frozen there, mouth half open, as if reaching for a small bite or kiss, his eyes in mid-blink, peeking out from under their fleshy lids, fixed on Felix.

Felix pressed the *Stop* button. But the picture didn't vanish. Instead it rewound itself. And then Duma spoke the words about dying again, 'I know how . . . where and when,' but this time leaning closer, his stare very direct, very intimate, his voice softer. Wet patches, as from animal breath, appeared on the inside of the glass.

Felix shied back, then laughed.

This was the dry world's own DTs.

When Felix pressed the remote control again, and when it still failed to work, and when he tried the panel on the television set itself, and when this wasn't functional either, he pulled the socket from the wall, and Duma finally vanished, with a little frying noise.

There might be a practical explanation for this, thought Felix, now on hands and knees, an explanation to do with faulty equipment or Third World wiring, but, on the other hand, there might not.

He reached for his chair, crawled into it like a disabled man, then waited, gathering his strength for the long journey downstairs.

three

'At least he made the trains run on time!' was one of the jokes among the non-Afs these days. Since Duma's overthrow, train timetables, bus and postal services, energy supplies and running water had all become unreliable. The servants of the non-Afs were affected more than their masters, who had jeeps and helicopters, cellphones, the Internet, and Perrier by the crate, but it was irritating nevertheless. Especially the power cuts. Electricity had become a valuable commodity, both its source and its means. Private generators were installed by those who could afford them, while batteries, plugs, fuses and other electrical goods were prized contraband products. At the Alex, all spotlights and lamps were kept under lock and key, for performance use only. The rest of the time, three naked bulbs hung above the vast stage, half-way down, out of reach.

Their weak wattage shed more gloom than light, robbing the theatre of its customary magic. It was like opening a radio to find just a dusty black box with a tangle of equipment. But as Felix tottered into the wings now, seeing the place again for the first time in five months, his gaze was full of love. He tilted back his head, smiling at the old walkways, air-ducts, swathes and loops of cable, the workings of it all hanging up there, making the space seem top heavy and perilous, and putting in mind the idea that actors should be issued with hard hats. On the colossal, black-painted walls of the stage, the brickwork showed through in dramatic red tracts, alongside fantastical whorls of orange, blue and white mould. Elsewhere, wiring and

girders twisted through the surface, and whole sections of the proscenium arch were missing, the plasterwork fallen away, leaving pale and
stringy holes. Out in the auditorium – where another two bulbs hung
on long cords – the balconies and boxes seemed to sag, as though
weighed down by all the chipped and dusty cherubs which deco-
rated their fronts, and the seats were balding, with no puff in them,
drained of their crimson colour.

'Beautiful,' whispered Felix, wishing he could transport this playhouse to Paris, New York or London, where it would be described
with that First World word 'distressed', and regarded as the height
of fashion. Here it was regarded as a disgrace.

He surveyed the expanse of the stage. Its bare boards stretched
away with the lonely lines of a perspective drawing. The only sign of
life was a skinny woman with a pair of garden shears, trimming
away the weeds that had sprung up here and there, turning the vast
surface into a kind of shrubland, a semi-desert.

This was Felix's stage manager: the half-Chinese Frankie Hoong,
intensely shy, efficient, and dogged. A woman of violent timidity, is
how he thought of her.

They peered at one another across the distance, then Frankie
Hoong called, 'You're back. Did you have a nice holiday?'

As Felix paused, wondering how to answer, she abruptly ducked
her head and returned to her task.

How odd, he thought, she's frightened of me, she thinks it's the
old me, she's cursing herself inside – for making small-talk – she
doesn't know that this me, the new me, would be happy to make
small-talk, any talk, if talking wasn't so difficult.

More than anyone else in the company, his stage manager had
borne the brunt of his rages. As Felix watched now, an apparition
appeared in the wings. *Ah,* he mused, *here you are, here we go.* He
was interested to observe that it wasn't transparent as in popular
myth, but made up of at least two if not three dimensions, possess-
ing the substance of dense shadow, like a figure glimpsed in the
monochrome glow of pre-dawn, and needing only one spill of illumination to bring it to life . . .

And indeed, now, as the ghost moves towards centre stage,
it shows itself with full clarity: purple flesh, hair damp with

whisky-sweat. Walking with a weaving yet deadly aim, it crosses to Frankie Hoong – who looks younger, and seems to be supervising a Tech – and booms at her, 'Yes, I am aware that you can't see the problem! And I am also aware of the reason! 'Cause you're not just slit-eyed, you rancid bitch – you're cunt-eyed! D'you hear me? You're *cunt-eyed*!'

Flicking his head wildly, banishing the ghost, Felix wondered whether to cross to Frankie Hoong, and kneel, and say sorry.

He was distracted by the sudden arrival of Charlie, hurrying from the direction of the stage door.

'Sorry, had to dash to a patient,' he said. 'Have we started – am I late?'

'Hmn?' Felix said. 'No, early. I think.'

'How you doing, buddy?' Charlie asked, as they kissed, looking at him closely. 'Bit of jet lag, huhn?'

But I felt like this *before* I got on the plane, thought Felix, I felt like this the moment I left the clinic.

He suddenly realised how frightened he was. The meeting – the board meeting – was upon him. Frankie Hoong was now arranging a circle of chairs in the centre of the stage. And other members of the board were appearing from the stage-left wings, heading towards the chairs.

'Felix,' said Charlie, with sudden, low-voiced urgency, 'pull out all the stops. You have fewer friends here than before.'

As if to emphasise this odd, unexpected warning, the first person Felix saw was a lemur-faced woman in flyaway specs and a turquoise wraparound. The woman from the airport. Of course – that's why she had looked familiar – *she was one of the trustees*! A new one admittedly – she'd been to only two previous meetings, and he was blotto at both – but even so he should have recognised her.

Felix swayed. He saw her notice, saw her thinking, *Sozzled again!* And, bizarrely, he felt she was right: he might not have had a drink in three months, yet his senses were more blurred than at any previous meeting.

'You sit down,' Felix mumbled to Charlie. 'I'll just gather my thoughts, collect my notes.' Moving in a shambling run, he headed not for his office but the stage door.

Outside, the greenish-grey light and heat hit him like a breaking wave, rushing through his senses, leaving him slightly off-balance, one foot hovering off the ground, a dazed look on his face. He let gravity slowly tip him against the big palm tree that stood next to the stage door; it was the same tree that waved its fronds at him through the attic window thirteen floors up. He leaned there, rubbing the sandy grey bark as though it was the leg of a tame monster. Across the wide road there was an astonishing curtain of bougainvillaea, as high as the theatre building, and as different in every other way. The apricot-and-cream stone of the one stood in direct sunlight, bright and dry; the other was in shadow, a luscious tumble of leafy foliage laced with huge magenta blossoms, which seemed to pour from the top and drop; it was as if they had been strewn on a river during some ecstatic ritual and were sweeping over a dark waterfall.

Felix felt a sense of some presence, a human-smelling presence, very near him. Close to his ear, just behind his head. Expecting another ghost, he spun round. Nothing. He looked up and down the long road. Apart from the trustees' bodyguards and drivers grouped round their vehicles, smoking, there was no one to be seen.

He was about to go back into the theatre when he noticed something across the road, under the curtain of bougainvillaea. Here were a few small shops, with iron grilles over their fronts, and signs that read, 'We *are* open – ring please.' One of the windows belonged to a butcher. Among the row of upside-down carcasses, glimmering with flies, there hung two sleek creatures – monkeys, perhaps, or dogs. One was not quite dead. It tried to feed on the shoulder of the other. This was done in a listless but determined way, as if hoping that, through nourishment, things might yet return to normal.

'Appetite,' whispered Felix, with his first longing for whisky since coming home. Shaking himself like a wet animal, imagining he was shaking away bad thoughts, he regained his composure. According to Charlie, there were more tangible dangers awaiting him inside the theatre. 'Pull out all the stops,' he told himself, and went in to face the trustees.

*

Determined not to sway as he crossed to the circle of chairs, where all the members of the board were now seated, Felix walked carefully, slowly, adopting the rolling, round-shouldered gait, reminiscent of a gunslinger's prowl, which used to disguise an inebriated stagger. As he drew nearer, and as the trustees went quiet and still, Felix was struck by a sudden awareness: like Frankie Hoong earlier, these people were *frightened* of him.

They were seeing the old Felix: black-shirted, black-browed and bearded, the famous scowl, the famous slouch; they were seeing the mask, the costume, the shape called Felix. Since they didn't know what he'd actually been doing over the last five months (they'd been told he was on a drama sabbatical in America), they braced themselves for his cruel wit, his muttered sarcasm and insults, his slurping foul language, all to be endured because the man was talented, very talented – so the experts said – with a weird but brilliant imagination, worthy of an overseas career.

If their perception of him was cloudy with prejudice, the reverse was quite different.

The lemur-faced woman – her name was Mrs Al-Qirib, he now remembered, she was from one of the top Arab families – look at the way she takes a little notebook and fountain pen from her hand-bag, look how diligent her gestures are, look at the tilt of her head, studious but glum, she's back in a classroom, the plain, hardwork-ing swot, and look how tidy the bag is inside, everything in organised rows, no debris, no scrunched tissues or wrappers. If she was to die unexpectedly today, and her possessions handed over to nearest kin, the inside of that bag would break someone's heart: it was *so like her*.

Or Lord Gomes, the British-Portuguese chairman of the board, a shipping magnate, a gentleman buccaneer, with his immaculate summer suits and his tanned, shiny, hard flesh – cured pork wrapped in silk – look at the way he sits forward now, and folds his hands on his lap, ready to start; someone taught him to do that once, and praised his efforts, and he does it still without thinking, like a good little boy, this dangerous, devious man.

Or Muriel Slackforth-Carter, heiress of the cobalt fortune, or the ancient university professor, V. K. Bukherjee, or the only black trustee, Judge Okoth-Ofumbi . . . and all the others, these rich and powerful people, who sit on the theatre board as a hobby . . . look at them.

Look at how obediently they've taken their places in the circle, look how respectfully they've gone quiet, look at their soft parts, their necks and eyes, picture the rest of their bodies, their flab, growths and scars, their genitals hidden away, bandaged by under-clothes, smell their scents and sprays, their roll-ons and odour-eaters, think of their shame, their adult shame in their looks, their marriages, their secret lives, think also how they love and are loved, each of them, imagine what makes them happy, what they dream of.

Charlie had warned of enemies here, but this seemed unlikely to Felix. They were too vulnerable. Too much like him – small, raw, naked – infants trapped inside giants, angels within demons.

The sobs came from deep within, giving no warning, no chance of stifling them, and he fell into his chair, doubled over, gasping and spluttering.

The circle was silent. Even Charlie was too surprised to help. Then Lord Gomes said: 'And how was your break, Felix?'

I'll tell them, thought Felix, tell them the truth, we're all in it together, this life – but as he started to speak, Lord Gomes, who was not in the habit of letting you reply to his questions, continued: 'Excellent, excellent, *muito bem*, let's make a start, mustn't be too long, I have another appointment, sure everyone does.'

Mopping his tears, Felix smiled to himself. Lord Gomes didn't mean to be brusque. He was a good little boy who sits up straight, folds his hands, and tries to take charge, tries to run things. Let him.

'On this historic day,' said Lord Gomes, 'the last day of the Hakika, whilst the rest of the nation prepares to set aside the horrors of the past and look to the future, I feel that we, in our humble way, might perchance think along similar lines.'

As the trustees smiled and murmured their approval, Felix looked up groggily. What a strange comparison to make. Between the Hakika – a confessional for torturers and death-squad commanders – and this, a routine board meeting.

'The future, Felix,' continued Lord Gomes, removing two bottles of chilled wine from a leather cooling sleeve, and passing round a small tower of plastic cups – this ritual, like the democratic circle of chairs, had been instigated by Felix himself long ago – 'We're all eager to hear your plans for the future.'

'Future,' Felix repeated slowly, in a dragged-out tone, like an imbecile, or a baby learning its first word.

The cups reached him. Quickly handing them on without taking one, he prepared for an outcry of astonishment. But no one noticed. Either that, or they assumed he was already tanked up to his limits. He patted his pockets, touching the reassuring shapes of chocolate peanuts.

'The future,' Lord Gomes said again, his eyes narrowing as he watched Felix slip something into his mouth – *was the man on drugs now?* – 'Your last show, the Genesis show, played to empty houses, you've stopped holding your "ethnic evenings", for what they were worth, or even showing films, and the Alex has now been dark for eight months.' He had begun with an unexpectedly brutal punch, and paused to let its impact settle. Raised both here and abroad, in the local Portuguese-speaking community and at British public schools, his accent had a precious, almost effeminate clarity, displaying each English sound like a calling card. Felix listened to these, more fascinated by the noise of Lord Gomes' speech than its content. Meanwhile the chairman launched into a long diatribe about, firstly, the new government's exorbitant taxes, and secondly, the running costs of the theatre building and its state of disrepair. Since the Alex was funded privately, mostly by the trustees themselves, the situation was critical. 'We are, Felix, in what my people call *uma grande porra*, and what I shall simply translate as something of a fix.'

Above his head, as if to help make the point, one of the three naked light-bulbs died with a mean little pop. Felix sighed, staring at a clump of pretty, saffron-coloured weeds peeping through the stage floorboards – *hadn't Frankie Hoong just cleared this area?, could they have sprung up since?* – then echoed, 'A fix.'

'Well, you've seen the auditor's reports, the surveyors' reports . . .'

'Have I?' mumbled Felix.

'I sent them to you in Long Island,' Charlie whispered out of the side of his mouth.

'Did you?' Felix replied, half remembering the fat, special-delivery package arriving at the clinic, and how it had remained in one corner of his room, unopened.

Lord Gomes smiled. This was an old Felix tactic: pretending not to have read documents, not to have had phone conversations, not knowing about things that didn't suit him. 'So we're all agog, naturally, yes?, agog to hear how you think we can make this place survive.'

'Survive,' Felix repeated drowsily, his head starting to loll.

Charlie was ready for this – Felix making a slow start – and came to the rescue, grinning at Lord Gomes: 'Carlos, isn't the problem that the theatre is being, like, upstaged by real life? How do we compete with the Carnival? 'Cause, y'know, that's what's been going on out there' – he nodded towards the streets – 'for the last year. One big rave-up. And it's terrific, y'know, a carnival, the people get to participate, they get stuck in, they get their hands dirty, their juices flowing, hearts thumping with the drums, it's wild, wild stuff. When you can do that, who wants to just sit in here again, just sit quietly in the dark watching others have all the fun?' He gave his shy laugh, his mouth twitching naughtily, and said, 'Who wants to *watch* when they can *do*?'

The trustees made an assortment of noises, disapproving but affectionate. All had either visited Charlie's famous wild parties, or heard the stories.

Meanwhile, Felix thought, Poor Charlie, he's making things worse, yet he's trying to help . . . He's a dear friend, he loves me . . . Aren't people kind? In their deepest hearts, aren't people good?

As he wiped away a new fall of tears, the trustees looked away squeamishly. They were fed up with his hygiene at these meetings: sweat, bile, mouthfuls of drink, all spilling from his damp, red-eyed face.

Felix popped some chocolate peanuts into his mouth, chewed rapidly, trying to draw energy from them, then said, 'The Genesis show . . . yes . . . played to poor houses. All our epics have, alas. The other Bible shows, and *The Iliad*, *The Odyssey*, the *Ramayana*. The only things that sold out were the jazz evenings, the film shows.

But you didn't mind before. In the bad old days. Because . . . what was going on here, in this theatre . . . it made us feel we were doing something. We lived in a society where no voice of protest was permitted, but . . .' He hesitated, grimacing – it was happening again – he was *hearing* himself – yet he must continue, must press on. 'By playing little daredevil games with the censorship office . . . or even just by putting five hundred people on stage, *people*, real people, and then adding a few actors, and telling one of humankind's great stories . . . this was, in its own small way, a political act, a lone voice of protest.' It was no good. His statements sounded pretentious, his accent sounded ridiculous – like Lord Gomes' – with dandified English sounds laced into it. Felix spoke a few more sentences, a dazed look in his eyes. He wasn't just hearing his voice any more, he was feeling its shape, touching it with his tongue and gums, and it was horrible, horrible, each vowel tasting like a sweet that had been in someone else's mouth, each consonant a fish-hook.

Lord Gomes was a bad listener. While Felix spoke, he gazed round the circle with a pouting expression, emphasising the dark skin of his eye-sockets and lips. But one word had caught his attention, and he repeated it now: 'Political?'

'Isn't it what we were doing here?' Felix said weakly. 'All of us.'

Lord Gomes smiled. 'Forgive me, Felix. I thought what *you* were doing was providing entertainment. What *we* were doing was providing a touch of moral guidance and business acumen, those necessary evils without which Art can't survive.'

A ripple of nervous laughter passed round the circle, and they all glanced towards Felix, awaiting his withering reply. In the past he would've smiled back and said something like, 'Oh, Carlos, I'd never call you a *necessary* evil.' But today he didn't, couldn't, rise to the bait.

Amazed, Lord Gomes said, 'Putting all this aside, Felix – the future, yes? – your plans?'

'Plans . . .' Felix thought and sighed, opened his mouth, closed it again. After a long silence, during which the only sound was of people sipping their wine and breathing into their plastic cups, Felix finally managed to say, 'A show about dictatorship, perhaps?'

'*Dictatorship?*' said someone.

'Oh dear,' said someone else.

'Gloomy,' said a third.

Lord Gomes gave a grim smile. 'Hasn't that show been . . . what's the phrase? . . . *been done*? In this country. Yes, surely. It was a big hit, no? Ran for over thirty years.'

'Precisely,' said Felix, fighting to keep focused. 'So now's the time to – to – finally talk about it. We could perhaps adapt *Ubu Roi* or *Arturo Ui*.' The trustees looked nonplussed. None of them knew these plays, and a few thought he was just making up gibberish titles. 'Or we could devise one from, from . . .'

[margin handwritten note: Ubu + the Truth commission]

It had all seemed so clear up in his room, so inspiring, with Duma staring back at him, lifting that demonic, buffalo head, scenting the air, curious, challenging – but now he couldn't remember the first thing about his brainwave. With jaw hanging open, he stared at Lord Gomes.

It was a fatal pause. 'I wonder, Felix,' said the chairman, 'if it isn't a more complete change of direction that we need.'

Picking up her cue quickly, too quickly, making Felix sit up in surprise, the cobalt heiress, Muriel Slackforth-Carter, said, 'My husband believes you could make a simply splendid shopping mall out of this place. One of those charming conversions, d'you see, like they do with warehouses and wharves these days.'

Felix blinked at her. A drooping, thin-shouldered woman, she normally gave the impression that her life of privilege was a form of martyrdom; she had been singled out for this burden and she would endure it without complaint, just a listless, irritable quietude. Yet she had spoken with real enthusiasm, real appetite.

'Beg pardon,' said Felix in a small voice. 'Are you suggesting we turn the Alex into a . . . ?'

'Or law courts,' interposed Judge Okoth-Ofumbi, who had decided Felix was drunk and not worth listening to. 'When the Hakika ends this afternoon, when its amnesty expires at midnight, we can start preparing for some spectacular show trials in this country. Army generals, cabinet ministers, newspaper editors . . .'

'Judges,' joshed Lord Gomes.

'Judges,' concurred Judge Okoth-Ofumbi, without smiling, his eyes bright with the gleam of integrity. A youngish man with bold black spectacles, a dramatic gap between his front teeth, and a thick Swahili accent, he had been one of the few lawyers whom the old regime failed to corrupt, and after Liberation he had been rewarded with promotion to the bench. 'And all the thugs from the SSU, all the torturers, all the death squads, all the ones who haven't come forward to the Hakika, all these people, they must stand in the dock now, oh, indeed, so we're going to need one damned big dock!'

'What? Turn the Alex into –' Felix started to say, before being interrupted again, this time by the ancient V. K. Bukherjee, whose dry, grey face was alight with excitement.

'Maybe they'll even find the big boys, bring the big boys to the day of reckoning, even the biggest of the big boys . . . him, y'know, *him*.' He muttered to himself in Urdu, cursing his failing powers. 'Oh, what's that one called again?'

'Duma!' everyone chorused, smiling at the old man, rolling their eyes.

'What if they found him?' V. K. Bukherjee said, one tremulous hand weaving through the air. 'Found him wherever he is, in hiding, in exile, the old devil, just think if they found him!'

Felix flicked his head several times, trying to clear his thoughts. Should he try a joke? – *Duma's upstairs if you want him, just look behind my television set.* He opened his mouth, but the ancient V. K. Bukherjee was still in full flow:

'. . . And *think*, just think if they trapped him, our emperor, and brought him back here in chains!'

'Just imagine!' concurred Judge Okoth-Ofumbi. 'What a trial! *Loo! – jamani!* The international media, you would not be able to keep them away – and the public! Ah, you'd certainly need a special courtroom for that trial!'

Everyone gazed round the auditorium. Hanging in the gloom, the great tiers of the circle and the gallery had the look of open, empty jaws; their expanses deep and dark, and only their long, white-and-gold façades showing toothily, curving round into a kind of smile.

'Eichmann's trial was held in a theatre,' Charlie told the hushed group. 'A converted theatre in Jerusalem. It was like a show, a blood sport, a sort of ancient Roman spectacle. They filmed it all, I've seen it, amazing movie.'

Felix blinked. Was Charlie behind this extraordinary idea – of converting the theatre into something else, of *closing* it?

'Hey!' V. K. Bukherjee said with sudden urgency. 'Maybe they'll even catch the big boys!'

The trustees glanced at one another. V. K. Bukherjee had reached the point, routine at these meetings, where he started to repeat himself. It was sad: he used to have a bright mind, used to lecture in philosophy at the university. Charlie was about to reach into his pocket and the emergency supply of medicines – sedatives, painkillers, snakebite antidotes – which he carried for his friends, when V. K. Bukherjee explained: 'Yes, the really big boys, the real culprits – *us*. We've all lived like fat cats off this fat land, we've all turned the blind eye to what was going on, all of us – me too, so I know what I'm saying, eh! I'm not bullshitting here!'

V. K. Bukherjee was on the edge of his seat now, voice quavering, wine sloshing from his cup, but no one seemed concerned. *Old age is like drunkenness,* Felix mused to himself.

'These two men contradict each another!' V. K. Bukherjee said, voice rising, crooked finger pointing at Lord Gomes and Felix. 'One says it was just *entertainment*, what we were doing here in this theatre, the other says no it was *political*. He says that when we told the great stories of mankind, the *Ramayana*, the Bible, *The Iliad*, when we did this, just by demonstrating this amount of *humanity*, with great heaps of the stuff, y'know, just by doing this, we were protesting against the regime. Which man is right? Which do we believe in our hearts? I'll tell you – both! On the one hand, of course, it was just entertainment, just stories, bedtime stories, fireside stories, but on the other hand, we wanted it to be more, eh?, we wanted it to be political! We saw what was happening in the streets, we heard about events in the villages, my goodness, you couldn't go for a picnic at the Minawa Falls without seeing a body or two come plummeting over with all the lovely water. We knew about all this but we wanted to be able to say to our children, to our grandchildren, to *ourselves*, "I didn't just stand by, I did something." So what did we do? We gave our money, we protested with our chequebooks.

And where, what place did we find to make our protest? Here – this building. And what method did we use? *Art!*' He gave a terrible laugh, his grey skin suddenly looking more ancient, more reptilian. 'Art with its obscure, coded messages! It's like dreams, my friends – it's nonsense, it's rubbish! What was it worth compared to the drama going on outside these walls, what was it worth? Nothing. And that's what we did – *nothing!*' Running out of breath, he gestured towards Felix and Lord Gomes again. 'These two men don't really contradict each other at all. One is trying to say, "We did something," and the other is saying, "Yes, we did, but it was so little, so pathetic, and we should be so ashamed of ourselves, let's just call it *entertainment*".'

I can't believe it, thought Felix – this senile old man has summoned his last burst of brilliance, of fluency to defend Lord Gomes and rubbish me . . . me and my life's work.

As the trustees applauded and cheered V. K. Bukherjee, it gradually struck Felix how much he was hated here. Glancing round the circle, he could see it clearly above the flutter of clapping hands. Such scorn and disgust, such fear. All focused on the outline they saw as *Felix* – their artistic director, the tyrant, the bully, the drunk, the man who treated his staff like slaves, his colleagues like inferiors, and them, the board, like idiots – nobody could see the new Felix, seated inside the dark shell, peering back timidly.

Felix remembered Lord Gomes' little flourish of grandiloquence at the start of the meeting – about the Hakika – and it seemed less preposterous now. He felt like he was at a kind of hearing. And he had been found guilty. And now he should kneel and ask forgiveness.

'So,' said Lord Gomes, stopping the applause with an ostentatious look at his watch, 'a shopping mall, a law court, or something else. All these things are viable possibilities for the future life of this building.'

Felix stared at his chairman across the circle. 'Or something else,' the man had said. He was up to something – Felix knew him of old – they were all up to something, even Charlie. Glancing at his friend, Felix saw a gentle look in his face, a doctor's look, which said, 'This is probably for the best.' Was the theatre's fate sealed, then?

Was there nothing to be done? Was he powerless? It was a strangely comforting feeling, not unlike the approach of sleep, even more blissful. Felix wept. To give up at last, to surrender, to fail, to lose the big battle: keeping this place afloat, this beloved place, the love of his life . . .

Through the smear and sparkle of his vision, Felix smiled at Lord Gomes – *The old me could've given you a run for your money, a fight to the death* – then he said, 'I should like a last go.'

Everyone stopped what they were doing and waited, frowning slightly. *A last go.* Did he mean a swansong or a final chance? Even Felix wasn't sure.

A last go.

The words hung in the air for several moments, then Felix found himself surrounded by brightening faces. It was as though, one by one, the trustees had deciphered the code, and persuaded themselves he was leaving.

Only Lord Gomes remained on his guard. This was tactics – this was his old adversary playing for time. 'Of course,' he said, with a steady smile. 'We've been waiting to hear your plans, dear chap, since this meeting commenced. A last go?' He dispatched 'last' like he might other four-lettered words, without quite closing his mouth round it. 'On dictatorship? *Ai caraças!*' He wrinkled his nose. '*Must it be on dictatorship?*'

'No,' replied Felix quietly. 'I'd like to do a compilation show . . . a compilation of scenes from all the shows we've done here . . . whether they were political or just entertainment, these shows, it's hardly relevant now . . . but I'd like to make one story out of all the great stories. One show out of all our . . .' He hesitated, then said it, 'All our great and marvellous shows.' He was aware of a new embarrassing sound to his voice – grand and sentimental – but it didn't matter. He was an artist, about to have 'a last go', and artists must risk such things. Holding his head high, he concluded, 'I should like to do a tribute to the work of this theatre, a celebration of all we've achieved here at the Alex over the years.'

'What?' Charlie said. 'You mean like, kinda, like *The Beach Boys' Greatest Hits*?'

Felix squirmed, suddenly seeing the idea in a different light, but the trustees became very animated – this was definitely sounding like a swansong! – and they began chattering like children, holding their hands in the air, asking to be heard.

'Oh, you simply must do the Creation sequence from the Genesis show!' exclaimed Muriel Slackforth-Carter, her dull, martyred tone vanishing for the second time today. 'The naked masses, it was very affecting, my husband talked about nothing else for weeks.'

'And that scene from the *Ramayana*,' said V. K. Bukherjee bubbling with excitement, his previous arguments forgotten. 'That scene . . . *that one* . . . oh, y'know!'

'Where the monkeys rescue Sita from Ravanna's palace?' prompted Mrs Al-Qirib, her lemur face shining, all disdain gone.

'That's the one!' whooped V. K. Bukherjee.

'Cyclops from *The Odyssey*,' said Judge Okoth-Ofumbi, as enthused as everyone else, but trying to speak in measured tones. 'And that way, Felix, you would cover your dictatorship theme in a way, would you not?'

In his production of *The Odyssey*, Felix had directed one of his actors, Mr Mmalo, to play the giant Cyclops as a dictator-like ruler of his island. Dressing him in Humpty-Dumpty costume and big one-eyed helmet, Felix avoided any reference to Duma – the concept was dangerous enough – but everything went wrong on the first night: Mr Mmalo suddenly launched into an astonishing impersonation of the leader, State Safety Unit men arrived within the hour, and it was the director, not the actor, whom they arrested on a charge of high treason.

Felix shivered, driving away memories. Then, eschewing the opportunity to make some cutting comment – 'It's a dangerous business, what?, *entertainment*!' – as the old Felix would have done, he dutifully inscribed 'Cyclops/Odyssey' on the list he'd started to make. 'And if I may venture a suggestion myself,' he said – again without irony – 'The Death of Hector scene from *The Iliad*.'

This was his own personal favourite: the chariot-torture played offstage, viewed by Andromache high on the walls of Troy, she expressing her grief through a kind of song, half blues improvisation, half tribal wail.

At exactly this point in the meeting, the actress who had played Andromache wandered onto the stage. Kaz. It looked like she was in one of the final scenes of the play, distracted with grief after the death of Hector. She even wore the same bomber jacket – it had come from her own wardrobe – and her hair was in the same crest-and-braid style, falling like a curtain round her face, with only a cigarette poking out.

Kaz

Felix and Charlie exchanged a glance. Something was wrong, seriously wrong. It was the way she was wrapped in on herself, the way the cigarette was kept close to her mouth between puffs, as if someone might snatch it away, and the way you couldn't see her eyes at all. And now they noticed that her braids were shiny with liquid, and that the cigarette, acting like blotting paper, was turning red. They both rose to their feet as she fell.

four

'Oh, yeahhh,' purred Kaz, as Charlie poured another bucket of hot water over her. It slid off the coxcomb in big, separate drops, failing to penetrate the seal of palm oil with which she'd dressed her hair, but melting the clay dirt on her forehead, sending a spill of ochre down the hanging braids and their sisal extensions, woven with tiny sea shells and wooden beads, and dripping onto her shoulders and throat. Her body was sinewy, rawboned; a fighter's body, a dancer's. Kaz was the company's choreographer as well as its leading actress and singer. Her whole being was tough, worn, uncompromising. Yet there was a softness too, a haze, a smoky light in her eyes. These were always half closed, and her lips were always half open. Everything about her was slightly ajar. Even the angles of her loose limbs, they were half turned too, turned outwards, questioning, inviting, saying, 'Hey, man, how ya doin'?'

'Holy shit, what *have* you been up to, baby?' Charlie asked as he scrubbed her. The bathwater was turning dark with dried blood and earth, and the floor was littered with bright red lumps of cotton wool; the attempts to staunch her nosebleeds.

'Don' ask, honey, don' ask,' Kaz replied, in her low, rough voice with its curious tunes, half this, half that, ajar again, rooted in Africa yet styled by a string of American boyfriends long ago – her mother was a cleaner at the embassy – and by American songs and movies ever since. Kaz was of the Tao tribe, one of the traditional enemies of Duma's own. During his reign, finding herself a target for his death squads, she had devised different survival techniques. Outwardly, she *blacked-up* her chestnut-coloured skin with grease-paint, to look darker, bluer, more like the Igisha, Duma's tribe. Inwardly, she turned away from Africa, and, like so many others on the continent, made America her dream-place. In Charlie's company, the dreams flourished.

'Oh, Mr Medicine Man,' she murmured, watching him clean her body as if it was happening to a third party, a dull amused look somewhere within the hanging braids; trying to provoke him, sometimes pulling his hand under the water, trapping it with her legs. Felix wondered if Charlie and Kaz were currently an affair. It was an on-off arrangement. As Charlie's hand soaped between Kaz's breasts, Felix thought, Now that's not strictly a doctor's touch. She purred. 'Oh, Mr Medicine Man, make me better again.'

Charlie smiled indulgently and opened his 'magic box': the doctor's bag he had fetched from his jeep after Kaz gatecrashed the board meeting. He gave her a hefty injection of vitamin B. She paused, eyes closed, feeling the warm hit, smiling in a manner that made Felix nervous. Next Charlie tackled the nosebleed, administering a classic but rarely used treatment: squirting the nasal capillaries with a 10 per cent solution of cocaine. Felix grew more nervous. But Kaz still wasn't satisfied: she ran her fingers over the supplies in Charlie's box. 'Gimme somethin' stronger, Mr Medicine Man.'

Charlie said, 'At this stage, anything stronger would finish you, Kaz. Even you. We've got to get you straight-line-mellow.'

'No-thank-you!' said Kaz, giving a husky bark of glee. Her hand now strayed up to touch Charlie's hair, and the kiss-shaped birthmark on his neck. 'You're jus' a big dumb blond, ehh? – my *mganga*?'

Charlie laughed shyly, then took a tiny plastic phial from his box, snapped off the seal, allowed her to sip half of it, and finished the rest himself.

Felix glanced away discreetly, prissily, while reminding himself that the Alex was lucky to have Charlie as its doctor. Kaz was only half joking when she called him *mganga* – a witchdoctor – for his skills were practised in unorthodox ways, and aimed at expanding the mind as much as healing the body. With access to unlimited pharmaceutical supplies – an American college friend sent them over – he was able to offer the company a variety of special aids (amphetamines to get them through the marathon epics, benzodiazepines to unwind afterwards, steroids for strained larynxes, analgesia for limb injuries), also minor surgery and pregnancy terminations, *as well as* tending to their basic medical needs! Charlie was a very popular man.

'Get some more water, yeah?' he whispered to Felix now, as he fetched Kaz's cigarettes for her. 'God knows what she's been on – palm wine, *bangi*, glue, gasoline – God knows.' When he lifted her bomber jacket, sand poured out of its folds. 'And she's been on a beach somewhere, for a day or two, I reckon.'

Is it because of us? Felix wondered, as he left the room, slowly swinging the empty bucket. Did she go on one of her benders because I was coming back, and she's fearful about what happens now?

Kaz had not looked at him once since she arrived. She had not yet said hello.

In the old days, Kaz had been Felix's great drinking partner. During their last binge, on the night before he left for New York, she had suddenly turned to him, eyes glassy with tears, and said, '*Ai mpenzi*, I wonder if we're gonna survive what happens next?'

The bathroom led onto a narrow corridor, its one side railed, overlooking a deep lightwell. Topped by a domed skylight, which either creaked with heat or dripped with rain, and leading down into the enclosed courtyard far below, known as the Green Room, this lightwell was the centre of the dressing-room area, where the company now lived. It was hung with washing-lines, decked with untidy flower-boxes, TV and radio aerials, and surrounded by a jumble of wooden stairways and passages, some exposed like balconies, others more like alleyways, burrowing darkly away. Footsteps made a hollow clacking noise down these, like old dentures; as though the building was swallowing up any retreating figure. Felix relished his travels through this warren of routes and dwellings. He felt he was in a biblical city, or a walled medieval town. At other times he decided that the German architect had simply doodled here, drawn a sketch of some magical location that he had seen or imagined during childhood.

I love this place, Felix thought – 'Old Alex' – am I really going to let it go without a fight?

The lightwell held another, special attraction. The windows looked into it, and one another. Although draped with a makeshift assortment of curtains and blinds, it was not difficult to spy a thing or two as you prowled along. Or to do more. Steal down this little cul-de-sac here, open that panel down at the bottom, and you could let yourself into the air-ducts. Then you could view the dressing-rooms from their other side, their inner side, through small, crusted grilles; you could see into showers and toilets too, and, with the sound of your mouse-like shiftings always disguised by the groans and sighs of the elderly playhouse, you could spend hours crawling along these clammy, silvery tunnels . . .

All you needed was a bottle or two of whisky inside you.

Now that wasn't a proposition any more – *of course it wasn't!* – but imagine, just imagine sneaking into the upstairs air-duct now, and peeking into the bathroom where Charlie was currently wash-ing Kaz, slowly, smilingly, using more than a doctor's touch . . . imagine being a fly on that wall, an eye in that grille . . .

Dropping the bucket to clutch the rail, Felix did battle with a rising, sickening thrill. *No, no, that was the old days, the old ways.* He stood there, the lightwell spinning round him, its different levels and layers unravelling like a long bolt of cloth, leaving him, naked and excited, in the middle.

He tried to calm down. 'Not well, are you?' he said, using that singular voice he saved for talking to himself: higher than normal, peculiarly quiet, almost disembodied. Ah, it's *your* voice, he thought, watching a small ghost descend the nearby stairs. A black-haired, runtish boy, aged about six . . . the child who was born late to a colonial auditor and secretary just as they were settling happily into middle age with its lack of surprises. 'Two of the most cautious people in the world had forgotten to take precautions,' he later told friends. 'I was a gift from God the Prankster.' The first word he learned, believing it to be a term of endearment, was 'Shush!'

Felix gawped at his younger self. Already an expert in solitude, yet brimming with ferocious curiosity, he has not yet discovered the scowling slouch that will help him through life; his stance is still upright and vulnerable.

'It's all right, you're all right now,' Felix said, in his private voice, suddenly picking up the bucket and manoeuvring past the boy-ghost by taking three steps in one. 'We'll go to bed soon, be safe there. You're all right, you're all right.'

He reached the Green Room.

Overcrowded with ancient furniture, unemptied ash-cans, cooking pots, and dried foodstuff hanging from above, it looked like a cross between a railway waiting room and a market-place. Here the impression was of people passing through, stopping for a moment and never moving on. Here the company played cards and dice, washed and fed babies, slaughtered and plucked fowl, cooked and dozed. Here they lived, and occasionally died.

Those present went silent when they saw Felix return for more water. They stiffened, came to attention, flattened themselves against walls. No one noticed that he was doing the same, flinching from them as well, wondering which ones he'd hurt, which he'd abused, wanting to mutter, 'Forgive, forgive me,' as he passed.

He had just filled his bucket at the open range in one corner, when he heard: 'Oh, good gracious me – and when did you return to these fair shores? How are you, sir?'

Approaching him was the sturdy figure of Mr Mmalo. As the senior member of the company – and a committed Christian – Mr Mmalo felt compelled to offer a greeting, despite being as intimidated by his boss as everyone else. He was a gentleman-actor of the old school – like Felix, he'd trained in the UK – always wearing jacket and bow-tie to rehearsals, his bald black head looking polished, his script carried in an attaché case along with a tracksuit and trainers for Kaz's movement sessions. It was Mr Mmalo who had played Cyclops in Felix's version of *The Odyssey* – losing control on the first night and mimicking Duma. The actor's physical resemblance to the great dictator was, in fact, particularly striking. So much so that it confused Felix now, his mind still fresh with images from the television screen upstairs.

'Mr Mmalo!' he said with a laugh – in case it wasn't.

'Felix,' replied the other, and cautiously extended a hand.

This is good, thought Felix, setting down the bucket to free his fingers, this is a good, worthy act of reconciliation. He had insulted and goaded Mr Mmalo terribly over the years – ever since he, Felix, was arrested on that fateful opening night. He had never fully recovered from what happened over the next few hours . . .

A memory was starting . . . he didn't want it . . . he shook his head violently, shook it away.

Misreading this signal, Mr Mmalo withdrew his offered hand. Felix whined, 'No-o-o!' Mr Mmalo decided his director was not only drunk but in one of *those* moods, and backed off, fleeing through the nearest door. Felix caught his breath, and looked round. Two children were in front of him, frozen with fear. He smiled at them. They ran, shrieking.

Sighing heavily, Felix left the Green Room and slowly climbed back through the lightwell, resting frequently.

On the corridor of bathrooms, the door was open to *that* room. Felix crept closer. He could hear Charlie and Kaz talking. Just a murmur through the open door, a murmur of their strange, hip accents. *We apes, we colonial apes,* thought Felix affectionately. America didn't even need to land in Africa to colonise it. It was like listening to an old B-movie buzzing through the wall, from someone else's TV or a fleapit cinema. Then he heard what they were saying:

'. . . with sections from the Bible, *The Iliad*, them all. A kinda *Beach Boys' Greatest Hits.*'

'*Felix's Greatest Hits* . . . ? That is one asshole of an idea!'

'You reckon? I thought it was quite cool.'

'Yeah, well, thass 'cause yous jus' one dumb blond. It's an asshole, an asshole of an idea! Those Long Island dudes, they's gone and lobotomised our man, fuck 'em . . .' As Felix walked in, Kaz reverted to her own language – '*Kuma zao!*' – then went silent.

Felix poured the fresh water over her. She ignored him. Out in the lightwell, someone was practising the saxophone. She jammed along; no words, just open sounds . . . *Zaa-za-zaa*. Her voice was raw, dry. It curled through the air like smoke. It made you feel sleazy, heavy-limbed, well past your bedtime; it made you smile. Felix longed for times past.

'"... And stars fell on Alabama last night,"' she crooned, finishing a song in her head.

'Hello, Kaz,' Felix said at last. She didn't reply. 'Hello,' he said again. 'How d'you do? The name's Felix.'

'I don't know no Felix,' Kaz said, talking past him to Charlie. 'Do you know a Felix?' Charlie retreated to the bathroom doorway and lit a cigarette, facing the other way. 'I *knew* a Felix once,' Kaz continued. 'He was a good, dark soul. Yeah. Passed away, I hear.'

'No. He just . . . got well.' Felix hesitated. He had sounded pompous. Embarrassed, he said, 'Anyway, you get well now, and . . .'

Her fists streaked through the air, and a wave of bathwater splashed him.

'No, I didn't mean . . .' He indicated the bloody cotton-wool balls scattered round the floor. 'You look like you've been through rather a ghastly time. I just meant . . .'

'I'm fine,' she said gruffly. 'Howsabout you?'

'Yes, fine too, ta.'

'Yeah?'

'Yes. Very chipper. This new . . . my new . . . it suits me, it's such a novelty, y'know, being well.' He paused, blushing again. Every statement sounded critical of her somehow. He laughed weakly. 'Apart from a slight problem with talking, walking or staying awake, I'm tickety-boo.'

She didn't smile. '*Yeye mshenzi!*' she muttered, head swaying. It occurred to him that she was still very far gone.

'Is that why you . . . ?' he asked, gesturing vaguely towards her sandy clothes. 'Was it because I was due back, and you were fretting about how we . . . ?'

She gave a bark of derision, and now the packet of cigarettes flew across the room, one sharp corner hitting him on the cheek. 'Have a smoke, sugar,' she said.

'I don't,' he muttered, stung. 'As you know.'

'So?' she scoffed. 'Start! A man's gotta have some poison in him. Isn't that what you always used to tell us, Mr Director Man? *Ehh?*,

Not South African space, but filled w/South African concerns. Makes the world difficult to place?

the Feast   53

ehh?' – she questioned, suddenly sounding like a Swahili market-woman, and then, as suddenly, a Yankee dame again – 'Ain't you the one who used to say, "There's nothing that's happened in this country that isn't in all of us, there's no us and them, no goodies and baddies, there's just human beings" – isn't that what you used to say, Mr God? Ehh?, ehh? So where's your poison now? Where's the baddie in you now?' Seeing Felix shift from foot to foot, she yelled, 'Hey, stranger, gimme my friend back!'

Felix's balance was starting to go. People were so demanding, so loud in the dry world; they loomed at you. Did they realise? Did they know how hectic they were? You wanted to say shush, be calm, try and stay still. 'Look, we'll talk anon,' he said, turning to the door slowly, determined not to bump into it. 'I'd like to discuss the new show with –'

'I heard it was an old show, an old, old show. *Felix's Greatest Hits!*' She gave a short, cruel laugh. 'Anyway . . .' She stretched up, showing thick curls under her arms, and stroked the wall with her knuckles. 'Anyway, you're gonna try kicking this place back into life, ehh?' Before he could answer, she added, 'This white, *white* elephant.' He flinched. Throughout his career, her collaboration, her approval, had been specially important. It made no real sense, but her blessing, as an African, was vital to him, an African. If Kaz deserted him now . . . it would be unbearable.

Sensing his distress, she softened her tone: 'We get to open this ol' house of dreams again?'

'We have a last go,' he drawled, trying to enter her B-movie world. He wanted them to smile together before he left the room.

Within the net of hair braids, her look was unfathomable. 'I get to do Andromache again?'

'But of course.'

She laughed. 'Wow, I better start practising some grief again, ehh?, start digging into my deepest darkest shit again.' She called over his shoulder to Charlie, 'Hey, Mr Medicine Man! Orders from the boss – undo your potions and get me back to Shitsville!'

Her head lolled back and the braids parted, showing her eyes for the first time. They were swollen. Hard, sore sacs of fluid. Not from bruising or drink or sleeplessness . . . something else. As though

she'd been crying for days. Felix longed to ask again about this
bender – what started it? – but now wasn't the time.

Back in his room, Felix plugged in the television set again. Duma
was still there. His face close to the glass, his eyes in mid-blink, his
lips in mid-utterance, an odd pull to his flesh. This is what he might
look like in private, drunk or ejaculating. It was a distorted version
of the famous image, the Big Man image, which used to be everywhere, magnified massively on the sides of skyscrapers and
billboards, or in miniature on stamps, currency, badges, stickers,
carried as placards and flags, framed in every office and home, or
indeed popping up unexpectedly on your television screen. Now it
was as though Duma was *stuck* in the airwaves. Felix tried various
procedures to shift the image, like he'd done earlier, pressing buttons, tapping the machinery. When nothing succeeded, he decided
that the tape must be tangled within the video machine. Reaching
his fingers into the slot, he got a fright. The interior was pliant,
damp, quite hot. It was like feeling inside someone's mouth or body.
Felix dared not glance up at the screen to see if Duma's expression
had changed.

The horror, the horror
chaos, Africa

five

'Horror,' said Felix. 'I'd like, if I may, to talk about horror.'

Emile stared back impassively. An elderly, thin figure, puffing at a cheap local cigarette, playing with his lank beard, trapping smoke within the twists, and then letting it escape in faint spirals, Emile was Felix's psychotherapist.

'I don't know if I've mentioned this before,' said Felix. 'But I've always felt a sort of . . . connection to horror. It travels with me *about* *horror —* through my life, shuffling along at my side. You know the way *Kurtz?* hyenas walk? You know that shuffling, limping, broken-backed walk? Well, that's how it feels. Horror. Like I've got a pet hyena at my side. It excites me just to say this.'

Emile shrugged. 'We're often excited by the same thing that frightens us, my dear.' The term was used lightly, with a Continental flourish. Born in the old Congo, Emile spoke with a lush Belgian-Jewish accent. Years ago, when he first started attending these sessions, Felix was struck by one of Emile's terms – 'You can *devil-up* this tendency', 'You might *devil-up* a resistance here' – thinking that it was shrink-speak for exorcising one's demons. He was disappointed to discover that Emile was simply saying *develop*.

'The cure in America went well,' Felix said, trying not to sound apologetic. When first consulted about the drying-out plan, Emile had declared, 'I'm utterly opposed to complete abstinence. You're just lighting a time-bomb my dear, that's all you're doing. Say to any human being, "You absolutely cannot do this thing that you passionately want to do", and sooner or later . . . boom!' But Felix was determined, and proceeded without Emile's blessing.

'. . . Extremely well,' Felix continued. 'Apart from a slight problem with walking, talking and staying awake, I'm tickety-boo.' His joke had as little effect on Emile as it had on Kaz. He ploughed on, grateful that his thoughts were at least coming out with some fluency. 'I mean, I may have lost my job today, lost the theatre, and yet I feel all right. Well, all right-ish. As though it happened to someone else . . . to this ghoul maybe, this ghoul that everyone seems to hear and see, that everyone cringes from. Meanwhile, me, the real me, I feel like I can make, invent, create myself from scratch. Who will I be, what will I believe in? On the one hand, it reminds me of tackling a part, y'know, as a director, or actor . . . what way shall we do it, how shall we play Felix? On the other hand, it reminds me of . . . Frankenstein.'

Felix gave a small abashed laugh, and went silent. An electric fan was propped on an empty kerosene tin in front of them. A cord trailed from it, all the way down the long wooden verandah, yet the fan's blades were rusted and still. The mid-afternoon heat was so thick you swallowed rather than inhaled, feeling slightly sickened by every mouthful. Roof to floor insect screens, opaque with age, added to the sense of airlessness. Felix couldn't see the overgrown garden beyond, but he could hear it: a noise like static. Although made by living creatures it sounded like telegraph poles in the *bundu*. Maybe underground pylons and satellite dishes buzzed like this too, he mused – these mysterious modern systems that could carry a word, a voice, a face, and God knows what else into your home, your television set . . .

Felix sniffed his fingers, recalling the moment of touching inside the video machine, and then the panicky drive across town to Emile's side. 'Anyway,' he mumbled, 'I wondered if we should talk about this feeling of horror?'

Emile shifted restlessly, the old cane armchair creaking around him. 'Tell me when you want to draw, by the way. You wanna draw now?'

'Ehrm, all right,' said Felix, feeling bullied into it. He tried to signal his displeasure, but it was no good. Even in the old days, when Felix's scowl wasn't just the chance arrangement of his flesh, but fully inhabited by his philosophy, even then Emile had seemed impervious to it. And worse, Felix often had the impression that he bored Emile. But how could that be? How could Emile ever have had a more fascinating patient? – or *client*, as the old man preferred to say.

Maybe it ran in the family, for Emile was Charlie's father, and boredom was a Charlie trait as well. Felix sometimes wondered if it didn't lie behind the pair's long and enigmatic feud: the physicians of Felix's mind and body hadn't spoken in years. Everyone assumed it was rooted in some terrible family secret. But maybe father and son simply bored one another?

Adding a fifth stick of Juicy Fruit chewing-gum to the wodge in his mouth, Felix selected his customary blue colour from Emile's dilapidated crayon box, and set to work on the sketchpad.

He tried to be open, unselfconscious; not to let the knowing, scheming part of his mind intrude between the crayon and the paper; the idea was to let what Emile called his *underself* spill out in the big doodle, which swirled, looped, knotted itself, and ran free across the paper. Today the loot from Felix's quiet inner chambers was a familiar assortment of eyes, fish and wings, but with something extra. A scissors-like shape. An image from the memory, which kept trying to surface – of *The Odyssey*'s opening night and his arrest. Ignoring it, Felix began the next part of the exercise: developing the whirlpool of shapes into one cohesive image. He made little grimaces and puffing noises as he worked.

When he was finished, and had woken Emile – discreetly, by knocking over the crayon box – they put the sketchpad into the centre of the reed matting on the floor, and leaned forward on their knees. A drop of sweat fell from each of their noses, tapping the paper.

'So now what do you see?' Emile asked.

'A sort of animal, me, I suppose . . . this over here, this is supposed to be an eye . . . and he's sort of got his arms wrapped round his face and . . .' He laughed uneasily. 'Portrait of the artist as a rather scared chap, I would say.'

'Looks strong too.'

'Oh, no!'

'Ah, yes. Strong defences. Those arms. Thick and powerful.'

Felix laughed. 'It's just because I can't draw straight.'

'Your underself can draw as straight as it needs, my dear.' Emile maintained that this therapy (his own invention, according to him) worked better for non-artists, who weren't distracted by issues of composition, anatomy, or whatever. 'Do a *gestalt* on it. What is the face saying?'

'*Aaaarrgghh!*'

Emile wasn't amused. 'What else you see there?' When Felix shrugged, he said, 'You wanna know what I see?'

'All right,' said Felix, with a nervous smile.

'Here!' said Emile, landing one long fingernail on the paper. 'Why is there a vagina here I'm wondering?'

'Because it isn't one,' said Felix. 'It's a pair of scissors.'

'A vagina,' insisted Emile. 'With the poor lady's legs spread wide.'

'Those are the blades of the sci–'

'How interesting,' said Emile, becoming more animated than he had been so far. 'You think it's a pair of scissors.'

'I don't *think* it's a pair of scissors. I *know* it's a pair of scissors. I drew it! You may *think* it's a vagina, that's up to you. My opinion happens to be the right one.'

'The artist speaks.'

'Tsk!' went Felix, feeling trapped. He didn't want to talk about the pair of scissors, to dredge up all that again. But nor did he want to surrender to Emile's train of thought. You dirty old man, he thought, you've just *devilled-up* a vagina for yourself! 'Look,' he said. 'It's just what we've often discussed. It's the lamentable standard of my drawing. If I was, say, Michelangelo sitting here with his shrink, there'd be no argument about whether this squiggle revealed a hidden craving for a bonk or a haircut!'

'That's an interesting view,' said Emile. 'So you'd go on to insist that Shakespeare is the only one who should interpret and therefore direct his plays?'

'Erhm,' said Felix.

'*Eh bien, mon cochon!*' cried Emile, rubbing his nose gleefully.

'Oh, bother!' said Felix animatedly. 'This drawing is just full of terror, horror – can we please talk about that?'

'Certainly, but I thought you were saying earlier how "ticketyboo" you feel.'

'*And* a sense of horror!' said Felix. 'The two side by side.'

'A tickety-boo sense of horror?'

'Look I know you don't believe in this recovery programme I've been through, and . . .' His voice suddenly began to rise. 'It's ruddy marvellous, y'know, my shrink doesn't approve of me getting better! Kaz – she's furious because I've changed! The board members – they're furious because they think I haven't! It's not just what I want from the new Felix! It's what everyone else wants him to be!' He paused – Emile was enjoying this anger-display too much. 'Can we talk about it, please – talk about the American clinic?'

'But of course,' Emile answered, smiling ominously.

'Well, the crew over there . . . they encouraged us to open our minds to this concept of . . . of a Greater Power . . .'

As Emile responded with a snort, Felix cried, 'And why not, pray? It doesn't have to be God, it can be anything, anybody you find inspiring, Shakespeare, Mozart, *you*. You've been a Greater Power to me. Freud and Marx have been Greater Powers to you . . .'

'Not any more.'

'No, I know not any more, but –'

'Two Yiddisher shysters who took this century for a ride!'

'Yes, all right,' said Felix, realising he'd pressed the wrong button, and desperate to avoid one of Emile's tirades. 'But what I'm saying is that Freud was –'

'A megalomaniac, a puppeteer, a cheat, *un faisan*, manipulating his patients, manipulating the evidence, I mean the stuff about child abuse – *pfff!*'

'Yes, all right, but like Marx –'

'Short-sighted, naïve! If Marx should've worked anywhere, it should've been here, in Africa, huge rural populations, huge opportunities for land reform, yet he fails here more spectacularly than anywhere, and why, why?'

'Yes, all right, but just –'

'I'll tell you why! Because he's limited to a tiny, tiny European model, which doesn't apply elsewhere!, and – *and* – perhaps more crucially, the fellow simply . . .'

'. . . doesn't understand about corruption,' recited Felix, giving up.

'Doesn't understand about corruption! Gramsci does. Gramsci says that between consent and force there stands corruption. Corruption, corruption. An effective strategy, Gramsci suggests, a strategy of rule. Others are less polite, they just call it the African disease. The Third World disease. No, no, my dear, it's the *human* disease! Here in Africa we are simply more ancient beings, truer to ourselves, in touch with this flaw in our souls.'

'Fine – so as good old Africans, good old ancient beings, can we now talk about gods and devils, please? *Greater Powers?*'

Felix sat upright, starting to preen. That was more like it, more like *him*, able to entrap any opponent, find the spot, deliver a crippling blow.

He checked himself. Emile looked badly winded. The joust had opened an old wound, one that hurt more than any other in his life. It was not just Freud and Marx who had been his heroes, his giants, his Greater Powers – if he allowed the word – and who had betrayed him. No, there was one other as well.

When Duma seized power back in the sixties, Emile assured everyone that it was a good thing. Duma was one of the first African nationalists, promising many social reforms, promising that the country's cobalt wealth would be converted into food and hospitals for his people. The new leader was clearly more aligned to Moscow than Washington (later Duma was also aligned to Israel and Islam *at the same time*, and even for a period to white South Africa), and Emile was one of the first to remark on the coincidence of *duma* being a word in both Russian and KiSwahili, meaning parliament and cheetah respectively. As Duma's regime became more sinister, with rumours about massacres in the villages, strange decrees about twins and half-castes, about not smiling in public or touching a soldier, Emile still argued that, although Duma's methods might seem eccentric or even brutal, his heart was in the right place. In Africa. He was forging a new kind of Afro-Marxist structure; this was bound to seem clumsy at first.

But last year, after Duma was overthrown, and his true nature finally exposed – the mountains of treasure in his jungle palace, the mountains of skulls elsewhere – then Emile could argue no more. His patients noticed that the old man suddenly aged fast, becoming listless, losing his combative relish, frequently falling asleep. His new catchphrase was: 'So – things have changed in this country – so what? Who says it's a change for the better?'

'Because the country's free!' his patients wanted to shout in reply, but nobody did. To debate the subject of freedom with this man required more courage than any of them could muster – Emile held too much intimate information about every one of them, about their private enslavements – so they stayed silent, each deciding that he didn't mean it; here was simply an angry old man refusing to admit he'd been *wrong*.

'Had this dream last night,' Emile said to Felix now. 'On the high seas, green light, deep green water, slow big swells. Me on some sort of raft. All my late relatives, all the male ones, all drifting round the raft like flotsam. One is in a body bag. I know it's someone dear inside. The only female. My mother perhaps. The bag is ripped and some of her is leaking out, green and runny like the water.' He hesitated, thinking, then asked, 'What d'you think it means?'

Felix laughed, and asked, 'Isn't this the wrong way round?' Emile looked at him, baffled. Felix laughed again, and then when Emile still didn't join in, said, 'Well, do what you always tell me to do – make everyone in the dream *you*.'

'Me,' Emile said slowly. 'So . . . I'm on a raft, surrounded by all my dead selves, another dead self is in a body bag . . .' He stopped, a look of fear in his eyes, then said grimly, 'Yes, fairly clear I suppose. Except – the one in the bag – why is that the only female self?' Felix shrugged, wishing they could change the subject.

'The imagination!' Emile cried suddenly, grasping his own head. 'What a gift. Even in that bleak dream, such beauty. The way my mind pictured the light, the heavy swell of the sea, the torn body bag, all the details. Such an achievement, such masterpieces, all going on, all the time. We're so gifted. Why d'you feel the need for anything else? This twelve-step, Bible-punching "Greater Power" bullshit your new American friends are filling your head with! This born-again crap! This –'

'That's not fair, that's –'

'Oh, my dear, just worship yourself. Please. There's nothing else, nothing finer. Our imagination – it turns us into our own gods.'

And our appetite? thought Felix. That turns us into the other things.

'Mr Chabecq,' said a voice. It was a plump Irish nun, one of the Sisters of Mercy who ran the place.

Emile looked up at her with dazed eyes, and then abruptly pointed at Felix. 'You know his problem? Hmn? His problem isn't drink, it's the same as yours – virginity.'

Felix's mouth fell open, while the nun repeated Emile's name, but in a cautioning tone.

'The drink would never've got out of hand if he'd've let me sort out the other thing,' continued Emile. 'Can you believe it? A man of almost fifty and he's never –'

'Emile!' Felix cried softly, half-standing.

'*J'en ai ras le bol!*' snapped Emile. He gave a small, ghastly laugh. 'And you know why he's a virgin? You know what I believe he wants to do, but dares not?'

'EMILE!' called Felix – from deep inside.

The old man finally heard, and checked himself. 'All just time-bombs, my dear,' he said, as a parting shot, then turned to the nun with weary, raised eyebrows. '*Ouais?*'

'We must wash your hands,' she explained gently. 'For supper.'

Emile smiled, relishing the prospect of both rituals: cleaning and feeding. He allowed her to retie the threadbare cord on his towelling dressing gown, and to help him out of the cane armchair. 'And where do these go back to, if you please?' she asked Emile, in a little-girl voice, collecting the box of crayons and sketchpad. 'Isn't the games room the place where we . . . ?'

'Oh, yes, yes,' Emile muttered, taking them from her. As she started to lead him away, he said to Felix, 'Our time is up, I'm afraid,' his manner cool and professional again, as though he was being hurried to another appointment. 'Same time next week.'

'Same time next week,' echoed Felix, trying to sound keen. The pair vanished round the corner.

Last year, after the fall of Duma, when Emile's health suddenly

declined and he had been forced to retire, he eschewed a more luxu-
rious refuge for old age, a bungalow along the coast with a private
nurse, and instead moved into this place: a small convent hospital
with one ward for the aged and dying. Being white-skinned and
Jewish, his admission by the sisters was remarkable, and seen as a
tribute to his work among the poor over the years, distributing
food, comfort, and generous portions of his wealth. Felix had felt
sufficient loyalty towards his mentor to continue their sessions in his
new residence. 'It'll help keep both our minds active,' he'd said to a
bemused Charlie at the time. But perhaps he'd been wrong.

The facts were unavoidable. His shrink was here, in an old
people's home, losing his marbles. 'Now d'you see what I mean
about horror?!' Felix muttered to Emile's empty chair. He ran both
hands over his face and hair, collecting the sweat. It was cold.

Emile had said it. The V-word. He had said it out loud.

Felix's car, a rusting green VW Beetle, slowed to a halt on the edge of
the *soko kubwa*, the central market; part of a queue of bicycles and
scooters, jeeps and lorries, donkeys and camels inching round and in
between the swarming scene. Felix gawped, smiling. Let Emile mock,
dismiss it all with the phrase *born-again*, but here was proof that it
was true. Felix had passed through this market-place a million times,
yet never really *seen* it before. It was astonishing. The mats heaped
with fruit, clothes, sandals, the cardboard boxes laid out with individual cigarettes, 'smoke-sticks', the cool-drink vans, the cooking
braziers, the optician's stall selling sunglasses or specs-made-while-u-
wait, the *uganga* table displaying little trays of roots, dried monkey
paws, hornbill beaks and dice-sized nuggets of animal bone. Multi-
coloured sun brollies and monstrous bunches of grey-green bananas
travelled around, head-high, with the shopping folk, above throngs
of traders, vendors, beggars, as well as long-horned cattle and
scraggy-haired goats. The whole spectacle was steaming in a haze of
sunlight, dust, and smoke from the food-stalls, clusters of flies too,
and the air was raucous with whistles, hair-clippers, sewing-
machines, ghetto-blasters, fowls and beasts crowing and baying, and,
above all, the cries of human beings demanding to be heard.

'Beautiful,' Felix whispered to himself, admiring the way that everyone swayed, hopped, danced, made way for one another or fitted together, and managed, in a mass display of balance and harmony, to avoid what any Martian observer would expect from this scene: a catastrophe of fighting or crushing. '. . . Beautiful.'

Bang. An open hand on the car roof. Felix leaned forward and peered out. No one there. No one even within reach. *Bang, bang.*

It must be the ghosts again, thought Felix, deciding to stay calm. *Bang, bang, bang.* And yes, here they were, jostling into view, consisting of two if not three dimensions, and at least all the primary colours, here they come . . .

ghosts

A crowd of revellers. The mood is special. People are happy, phenomenally happy. Laughing, crying, singing, bouncing on the spot like Masai dancers, climbing on one another. Their wildness is tempered with kindness; no one is being hurt. Here's a group lifting someone to safety. Here's another carrying fire, protecting one another from the flames that fall away. They're burning flags and placards, all with Duma's image. This must be one of the ecstatic processions following Liberation last year. Yes, yes. And here's a group from the theatre, Kaz among them, and Mr Mmalo, and Frankie Hoong, and . . .

Felix recoiled in his car, accidentally slamming the hooter, instantly banishing the ghosts.

He didn't want to see himself during those celebrations. He was so happy then – too happy. It wasn't just Liberation. The world had caught up with him at last – *everyone* was drinking before breakfast! For a few days, about a fortnight, he became normal. It was incredible. And then when the others went back to it, their normality, he couldn't bear it. In fury, he accelerated his habit, it grew feverish, and of the next few months he remembered nothing. Nothing.

Looking round the market-place now, Felix realised he truly hadn't seen this place before – not with clear eyes. What had changed since Liberation?

That gang of *magendo* kids over there. Of course there had been a contraband market before, during Duma's regime, but not run openly, and not by these strange children. They had driven a fleet of cars onto the square at dawn, when this was still possible, and now, inscrutable behind shades and low-brimmed baseball caps, they stood over their open boots, laden with the latest precious commodities: butter, bottled water, light-bulbs, and, most prized of all, cellphones. Like other public services, the telephone exchange barely functioned any more. On the rare occasions when it did, you were taken into an echoing tunnel of voices, all speaking together, *cacophony* thousands of conversations, each audible, except your own. Cellphones were no longer a luxury item. Families sold furniture or traded cattle to get one. Here in the market, scores of them were in use at the moment; it was as though the area had been beset by a plague of fat black insects, all stuck to people's ears, making them twist this way and that. Cellphones and rifles . . . rifles were another vital accessory, carried by everyone, not just soldiers like in the old days. Determined to deflate the country's reputation as a repressive state, the new government had decimated the police and armed forces, creating a Wild West atmosphere, which the poor relished more than the rich. And the stall over there, that was new too – heaped with skinflick magazines, videos, ointments and toys. And the stall next to it, selling *khat* leaves, ready-rolled reefers and little foil twists.

Nearby stood a lorry loaded with elephant tusks. The new president, John C. Guwedekko, was passionate about the restoration of the ivory trade; it was, he argued, an African solution to African poverty. In the back of his lorry, the tusk-merchant also offered rhino horn. He still did it secretly, but, who knows, John C. Guwedekko might eventually argue for this too. Young and heroic, 'Africa's Guevara', a David who had felled Duma's Goliath, the president had the ear of the international community. 'A tough pragmatist in terms of wildlife conservation perhaps,' said the overseas papers, 'the twenty-one-year-old arrived on the scene as a "rebel leader" and is still flaunting the label – however, he is also a humanitarian of exceptional courage and vision.' After all, Guwedekko had opened his arms to large numbers of refugees from neighbouring states – their tents, boxes, and washing lines surrounded the marketplace like a frayed edge; he had done this despite warnings that his own people could become swamped by a new *mki-mbizi* population, he had done this in the name of decency.

'So – things have changed in this country – so what? Who says it's a change for the better?'

Emile's catchphrase rang in Felix's head as he surveyed the new features of the market-place. Were they good or bad signs? Difficult to tell. The State was in limbo. Since coming to office, Guwedekko had rejected calls for elections, laid out a two-year timetable to create a new constitution, and, apart from essential law-changes and assembling the machinery for the Hakika, he had virtually put the country on hold. On holiday. If, immediately after Duma's fall, it had seemed to Felix that the whole world had joined in his drunkenness, now it seemed he was the only sober man at a long and uninhibited party.

Bang! went a hand on his car roof again. The ghosts were back. He ignored them. *Bang, bang!* A face slid down the windscreen, leering at him. Two, three more. These weren't ghosts, but a mob of beggar boys, aged about eight. They operated like hyenas or wild dogs, working in deadly little packs, able to bring down much bigger prey than themselves. Felix's forefinger darted round the lock-studs on the car doors. All were fastened. It might not be enough though. The windows could easily be smashed. He wished he had a rifle in the car, a cellphone, both. But he had stubbornly refused Charlie's offer to supply him with these, or indeed a full-time bodyguard, saying, 'This is my city, my home, I refuse to be terrorised by my own home!' The car began to rock. God, how many children were in this pack? Some of them were so young their heads didn't reach the windows. If only the traffic jam would free up, if only he could drive away! Perhaps he should try to reason with the kids: 'You see me as non-Af, privileged, rich, but it's not what you think, ask your parents, they'll know who I am, they were probably in my shows, we worked together for a better life, my theatre stood for it, I was arrested once, I was –!'

He checked himself. The children were gone. They had spotted easier prey and were gone. He breathed again, and noticed his right leg. Desperate to flee, it was still kicking impotently at his accelerator. He saw an image of himself a moment earlier, cooking up arguments to save his skin. Yet his miniature attackers probably didn't speak English, or even KiSwahili; they probably didn't speak at all. So the idea of offering up his artistic credentials, *his CV*! He began to giggle.

The traffic moved forward a little, then stopped again, more solidly than before. Felix's smile dried on his lips, and he sat back, panicking quietly.

New state a country on a drunken revel of a holiday
beautiful chaos + horror
disillusioned liberals + displaced whites who also struggled
in their own way - "I was arrested one, I was—!"
tortured.
New generation of unspeaking young animals - hunting
in packs like wild dog + running the underlife.

s i x

By the time Felix reached the theatre, he was feeling very strange indeed. He parked his car outside the stage door, and sat with the door open, his feet in the gutter, wondering if he was going to throw up. Perhaps it was the scare in the market-place, or perhaps jet-lag, or a side effect of the anti-depressant pills, or just the result of not eating properly. Today's sustenance had come from chocolate peanuts, chewing-gum, and ice-cream. He'd spent years living off a purely liquid diet, and now the task of cooking for himself seemed superhuman; he would square up to it later, tomorrow, soon. In the meantime, maybe sleep was the best thing . . . abandon plans of driving up to Charlie's mansion later, to see Alys, his beloved god-child, and just go to sleep now. Or was it too early for bedtime? He peered up at the dull greenish sky, having no idea of the hour. Sleep seemed out of reach at the moment, and dangerous somehow. Near the television set and whatever it held inside.

Stepping through the stage door, he lurched wildly. It was no good. He was close to fainting – he must eat something. There was nothing in the fridge upstairs, he would have to knock on someone's door, ask for some food. As he turned this way, then that, wondering which direction to take, a different and disturbing notion struck him. What if some of his old hiding-places were still stocked? The nooks and crannies where he'd stored bottles for times of emergency. He had better check them before seeking food, check and clear them. New times of emergency might arise at any moment, times when temptation comes, the *cravings* of which everyone talked in the clinic.

Touching the walls, his balance perilous, a flutter going like mad in his chest, he wandered backstage, into the wings, drawn towards the quick-change room on the prompt side of the stage. Didn't he used to keep a bottle somewhere in that little cubicle?

Pushing through the dusty black drapes, he was surprised to find someone inside: a man wearing dark shirt and trousers, slumped in a chair, elbows on knees, head bowed, dripping with sweat.

Felix was about to apologise and withdraw when the man raised *ghost of* his head. Felix rocked back in surprise. *self*

It was himself.

Crystal clear. Three dimensional. His breath, his smell, his blotched flesh, his creased clothes – everything real, solid, *there*.

Their eyes met. The sitting Felix looked straight through the standing Felix as though *he* was the ghost.

The standing Felix could do nothing but watch.

The sitting Felix seemed intensely troubled. *The arrest*

He had good reason to be. He was arrested last night.

He was arrested – not Mr Mmalo. How could that be?

Normally a reliable but uninspired actor, something happened to Mr Mmalo last night, Sunday night, half-way through the marathon three-day opening of *The Odyssey*. In rehearsals and pre-views, the resemblance of Cyclops to Emperor Duma had been negligible. But yesterday Mr Mmalo received news that a favourite uncle had fallen victim to one of Duma's death squads, and when it came to the performance, he took an unexpected and reckless leap. Felix watched with horror as Mr Mmalo threw aside the Cyclops helmet, revealing his own startling physical similarity to Duma, and then began to adopt every vocal inflection and physical gesture of the great dictator, as well as the quality that made him so spe-cially dangerous: his *passion*. During Cyclops' meeting with Odysseus, Mr Mmalo leapt into Duma's famous pose, knees slightly bent, arms reaching for the earth, head thrown back, and parodying the dictator's most celebrated quote – 'I *am* Africa!' – roared, 'I *am* this island!' The audience, most of whom had lost relatives or friends to the death squads, made an extraordinary noise – a kind of snarl, thunderous and gleeful – and the show stopped for several minutes while Mr Mmalo repeated the action, to wilder and wilder cheering and, eventually, a standing ovation.

Half an hour later, the State Safety Unit men arrived at the stage door, and it was Felix, not Mr Mmalo, they took away.

As someone who had always fantasised about the day that Horror came visiting, Felix was surprised at how calm he was while they bundled him into the car – with unnecessary roughness, almost hysteria, yelling, shoving, like he'd seen happen to others – and during the drive. His main concern was that, having been caught unprepared, he was without even a hip-flask. This could be serious. His drinking had developed its own clock, and any interruption made him very angry indeed. He needed to keep this in check. Such preoccupations vanished on arrival at the police station and he realised there was to be no formal procedure, no filling-in of charge sheets, no phone-calls to lawyers, no discussion at all. The oldest policeman simply said, 'We've been waiting for you' – and Felix knew exactly what he meant. Then they locked him in a cell.

That was six or seven hours ago.

Now his sweat is stinking of whisky – a cold, early-morning purée of last night's consumption – the beads crawling over his flesh like insects, a thin film finding its way along each hair of his head and beard, forming big slow drops at the nape of his neck and underside of his chin.

Despite the heat in here, he is shivering all over: tiny, almost comic movements of his skin, jerks and tics which he can't control, and which cause little whimpering intakes of breath. It's only partly from fear. He has a terrible thirst. Even water would help. He swallows constantly and licks round his mouth, but it's a losing battle. His gums are slowly sticking to the inside of his lips. It feels like his face is being fastened in a grip.

A man arrives. Shortish, a soft body, clerical-looking. He is wearing a shabby suit and carries a cheap aluminium attaché case.

Ignoring Felix, he sits in a chair, and has a private moment, resting his chin on his chest and blowing his lips, a faraway look in his eyes. He seems irritable, sulky. It is Monday morning. He doesn't want to be back at work. Maybe he has a hangover too.

He makes a phone-call and talks for a long time, listlessly.

Felix speaks only rudimentary KiSwahili, but it's enough to reveal that the conversation doesn't concern him. The man seems to be picking over some disappointment from the weekend – a row with his wife, a bet on a sports event? – saying the same phrases again and again.

Eventually the call finishes. The man heaves himself to his feet, and without looking at Felix – he hasn't done this once yet – says, '*Vua nguo!*'

Felix stands also and swallows hard, trying to lubricate his parched mouth. 'Frightfully sorry . . . my Swahili isn't . . .'

'*Vua nguo!*' the man says again, pointing his chin at Felix's torso and giving a downward nod.

It's clear that he wants Felix to undress.

Felix hesitates. There's something about the man's manner that both intimidates and reassures. You feel scared of irritating him, yet sense he isn't here to harm you. He's too bored. The instruction to undress was delivered as a doctor might – in fact, the man's air is very similar: weary, disinterested, seen-it-all-before. Perhaps he *is* a doctor. Perhaps this is a routine medical examination, which they give all prisoners; to cover themselves, to counter accusations of police brutality. They must know that Felix is an important person, or at any rate has important friends. And Felix is white-skinned, *non-Af*, protected from Duma's crazy laws. It might be best to co-operate. To adopt the same cold but civil behaviour as this man. Like now: he's patiently waiting for Felix to do as told. He's not shouting or pushing, like those thugs at the theatre. If anything, he looks like he doesn't really care. His small eyes are blank, his mind elsewhere.

Felix unbuttons his shirt and trousers and removes them.

A voice in him asks, 'Why are you letting this happen?' Another answers, 'Can't think clearly, need a drink.'

He waits.

The man repeats the previous gesture: pointing his chin at Felix and giving a downward nod. His weary look is almost apologetic – a doctor again, saying, 'Sorry but we are going to have to take the lot off.'

Felix climbs out of his vest and underpants, more embarrassed by his shaking fingers and funny muscle spasms than anything else. He wants to say, 'This isn't because I'm frightened, I'm *not* frightened, I've no need to be frightened, have I?'

Now he stands with his hands crossed in front of him, thinking that it reminds him of a photograph of something he can't place.

'*Keti hapo!*' instructs the man, nodding towards the chair.

Felix sits, hands in his lap.

The man opens his attaché case and removes a bundle of coiled rubber tubing. This is for taking blood pressure, Felix decides. He wants to believe this. He tries to hold on to the idea even as it becomes clear that the tubing is in three pieces. But when the man lifts his hands from his lap, and starts tying them behind the chair, Felix begins a dream-like moan, 'Nnnn – ! Nnnn – !' He's scared to say the word no. It would trigger the query what? He would have to explain: 'Don't hurt me.' The man would answer: 'Hurt you? But you're in a police station – this is Monday morning – we don't hurt people, we restrain them, the law allows me to restrain you.'

As the man bends, aiming to fasten his prisoner's ankles to the front legs of the chair, Felix finally begins to struggle, thrashing in a slow, strange way. The man pauses, patiently, and glances to the door. The message is clear: we can either do this calmly or I can summon assistance.

In a state of shock, Felix watches himself go still, allowing the rest of the binding to proceed.

The man makes the knots very tight. Looking down, Felix sees his feet turn yellow, then white.

He wants to say, 'This isn't necessary,' but to do so would be to criticise the man's professionalism. He must know how tight to tie the tubing.

At the theatre, Felix wouldn't hesitate to challenge people about their skills, snarling abuse at them, uncovering weaknesses they didn't even know they had. Here he sits timid and naked in a chair.

The pity of this strikes him. He feels a warm rush go down the inside of his left thigh. He doesn't want to look. He remembers videoing an execution – a woman tied to traffic lights – no blood, no visible spillage, except for three, almost pretty rivulets down one leg.

The man glances at Felix's mess and tuts. He doesn't look angry or disgusted, only tired. His expression seems to say, 'I hate work, especially on Monday mornings, when all the old routines start up again.'

He goes back to his attaché case and rummages in it. A clutter of objects – little bottles, wads of cloth, pieces of bamboo, metal things – some in compartments, some rolling free. It *could* still be a doctor's kit . . . the kind of doctor who works in the villages or squatter camps, say . . . Felix asked Charlie to take him to one of those medical centres for leprosy-research on the New Testament show, and was astonished by the hygiene of the staff, their unwashed instruments and old syringes. Or perhaps this man is a disgraced doctor. He'd have to be, to do this job – *what job?* – Felix doesn't know, doesn't want to know, his mind is jumping about, skipping connections. Maybe the man will inflict some damage – but using a doctor's methods, with pain-killing injections first. Felix fastens on this idea now. He needs the present situation to belong to a world he recognises. The alternative is unthinkable.

The man finds what he is looking for. A half bottle of Johnnie Walker.

Felix's heart lifts. As he suspected, the man has a hangover and knows only one cure for it, even first thing in the morning. They have something in common.

'Yes, yes, and for me, please,' says Felix, surprising himself with the commanding tone of his voice.

The man lowers the bottle from his lips, meets Felix's gaze for the first time, and frowns. He must understand, surely. He must speak English. It's still the country's second, if not *first* language! Anyway, Felix knows the Swahili for this: '*Wiski tafadhali.*'

The man stares at him. From across the room, Felix can smell the harsh aura of the malt, that most male of booze smells.

'I think you'll find it'll be easier for us both,' Felix continues, unsure what he means (*you can do anything you want if you give me some?*), and not caring. The whole chair is beginning to shake with him. 'I know that sounds rather barmy, but I promise you, fellow, I promise you . . .'

The man screws the top back on the bottle.

'You sod!' Felix splutters. He hesitates, then becomes fearless.

'You fuck, you selfish fuck! Right, I want to see a fucking lawyer now! You, yes, *you* – don't stare at me like that – get me a lawyer, *and now*! I have powerful contacts, chum, so you ought to think about that. And you can begin by freeing me from this cunting chair . . .'

He stops. The man has collected a pair of scissors from his case.

For a moment Felix thinks he is to be cut loose and says to himself, 'There, see, it was worth being firm.'

Then things go into slow motion.

As the man approaches, Felix is struck by the fact that, although clearly sharp, the scissors are filthy, with congealed bits on the joint of the blades. This outrages him somehow, yet on the other hand it makes sense. Why bother to clean these instruments?

The scissors descend.

Felix's testicles think they're the target and retreat, leaving just a frail cage of hair.

But in fact the scissors enter his flesh just below his groin, on the right-hand inner thigh, the dry side. Having used both blades, closed, to stab open a hole, the man now separates them, slides one in, and, working with some difficulty, huffing and puffing, snips all the way down to above the knee.

Felix is too shocked to feel pain. He watches the inside of his leg open like a big leather purse. Before any redness, there is yellow, a layer of fatty yellow; it is surprisingly and weirdly bright, as though lit from within.

Then, to Felix's utter astonishment, the man undoes the fastenings round his ankles and steps back with a polite little flourish, as though saying, 'You're free to go now.'

Although his wrists are still bound, Felix is able to slip them over the back of the chair as he rises.

Then the pain comes. The pain of one inner leg touching the other.

With a shriek he goes onto his knees, into a puddle of blood that he hadn't even noticed. The pain is still unbearable. He flips onto his back, legs in the air, held apart.

Now he understands.

This wasn't the start of it. This was just to incapacitate him. And to lay out some ground rules.

The man is serious; a true professional, so good at his work it bores him.

Look at him now: returning the scissors to his case without wiping them – or his hands – and lighting a cigarette.

'*Wafanya kazi peke yako?*' he asks Felix. '*Au kwa Waamerika?*'

Americans . . . something about the Americans. Oh, *that's* how they're going to play it. They're going to say that the events at the theatre last night, the mockery of the emperor, were part of an ongoing plot which obsesses Duma, a CIA plot to dethrone him.

The charge will be high treason. Felix's non-Af status won't save him. Things are much, much worse than he imagined.

The blood from his upturned leg is collecting on his stomach. He feels it cooling at the edges. The iciness spreads through his entire being. A voice inside says, *There will be hours and hours of this.*

Then Charlie rushes in.

Charlie – still in his suit from the theatre, unshaven, drawn, panicky. He's been up all night trying to find help. And he's finally succeeded. Following him into the cell, wearing bathrobe and shortie pyjamas, is a huge white man who has been a regular guest at those famous parties of Charlie's. He bellows instructions to the man and apologies to Felix in the same breath.

Felix blinks. Even from his upside-down position on the floor, the face of the new man is familiar, more than familiar. From the papers, the television. This is Bull Brak. Colonel Bull Brak. The country's senior police chief, and Duma's right-hand man.

Originally from white Northern Rhodesia, where he was an Army officer, then working freelance, hiring himself out as a mercenary in assorted civil wars – the Congo, Sierra Leone and Angola – and throwing in a stint as a secret-service boss in the old South Africa, Bull Brak had changed sides more often and survived more African upheavals than seemed humanly possible.

'Brak's A Cat With Nine Lives!' shouted the local paper when he first sought political asylum in this country, while its cartoonist, noting that the tall, big-boned man had something of the cowboy about him, with hooded eyes and lethargic swagger, portrayed him as the chief cowboy of them all, the *Dook*.

I've been saved by the Dook! a triumphant voice yells in Felix's head. *It's like being saved by the cavalry – he is the cavalry, the rough-riding law of the land, and he's on my side! – I'm safe, I'm invincible again!*

Brak dismisses the man with the attaché case. Before he closes it, the bottle of Johnnie Walker attracts Charlie's attention. He passes it to Felix, knowing that his patient needs this more urgently than anything else.

And then it's all over. Felix's wound is being administered to by Charlie, with supplies from his doctor's bag – a *real* doctor's *real* bag – and Brak is sharing the whisky with him. The colonel is surprisingly good-humoured about Felix's crime, giving his distinctive laugh – '*Haw!*' – and saying, 'It's only a theatre show, hey?'

In exchange for the promise that tomorrow night Mr Mmalo will simply play Cyclops as a giant with one eye and a Greek accent, thus avoiding any confusion in the audience, Brak sums up: 'Both sides in the wrong, apologies all round, centre of gravity secured, stability restored, and no real harm done. I think we must just all forget this ever happened, and be thankful that our society isn't as bad as they say, hey? *Haw!*'

seven

The early-morning air was wet and fresh, and still noisy with the soft row of the night; its last ringings and clickings. Felix stretched luxuriously, enjoying the way that consciousness came over him like cool water, with such clarity, such variety of patterns and lightness.

In the bad old days, there would have been only one topic struggling up through the sludge: How bad do I hurt? . . . Better start again straightaway.

He beamed, eyes shut tight, embarrassed by his own happiness, then slowly sat up and looked around. From this vantage point on the roof of the Alex, he could see over the wall of bougainvillaea opposite to the town with its rusting white-and-brown tin roofs, the domes of mosques, the spires of British and German churches, a rose-coloured skyscraper (belonging to Lord Gomes), and beyond, right down to the harbour with its cranes, palm trees and dhows, and finally a wide stretch of Indian Ocean. One vessel was crossing the horizon: a container-ship, its cargo in different colours, blues, yellows, reds, all piled high. It looked like a floating apartment block.

If there were people in those apartments, thought Felix, the view they would have of my home is a mountain, a mountain first and foremost.

The port was built in the crater of an extinct volcano, its seaward side having fallen away many millennia ago. Known as the Kwatokuu, the mountainscape looked like a headless figure with open, curved arms. One elbow was more prominent than the other, jutting aggressively at new arrivals, while protecting those who stayed within her embrace.

Felix climbed to his feet, happy and naked, his morning erection still tight, bobbing in the air. The sunrise was starting, approaching from behind, from the land, from Africa, up over the rim of the ancient volcano. It touched the back of his head like a warm hand, and within seconds was flooding the roof with its unique, peculiar, flaming hue. The locals had a saying for the phenomenon: 'Each of our days is born on fire.' Charlie had once tried to explain it to Felix, but it was too scientific for his sensibilities; something about the pollution from the docks and town, and all the cooking fires in the shanty towns, something about this invisible haze breaking up the light, scattering the shorter blue rays and only letting through the red ones. But Felix didn't buy it. Why, then, were there reports of the first settlers panicking as they awoke on their first morning, thinking that the volcano had come back to life? There had been no pollution from docks and shanty towns then – yet clearly they had seen the same red-gold brightness flow over their world like molten lava.

This colour fell now – as Felix watched – on the wall of bougainvillaea across the street, setting its blossoms alight one by one, lower and lower, the cool night shadow of the theatre dropping out of its way like a gauze.

It was so beautiful that Felix wondered if he should call someone. But no, it would only disappear when they arrived, or be over.

He reached down, tracing the old scar ridge that stretched from under his groin to above the knee. His own miniature mountain range, like on a relief map. He felt proud of the scar, yet hated reliving the incident. He wondered why it had surfaced so vividly in the quick-change room.

Oh, all the strangeness of yesterday – it all started and ended with that bloody television set! When he returned upstairs last-night, having failed to find food and overcome with tiredness by then, he saw that Duma's face was still on the screen, pulsating slightly. This was especially disquieting since there was now a power cut in the building. Felix stood frozen in the black room, eyes downcast, watching the loose, grey-green light playing on his hands. Then he quickly climbed out of the window, and onto the roof. Which was ridiculous. He shouldn't be the one to move out. The television should.

He turned towards the view again. It had begun to echo with the cries of roosters and seagulls. Both such burly, vicious-faced birds, they shared a kinship, Felix thought. Although one was earthbound, fussing in the dirt, and the other adrift in fresh ocean skies, there was a similarity to their call. The tone grated, it sounded unoiled, yet roused something in him; a yearning he couldn't explain.

He grinned, catching himself out. His life went wrong, he decided, when he went into the arts. Artists picture themselves as threaded into the circumference of the globe. They think this roundness includes them, that they are an indispensable link in the loop, that everything, *everything* comes to them, and through them, and is passed on by them. It had happened just then. The sweet, harsh tune of cock-crows and seagull calls, these were for him, *in* him somehow. And the flaming spectacle of the sunrise too. Even the shape of the bay itself: it began here, in the left-hand corner of his vision and travelled round in one great loving curve to over here, the right-hand side; all part of a sphere that needed him to complete it.

But Emile was wrong. There wasn't just ourselves to worship, ourselves, ourselves. Absurd. That was how children thought, or fools, or dictators. Or artists!

Well, he had failed as an artist. 'A last go,' he'd requested from the board. What did he mean – swansong or final chance? It didn't matter. He must find a different, humble, generous way of living his life. For so long he'd tried to be clever, sophisticated, calculating, selfish – *an artist* – now he would be the opposite, now he would be . . . He hesitated, wondering what the opposite of an artist was, and, unable to decide, began to dance.

Maybe he would find love along the way, maybe lose his virginity, maybe lead some kind of conventional life. 'Maybe this, maybe that,' he chanted, allowing himself the see-sawing signature tune of his ancestors. 'Maybe-schmaybe, yingelbee-yaybee.' Anything's possible, he thought, waltzing across the roof, I'm starting from the beginning again, I'm a foetus with a stiffy, I'm a twinkle in my own eye . . . !

In the blur of the dance, a pair of watching eyes. Felix stopped and spun round. A head was poking out of the skylight – Kaz, her feet on his table below.

'You bin drinking?' she asked.

'Oh, goodness, what? No, no,' he flustered, folding his hands in front of him. The two were used to seeing one another unclothed, but not in a state of arousal.

'There's some breakfast here,' she said gruffly, as one offering friendship after a fight.

'Oh, that's kind!' His excitement having subsided, he reached for her hands. As she helped him into the room, he caught a whiff of booze on her breath; a chemical odour, almost medicinal. The shock was strange, gentle, almost nostalgic, coinciding with the moment that his naked body, an innocent thing now, descended into strong, uplifted arms. He wondered when he'd first smelt alcohol on an adult, and who it had been? Both his parents liked their whisky. They used to drink it at this very table, the family dining-table back at the old house in Jamutiri Street, when they cleared it to play poker with Mr and Mrs Carrington on Wednesday nights.

Kaz had brought a bowl of maize porridge with honey, and a big slice of paw-paw. Pulling on a T-shirt and bathing trunks, Felix ate hungrily. She made coffee. Neither spoke, but they felt easier with one another again. He waited, knowing she wanted something from him.

Later, when they were drinking their coffee, a potent local brew, she moved his feet into her lap and began kneading them, going everywhere, the thin, almost sharp bones of her fingers rubbing round his heels, pressing into the arches, searching between his toes.

'My son,' she said.

'Hmn?' he replied, wriggling with pleasure.

'I used to do this when he was small, that damned beautiful child, soothe him like this.'

Felix reached across to her head, touching the coxcomb, tracing the paths of scalp where she had divided her plaits, and scratching gently. She began to murmur deep in her throat. It was like the old days, when they would groom one another for hours, like animals, entwined in lazy, sprawling positions, talking together or Kaz singing; and drinking, of course, passing out, drinking some more –

'Letting the spirit sink into us,' as Kaz put it – laughing wildly, some-times wetting themselves where they lay.

Still working his foot with one hand, Kaz lit a cigarette. The flame illuminated her face inside the hair braids; it was running with tears. But her voice was as rough and playful as always. 'Can we talk? Have I got my friend back? Can I talk to him?'

Instead of replying, Felix took the cigarette from between her fingers and, handling it like a peace pipe, carried it to his lips. He sucked gingerly. The taste made him sit upright in shock, his head and stomach threatening to change places.

'Talk,' he gasped.

She gave a small laugh, then bowed her head, hesitating. 'The Hakika ended yesterday.'

'Yes.'

'I kept hoping someone would confess.'

Felix nodded. Fourteen months earlier, just before Duma's over-throw, Kaz's son, a student at the local university, had been arrested during a campus demonstration – protesting about the censorship of educational books – and died in custody. Felix couldn't recall his name now . . . even though he'd often been in Kaz's dressing-room as a baby, and, later, played one of the Chorus in *The Iliad*. Names were not Felix's strongest point. What with various five-hundred-strong Choruses swarming through the theatre over the years, adults, infants, children, all changing from show to show, he'd given up on names long ago. He just had vague images of a handsome, humor-ous face, a sinewy body, his skin much lighter than his mother's. He was a mulatto, one of Duma's hated 'mongrels'. A mongrel *and* a student – the kid hadn't stood a chance in the hands of the police.

'I watched every session on TV,' Kaz continued, 'read every report in the papers, some days I went to the cathedral where they held it, sat through hours and hours. I kept hoping someone would mention him, say what happened. Just to know, just to know. I prayed every way I could, even went to the *mganga*, sacrificed a white fowl. Just to know.' Her fingers strayed restlessly over the crucifix round her neck. 'But, hey, listen – even a day or two before it ended, what I did know then, what I knew *for sure*, is that no one was gonna speak about him, confess what happened, so . . .' She shrugged.

Felix smiled wryly to himself – and he had thought her bender was prompted by fears for their friendship! He tried another puff of the cigarette. It was getting easier, the revulsion and dizziness becoming restful in their own way. It reminded him of first learning to drink.

'Well,' he said, 'the round-ups start today, so if his killer didn't confess during the amnesty, well, one must hope that they seek him out now, catch him now.'

'*Ahm*,' said Kaz. It was one of those pure African sounds, which Felix regularly heard her make. It was like a grim word for yes; a doleful confirmation of things. 'You reckon so?'

'I do,' said Felix, hearing how small his commitment sounded, and glimpsing the television set over her shoulder. Its grey screen stared back, a glassy coldness in the bright morning light of the room. Duma's face was gone, but Felix remembered the images of slaughter on the video he'd watched yesterday. There were thousands of Kazzes now: people who'd lost relatives when they went into police custody, or were picked up by the death squads; people who were currently hiring bodyfinders – a lucrative new profession in the country – to sift through the mountains of skulls, the deep pits of bones. Well, a few lucky ones might find their missing body, but justice, revenge, or even comfort? – this was harder to unearth. There were no records of what went on; there were barely statistics. Just gaps in the population. One grim joke going round a few years ago summed it up: *You know what they say about victims? – They all look the same.*

Felix thought this true. When you studied photos of inmates in a German concentration camp or bodies in a Vietnamese ditch – and he had a whole library of these images – you saw the same expression, the same *face* really: a disbelieving frown and a slightly open mouth, lips forward, as if trying to formulate a question. Everything else was missing, drained away in shock, all the features that make people special to their loved ones – all gone. Viewed both from outside and within – for Felix had, of course, his own first-hand experience of this emptying, this numbing, this fright – fear was a great leveller.

Kaz passed her palm across one cheek, wiping it dry. 'Still hurts?' Felix asked.

'Oh, boy,' she said, smiling at his naïvety. ' It just rolls on and on. It's like my life's broken in two pieces. Before and after his arrest.' She fetched a piece of toilet paper, and blew her nose. 'Maybe I was holding it all back. I thought that, y'know, the Hakika would grieve for me, punish for me, but now . . . it's like he died yesterday.' She went quiet, toying with some loose change Felix had emptied from his pockets: American cents and quarters. 'Can I?' she asked. He nodded, and watched her weave one of the coins into a braid of hair. Her head was hung with small dappled pebbles, aromatic seeds, beads of wood and eggshell, tiny animal bones, a child's tooth. 'D'you remember,' she asked, 'years ago, when we were doing *Iliad*, you asked how I did the big scene?'

'Indeed,' Felix replied, picturing the moment: the stage was abruptly cleared of the Chorus, and left to Kaz, high on the scaffolding that represented the walls of Troy. During the offstage death of Hector, she began a wail that lasted for the next few minutes – it was as much a feat of singing as anything else – a high, almost euphoric, open-throated wail, lifted from her depths.

'And you asked . . .' Kaz said, starting to laugh in her husky way, while tears still rolled down her cheeks. 'You asked, "Is it the situation in the play, Andromache's situation, or is it the situation in this country, *our* situation, which is moving you so much in that scene, which one is producing that noise you make?"'

'And you wouldn't tell me,' grinned Felix. '"Professional secret," you said, "don't prick the magic, spoil the mystery."'

'*Yaiy!* Well, it was only because the truth was so fucking dumb, it had no fucking mystery or magic at all!' They both laughed loudly, then Kaz went on: 'We'd all lived on the emperor's funny farm for years, it was just ordinary life, it didn't make our hearts sore any more. Did it?' Felix shrugged. 'Well,' she said, 'it had stopped making *my* heart sore. When that scene started and the music was creeping under my skin, and I knew in a moment I had to produce the goods, I'd think of something smaller, closer, something shitty, something that's happened during the day, a car crash, someone in the company who's damn parrot has died and – *ai kadogo!* – they can't bear it, anything, just ordinary, everyday tragedies, it didn't have to be because of the *system*. Or people close to me, family or friends who'd been sick or died their ordinary little deaths, I'd dredge up one of those sad times, and gorge on it in a kinda way, feeding on every little detail. And when you've been through them all or they've lost their impact, after a few dozen performances or so, then you start making them up. It's like a fantasy to help you in the sack, help you cum. Same principle. You play with people in your mind. You take loved ones who are alive and well, and hurt them in your imagination, and I mean really badly hurt – rape, torture, all the worst shit – you must really make the hurt as bad as possible, you must really stick your face in it, really make a very fucking vivid snuff movie out of it, and then one way or another you'll get to the point – and it really is just like cumming – the wow-wow-wow point when your skin feels thin as paper and everything's ready to break, to spill, and hopefully you've timed all this to the cue.'

Felix nodded slowly; he was fascinated by the different work methods of performers. 'And what? You used . . . ?' He hesitated, cursing himself, still unable to remember her son's name. 'You used, ehrm, as one of these . . . ?'

'Zach.'

'. . . Zach as one of these fantasies?'

'Oh, for sure, all the time, I whored the boy, I put him to work on that ol' service,' she said, still smiling, but her voice going dull. 'And then, of course, when I got the news, the actual news, well, the joke was on me. His death was exactly like I'd imagined it. Going into police custody and disappearing without trace. It was almost as if I willed it. Wanted it to happen. Made it happen. Almost as if they'd seen my snuff movies, in here.' She tapped her skull. 'Like the cops had seen in here and copied it.'

'Dear me,' Felix said softly. He felt a peculiar shame. His own arrest, his own brief experience of Duma's police cells, terrible though it was, didn't compare to what other people had experienced. To mention it now, for example, to Kaz, in the same breath as her son, was unthinkable. Even at the time she had been unsympathetic. Soft-glove treatment, she had called it, honky treatment, just honky-tonk. There was a gruesome status game sometimes played in this country; people would start telling their horror stories, and, without anyone intending it, a competition would begin.

Kaz sighed. 'I always promised myself that if his killer wasn't nailed in the Hakika, I'd go after him myself.'

'Won't that be rather hard to – ?'

'No,' she cut in. 'No!' she said again, jabbing her forefinger to her cheek – the gesture says, *Look deep in my eye, this is the truth* – 'No, killing Zach, that was the hard bit. Finding his killer, punishing this animal, that's *meant* to happen. *Ahm*, it is! You remember he was arrested with his girlfriend?'

'Do I?' said Felix with a foolish laugh. 'It was a long time ago, I was so pissed at the time . . .'

She stared at him in amazement – as though either fact should impair one's memory of that event! – then continued, 'Well, this girl, she's of the Igisha, the emperor's own tribe, so she got off lightly, she was just gang-raped a few times, and . . . I dunno the details, but anyhow, she came back alive. So I guess she's where I start.'

'Why haven't you spoken to her already?'

'She disappeared after it happened. They say she was in a pretty rough way. Anyhow, she's back now, she's been seen, she's got this kinda job I hear.' Kaz paused, then spoke quietly, without any drama, 'Come with me to this girl. Help me.'

He answered without hesitation, 'Of course.' This was perfect. This was the new role he was looking for. Himself as friend, as champion of others, as a good and selfless being.

Kaz's reaction was surprising. Before the smile of gratitude, before taking his hand, she asked, 'You promise, ehh? – to the finish, ehh?'

'To the finish,' he echoed solemnly. 'On one condition. I need your help too.' He broke into a smile, nodding towards his television and video sets. 'Help me lug these downstairs.'

'Where they heading?'

'Through the stage door. Onto the road. I'm donating them to the people.'

eight

It began. Darkness, then light, then the flesh of people. And animals, and birds, fish too, these in wheeled tanks, and wearing collars and top hats. Some of the land creatures wore waistcoats and boots, while the men and women wore very little, just pouches and straps, paint and powder.

The smell of human nakedness and animal hide spilled towards the watching crowd, along with the smoke that was travelling around the circle, low down, caressing the passing heels and hoofs, kicked by them, billowing and dipping.

The child began frowning; the look came from deep inside, the centre of her innocence. Was the spectacle *real*? Or – despite the smell of bodies, the heat of the lights – was it magic, a film, a dream? As a band struck up now, adding music to the strange parade, she shifted to the edge of her seat, and stretched her hands towards the circle of light and smoke, trying to touch, trying to understand, trying, at the very least, to put the outline of her own hands into the picture.

It's like the time, mused Felix, the time she visited the theatre, her first-ever visit, for a preview of the Genesis show . . . so rudely interrupted by Duma's downfall that day.

'Love you, little one,' Felix whispered reassuringly.

'Love you too,' came the hushed reply.

'Love-love-lub-lub-blub-blub,' he chanted softly.

'Lub-lub-blub,' she echoed dutifully. This was Alys: Charlie's five-year-old daughter, and Felix's godchild. An hour or so earlier, his reunion with her – *at last* – had been joyous; a hugging, romping tumble of a reunion, an animal-and-cub reunion, the best of his homecoming. He felt so proud. After all, in pre-clinic days, no one had known him more intimately than Alys. During the cuddling and carrying, the hello and goodnight kisses, she actually got to touch the slime of his whisky-flesh, inhale the fumes of his breath. Felix didn't allow any other human being as close, as physically close. And she had accepted the reeking, trembling creature that he was, trusted him in spite of it all, forgiven him in a way. Now, more than anyone else, she deserved the new him – clean-smelling, with calm dry hands, his purity restored – now she could finally have a decent guardian.

Alys was equally enchanted by their reunion, but since then the day had produced an even better treat. Together with Charlie and Kaz, they climbed into the Land Cruiser and, with Noah driving, sped out of town, past the *mki-mbizi* camps, with all their makeshift tepees and Red Cross tents, to where the sloping lines of guy-ropes suddenly soared, taking flight, into the shape of a Big Top . . . CIRCUS ZIKKI.

This was where, according to Kaz's contacts, they would find her son's girlfriend. Felix had asked Charlie along for moral support, and although Kaz seemed faintly uneasy about this, she didn't say anything. Her tears flowed ceaselessly, even when her mood was sassy and frivolous. Her grief was like a bad cold; you tried not to notice.

Now, as she lit another cigarette from the one before, he collected the stub from her fingers and finished it – the taste was growing on him – and then leaned forward, copying her position, to study each of the female figures in the circus ring.

Who might it be? The snake charmer, the elephant girl, the one carrying a vulture, the fat clown woman? Felix's gaze alighted on a tall black girl among a group of acrobats – or were they animal trainers? – who, semi-naked, except for hoods and G-strings, were carrying whips, cattle-prodders, pincers and electrodes. These were applied to one another's bodies as they processed, gyrating, bending double, doing backflips, all in time to the fanfares of the march. No, it couldn't be her. Dressed like a joke torturer? – after what she'd been through? – no, surely not.

The opening procession was finishing now, winding towards the far end of the tent, where a flap was hoisted up to let them through. The daylight blazed in, flooding the darkness, clashing against the pink and amber spots of the ring, thinning their power, and falling cruelly on the performers. The animals could have been from an impoverished Noah's Ark, with room for just one of each. The elephant was malnourished, the vulture had a thin, dragging wing, the monkey was listless, the snake looked dead. As for the people, their costumes were made of patches, string and cardboard, while flaking clay mixtures served as make-up. They looked like lunatics or prostitutes, or children in fancy-dress.

Felix watched, eyes bright with emotion.

During his childhood, one of the big British circuses had toured Africa regularly – 'From Cairo to Cape Town' boasted the sign – in a mile-long train, its carriages providing homes for the performers, cages for the animals, and haulage containers for the mighty tent.

When, like Alys today, Felix had been brought to the circus for the first time, it wasn't the new smell – that blend of pine sawdust and horse manure – or the music or costumes that struck him most. It was the image, again and again through the afternoon, of daylight coming into the dark tent. The shock of it: reality and make-believe existing so close together, just separated by a layer of canvas. Within the Big Top, the world was mad: beautiful and grotesque. Elephants were dancing, lions and tigers were leaping through fire, red-nosed men were falling over, always falling over, beaten, thumped, doused, hurt terribly, yet springing up, always springing up too, while other people were flying – *they were flying* – high in the air, or walking around in it, from one end of the stuffy, orange, cloth-like sky to the other, and some of them were falling also, falling, falling, into nets that were big and safe as swimming-pools. Within this place, some conspiracy between the watchers and doers upturned all laws of gravity and animal behaviour. And yet every now and then, the circus people lifted a flap of their tent, as though saying to the audience, *Look!* . . . look how thin this wall is, it's soft, it bends . . . look what's beyond, that patch of dried grass, that telegraph pole . . . look at the ordinary air and light. It was astonishing. It made the magic very fragile, and all the more precious. Felix fell in love then and there.

Circus Zikki wasn't quite the same. German-run, it was a *modern* circus, a bizarre mixture of traditional skills, tekno-tricks and market-place entertainment; Eurotrash meeting New Africa. It ushered in the daylight aggressively, hauling up one whole side of the tent to let in two roaring, stinking motorbikes for a jousting act. The gymnasts wove stripteases into all routines, and the clowns joked about the unjokable: Aids, genocide, and – with raisins bobbing round their heads on sprung wires – fly-plagued famine. The magician really did saw a lady in half. A lady goat, batting its mascaraed eyelashes as the screeching chainsaw was first juggled in the air and then aimed at its middle. And one of the acrobats, a child, really did fall off the high wire. There was no safety-net, so the small figure crashed on to the floor of the ring with such impact that it scattered the sawdust and split the coconut matting beneath. The audience's gasps didn't turn to cheers of relief until the body was stripped of its hooded jumpsuit and revealed to be just a baboon.

'All meat goes to the hungry, ladies and gents, *meine Dame und Herren, mabibi na mabwana*,' announced an odd little chap in heavy blue make-up – eyebrows, nose and lips studded with black metal – who, although dressed like an animal trainer, also seemed to do some clowning and a dozen other jobs, scurrying round constantly. He had introduced himself as the Great Zikki, so perhaps he was the owner. '. . . The hides make sandals and caps, the skulls make ornaments, the teeth jewellery, the paws are used by *mgangas*, nothing is wasted!'

These sentiments were important. The audience prided themselves on being liberated. Newly liberated – by their hip young president John C. Guwedekko – and now able to forge new rules for their society, borrowing what they wanted from foreign culture and adapting it to their own. Violence, even cruelty, was part of the cycle of life. The doing of it was instinctive to animals, the watching of it compulsive to humans. Both things were natural. There was nothing wrong in it, as long as it wasn't pointless; as long as it provided entertainment, food, or other forms of sustenance.

Felix glanced at Alys during the bloodier interludes. Her expression was thoughtful and private. She had seen things like this many times – the comedy of death, animal torture – it was there in the streets every time she was driven through them. And Circus Zikki's other acts, like the rough-rider now, mounted bare-back on a zebra, flicking its ears to make it change direction, didn't enthuse her. Nothing had lived up to the opening parade. Now she looked vaguely bored. Felix sometimes feared that she had inherited her father's one flaw, along with his angelic blond looks. She had barely known her mother, Isabeau, a French-Canadian photographer, who died when she was only a few months old.

'Love-love-lub-lub-blub-blub,' Felix whispered again, smelling her hair. That abiding drowsiness hung over him as usual, but the sensation was melodious today; he felt calm and strong. Nudging Charlie, he observed, 'Quite a house!' Scanning the large audience, they both noted there were fewer non-Afs than you would have seen a year or two ago. 'Better than anything we get at the Alex.'

'Yeah, well,' replied Charlie. 'This is what the people want. You know what they say. The people only want – or need – two things.'

'What?'

'*Panem et circenses.*'

'Ah,' said Felix, smiling affectionately.

Charlie's obsession with the Roman Empire went back to child-hood. Closing his eyes, Felix was bathed in memory . . . a screening of *Quo Vadis* at the King George cinema one Saturday afternoon, and the look of Charlie's face as they re-emerged into the sunlight. His hand was held over his brow, and it wasn't just the glare. The friends had never seen one another's tears before. Even more sur-prising, this was from a kind of joy.

. . . Felix stirred, feeling confused. There was a chilly moisture at the side of his mouth, threading into his beard. He'd been drib-bling . . . he'd been asleep! A brightness on his eyelids, a jelly-like shiver. Opening them, he became more disorientated. The whole tent was infused with the quivering presence of water, and of lights shining into water, and of the reflections of both; loose, complicated patterns were everywhere, even on the underside of things. The trembling, troubling light reminded Felix of hangovers. He frowned, working it out. The ring had been flooded with water for the aqua-circus, the big finale. *Good grief, how long had he slept?* A man and two women were doing a lacklustre version of formation swimming, mostly lifting one another out of the pool, or doing handstands, to show off their bulging bikinis.

As his eyes adjusted to the wavering darkness around him, Felix saw that Kaz was missing. *Oh, no!* His torpor felt like a kind of self-ishness. He shook himself awake angrily, and unwrapped three sticks of Juicy Fruit in quick succession.

Charlie was talking to the Great Zikki, who was slouching in the aisle, a towel round his neck. It was hard to tell whether the little fellow was a child or a midget, young or old. Underneath the blue make-up, his skin looked corrugated. Was this acne or wrinkles? Or neither . . . a skin graft, perhaps?

The audience gasped as a shark swam into the flooded ring, showing first just as a fin, and then, as the follow-spot found it, in all its long, dark glory. The swimmers scattered onto little poly-styrene islands, feigning fear, grasping one another, ripping away the bikinis, teasing you with their nakedness, never showing full-frontals.

'Tsk!' went Zikki. There was something wrong: the shark seemed lethargic, lolling slightly to one side. 'Just can't get the water right,' he complained. 'It loses air or something – tsk! – just in the short ride from the beach. And look . . .' He pointed to the basin of the ring: it was leaking in several places. He smiled at Felix, his small teeth shining in the fluid light. 'I'm a taker if you ever want to flog the Alex, I am, yes-yes . . . or may I call it Die Hatzfeldt Oper?'

Felix was aghast. This little fellow knew who he was. He also seemed to know about the theatre's troubles. He even knew its origi-nal name. He was probably from the German community here. Although he spoke English without an accent, and fluently, his vocabulary was limited, and Felix decided this was a clue to his youth. His mind seemed a few steps behind his manner, which was boastful and speedy. Unable to find words fast enough, he just gab-bled appropriate sounds, almost creating a stutter.

'I'm crazy about your work, by the way,' he said now. '*The*

Odyssey, the Bible shows, wild stuff, and *ja*, wa-wa-wild!, it's given me lots of ideas, gotta admit that it has, it has, gotta admit I've thieved this, thieved that, thieved a bit, gotta admit.'

'Goodness me.'

'Sure-sure. The way you mix the old, the new, Third World, First World, tribal, rock, Sinatra favourites, bit of nostalgia, bit of horror, all the bare-arse stuff, and all-all-all of that.'

Unsure whether to be sniffy or gracious, Felix said, 'Well, have to confess one was influenced by the circus too in one's time, the old British outfits, y'know, when one was growing up.'

'Is that for real?' said Zikki, sitting forward and fixing Felix with his weird, bright look – it held a touch of mockery. 'And yet you missed the best bit today, the best, the ba-ba-best, you slept through my disappearing-lion act!'

'Ah, apologies,' mumbled Felix.

He was saved by Kaz suddenly appearing out of the darkness. 'Where've you been?' he asked.

'Thought maybe she worked, like, backstage,' Kaz replied. 'But nope – she is *nowhere*!'

'Who, please?' asked Zikki, instantly turning his piercing focus onto Kaz. 'Who-who-who?'

Felix wanted to tell him to keep out of it, mind his own business, but Kaz was already explaining. 'Ach, yes,' said Zikki, and stood, inviting them to follow.

Outside, the daylight was overpowering, making everyone reach for their sunglasses. Felix lifted Alys onto his hip and carried her. She held the lobe of his ear – this was one of her favourite rituals – pressing it gently, curiously, keeping time to the rhythm of his walk.

Zikki led across a stretch of sandy grass. Watching his swanky stride, Felix calculated that he was no more than eighteen, small for his age, but wunderkind rather than midget; one of the city's new breed of brat-sized entrepreneurs As he walked, he wiped the blue make-up with the towel. It *was* a skin graft, Felix realised, peering discreetly at the rippled hardness on the face. Its colour, a lifeless white, was different from his neck and hands. These were light brown. Kaz had noticed too. He was mulatto like her son, a 'mongrel'.

What was his story under the old regime? Felix wondered, as Zikki kept up his high-speed patter: 'Want to explore it all, modern circus, trad circus, people've seen everything now, seen it all, but I still want to make them say, "Ga-Ga-God, is someone doing this?!", I still want to get a *reaction*, see whaddem saying?, how to get a *reaction*, how-how-how?'

'To get that wow-wow-wow,' added Kaz, as if jamming with a musician.

Zikki headed through a clump of euphorbia trees. With their thick twists of quadrangular branches, their latex-stained trunks, their flowers like blobs of plasticine, they provided effective masking to what lay beyond . . . a long, low tent.

'So this,' Zikki explained, 'this is a new thing of ours, but like all new things, it's an old thing too, been done before, ach sure, in England, Victorian times, they did it, sure-sure, but I say it's African through 'n' through.'

Felix noticed a little group sitting outside the tent. He couldn't work out what, but there was something odd about these people.

'Shoo!' Zikki shouted at them, clapping his hands. 'No more jobs left, *kwenda huko*!'

The figures moved off, stumbling and limping. As one man tripped wildly over a guy-rope, even though it was painted bright red, Felix realised he was blind. They were all disabled. Felix narrowed his eyes. Two of the figures were familiar: an old legless man travelling on his fists with ape-like dexterity, and a boy on crutches. They were the pair he'd seen on his first day home, driving from the airport.

Some instinct made Felix want to raise his hand and wave, but Zikki had already led into the tent, and Noah, keeping up the rear as always, rifle at the ready, bustled the party along with firm but caring nudges; a hen preventing its brood from separating.

Inside, the light was dim, so everyone was struck by the odour before anything else. Human, definitely human, but with something wrong, a dampness, a sharpness. It reminded Felix of his research trips with Charlie to rural hospitals.

Now, as their eyes adjusted, and as they saw the inhabitants of the tent, Felix said to Charlie, 'I'm taking Alys out!'

A flash of surprise went across Charlie's face. Alys's education was *his* affair. As her father, and as a doctor, he had decided that, so long as he was present – to explain, to identify things as the stuff of life and not nightmares – there were few sights she shouldn't see. But maybe this was one of them – maybe Felix was right. Since the death of Isabeau, Charlie's wife, Felix had become much more than just a godfather to Alys. 'Your bearded mommy,' is how Charlie put it.

The friends retreated from the tent – Noah alongside, walking backwards, covering them – and Charlie activated a number on his cellphone. Within minutes a helicopter appeared out of the sky, landed on the grass nearby, and took off again, with Alys inside.

She made no protest, simply adopting that manner of hers, that odd, adult composure, which sometimes troubled Felix. A shiver went through him as the helicopter lifted away. Isabeau had died in a plane crash – a ranch-hopper plane, from which she was photographing wildlife – and although Alys could have no recollection of the tragedy, there was something about her now; her small, silent face rising into the air, looking down; her helplessness set against the force of the machine . . .

Felix glanced at Charlie. He was, perhaps, thinking similar things. The friends smiled gently at one another.

Back in the tent, the party followed Zikki down the central aisle. On either side were living exhibits on plinths or little stages, one or two in cages: giants, dwarfs, hunchbacks, Siamese twins, a real one-eyed cyclops, and others, some with signs above them – Our Own Elephant Man, the Bird Woman, the Inside-out Child. They sat or slept or posed or danced or stripped, chatting among themselves and to the crowd of customers who jostled through the gloom.

As different, half-formed feelings bubbled up inside him, Felix whispered to Charlie, 'I don't get the point, frankly. One can see all this out in the streets.'

'But without the Art,' interjected Zikki, overhearing. He gestured to the signs above the exhibits, to their sets and costumes. These were makeshift and amateur. Felix started to smirk, but was halted by an exhibit entitled 'The Skeleton'. It was a *mki-mbizi* man, a stick-figure, brittle and wasted, too weak to wave away the flies round his head. He was exactly like the dozens, the hundreds you saw every day on the roadsides, except that someone, perhaps the man himself, had painted the stark bones and hollows of his frame in black and white – ash and clay – adding a varnish of palm oil. It made him look both plasticky and real, alive and dead, a fairground ghoul and a walking spirit. He was beautiful. Felix shied away, sweat breaking out on his forehead.

Zikki noticed and gave a chuckle. 'We house him, we feed him, and when he starts to get fat, we replace him.' Switching to a burlesque German accent, he asked, 'So – zere's a pickle, *ja*?, do ve do good or bad, vot you reckon?'

Unable to think of anything else to say, Felix asked, 'Why are you talking in that voice?'

The teenager grinned, as though he'd been waiting, praying for this cue, and out it poured: 'I vas not made velcome, *ja*?, here in ziz country, *my* country, ze country of mein forefathers. Und ze men in uniforms, they had a little accident. On me. Just a little boy. Heil, Duma!' Touching the peculiar, wrinkled skin of his face, he told the story of a strange childhood: being smuggled out of the country after his encounter with the police, and going to live with his father's people, a wealthy circus family in Munich. There he became fascinated by First World culture – the feverish explorations of Sensational Art, Tekno-rock, Eurotrash. 'Und zen, ven Führer Duma vas deposed, I came home und lived happily ever after.' Suddenly dropping his act, he said quietly to Kaz, 'Is this who you're looking for?'

They had reached the far corner of the tent. Here, under a sign that read 'The Nightmare', a young woman was curled on a mattress, dressed in a short nightgown. Her hands and feet were missing.

Kaz, tears streaming down her face, knelt alongside her. 'I didn't know,' she whispered. 'They just said you were better.'

'She is,' said Zikki. 'She's got a roof, got food, got clothes, got safety, got *work*! Isn't that better than lying in a hospital bed?' As Kaz started to protest, he pointed to the other spectators in the tent. 'She's showing them what happened in this country – *Sie sagt als Zeuge aus* – she's a witness, *ja*, isn't that good-good-good?'

Kaz watched the spectators. As they reached each new exhibit, they began giggling.

witnessing

'*Ja*, well,' said Zikki, shrugging. 'That's the work of my god, and his name is Hugh. Hu-hu-human nature. Nix we can do about Hugh.'

'They're going to come here and *laugh* at her?!' said Kaz, rising to face him.

Zikki shrugged again. 'She's free to go at any time, no ropes, no chains, whenever she wants she can get up and walk away from . . .' Realising what he'd said, he stopped and mouthed, Oops!

Kaz grabbed the towel round his neck, like lapels, yanking him forward. A tough and capable brawler, she was about to strike, when the girl suddenly snapped out of her wide-eyed reverie, and mirrored Zikki's expression of comic blunder. Nonplussed, Kaz loosened her hold.

Zikki smiled, brushed himself down, then touched the girl's hair. 'These people wanna talk to you, that OK, *ja*?'

She thought for a moment, then sat up, looking reluctant. Putting the stumps of her arms together, she slowly jigged them up and down. Charlie reached in his pocket, and slipped a wad of notes under her pillow. Now she nodded enthusiastically.

Kaz settled onto her haunches, and spoke to the girl in street rhythms: 'This face on me, you don't recognise, ehh?, isn't it?' The girl shook her head. Kaz stroked her shoulder. 'You don't worry, we only met one time or two. I'm Zach's mother.'

The group braced themselves. It looked like the girl would break into panic. But something else took over, something way beyond tears or pain. She went still, her neck softening, her gaze very steady.

Kaz lit a cigarette and half offered it, unsure whether this was appropriate or even practical. But the girl accepted it, expertly, between her stumps, and smoked greedily. Kaz lit another for herself – barely noticing as Felix helped himself to one as well – then she said to the girl, 'This thing that happened, can you tell me, *kipenzi*?'

The girl's eyes brightened again, with amusement – like when Zikki talked about her 'walking away' – then she shook her head.

'You can't? You won't?' Kaz prompted.

Leaning close to Kaz, showing her only, the girl opened her mouth. Puzzled, Felix turned to Charlie. The doctor had been studying the girl closely, and noticed how she had to keep throwing back her head to swallow her saliva. 'Her tongue too,' he whispered.

'*Ai kipenzi*,' Kaz said to the girl. 'You are in hell, ehh?, isn't it? But why – *why* – did they have to do this thing as well?'

The girl shrugged in her odd, peaceful way, while Zikki answered for her: '"Why"? For this reason, this one, this, this, here, now! She's the witness – *Zeuge, ja*? – but she can't tell us nothing!'

'Oh, yes, she can,' said Felix stepping forward, a bizarre idea surfacing through his shock and queasiness. 'D'you think if . . . ? None of you know *Titus*, do you?, because . . .'

'Titus?' said Charlie. 'Who finished building the Colosseum? The Emperor Titus Flavi–'

'*Titus Andronicus*!' Felix said impatiently. 'Shakespeare's Titus. The daughter, Lavinia, is, sort of . . .' He gestured apologetically towards the girl. 'They have to find a way of getting her story. So what they do is this.' He smoothed a section of the sandy earth, then picked up a stick of bamboo lying nearby, and used it to sketch a ground-plan. 'All right, here's the police station,' he said to the girl. 'The compound where they drive in and park, the entrance, the front desk, the corridor with cells, and . . .' He paused. 'The cell at the end.' Hearing a murmur of confirmation, Felix glanced up and saw Zikki nodding intently. So it had happened to him there as well – whatever led to the skin graft, it happened in *that* cell.

Felix offered the bamboo stick to the girl. She took it between her stumps. The game seemed to excite her. Felix's pulse quickened too. 'So show me,' he said. 'Where are you and Zach?'

She pointed the stick to the desk area.

'All right, and then you were taken here' – he indicated the end cell – 'am I correct?'

She hesitated, then both nodded and shook her head.

'I don't understand. Try and explain.'

She drew two stick figures in the desk area.

'You and Zach?'

She nodded, then drew another clump of figures near the desk itself.

'The police?'

She nodded, and then dragged the stick over to Zach.

'They came to him . . .'

Her stick went to the doorway.

'. . . and took him somewhere else.'

She nodded.

Trying to keep his own disappointment from showing, Felix glanced to Kaz. She had taken her hair braids and folded them over her face like a curtain.

Meanwhile, the girl was becoming agitated. She needed to tell the rest of the story. What happened to *her*. Twisting the cigarette around between her lips and puffing on it deeply, she took the stick to the other figure, and then down the corridor to the cell at the end.

'Was there a man waiting for you?' asked Felix. 'Shortish, fattish, in a suit, with an attaché case?'

The girl looked surprised, then nodded. Zikki gave a murmur of recognition as well. The girl drew a host of single lines in the cell. 'Others?' Felix enquired. 'Others came in as well?'

She nodded, and kept drawing, just notches now, notch after notch, the end of her stick beginning to stray, the sketch becoming freer, madder, reminding Felix of his doodles with Emile, and then, without warning it ended. The bamboo fell away, leaving a wild mess in the dust.

Throughout the group's visit, the girl had managed to stay composed. Now the cigarette slipped from her mouth and she lay back shivering.

Charlie made a quick call on his mobile, then drew out a bank roll of dollars, and peeled some into Zikki's hand. 'Here's for your trouble, friend, 'cause I'm afraid you're gonna have to find yourself a new exhibit. My helicopter's on the way back. Help her get ready, OK?' Kneeling next to the girl, he explained that there was a clinic specifically for the victims of the old regime, and that he could have her transported there. She nodded gratefully.

They were about to withdraw from the tent, when Noah, who had been standing thoughtfully to one side, suddenly said to the girl, 'But the boy Zach – where did they take him?'

Still trembling, she reached for the bamboo again.

'You *know*?' Kaz said incredulously. Like the others, she had assumed this was a lost trail. 'They *said* where they were taking him?'

The girl hesitated, then slowly nodded.

'*Where?*' the group cried as one.

The girl guided the bamboo stick to a fresh patch of earth. Everyone leaned forward, expecting another drawing. Instead they saw letters forming: P . . . O . . .

When she was finished, Felix couldn't understand the look of shock on everyone's face, or the hushed tone with which Charlie spoke the name: 'Popo-boy!'

nine

'Mega scandal while you were away,' Charlie explained to Felix as the Land Cruiser cruised into town, after the group had supervised the girl's departure from the circus. 'His was the *numero uno* name on everyone's lips for a week or so.'

'Popo-boy, Popo-boy,' Kaz chanted quietly.

'Came out at one of the Hakika hearings. One of the cops who was confessing, he told how, y'know, if they wanted a prisoner to disappear, he'd be "sent to Popo-boy".'

'Popo-boy, Popo-boy,' went Kaz. Felix noted that she'd already consumed a third of the bottle of whisky. It was Chivas Regal, his old favourite, his poison, as the saying goes. Was it a deliberate choice? he had wondered when they stopped for refreshments at a *magendo* dealer. Difficult to say. Kaz was in a dangerous mood. Felix kept his head down, tucking into his tub of Ben and Jerry's ice-cream.

'A pseudonym, of course,' continued Charlie. 'In fact, the word *popo* means something . . . uhh . . . ?' He turned to Noah for help.

'It is the word for the bat, Mr Charlie, for him that sleeps in the day.'

'Yeah. Sick joke, I guess. The prisoners who went to him ended up sleeping in eternity. The guy we were hearing about was some kinda monster, some special torturer, our own Torquemada or Mengele or whatever. We never got to find out. The cop who had the information, the one who was singing, he was half-way through his story, the court adjourned for the day, and that night he suffered a "fatal cerebrovascular accident".'

A bitter chuckle went through the jeep. Even Noah joined in. They'd lived through years and years of this kind of thing, but who would've thought it would still be happening now?

'So, that's it,' Charlie summed up. 'That's all we can tell you about Popo-boy.'

'Popo-boy, Popo-boy,' Kaz hissed through her teeth.

Charlie twisted round to face her and spoke frankly. 'It's not good, baby. Not hopeful. He'd have fled with the first lot, Duma's nearest and dearest.'

'Probably be easier to find Duma himself,' added Felix.

'You should put it out of your mind, whatever's in there,' Charlie said gently, reaching to touch Kaz.

'*Acha!*' she muttered, swiping away his hand.

Felix shifted further away from her, burrowing into the corner of the back seat. It was amazing, he mused, in no time at all, in less than half an hour, Kaz had changed utterly. Her gaze was slipping like her speech, missing its aim; her skin seemed to hang on her frame; her very being seemed different – fiercer, hotter. She could've been swallowing petrol instead of whisky. He dreaded the thought of the hours ahead. Despite his promise to Kaz this morning – to help her to the finish – he would have to hide, lock himself in his room, or whatever; he would have to stay away from the bottle she was holding. Oh, that stuff slopping around inside it . . . that luscious, honey-coloured sphere see-sawing this way and that. Oh, that *smell*! It was curling, climbing out of the bottle, opening its arms to him, offering three wishes, anything, everything, the world.

Charlie had gone still, his slapped hand in mid-air, his gaze fixed on Kaz. It looked like he was going to say more, but he sipped his beer instead, then rested his lips on the bottle, plugging them.

Felix sensed the prickling vibrations of their old, complicated relationship. He saw a flash of them making love, or fighting – entwined anyway – the boy-man with his blond locks and kiss-shaped birthmark, the mother-woman with her braids and bony brown hands. Felix's veins surged with a familiar cocktail of envy and strength, of being both feebler and purer than them.

The Land Cruiser turned into the market-place, and began inching through the crowds.

'*Uhuru!*' said Kaz. Following her eyeline, Felix saw that she had read the word on a stretch of pavement nearby; it was being woven out of different-coloured reeds and grasses by a group of women.

Others were fixing the giant letters onto a framework of cane and liana. This would be hoisted above the *soko* for the festival in a few weeks' time; the first anniversary of Duma's overthrow. Freedom! the sign would boast, in both national languages. '*U-hu-ru! Free-dom!*' intoned Kaz, slowly, hoarsely, imitating the sound of a great crowd. She took a deep slug at her bottle. '*Free-dom! U-hu-ru!*' she cried, pumping one fist in the air, mocking the pedestrians who were pushing through the traffic. 'Yaiy!, happy, happy, ehh?, everyone's happy, ehh?, it's over, the Hakika's over, and everyone's got what they wanted . . . got justice!' She gave a bark of derision, and jerked one forefinger into her other palm. 'Well, I wanted it also, here, in my hand, *here*! Eye for eye, tooth for tooth, that's what they teach, isn't it? Bu' no, no – there's no eyes, no teeth! The dog is gone, the Popo-boy dog, he is gone, gone!'

Everyone ducked as Kaz swung the bottle round. 'I don't want it to hurt any more!' she cried suddenly. 'It's supposed to be fair now . . . everything's supposed to be fair. But it isn't. It's still hurting. Make it stop hurting!'

Felix chewed his lip, wondering whether to say anything.

He knew what she meant, certainly. He was tempted to give his own little cheer of *Uhuru!*, for he had won his own liberty, wresting it from his own private tyranny – one that came distilled and bottled. Yet the victory hadn't produced what he expected. Life held so many options now, too many, and most of them were traps. It didn't feel fair. It didn't feel safe at all.

'It's hurting,' Kaz said again.

'I'll drink to that,' Felix replied, with a little laugh.

She peered at him, and then, as though conducting a scientific experiment, wafted the whisky past his face, back and forth. He turned away, trying to seem amused and untroubled, while his eyes stung – from anger and hurt, and *that smell*. Hard to resist. Yet he must, he must. Kaz laughed, as though reading his thoughts. It was a cruel, violent laugh; it wasn't Kaz's laugh at all. Or maybe it was truer to her. Maybe he just hadn't noticed before.

The car thumped over a pothole, jolting Felix forward, drawing his attention to a small crowd in the distance: the majority on ground level, a few raised higher. Both groups appeared to be dancing. Was it a form of market-place entertainment, with some people on stilts, perhaps? As Noah accelerated slightly now, Felix caught a second, clearer glimpse, and new information. The figures capering on the ground, they were hurling stones, and the jigging figures in mid-air, they were hanging from a makeshift gibbet.

'Holy shit,' whispered Charlie, noticing as well. 'But . . . the round-ups only started today.' Noah smiled and cursed the corpses in his own language, while Kaz just exclaimed: 'Popo-boy!'

'No, baby,' said Charlie. 'Those'll just be small fry. Reserve cops, apprentice torturers.'

'Popo-boy!' she growled, reaching for the door-handle.

Noah reached his controls first. 'Huh-uhn!' he went, and activated the locking system – *tshunk!* – incarcerating them in the tinted, bullet-proofed interior.

'Open this!' Kaz commanded fiercely, rattling her handle.

'Kaz . . . baby,' Felix and Charlie said, at the same time.

She went still, then spoke quietly, 'You fools, ehh?' Felix realised she was speaking without her American accent – she had been doing so for some time – her drunkenness had shrugged it away, sloughed it off; the complicated disguise she normally wore. The look on her face now, tired and angry, it wasn't imported; Felix saw it everywhere in this country, on this continent. With eyes creased and bloodshot, Africans squinted at him, an African, as though he was standing somewhere far away. Kaz muttered under her breath, her tone quite gentle, pitying him and Charlie for not understanding, then she prodded Noah's shoulder. '*Fungua, fungua.*'

'Open it,' Charlie said to Noah.

Kaz sprang from the vehicle and dashed towards the gibbet, scooping up stones as she went. She pelted the corpses. Felix watched, open-mouthed – could this be his friend, a member of his company, an actress, a singer, *an artiste*?! Of the four Kazzes he had seen in the last hour – sober Kaz, drunk Kaz, American Kaz, African Kaz – which one was this? Running out of stones, Kaz attacked the legs hanging in front of her, punching the ankles, the knees, now aiming higher with her Chivas Regal bottle.

For more than one reason, Felix had to look away. 'What do we do?' he asked Charlie.

'We leave her,' came the reply; Charlie speaking in that dry, no-nonsense tone that he occasionally adopted, in professional mode. It always seemed out of character, making him sound more like Emile, his father. As they left the market-place, Charlie asked, 'Where d'you wanna be?'

'The Alex,' replied Felix. He would go back and work, start preparations for the new show. Not an attractive prospect, but probably the best thing, the best way of holding off this heaviness that kept threatening to descend. He noticed that his finger was rubbing one leg, tracing the scar there, enjoying the rise and dip of the long ridge. It used to be one of his habitual gestures a few years ago, accompanied by an extraordinary notion. What if the man in the police cell had inflicted more damage? Nothing too gruesome (not as much as the girl in the tent), but enough to disable him . . . to excuse him from duties. Like when he was a schoolboy. Oh, that blissful feeling. In bed, at home, safe, for a day, a week – once it was much longer; a childhood illness?, he couldn't remember – absolved from responsibilities and expectations, and yet conferred, curiously, with the qualities of bravery. If the man in the cell had done just a little more, he could have made a hero of Felix.

The jeep turned into the road alongside the theatre. Felix narrowed his eyes. There were two objects on the ground outside the stage door. Exactly where he and Kaz had left them this morning. His television and video sets. But this was impossible. Two valuable pieces of equipment had stood in the street for half a day *without going for a walk*?! Impossible. Since the dissolution of Duma's police state, nothing was safe. Manhole covers went missing; tarmac was ripped up and water pipes removed; telegraph poles were hacked open for the wiring inside. In the buildings, anything could vanish: ovens, bathtubs . . . Felix's *bed* had disappeared a few months ago! So how could these two machines remain untouched?

The answer became apparent as they drew closer. Although the plugs were lying lifelessly on the ground, like upturned beetles, little legs in the air, both the television and video were functioning. Any thief would think twice about touching them at the moment, for the face of Emperor Duma was swollen against the glass of the TV screen. He filled it completely, except for the corners, and these little spaces swam with a glutinous substance, threaded with cloudy pigments – sperm white, blood black – trailing onto his skin, half caught over one ear. He looked like a reptile being born, breaking through its egg.

Felix glanced to Charlie and Noah. They hadn't noticed anything odd. He was on his own. This thing – it was just between him and Duma. He went cold, suddenly realising something, knowing it for absolute certain. This was only the beginning. The manifestation of Duma on the screen – it was only the messenger.

'On second thoughts, old chap,' Felix said slowly to Charlie, 'may one trouble you for a bed tonight?'

'Sure. Alys'll be over the moon!' replied Charlie, while Noah, who had been about to brake, accelerated again.

Finding Kaz's cigarettes on the seat, Felix lit one absently, and it was several minutes before he thought, Oh, I'm a smoker now. He gazed ahead drowsily. Noah was a fast, deft driver, handling his steering-wheel like a drumskin, fingers fluttering round the rim, fist thumping the centre, lightly, often – *paa-pi-paap* – adding his beat to a swinging, swerving din of horns and bells . . .

Opening his eyes, Felix smiled. They were travelling down an oak-lined avenue now, with modest colonial villas nestling in its patchwork shade; the shadows sepia-coloured, the sunshine like clusters of ghosts; little white-faced clerk-kings and their wives, people like Felix's parents. And there he was, he and Charlie, walking back from school – just imagine, you could *walk* in the streets then! – aged about ten, dressed in their uniforms: aubergine jackets, charcoal shorts, striped little bow-ties. And now they were turning into a particular driveway, across a freshly mown lawn, returning the wave of old Milton, the garden boy, and heading round to the French windows at the back, where a small, upright figure would be waiting, in a bright cherry-blonde wig and lavish make-up, always

carelessly applied, slightly smudged, her knuckly hands gleaming
with bracelets and rings.

Felix leaned forward in the jeep and touched Charlie's shoulder.
'D'you remember Miss Rosewood?'

Charlie grinned. Miss Rosewood was their English teacher at
school, who gave private lessons in elocution. 'What a character,
huhn?! Everything was a *nightmare*, a *disaster!*'

'*This is a tidal wave, darling, this is Hurricane Mary.*'

'Or else,' said Charlie, beginning to shake with laughter. 'Or else
she'd say such-and-such *isn't* a tidal wave, it *isn't* a hurricane.'

'That's right!'

'You'd fall and graze your knee and she'd say, "Well, it's not the
atom bomb now, is it?" Which made you think, You mean it *could*
have been?!'

'Where did she get all that from?' asked Felix, wiping away tears
of mirth. 'She wasn't a refugee from Tsarist Russia or Nazi
Germany.'

'How d'you mean?'

'She was Jewish. Rosenblatt. Changed it to Rosewood.'

'Hey – never knew that. You couldn't tell.'

'No indeed – the point of the exercise. But anyway, she was born
here, in Africa, she led her whole life as a Mrs Bwana, a *mamsap*, a
madam, she never had to lift a finger, worry about anything. Where
did the notion come from that round the next corner there might be
an atom bomb or Hurricane Mary?'

As their laughter subsided, Felix felt a different kind of hysteria
stirring in his belly. Miss Rosewood had frightened him in a particular and unexpected way. Unlike his elderly parents, she took a fierce
interest in him, she *believed* in him. The lessons were more than just
speech training, they were acting classes. With his almost palpable
charisma, Charlie should have been the natural star, but Miss
Rosewood had decided this was skin deep, a trick of the light – his
white-blond hair caught it like a halo – and she certainly didn't
approve of his infatuation with America, and America's lamentable
way of speaking English! While Charlie began playing truant from
her lessons, eventually persuading Emile to stop them altogether,
Miss Rosewood put all her faith in the runt, the underdog, Felix.

Felix and his quirky character work – or, as she liked to say, 'My Feelie and his *imagination*!' Miss Rosewood's belief in his future was so fervent it scared him. What if something went wrong? It couldn't, of course – she seemed so *sure* – she seemed to hold his future in her hands; those knuckly, ringed and bangled hands; she seemed to have direct access to God, Satan, the Fates, or whoever it was that arranged these things. 'I've got grand plans for you, my darling,' she would say, crossing every T, sucking every vowel. 'But not here, Feelie, *abroad*! Here you can have every luxury under the sun, save one. Culture. Culturally, this place is, alas, a disaster zone, it's Hiroshima, it's Pompeii, it's Krakatoa, it's the San Andreas Fault! Take flight, my precious, take flight!'

After school, Felix travelled to the UK and was accepted at a top drama school. But the moment his training finished, he came home again. There was no question of a British career. It wasn't a matter of talent, simply of a work permit. By now Duma was in power, and his non-Af citizens were particularly vilified internationally for their passive acceptance of his regime. Felix swapped acting for directing but, despite his success, something troubled him deeply. Although Miss Rosewood had passed away by then, he could still hear her voice, it was often in his head – not like a memory, but closer than that, clearer, crossing every T, sucking every vowel, 'Such plans, oh my darling, I had such plans for you.'

'What made you suddenly think of Miss Rosewood?' Charlie asked, still chuckling. Turning round, he was surprised to find Felix's eyes shut, and his hands clamped tightly over his ears.

ten

The ocean came into view now, reflecting the sky so completely, with such blueness, that it looked like a child's painting of water, and a glorious, seaweed smell drifted into Felix's nostrils, joining the mixture of hot dust, sudorous foliage and animal dung, the smells of home, which were filling his senses.

Noah had protested when Charlie opened all the windows, but his boss ignored him, and tickled the set of controls that brought the CD player to life, loudly playing the Eagles. And so to these old, sweet ballads of Tequila Sunrises and Hotel Californias, with Charlie singing along and Felix puffing at one of Kaz's cigarettes, they climbed the northern ridge of the primitive African volcano – the longer, more bent arm of the Kwatokuu.

Here were situated the prize homes of the district, each with private electricity generator, satellite dish, helipad and funicular to the sea; homes of the plantation and mine-owners, the fishing and shipping magnates; the same non-Af millionaires who'd lived in luxury under Duma. When John C. Guwedekko took over, they won favour by voluntarily redistributing their wealth in the form of colossal donations to the new government.

Charlie's house – like its owner – had a remarkable and simple beauty. Constructed in natural colours, terracotta, white, blue, it seemed to grow naturally out of the highest point, the elbow, of the Kwatokuu's arm. Built in the style of a private mansion, a *domus*, from the Roman Empire, and of the Pompeian type, it sprawled

Charlie's domus.

horizontally across the mountain-top, having no need for further leverage. Its blind, unbroken wall – its street-wall, in Roman terms – was turned to the driveway and the extensive security systems situated there. Within, all doors and windows opened on its interior courtyards, except for the seaward side of the building where, breaking with the design of its model, and finally safe from intruders, the walls were made of glass and led onto a vast sundeck, complete with swimming-pool.

It was here that Charlie brought Felix, while a servant walked alongside whispering in Charlie's ear. 'Oh, wow,' said Charlie. Waiting for him on one of the sun-loungers was a big man in a white safari suit.

As Charlie hurried over and began a private conversation, Felix turned to face the sky and sea. Breathing deeply, he decided it was a view of time not space: a view of today at exactly half an hour before sunset. The feeling of openness intoxicated him. He wanted to run forward, but instead crept towards the parapet. The deck was so high in the air you had mixed feelings about venturing to the edge. Wide-eyed and agog, but behaving like a blind person, you tested the last bit with your toe and reached for the rail.

Smiling at the stupidity of this, but still maintaining a vice-like grip, Felix peered over.

Not another dwelling in sight – the mountain somewhere underneath you – just a giddy drop of sky all the way down to the ocean. You could watch seabirds, the occasional helicopter, and even small clouds drift by below. On windy days, when the town was tugged this way and that, with thrashing palms, torn awnings and rolling debris, up here it stayed perfectly calm. And there was never a grey-green overcast above, always clear blue sky. These phenomena were caused by convection and air currents just in this spot, Charlie once tried to explain to Felix, but it was all too scientific for him.

Hearing the volume of Charlie's voice rise – 'Just get that for you' – Felix turned from the rail. Charlie had gone into the house and the big man was rising.

Felix blinked.

That lazy swagger, the hang of those arms, as though hovering over six-shooters . . . it was *the Dook*. Colonel Bull Brak. Duma's right-hand man.

Felix blinked again. Was he experiencing another of those time warps, his ghost stories, the dry world's own DTs? Was he somehow back in that police cell again, with Charlie and *the Dook*, on that Monday morning six years ago? There couldn't be any other explanation. After Duma and this Popo-boy character, Colonel Bull Brak must be the most wanted man in the country!

'Hi,' Brak growled, strolling over. 'I'm one of Charlie's neighbours.' No name, Felix noted – a policeman's precaution. 'Just popped over for a cup of sugar. *Haw!*'

Felix gave a faint, involuntary copy of the famous laugh, while thinking, *He doesn't recognise me!*

For Felix, too, there was novelty in the encounter. When they met before, he had been somewhat preoccupied. But now . . .

Brak's hand was massive – it was a paddle! – and his wrist had the thickness of an ankle. As the greeting finished, Felix's fingers were fluttering like his heart.

The policeman possessed a magnificent, sore air; his nose and cheeks so ablaze with veins, it was as though his face had been splashed with fresh blood. His thin swept-back hair was dyed ginger, and his domed forehead and jowly jaws loomed towards each other, giving his mouth a sloppy, toothless look; though as he smiled now, Felix saw that he had a full set of small teeth. The eyes were small too, blue and hooded, while the ears were particularly large. It was a baby's face on a man who had surely never been one.

'Fantastic setting Charlie's got up here, hey?' Bull Brak drawled in the accent of his birthplace, 1930s Rhodesia.

'Fantastic,' echoed Felix, then began to babble: 'Even when the north-easter's blowing it's always so splendid up here, isn't it?, and the sky's always so blue!, and, and it's simply marvellous, it's . . .'

He dried. Brak allowed the silence to stretch, perhaps enjoying Felix's excitable unease, then commented, 'Well, you know what they say . . . with enough cash you can even buy the weather. *Haw!*'

Felix laughed long and hard, in a panting kind of way, followed by little sniffs of amusement, as if recalling the witticism and committing it to memory.

'My cup of sugar,' said Brak, glancing over Felix's shoulder.

To Felix's surprise, Charlie *was* carrying a porcelain demitasse, heaped not with sugar, but greyish tablets, home-baked, some broken. Felix had noticed them in Charlie's magic box before. Brak licked his lips. 'How much do I owe you?'

'My pleasure,' replied Charlie.

'This bloke is too bloody generous,' Brak told Felix.

'He is, he is, he is!' chuckled Felix.

'Nice to meet you, sir,' said Brak, then slapped Charlie's shoulder and lumbered away.

Felix exploded. '*That was Bull Brak!*'

'Sure was.'

'But . . . but . . .'

'Oh, yeah, you missed it,' Charlie said. 'His performance at the Hakika. I'll see if I've still got some of it on tape. It's worth studying – for any connoisseur of acting. Contrition ain't the word. Tears, swooning fits, you name it.'

'So now he's free?!'

'Free? He's been promoted! He's now Inspector-General of the Police.'

'Good gracious!'

'"Brak's A Cat With Nine Lives!"' chanted Charlie, recalling the local paper's headline when the man first arrived on the scene, after surviving the collapse of old Northern Rhodesia, years of serving as a mercenary in the Congo, Sierra Leone and Angola – on whichever side paid most – and a stint in the secret service of white South Africa. 'That guy'll be here when the rest of us honkies have all been blown into the sea. I tell you, that guy'll be the first President of the United States of Africa.'

'Gosh,' said Felix quietly.

Charlie gave a sympathetic chuckle as he went to fetch refreshments. 'You've been away.'

'I've been away,' Felix echoed softly, surveying the vista below again with a smile. Africa. Massy and molten, still tumbling into shape, the land was *alive* – it was half rock, half beast, made up of earth and flesh, fire and blood. A dinosaur thrashing around in the modern world, clumsy, lost and violent, yet able to mutate itself with prodigious lightness of touch, faster than any computerised society on earth. It was bewildering. You could only seek refuge in laughter, as he and Charlie did, often triggering it with one of their catchphrases, 'Jews in Africa!'. The words didn't seem to fit together. The friends often remarked that only a Blessed Prankster could have deposited them here, and then vanished Himself! The little synagogue in town had been closed for years. There weren't enough men to make up a *minyan* and hold services. Among the half dozen families left, no one practised their religion any more. The Jew was always talking about the Old World as somewhere to yearn for, and the New World as somewhere to conquer, but Africa was neither. This was a world before the Holocaust, the pogroms, the Diaspora, the Old Testament itself. This was the chapter before 'In the beginning'.

Felix was lost in fantasies of flying, when he felt something nip his bare heel, just above the flip-flop.

Looking down, he saw what seemed like a species of bat. It certainly had a bat's head, with big ears and black snouty face, though it was on the body of a scrawny puppy. A peculiar scent emanated from the animal – sharp and penetrating.

There were more of the creatures – five or six – crossing the sun-deck towards him, their little paws scrabbling over the varnished wood like so many fingernails clawing across a blackboard.

They fell upon his heels and toes, snuffling and nipping. Nothing hurt, but it was disgusting. And their smell was overpowering.

Then Alys came running from the house and, befitting her angelic looks, flew through the air into Felix's arms, her airborne shadow scattering the tiny bat-dogs.

Although they had been together just two hours earlier, Felix and Alys cherished every reunion. Whenever they parted, Charlie was under strict instructions to ring Felix and say, 'She got home safely.' Her godfather was in constant anxiety about her safety. There were so many car crashes, plane crashes, kidnappers, kid killers, kid rapists, on and on it went, the possibilities of harm. What would he do if anything happened to her? Sometimes he pictured it – the small coffin – just to release the tension, like Kaz trawling ugly memories for her acting work.

The wild dogs

Felix and Alys covered one another's faces with kisses, while making smack-smack noises so that neither should take the affection too seriously. 'What are these horrid little beasts, Lys?' he asked.

'Our new babies,' she said, and then, pronouncing the unfamiliar words carefully: 'African wild dogs.'

'*African wild . . . ?!*'

Still holding Alys, Felix jumped onto the nearest sun-lounger. This excited the puppies, who surrounded the base, squeaking and twittering, some trying to leap up and then falling backwards with small soft-boned thumps.

'Charlie!' Felix exclaimed, as his friend returned with a jug of iced watermelon juice. 'These aren't really wild dogs, are they?'

'Ran over their mother sadly. They were only days old.'

Felix groaned. Charlie was always rescuing young animals on his farm – actually a private game reserve – and bringing them back here, where he maintained a small menagerie. Felix had encountered sizeable cheetah cubs on this sundeck and, once, a baby hippo in the swimming-pool.

'How can you bear them?' Felix asked Alys, wrinkling his nose at the puppies. 'They stink.'

'Nature doesn't stink,' said Charlie, lifting one of the animals and letting it lick his face. 'It's one of the most vital things to teach her.'

'I hope you're also teaching her how dangerous it can be! These things are like hyenas. Very bad table manners. They eat on the move. While the prey is still running.'

'That's right,' said Charlie. 'Only way they can bring down game that's bigger than them.'

'Like Alys.'

'Don't be an asshole.'

'Charles!' said Felix, using the French pronunciation – *Sharl* –to temper their souring banter. 'I'm really not happy about this.'

Charlie smiled, and said to Alys, 'Your bearded mommy is hassling us again.'

'I'm serious,' persisted Felix. 'Their instincts . . .'

'Animals are motivated by only two instincts,' said Charlie. 'Feeding and fucking. And they don't need Alys for either.'

'Until something goes wrong one day.'

'And long before that day, they're going back into the wild – *aren't you?*' he asked the puppy in his hand. Dangling it as bait, he led the rest of the scampering litter back into the house.

'And wash your hands!' Felix called after him. He kissed the top of Alys's head. 'I'll take you away with me, Lys. D'you want me to steal you?'

'OK,' she replied, smiling in that way of hers, as though suddenly revealing . . . something. It was very adult. When she peeked at you from underneath a drape of blonde hair, her green irises simultaneously coy and amused, it was hard to believe she didn't know what she was doing.

Felix looked at her, their eyes only inches apart, then averted his gaze as Charlie returned.

The two men sat on the lounger and drank, the girl flopping from one lap to the other.

'I was thinking at the circus today,' said Felix, 'of the first time we took her to the theatre. The way she tried to . . .' He reached out his arms, imitating Alys.

'I'm surprised you remember!' laughed Charlie. 'You were so bombed that morning.'

'Oh, don't be silly. The day of Duma's downfall – how could one forget that? Preview of the Genesis show. Popped upstairs for a drink, heard it on the Overseas Service, and . . .' He hesitated. 'D'you know the first thing I felt?'

'Hmn?'

'Never told you. Never told anyone.' Charlie waited, raising his eyebrows. 'Disappointment,' said Felix. He nodded towards Alys. 'One was touched by a child's first visit to the theatre, yet this event, this longed-for, momentous event . . . politics suddenly rearing up with all the force of Nature, huge and unstoppable – politics behaving like history! – this great event just produced a sort of flatness. The head, not the heart was full. And . . .'

He stopped, his head loud with his grandiloquence. Oh, this accent of his! Trumpeting opinions and airs, it allowed him to be both pompous and self-mocking in the same breath. What a thoroughly British product it was. He glanced at Charlie. The man was as much a colonial ape as he was – adopting that silly American voice! – yet it didn't seem to trouble him. He was so sure of himself in every way. So experienced. Charlie's handsomeness, the rich, yellow light of late afternoon, and the luxury of the home framing his profile, all combined to make him look like he was from an earlier, more carefree era: a playboy in the twenties or thirties, endowed with good looks, untold wealth, and no problems whatsoever. Viewed like this, in the luminosity of sundown, Charlie's features, his skin, his very being, seemed flawless.

'What's the matter?' Charlie asked.

'Gosh, no, I was just . . .' spluttered Felix. 'Nothing.'

'Carry on. What you were saying. About the day Duma fell.'

Hurriedly lighting a cigarette, Felix explained, 'Well, no, I think I just knew it was over – me and the theatre – our best days were over. Freedom's a fine thing, but dull.' Charlie gave a little laugh. 'Well, yes, might sound awful, but it was inspiring – repression. How is one going to deal with the Public Info Office, dodge round the censorship laws, find a way of representing freedom, yet not end up behind bars?' He grimaced and touched the scar inside his leg. 'Didn't always judge *that* perfectly. Nevertheless . . . the solutions you come up with! Nothing like stricture to produce one's best work. Budget, resources, staff, material – restrict these things a trifle, and the creative imagination will become so bloody inventive! We were talking about animal instincts earlier. That's what the creative imagination is like. A wild animal. Trap it and it'll find a way out. Or kill itself in the struggle. Beautiful stuff either way.' He flicked ash from his cigarette, and watched it float on to the sundeck and rest there, poised . . . the air was so still up here. 'Anyway, that's all finished, and now . . . as I expected, everything has gone from bad to worse, and the board wants to get rid of me, and . . . I think I knew it all in that first instant, when I heard the news on the radio . . .'

'Do you regret it?' Charlie asked abruptly. 'Do you want Duma back?'

'Of course not!' Felix was about to laugh, when he thought back to Brak's appearance here on Charlie's sundeck. He said slowly, 'Do you?'

'No. But . . .'

'*But?!* How can there be a but?'

Charlie scrubbed his face bashfully. 'Ah, shit, man, whenever we talk like this, talk politics, I feel so . . . !' He became more agitated. 'What did Kaz call me yesterday? – a dumb blond. A poor little rich boy, she calls me that too. She's right. Y'know, life in these homes up here . . . without Duma, with Duma, *before* Duma . . . if you're rich in Africa . . . well, you know the score.'

'I most certainly do not!' guffawed Felix. 'Haven't got two pennies to rub –'

'No, but you know the score, c'mon, c'mon, you know what I'm talking 'bout here!' Charlie's words were beginning to race, and his eyes were brightening (Felix wondered if, while fetching Bull Brak's 'sugar', the doctor had sampled a grain or two). 'She says to me the other day, Kaz, she says, "Why do you stay in Africa? You could be anywhere, you could be more comfortable, more safe, you could be in Manhattan or Knightsbridge or Monte Carlo or wherever." Shit, man, she doesn't understand. And I can't explain without it sounding like a joke or an insult. *Comfortable? Safe?* If you're rich, why would you want those things? Boredom lies thataway. But here . . . being rich here is so . . . intense! It's like everything else here, it's like, like . . . !' He gestured to the slopes of the Kwatokuu above them, his fingers opening and closing sensuously. 'It's thick rich, it's wet rich, it's jungle rich, it's like raw rich, it's lush, you can hold it, smell it, eat it, stick it in your veins! You end up not thinking straight, certainly not thinking *politics*. You're lucky if you end up thinking at all!' He broke into laughter, covering his face. 'Wow . . . sorry . . . where did all that come from?'

'I don't know,' said Felix, laughing as well. 'But I think it answers my question.'

Charlie looked up. 'What was your question?'

They laughed louder. Which of the other millionaires on this mountain-top would make such confessions? wondered Felix. Which of them would admit that life here was simply a gorgeous paradise, *their* paradise, and that Dumas might come and go, but nothing would ever spoil it? Charlie's honesty enchanted Felix, and Charlie's innocence, and . . .

[handwritten marginalia: "In ♡ w/ Charlie? homosexuality?"]

And Charlie.

He had saved Felix's life twice, this unorthodox doctor . . . the first time was in the police cell on that terrible Monday morning, the second was when he proposed the idea of the Long Island clinic, and organised everything, and picked up the bill. Perhaps he could help again? Help shape Felix's new, unformed life, help make sense of a host of confusing new emotions. Perhaps, when dancing on the roof this morning . . . when those strange ideas occurred . . . about love, daring to love, to touch . . . perhaps it was Charlie he had in mind? Felix began to redden. In the past, emboldened by drink, he'd been able to declare, 'When it comes to the bedroom department, the goods seem so terribly limited. There's the straight mattress, but – pshaw! – it's so infantile, that constant return to the breast, the womb! And then there's the bent mattress, but – ugh! – who wants to take on another man? It's akin to wrestling!' Now both prospects simply made him tremble.

Charlie was looking at him intently, lips twitching with amusement. 'What is it?' Charlie asked. 'There's something . . .'

'There isn't, there's nothing,' Felix replied briskly. 'Ah look!'

Alys had fallen asleep across their laps. Felix gathered her into his arms, and nuzzled her hair. 'Smell this,' he said softly, offering the other side of her golden head to Charlie. 'What is it, what is it?'

'The dogs?' grinned Charlie.

'No. A good smell.'

They sniffed her hair, their noses almost touching.

'She's been outside since coming back,' said Charlie.

'The sun, yes.'

'And she had some toast for tea.'

'Toast, yes.'

'And . . .'

'And?'

'I dunno – childhood, I suppose.'

'Yes.'

[handwritten marginalia: "Joy! object - Alys."]

They both kissed her head, and Charlie said, 'To bed, to bed, sleepyhead . . . oh!' He held his breath. But it was no good. She had woken.

'It's all right, I'll do it,' said Felix, and lifted her. They strolled

into the house. The living-room was furnished in the minimalist
style, with just a few exquisite pieces, mostly Roman antiquities.
The walls were big, white and bare, except for a small but priceless
first century mosaic panel at one end, and, at the other, a framed
photograph of Isabeau, Charlie's late wife and Alys's mother. Since
she had been a professional photographer herself, the image –
Charlie's favourite Instamatic snap of her – didn't seem adequate
somehow, despite its expensive frame. If anything, the silver and
velvet mount demoted its subject, pushing her deep into the wall, or
even further away, creating the impression of a peephole. A deli-
cately pretty woman with ginger hair, washed with sunshine, caught
in mid-movement, she seemed somewhere beyond the room, passing
by, glancing in.

'And what's this?' Felix asked, noticing a book on the marble
coffee table – *Private Life in the Ancient World* – with lists and
sketched ground-plans surrounding it.

'My next party,' the other replied, grinning. 'The biggest 'n' best
yet. Over the long weekend next month.'

Felix gave a mock-groan. He wondered what Charlie looked like
in the middle of these parties, these famous wild parties, held at his
farm, with planeloads of guests flying in. The weekend's itinerary
was modelled on Roman feasts, it was said, down to the last detail
of culinary and sexual ritual. What did he look like at the height of
it all, this emperor of revels, with his strong, straight profile and
fringe of curls, what did he look like then?

'Why don't you come along this time?' Charlie asked now – as he
always did. And, as always, Felix dismissed the suggestion with a
prissy wave of his hand, while – as always – a strange, unformed
excitement crept through his guts. Quite soon, a favourite phrase
would crop up in his conversation: *fly on the wall.*

Felix left the living-room, carrying the drowsy Alys. He sometimes felt troubled by Charlie's addiction to ancient Rome. It was
fed in every possible way: history books, Hollywood epics, overseas
auctions. The two columns in the corridor down which Felix
walked, they were original, in marble, from the Severian era, but
altered to fit this house, the one cut down, the other topped with
plaster, stained to match it, so that they appeared to support the

this *book*

ceiling. There was something about this act – it was like a piece of forgery or vandalism – something barbaric and vulgar.

In Alys's bedroom, the prize piece was a marble peacock, still boasting a last crust of the brilliant colours that were the speciality of Roman sculptors. It stood at the window, its silhouette fanned out against a flaming view of sky and sea. The end of the day. Felix watched it in ecstasy, while absent-mindedly helping Alys into her pyjamas. The sun set with African speed: an orange egg dropping onto the horizon and breaking there.

'A story?' he asked.

She thought about this and held back her answer until she was lying in bed looking up at him. 'OK.'

'What's the little word?'

'Please,' she answered, and then stroked his hand. 'Please.'

He smiled back. 'You're very controlling, d'you know that?'

'What's very controlling?'

his life story

'I'll tell you.' He took a deep breath. 'Once upon a time there was a witch who cast a spell over a child so that he could only think of fame and fortune. She did this by first teaching him to speak in a funny la-di-da way. By going *T-t-t*, or *P-p-p*.' He saw Alys grin with pleasure. 'Or *maa-may-mee-maw-moo*, and by making other funny sounds, so she cast her wicked spell. Then one day . . .' *doesn't give it*

His bedtime stories only needed a trigger and they tumbled out, going this way and that, with fantastic convolutions and elegant, nonsensical resolutions. Both he and Alys found them captivating while they were happening and completely forgettable afterwards. They were like dreams, like doodles.

Our imagination! thought Felix, when Alys was asleep. He grasped his head with both hands, like Emile had done yesterday.

Emile had never been allowed to see Alys, his granddaughter, but Felix saw it as his personal mission to arrange a meeting, one day, somehow, and to be present at it. He wanted to see Emile – hard-nosed, heard-it-all-before Emile; Emile the shrink, Emile the Communist – he wanted to see Emile the old man meet this golden-haired angel, and melt.

Felix stood slowly, one finger lingering on her hair, drifting across

the bedhead, and onto her big cushion-dolls, the Scarecrows, which
he had commissioned from the Alex's prop-maker for one of her
birthdays. Child-sized, made with the rude comic energy of local
sculpture, they were much cherished; she loved pummelling them, or
dressing them in her clothes. Sometimes, spying her in a long private
embrace with one of them, Felix fretted about her solitude. Sighing
fondly now, he switched off the light.

As he strolled back across the main courtyard, its stones still
warm from the day, its foliage beginning to buzz and tick with the
night, he wondered where the litter of wild dogs slept. A ghastly
picture rose in his mind: a basket filled with bat pups all wrapped
into one another like a pile of intestines; a basket of baby devils.

Passing a lit doorway, he saw Charlie inside. The room was his
surgery. Cluttered in a way that Felix found romantic – it reminded
him of doctors' stations in black-and-white films about colonial
life – it was here that Charlie saw patients, performed minor
surgery, and dispensed medicines. He often worked long hours,
tending his circle, their staff and the staff's families. He was a good
doctor; a fact that always surprised Felix. In a side chamber (Kaz
called this 'the *mganga*'s hut'), arranged like a little laboratory,
Charlie sometimes whiled away the evenings concocting new treats
for himself and his friends, mixing solutions, baking little tablets
like those he'd given Brak. But none of it was enough for Charlie,
neither the work nor the play; he practised both restlessly, as
though there was something better just round the next corner. Felix
understood the feeling.

'Can I smoke in here?' Felix asked from the threshold.

Charlie shook his head mutely, swallowing something, and
strolled out of the room, locking it securely. Felix lit two cigarettes,
like characters did in those old films. 'Are you all right?' he asked,
noticing how listlessly Charlie received the little gift.

Blinking rapidly, like someone waking, Charlie said, 'Just thinking. Those people we saw in the market-place. The hangings.'

'Yes,' sighed Felix.

'They said that kinda thing would start.'

'Kangaroo courts, presumably.'

'Guess so.'

'Terrifying!' said Felix. 'Imagine being a fly on the wall at one of those hearings!'

'No thanks.'

'And, I mean, if people are simply going to take justice into their own hands, how are we ever going to find out what went on?'

'Never really found out during the Hakika,' said Charlie. 'Won't find out now, so what's the diff?' He arched back into a yawning stretch.

Felix persisted. 'Yet someone like Kaz won't rest till she does find out. Exactly what happened. To *her* son.'

'Then let's tell her to stop stoning the stooges. As I tried to do this afternoon. Stooges, small fry. That's all those guys were. Just following orders.'

Felix gave a humourless laugh. 'Heard that one before.' *So obvious*

'Yeah. Well.' Charlie started to move away. 'Supper-time.'

'This "Popo-boy",' Felix said, refusing to let it rest. 'You could ask your chum Bull Brak who it was. Who it *is*.'

Charlie stopped. 'I could. Unless it's *him*.'

'Are you serious?'

'Naa. Don't think so anyway. Brakkie's a two-faced slob, a bully, a mean bastard when his back's to the wall, but I don't reckon he's a sadist.' He thought for a moment. 'One rumour going round about Popo-boy is that it was Duma himself. Y'know he's supposed to have practised blood rituals. Igisha stuff. Eat a piece of your enemy and gain his strength, that kinda thing.'

Felix sighed grimly. 'Oh, well, I'll tell her to go and ask Duma, then.'

'Do,' replied Charlie, amused by the idea.

'And where should I tell her to start looking?' scoffed Felix. 'Where was the last reported sighting? Libya? Iran? South America?'

'Naa, much closer – walking distance,' said Charlie, and before Felix could laugh, added, 'I treated him yesterday. It's why I was almost late for the board meeting. He had a migraine.'

PART II

the Great
Dictator

charicature!

eleven

As he climbed the steep hill towards the cave, Felix's body felt as if it didn't fit any more. What with the sweat pouring out and the air trying to squeeze in, he had become either too small or too big for himself. He was out of condition, certainly – his old liquid diet was arguably healthier than the new one of ice-cream, chocolate peanuts, coffee and cigarettes – but he suspected it wasn't just a physical problem. Nor was it anything to do with Nature, who had sloped this piece of land at such a preposterous angle that the task was comparable to running through water, or reaching an urgent appointment in a dream. No. Much hotter and noisier than the undergrowth through which his feet churned, crashing and slipping, was the inside of his head.

He wanted to fall back and fly forwards at the same time, he wanted to run screaming from the place while also bounding onwards with a whooping war cry.

I can't wait!

The phrase went round and round his head, teasing him with its different meanings:

I want to be there.

I mustn't stay for this.

He watched his perspiring hand shoot out to steady his balance for the umpteenth time, and then check that the locks hadn't sprung open on the case he was carrying. Now his hand moved up to his face and felt the unfamiliar smoothness of his chin, cheeks and skull.

Bald as an egg, bald as a stone.

Eggs can break, stones can hurt.

The hillside's vertiginous slant was intensified by the angle of the palm trees that rose from the thick green bush: high and thin, they leaned towards the sea with strange elastic curvature, seeming to defy gravity, creating the impression of a hurricane in full blast, even on a beautiful still morning like this. Ahead on the slope, Charlie stopped again, pretending to take in the view of the bay while waiting for Felix to catch up.

It wasn't fair that Charlie should be bounding up the slope like a mountain cat – Charlie abused his body with more than just sugar, caffeine, nicotine – *it wasn't fair*.

The two friends waved at one another, and Felix hauled himself onwards to the cave.

Two evenings ago, standing on Charlie's sundeck, when Felix learned that Emperor Duma was not in exile as everyone thought but just a few miles away, the second surprise was the location of his hiding-place.

'Bull Brak's land?!' spluttered Felix.

'Yeah, and I know what you're thinking,' Charlie said. 'Did Brakkie fool the Hakika after all? Everyone said he couldn't've acted all the tears and stuff. But who knows? Personally, I reckon he's just biding his time – waiting to see what happens in this country after the party's over.'

Felix shook his head, trying to absorb it all. 'So what is Duma in all this – in Bull Brak's master survival plan? The card up his sleeve? Tomorrow's meal ticket?'

'Dunno. Don't reckon Brak thinks about it much. Doesn't seem that interested in Duma. He hardly visits him, hasn't posted a guard, doesn't really care what happens to him. He's granted him, like, sanctuary for old times' sake, and now he's keeping his hands well clean. You know what I think Duma is to Brak, more than anything else? Just one helluva status symbol!'

'Status symbol?'

'Well, it is impressive! To the handful of us who know. C'mon, *you*'re impressed, right now. Own up.'

Felix stared back sourly, while his heart pounded.

'It's brilliant,' continued Charlie. 'Half the world's looking for him.

Different secret services with different agendas, all looking for him, and where is he? In the one place no one expects. Here. In his homeland. In a cave. All on his own. Without . . .'

'Is it brilliant?' Felix asked. 'Someone will find out. Just someone local, I mean. One of Brak's herdboys or . . . I mean, you've just told *me*. Aren't you sworn to secrecy or something?'

Charlie shrugged and gave his shy-naughty smile.

'It's just a question of time,' Felix said. 'He'll be murdered in that cave.'

'Exactly!' laughed Charlie. 'That's why it's brilliant. From both sides – Duma's and Brak's. If Duma's murdered, Brak says he didn't know he was there, or more likely does another confession-number and claims *he* killed him, and poses next to the body. "The man who shot Emperor Duma." He'll be a world hero.'

'And Duma? You said it's brilliant from both sides. How, pray, does Duma come to view his own murder as brilliant?'

'Because *that*'s what he wants!' exclaimed Charlie, leaning forward, eyes blinking rapidly. *(How many of his own potions and powders had the doctor sampled tonight?)* 'Remember the famous speech? "I know when I will die, when, where and how."'

'So – wait, wait, wait – if he wants to die, the mob would've obliged him happily, so why did he run away in the first place?'

'He didn't. He's here. He stayed. And as you say, he'll pay with his life. But he doesn't want to die at the hands of the mob. He wants something nobler – like an assassination – something more in tune with his story. I mean, you know better than anyone – it's like he's scripted the whole thing. The humble tribal beginnings, the rise to power, the dictatorship, the cruelty, the crazy lifestyle, like Nero or Tiberius. And now he wants to find the right exit. The grand exit.'

Felix listened carefully. Did it make sense? In a dreamy kind of way perhaps. Particularly when spoken by a handsome ageing hippie with a shy smile and a peculiar look in his eyes . . . a look of boredom? of wisdom? of being stoned out of his mind?

'And you?' Felix asked. 'What's your involvement?'

Charlie grinned. 'Me? Naa, I'm just the medicine man, the *mganga*, just here to patch 'n' mend, to soothe 'n' save. Bull Brak called me in because Duma's been getting these headaches. It's a laugh, really. He lost his glasses in the flight from the palace, and –'

'Glasses?' exclaimed Felix. 'But glasses were outlawed. Glasses branded you as a student or an intellectual.'

'Or one of Duma's family,' laughed Charlie. 'They were all blind as bats, the Scourge of Africa included. But he's been without them since he fled, and now he's getting these mega migraines. How the mighty doth fall, huhn? So I gave him some pills.'

'Wouldn't new glasses be better?'

'Well, his optician isn't around, of course – fled with the rest of the nearest and dearest – but yes, one of Brakkie's guys and me, we went to the guy's ex-premises. But no prescription. Just a note in his file – "Records are at patient's address". Apparently Duma hoarded all his medical files, kept them under lock and key. Very anal that way, apparently. So, yeah, will keep looking.'

After supper Felix changed his mind about staying the night, and returned to the Alex. Outside the stage door the ground was clear; his television and video sets had gone. 'It *was* only the messenger,' he whispered to himself. Fearful of bumping into Kaz, maddened with drink, he darted upstairs, then barricaded his door and crawled straight into his bed under the table, feeling exceptionally tired.

He'd always liked the phrase *dropping off* because it precisely described the strange function of voluntarily passing out: his feet really felt like they were dropping off, or dropping from one ledge to another, and another, each lower than before, and then again, he felt the jerk go through his leg, it was surprising, clownish, dog-like, just one more time and . . . but tonight this last step turned into a kick, and its force made his eyes pop open. Now his mind was caught in a limbo-land between consciousness and sleep; teeming, doodling, tying itself in knots, coming round in circles, and eventually formulating a most bizarre idea. He lay restlessly, stroking the underside of the table, trying to quell the new idea, the growing excitement. *It's night-time rubbish,* he decided, *small-hours' stuff*, and resolved to clear his mind and rest. If the first part of what he would later automatically call 'my night's sleep' had seemed like a landscape, with stone stairs safely leading him lower and lower into his underself, the second part was more like water. He skim-slept, dipping in and out of brief, baddish dreams – one featured a short man with nose-studs who was teaching him German elocution – and then, just as he was finally plunging down successfully, being enveloped by a deep, warm darkness, he was instantly woken again by a small noise. The kind that can reverberate through the half-conscious mind, less a sound than a sensation, a chill, a terror, some nightmare from childhood, real or dreamed, come back to touch you. So this noise – in fact, just birds scrabbling on the roof above – twisted through Felix, leaving him aghast and wide-eyed.

As soon as he saw the outline of the table separate itself from the rest of the darkness, he crawled out of bed, made himself coffee, then picked up the phone. He fully expected it to be dead, as usual, but no, it was working. Of course it was. For *this* call.

'Yeahh?' Charlie's voice was slurred.

'Sorry. Were you asleep?'

'I never sleep,' came the reply, and Felix thought he probably wasn't joking.

'Sorry,' Felix repeated. 'But it's urgent. I want to –'

'Hang on,' said Charlie. Felix heard whispering. A woman, possibly two – or was one another man? A door slammed. Then Charlie back on the line. 'Yeahh, fire away, yeahhh.' His voice sounded like it was being played at the wrong speed.

'You all right?' asked Felix.

'Will be in a sec,' croaked Charlie. A tiny snap – perhaps the top coming off a plastic phial? – a sipping sound. And now, when he returned to the mouthpiece, his voice was miraculously freshened. 'Yessir, and what can I do for you?'

'I want to ask a favour.'

'Name it.'

'Take me to see Duma.'

'No way.'

'Charlie . . .'

'*No way!*'

'Oh, for goodness sake, what d'you think I'm going to do? Pull out a dagger and carve myself a niche in history? You know me. I can't cut steak without feeling faint, I'm –'

'Felix, this is crazy, man. Just because Kaz wants to find her son's killer . . .'

'What? No, no, it's not for her. I'd forgotten about that. No, this is for *me*.'

'Felix . . .'

'Just listen, just hear me out – all right?' As the silence sharpened at the other end of the line, it felt like Felix's own ears popping. How to phrase his argument? How to explain that he and Duma *had already made contact?* The invitation, or challenge, had been issued. This was simply the next stage, pre-ordained and inescapable. Taking a deep breath, Felix launched in: 'Last night you said you weren't really a political creature. Well, neither am I. Always wished I was, but I'm not, never will be. Art is about asking questions, politics is about concocting answers. People thought I was political, they said I was. But I was just an artist in a rather dramatic environment – a police state – working in it, exploiting it, doing what artists do. I am an artist. Not an easy thing to be. Not even an easy thing to say. *I am an artist.* Sounds unlikely. Sounds more like the speaker is a masturbator. Maybe I am that too. Well, no, I *am*. But I am also . . . well, I am an artist.' Felix paused briefly, thinking he'd put all that rather well and wishing he had a pencil to scribble it down for his journal later. Finding Kaz's cigarettes instead, he lit one and reeled from its first cruel invasion of his being. 'So it's as an artist that I'm asking you, begging you, to do me this favour. An artist needs to see everything he can . . .' He puffed twice at the cigarette, quickly, nervously, with little kissing noises.

'Charlie, look at the big stories that man first told, and you keep coming up against different writers' ideas of our dark forces, whether it's the resident reptile in the Garden of Eden or a one-eyed giant on an Aegean island. Fair dos, we're dealing in symbols, basic, crude, effective symbols. And so you look at Shakespeare, the greatest of them all. And his villains are deformed or possessed by witchcraft or born out of wedlock. And you think we're still dealing in symbols. But what was it like to have tea with Hitler or Stalin?

Symbolic evil /Real evil.

How did their handshake feel, what did their breath smell of? Were they listeners? Could they make small-talk? Did they smile at you – what were their teeth like? Charlie, all my sensible, intelligent, politically correct, stone-cold-sober instincts make me want to run a mile from any contact with Duma, and all my other instincts, animal and artistic, these drag me towards him, sniffing and curious. Charlie, I want to, I *must* do this thing. I must –'

'Meet with the devil?' joked Charlie, but at either end of the phone neither of them was smiling.

'Call it what you want,' replied Felix.

'I call it wild, old buddy, *wild.*'

In that moment, Felix knew his friend was up for it. They both held their breath.

Then Charlie asked slowly, 'But how would we actually . . . ?'

'Well, yes,' Felix said, having feared it would come to this: some foolproof plan; he'd been struggling to solve this. 'Well . . . you said Duma had lost his glasses, and you couldn't find his prescription. Well . . . what if you had to take an optician to see him? An optician whose trustworthiness you could vouch for with your life. And what if this optician does eye tests on him, or seems to? And . . . what d'you think?'

Charlie laughed. 'I'm thinking – what happens when Duma fails to *get* any new glasses? Y'know, as a result of the visit. The visit of this optician that I've vouched for with my life. What happens then?'

'Well, yes.'

Felix felt ashamed for Charlie, sensing his fear underneath the jokiness. Duma might be without his spectacles, but his all-seeing, all-knowing eye still seemed to menace Charlie.

'Naa, it'll only work,' Charlie said thoughtfully, 'if the optician really does his stuff, really produces the goods.'

Felix frowned. Had Charlie's night been so debauched that he wasn't concentrating? Had he not realised who the optician was?

But Charlie didn't sound fuddled, only like a man who suffered from chronic boredom and whose juices were activated by a plot, a puzzle. He thought for a moment, then repeated, almost to himself, a phrase he'd quoted last night: '"Records are at patient's address".'

*

The road to Duma's main palace, his favourite, the jungle palace, was anonymous. It could have been any one of a thousand roads that traversed the countryside just out of town: crudely routed, untarred, coming and going with the seasons – droughts cracked them open, flash floods washed them away – sometimes resident to bandits or elephant herds, these were quirky sketch-roads, rough and ready affairs with their own lively beauty; red dirt roads winding through green bush under humid grey skies.

This particular one came to a sudden dead end in front of the palace gates. Its wrought-iron was shaped into an outline of Duma's emblem, the African buffalo. 'The most dangerous of our wildlife,' Charlie once explained to Felix. 'Wounded or angered, it'll ambush you – it will, deliberately and cunningly, *get* you!' The gates were suitably huge and imposing, but presently in poor shape: rusted, dented and, most surprisingly, held together with only a padlock and chain.

One sun-sleepy soldier was on guard. In sharp contrast to the muscular, immaculate men of Duma's forces, this chap was half starved, without beret or helmet, the knees of his camouflage uniform worn through, and instead of boots he wore green rubber wellingtons.

There was no difficulty in persuading him to open the gates. Bull Brak's man, Captain Kyolaba, a policeman in civilian jacket and tie, didn't even have to show any papers: just a few cigarettes did the trick, supplied from the carton that Felix now possessed. (He'd discovered that chain-smoking allowed you to bypass the awful nauseous hit of the first puff; this way evened it out, giving a constant, grubby dizziness, which you could learn to live with.) The soldier seemed excited by the visit. Hardly anyone came here any more – not like the flocks of international journalists and hordes of citizens just after Duma's fall.

Then there were extraordinary scenes at these gates. Felix watched every news bulletin, both CNN and the local ones, preferring the latter because of their astonishing, uncensored scenes of celebration and catharsis, of mob violence and mob grief . . . one of the palace guards being torn apart, literally, his body separated by people's bare hands, Duma's statue being lassoed and toppled, people dancing and urinating on his upturned face, smashing it

Duma's palace

with iron bars, riding it to its final resting-place, the palace swimming-pool.

The statue was still there today, still in its drowned pose, face down in the great, empty pool. The raised fist lay in one corner, half covered by a puddle of litter and moss, while at the other end the huge feet rested clumsily on the diving-board and steps. It looked more comic than tragic, like a stupid accident: a pissed giant who'd died at a party.

Felix gazed at the pool. According to rumour, the emperor used to fill the water with crocodiles, and then, one by one, live students.

(Students like Kaz's son . . . ?)

As Captain Kyolaba led them through the palace grounds, Felix was struck by the lack of grandeur. Even given the state of disrepair – for anything that could be looted had been looted, anything that could be broken had been broken – even so, there had clearly never been formal gardens here. Duma's much-publicised private zoo (he was amused by unAfrican creatures, llamas, kangaroos, polar bears, and imported them from round the world), this was just a huddle of little cages on wheels, like a downmarket travelling circus, the doors hanging open and the animals missing, looted as well, for food.

As for the palace itself, this looked like a civic office-block; its huge, orange-brick ugliness emphasised by the lack of windows. The only ones were right at the top, just under the grey corrugated-tin roof.

What a tawdry Third World idea of majesty, thought Felix – until they went inside.

To his amazement, there was only a single room here. A colossal hall. It was not made of brick at all (that was just a weatherproof outer casing), but red stone, carved directly out of the landscape. One massive red rock had been hollowed out. The palace was, in fact, a whole small hill.

If it wasn't for the tin roof way above them, there would be nothing at all, the space open to the sky, and now Felix understood those windows at the top: empty of glass, they were simply there for ventilation, and for the long, tall slants of light they threw. The walls were overpoweringly beautiful. You wanted to touch them immediately; you wanted to spread your arms wide against their rounded expanses or nestle in their hollows. As old as time, they were patterned with all the fantastic birthmarks and growth pains of the planet: lines, ridges and fillings of different minerals, layers of cooled molten lava, the petrified shockwaves of earthquakes which had bent, dropped and folded the land; all on display, the undulating floors, shores and surfaces piled one upon the other, each section travelling right round the incredible room, the predominant red colour changing from place to place, wet and purply here, like meat on the turn, or soft, clayish and yellower over there, and infused with every other hue in the universe, and some from underneath it, pure whites, gleaming blacks, soft charcoals, golds and silvers, a turquoise sheen, glittering azure grains, the delicate lime contours of coral and shellfish fossils, which studded sections of the walls like little inlaid gifts . . . fragile shadows from long ago, when the continent lay deep underwater.

Felix imagined Duma's famous cry – 'I am Africa, and Africa is me!' – echoing round this room (this is where he had made the speech, after all), and not sounding at all preposterous; no, it would make complete sense in here. You felt you were *in* the earth, not on it. You felt safe as a child, strong as a superman. You felt immortal, invincible.

Duma had both lived and worked here – according to Captain Kyolaba. At one end had stood the famous three-square-metre ebony desk, under the famous portrait, its proportions like a New York billboard, yet executed in oils by a team of Dutch painters specially flown in for the job (it *had* to be oil paint, it *had* to be Dutch painters, it *had* to be like an old masterpiece). Felix half hoped to see the outline of the painting – burned publicly after the dictator's fall – left up there, ghost-like, as on a dusty wall, but the ancient rock had remained impervious to its brief presence, a mere three decades or so. However, at the other end of the great chamber, patches of the floor and walls were stained black with smoke: evidence of the cooking and ceremonial fires that had characterised Duma's private life. Here he had slept with his twenty-odd wives, here he had engendered his sixty-odd children, here he had been serenaded by praise-singers. Felix never realised from news footage that the palace possessed this earthiness, this awesome, shadowy presence. During the big rallies, the interior was covered in flags, banners and other Dumanian paraphernalia, and crammed with crowds. Coachloads of supporters were brought in, there were free banquets, cauldrons of homebrew beer, whole oxen roasted on the spit, there was mass dancing, with people on hands and knees, ready to pray, ready to copulate, their torsos undulating to thunderous drumming – they were *throwing the dance at the drums!*, as the saying goes – while cheerleaders with microphones led the chants, 'EEE-OH, DU-MAAA!, UUU-OH, DU-MAAA!, sounding like elocution lessons on a gigantic scale.

Revolving slowly, Felix whispered, 'Crikey!' This chamber had served as tribal village, as imperial court, as political stadium, as governmental nerve-centre, once as the location for a celebrated international boxing match and, for a few months, as a film studio, when it was fitted with lighting rigs and scaffold-towers, and Duma starred in a film of his life.

Felix and Charlie were puzzled to see other people in the room today, a smallish group clustered half-way along one wall. Were there squatters even here? Were they remnants of Duma's family – the ones who hadn't fled or been murdered? Surely not. When questioned, Captain Kyolaba was enigmatic: 'Part of a cult – I think.'

A cult? What were they worshipping, these robed figures huddled round what looked like an eternal flame, and why were they worshipping it here, in this unholy church, this temple of Duma?

Captain Kyolaba led to a gap in the far corner where, he explained, there used to be a secret door – now stolen.

It led down a flight of stairs to the lower level: sprawling underground premises that could be sealed off in the event of nuclear or chemical war. This area showed signs of a grander lifestyle: archways with pillars, and apartments with moulded ceilings. There were peeling traces of flock wallpaper, spiky wooden strips framing missing carpets, and *en suite* bathrooms where everything, from toilet bowls to taps, had been ripped away. And there were dressing-rooms: row upon row of narrow, passage-like chambers with built-in cupboards, their mirrors and gilt surrounds thieved. Here had hung all the costumes of the emperor-dictator. From the traditional tie-dyed *kitenge* shirts to the Napoleonic coronation robes;

from the evening dress and top hats to the togas and solid gold garlands; from the Castro fatigues to the white field-marshal uniforms laden with braid, sashes and medals. Felix was surprised to see that the empty coat-hangers came in many different sizes, some quite miniature, then remembered that all Duma's children were high-ranking army officers too.

There were many other rooms Felix wanted to explore (the kitchen in which Duma was rumoured to have cooked and eaten a political rival – where was that?, what did the oven look like, or the gargantuan fridge where he reputedly stored other bodies?), but now the sightseeing was over. Captain Kyolaba retreated discreetly to the entrance of the underground bunker, as instructed by his boss, for Felix and Charlie were here for a purpose: there was something to be found.

If Felix had been inventing this visit, as part of a bedtime story for Alys, or directing the sequence in a play or film, he would have ended it with the hero – himself – somehow, incredibly, miraculously, among all the rubble and, despite all the theft, suddenly finding a pair of glasses. The great dictator's specs. His spare pair. Perhaps in a bathroom cabinet or a toiletries bag.

But instead, many hours later, when the magic object was found, it was not a pair of specs but a piece of paper, and Charlie was the lucky one, the hero of the day.

A piece of paper – from a file marked *Medical*, on a floor of scraps and waste, in a small office with an overturned filing cabinet.

No looter would have bothered to steal this piece of paper – it merely held typed information, with lists of numerals and abbreviations – but to Felix, at this moment in time, it was the most valuable thing on earth.

As Charlie said on the way back to the car: '*Now* we're cooking. *Now* I can take an optician to Duma and vouch for him with my life. Because a week after this optician has done his little ol' test, Duma's gonna get a pair of new specs and they're gonna be prescription-perfect!' He waved the piece of paper in his hand. 'So – our man, the big bogey man, he'll be happy, and I'll've done well, so I'll be happy, and you, well, I don't know what . . .'

'No, I don't know either!' said Felix, suppressing a fit of mad giggles. 'But it feels rather promising, what?!'

Charlie shook his head and smiled. 'If you're expecting to come face to face with some kinda "evil" or whatever, you're going to be very disappointed. He's very ordinary.'

'Ordinary, right, okeydoke,' said Felix, his hysteria growing. 'When we get to the cave tomorrow, I'll look out for the ordinary one!'

twelve

As Felix reached the mouth of the cave – the cave set into a steep hillside on Bull Brak's land – about half an hour after Charlie, he was pleased to see that it looked exactly like it ought, like a mouth, a mouth in a dream, a dream, not a nightmare, and that it offered a sucking not biting opening (about which Emile would probably have had something to say); the shape being oval not jagged, and the lips soft with moss and vines.

Catching his breath, Felix did a final check of his optician's equipment, and of his freshly shaved bald head and chin. The disguise was simply an extra precaution – they didn't actually believe that Duma knew what a mere theatre director looked like – but Felix liked it. His recovery was now marked in an explicit and dramatic way: he *looked* like a new man.

The friends grinned at one another. The climb had filled their lungs and chased the blood round their bodies and, now that it was accomplished, even Felix felt better for it. The morning was bright and fresh, the world looked safe, and the next step, into the mouth of the cave, seemed no more dangerous than climbing through the torn fencing round the Queen Mary Hotel when they were kids, for an hour of play in the lush shadows of its grounds.

It would be exciting, it would be an adventure, but light years away from the appointment with the devil that Felix had previously imagined.

They stepped into the cave.

Felix's senses were immediately alert. The smell of the rock; that cold smell of inside the earth, its first layer; a smaller, colder version of the palace. The curve of the walls, like a subway or, no, something fleshier; a womb or a whale came to mind, though Felix had no recollection of being inside either. He listened. A crunch. Was that a footstep? Only his own. Something soft and brittle under his boot. Squinting through the gloom, he saw a squashed baby bat on the rock floor. This felt familiar. Peering down at a small snouty face with big ears, he assumed it was an image from his skimming-sleep last night.

The two men stopped – just a metre or so from the entrance – and stood motionless, their heels a fraction off the ground.

A rustle. It definitely wasn't from them. There – again. Coming from the belly of the cave. They narrowed their eyes.

The place seemed less dark than before. Light from the hill touched the far wall with an almost watery spill.

It was against this cool luminosity that he now appeared – slowly – his silhouette rising from the shadows, where he had either lain asleep or in wait.

'Dr Chabecq?'

Felix went cold. *That voice.*

'Is it you, Dr Chabecq?'

That voice. A hundred news broadcasts. All the great speeches – mostly delivered in English, which helped to make them newsworthy abroad. If voices have colours, and Felix believed they did, then Duma's was an umber voice, earth umber or shit umber, depending on your point of view, but it was certainly mined from some deep and powerful place.

'Dr Chabecq?'

Felix realised that Charlie wasn't answering. Turning, he found his friend locked with fear – as if only now struck by the danger of this game.

'Yes, hi,' said Charlie, snapping out of it. 'This is Mr Rosenblatt, the optometrist I've brought to test your eyes . . .'

Felix tensed. He thought they had agreed to say 'optician'. *What was the other word again?*

'You got my message, I hope?' Charlie asked.

'I did. Thank you for coming, Mr Rosenblatt,' said Emperor Duma, and shuffled forward. His slow entrance was emphasised by the strange light of the cave: he left the monochrome of the shadows, where his flesh looked dotted and blocked like newsprint, and entered a humid grey-greenness, the colour of local television, which is how Felix was used to seeing him, both during his heyday and in the recent apparitions, nudging at the screen of the set, making it bend like a reptile's eggshell, bend and yield . . . breaking now . . . now at last . . . delivering him into the same space as Felix, breathing the same air, standing here, *right here* . . .

Duma was a short man, who seemed even shorter now. He'd lost weight since his sudden departure from office, and was further reduced by the absence of his bulky uniforms, robes and togas, and the bullet-proof vests they concealed. It was a surprise also to see him life-sized, rather than on screens and billboards. On the other hand, those giant impressions travelled with him like an outline in the air; all the legends, real and fictional. Here was the man who, as a youth, had killed a lion with his bare hands, and who, as an adult, had cannibalised his enemies; here was the soldier who had joined the King's African Rifles of the British colonial army, went on to train as an officer in England, reached the rank of sub-lieutenant, returned home and promoted himself to field marshal; here was the commoner who had crowned himself – not king, which would have linked to his tribal past, but emperor; here was the great dictator whose powers of oration were compared to the greatest of them all; here was the political juggler who had, over the years, been both Marxist and capitalist, African nationalist and trading partner of the Old South Africa, friend to both Israel and Islam; here was the visionary who wanted to infiltrate black America with the language KiSwahili; here was the human being who had said the words, 'I am Africa.' Aura, charisma – these words were insufficient for Duma. What on earth had Charlie meant about him being ordinary?

In the flesh, Duma's large head, with wide-spaced bulging eyes, looked more frog than buffalo, but it held phenomenal energy. His thin moustache and goatee were neatly trimmed – circling the famous mouth – and his skull was shaved clean. (Felix wished he'd chosen a different disguise for himself; he felt like he was the dictator's albino twin.) Duma had clearly managed to bring a razor-blade with him, but in every other respect he looked impoverished. He wore only a pair of dark charcoal shorts – reminding Felix of school PT kit – which merged with his skin colour to give an impression of nudity.

'I'm Gomgom the hermit,' said Emperor Duma dully, with little commitment. 'How do you do?'

'Gomgom – hello.' Felix's greeting was barely audible. It had been overwhelming enough to stand face to face with Bull Brak, but Duma . . . *Duma!* Felix almost jumped as they shook hands. The dictator's was unusually heavy, the skin scaly and cold. Once introduced to a tame silverback gorilla at Charlie's menagerie, Felix had had the same sensation as now: a hand yet not a hand.

'Why do I feel I'm meeting my executioner?' Duma asked quietly.

Felix blinked, remembering the moment when Duma's face froze on the TV, becoming stuck. He had been talking about his death then: 'I know how, when and where.' Felix started to reply, found his lips stuck to his gums, quickly swam round them with his tongue, then said meekly, 'Dunno, I'm just your optometrist.'

(The word came out as *opthwomethwist*. Felix wondered if he should keep the lisp.)

Duma nodded. 'Of course. My remark, it was a joke. Why would anybody bother to execute Gomgom the hermit?' He sat on a rock column and began humming in a quiet, broken way – it sounding more like eating noises than a recognisable tune – while one hand busily scratched his shins. Felix wondered if he was trying to play mad. On the other hand, when he was in office, it was widely believed that he *was* mad, certifiably so. Felix felt himself stepping into familiar territory: a hall of mirrors.

'Well?' said Duma.

'Well?' echoed Felix.

'May the test begin.'

'Sorry?'

'My eyes.'

'Indeed,' said Felix, just stopping short from adding 'Your Majesty', then sprang into action. His ensuing performance surprised himself, amazed Charlie and impressed Duma. Partly through fear, partly through a sensation that this wasn't really happening, Mr Rosenblatt the optometrist became a light-footed, quick-fingered, slightly camp individual, with a touch of bravado to his work. From watching the market-place opticians, Felix had only a rudimentary impression of their procedures, but he was able to put into action one of his own directives to actors in trouble – 'Do it fast and no one will notice.' He scurried around Duma, pretending to fill in a Snellen chart, and perform examinations with the retinoscope and ophthalmoscope.

It was when he began slotting trial lenses into the frame-apparatus on Duma's face, when his touch skimmed the man's face – the black skin had a silvery sheen, as though polished – and when he aimed his torch-microscopes into those eyes, like boiled eggs gone bad, it was now that Felix's innards began quavering, and he fought to stop it reaching his fingertips. At the same time, he was tormented by an overpowering image from *The Odyssey* – the blinding of Cyclops.

Charlie watched anxiously. But Duma himself seemed barely present, humming to himself, or listlessly answering Felix's questions about which letters showed clearest on the distance-panels.

His voice suddenly became more animated as Felix leaned closer than before: 'Lemon Lime.'

'Sorry?' said Felix.

'Your shaving cream, Mr Rosenblatt.'

Both Felix and Charlie froze. Then Felix licked his gums again (was Duma detecting any nervousness? – yes, probably, but he'd be used to nerves in his presence) and said brightly, 'Lemon Lime. Yes, indeed. Gillette Foamy.'

'My brand too,' commented Duma, his tone fading back into apathy, while he scratched his legs.

'Your brand – that a fact?' said Felix, changing lenses in the apparatus.

'Tangy.'

'Isn't it just?' Felix felt himself relaxing again. He was enjoying the way he could make chit-chat and work at the same time, improvising questions about the lenses and jotting down answers on the printed card; it seemed like kosher medical behaviour. 'Now,

Gomgom, which is brighter – the red or green? And I don't want you saying green just because Lemon Lime was the last thing on your – !'

He stopped, amazed, his lips clamped round a pistol.

It had happened so abruptly. In one movement, Duma's scratching hand had collected the weapon from his back pocket and smacked it into Felix's mouth, clipping his teeth and making his skull ring.

Felix's first reaction was, illogically, one of outrage: *Shove a gun in my face by all means but must it be so rough?!*

They stayed like this for a long moment, Felix's eyelids closed and fluttering. When he looked again, he saw Charlie – white-faced, rooted to the spot.

'You can go,' Duma said to Charlie.

'Your Royal Highness . . .' spluttered Charlie.

'Gomgom,' the other said, flatly.

'I'm –'

'Just go,' Duma said again, without raising his voice.

'Felix?' Charlie asked anxiously.

'Ymbddmgghh,' Felix replied.

Duma released the safety-catch on the pistol and quietly repeated his order.

Charlie turned and fled.

In the cave the two men stayed motionless, listening to Charlie's dusty, slaty scramble down the hillside.

Be all right, Felix told himself, *he'll fetch Brak, I'll be all right, be all right, be all right.*

Now Duma withdrew the pistol from Felix's mouth and, in the same muted, almost disinterested voice, asked, 'Who are you?'

'I'm Mr Rosenblatt the opthwome–thw–thw–'

'And I'm Gomgom the hermit.'

'I *am* Mr Ro–'

'No.'

'Why not?' asked Felix, with a small, foolish laugh, his saliva activating the taste of metal in his mouth.

'A scent of . . .' Duma searched for the word. 'Something we share.'

Felix frowned and proceeded carefully. 'Gillette Lemon Lime Foamy?'

'That too,' replied Duma, without a smile. 'But no, I meant, the scent of . . .' Again he hesitated, then sighed and said, 'Heroic destiny.'

Felix's mouth fell open. He tried to disguise his surprise by checking his front teeth for chips.

Now Duma smiled. 'You're flattered. Don't be. My sense of humour. People – they don't always appreciate it. No, forgive me – it *was* the Gillette Foamy. Or, to be more precise, and I value precision, the lemon-lime smell of Gillette Foamy provided an explanation for something that was troubling me – namely some very white patches on your head. I did not believe these to be a form of psoriasis.'

Felix cursed himself. He and Charlie had, of course, noticed the disparity between his tanned face and his newly shaved pate and chin, and they had evened out his skin tone with Panstick. But the climb up the hill, the pouring sweat . . .

'Who are you?' Duma asked politely. 'Heh? What are you? Have you come to kill me?'

As he said this, Duma laid down the pistol – its safety-catch still open – on a rock between them, almost inviting Felix to reach for it.

Felix watched, uncertain, sensing danger. 'I'm a theatre director.'

'Aha. Of course. An artist.' Felix flinched. Last night he had remarked that the word artist was difficult to say or own, carrying, as it did, delusions of grandeur. This was not so when Duma used it. He made it sound like a paltry, miserable thing. But now the dictator's tone brightened: 'Artists, they always want to meet me. Artists, they are so well behaved, so easy to impress. I am not required to, y'know . . .' He rose and began a silent pantomime of command and beckoning gestures, but in an odd, half-hearted way, as though performed by a poor mimic. Then he went into *the* pose, head back, knees slightly bent, arms reaching for the earth, and Felix thought, *He's going to do it, he's going to roar, 'I am Africa!'* – but again his energy drooped, and he uncoiled from the position like a dissatisfied dancer. He sat. 'With artists – I don't have to do this. I have only to be myself, and artists – they can't take their eyes off me.' He stared at Felix, then laughed loudly. 'So, that is why you looked so flattered – "heroic destiny" – forgive me, very amusing!' His mirth abruptly changed to an expression of wonder. Reaching into a small rock pool, he cupped some water in his hand, and dribbled it over his bald head. 'My imagination!' he whispered, making Felix go cold.

Duma looked at him cheerfully. 'Ask me anything. Go on. Anything. I'll answer.'

The first thing that came to Felix's mind was, 'D'you mind if I smoke?'

'Please do. I'd like one also.'

Felix lit the dictator's cigarette, while battling to absorb the reality of the situation. As the match illuminated Duma's big boiled-egg gaze, Felix was again reminded of wild animals in Charlie's menagerie: you see light in their eyes, but it's not familiar.

Duma inhaled deeply and happily on the cigarette, then rose and began searching through a cardboard box of supplies. 'Will you take tea?'

'I won't, thanks,' Felix said quickly.

Duma looked offended. Felix glanced at the pistol on the rock – presently closer to him than Duma. Before he could reach any decisions, Duma strolled back and said, 'My people, the Igisha, we have this saying, "The eel is best eaten hot."' As Felix struggled to decode the message – *did he mean the gun, did he mean Felix had missed his chance?* – Duma smiled and sat again. 'Where's your theatre, Mr Director?'

'Here. In town. The Alex.' Remembering, he said quickly, 'The, the, the State Theatre.'

'Oh. You are local. You don't sound local.'

'Neither do you.'

Annoyance flashed across the dictator's face, and Felix bit his lip. Probably not the best thing to have said to a man with the catchphrase, 'I am Africa.'

After a moment, Duma shrugged and said, 'I studied in the British Isles. Sandhurst.'

'So did I. RADA.'

'There we are, then. So. Tell me about your theatre.'

Felix's eyes narrowed. Did Duma really not know? When *Newsweek* magazine did an article on the emperor's regime, the theatre was mentioned. Briefly. But it was a mention nevertheless! However, as the same journalist noted, 'Only 60 people are important at any given time in Duma's state; 20 of them are ministers, 20 are ambassadors, and 20 exiles. Then, every few months, the music stops and the emperor forces everyone to change chairs.' And Duma was famously disinterested in the arts, famously contemptuous. 'Art is a poor substitute for Life,' was one of his maxims.

'Tell me about . . .' Duma started to say, before an expression of surprise lit up his eyes. As though suddenly discovering it, he lifted the pistol from the rock. He turned the muzzle now towards himself, now towards his visitor.

Felix flinched. Was the safety-catch still off? Was the gun loaded? Should he say something? How would one phrase it? 'Ehrm,' he said. 'The theatre? Well, what to tell you? Things have gone a bit downhill since you left.'

Duma glanced at him – warmly, gratefully – then put the pistol to a point exactly between his own brows, and used it to rub the skin there. 'Terrible thing,' he whispered. 'To be without one's glasses.' Suddenly leaning forward, he asked, 'Have you come to kill me?'

'Of course not. I'm a theatre director. I'm –'

'Not important enough.'

Felix smarted.

I was important enough for your police to arrest me once – for high treason! – important enough for them to start the process of eliminating me.

'Who will it be?' mused Duma, 'Kennedy was killed by a book-depository worker, Mahatma Gandhi by a Hindu fanatic, Indira Gandhi by a bodyguard, Rajiv Gandhi by a woman with flowers, Verwoerd by a parliamentary messenger, Sadat by soldiers, Rabin by a law student.' He paused. 'So why not an optometrist?' The word was pronounced perfectly, with a little sneer.

'But I'm not an opthwo– I'm a theatre director.'

'And Lincoln by an actor, so, indeed, why not?'

'Look, I haven't come here to –'

'What then, heh?'

'Just to see. It's what you said about . . . "artists". I wanted to see you.'

'Mm. Well,' said Duma, thinking about this. Then he pointed the pistol at Felix. 'You've seen. Now go.'

Felix leaped to his feet and started to run. Until this moment, he hadn't realised how frightened he was.

As he reached the mouth of the cave, Duma's great voice reached out like an arm: 'What's on?'

'Sorry?'

'At the State Theatre. Tonight. What's on?'

The banality of the question flummoxed Felix. Was the devil making small-talk? After a long silence, he replied, 'Nothing.'

'I beg your pardon?'

Felix swallowed hard, then said it again: 'Nothing's on.'

'Nothing's on,' echoed Duma slowly. It was as if he sensed the other's shame

'No,' Felix said, feeling an inexplicable, mounting anger. 'But come along in a few weeks' time and you can see . . .'

(How to put it? *Our Golden Hits*?)

'Yes?' said Duma.

'Yourself,' Felix replied boldly. 'The highlight of our next piece . . .'

He started to explain about the compilation show, but got no further than the Cyclops scene. Duma's narcissism fixed itself on this. Mr Mmalo played the part like *him*, did Felix say? How accurate was he? What did he wear? The gestures – were they as powerful? The voice – was it as deep, as rich? 'And the words?' he asked with fierce interest. 'This performer, what does he actually say?'

'I haven't written it yet,' answered Felix. 'But it'll be terrifying. You in exile. Finally saying it all. I can't wait to start it.'

Duma frowned deeply, then said, 'No. Let *me* do it.'

Felix was so surprised, he walked back into the cave.

'Let me do it,' Duma said again. 'I'll do it better. I've had more practice.'

'I couldn't allow that.'

'Why not?'

'One of your speeches on my stage. Unthinkable.'

'Why? You're planning to parody them, why not the real thing?'

'Because the parody will be funny.'

'I thought you said terrifying.'

'Terrifying too, but funny.'

'Whereas the real thing?'

'Would be obscene!'

'Doesn't sound like a very good parody you're planning.'

Felix laughed, feeling his power over the great man. Duma showed no anger. He had a defeated, sad look.

'Mr Director,' he said, 'please let me–'

'Listen, *Gomgom*,' cried Felix, intoxicated with a rush of joyful strength. 'There is no way that I will allow Mr Mmalo to mouth your words on my –'

'Oh, I was not intending *him* to do them.'

Felix froze, his mouth hanging open. After a moment, he closed it and said, 'You mean – ?'

'Yes.'

'You'd be torn to pieces. You'd be lynched.'

Duma smiled grimly. 'Who would know? You say this performer, he wears a bloated costume, a helmet with its visor shaped like one eye. You say he sounds like me, moves like me . . .'

'Yes, but . . .'

'. . . so no one would know. It is not unlike the situation with regard to this cave. No one expects me to be here. No one would believe I could be here. So thus I'm able to be here.'

Felix swallowed hard, trying to clear his ears, feeling he was in a fast-descending plane, a crashing plane.

It's happening . . . we joked about meeting the devil . . . but who else would tease like this? It's happening.

Duma stood, and spread his long arms towards the earth.

He's going to do it! thought Felix, tingling with horrible excitement. *He's going to do it this time!*

But, speaking in his quietest voice, Duma said, 'Mr Director, I don't know how to put this . . . you probably know that I have little respect for artists. Art is a poor substitute for Life . . . but I am told and am prepared to accept that you artists do become possessed by the same thing that has driven me, a feeling of specialness. I joked about heroic destiny earlier – you must excuse my sense of humour, heh? – but whatever we want to call it, let me appeal to that bright, glorious, sweet thing in you.' He paused, letting his words have their impact, then, raising his little finger with curious daintiness, continued: 'Point number one. I need to make a final statement. I have been sitting here going insane with the need. Now you've shown me a way. And – this is point number two – I am prepared to make my statement dressed as a clown and with the assembly laughing because you've advertised it as a parody and so they'll *think* it's a parody. But let me make my statement. And let me make it in my own voice. Will you?'

Felix's head was swimming. He tried to formulate Duma's request in a way that made sense to himself, or at least his underself.

To see you on stage, you, I'd part with a limb . . . but my soul – will I give that?

He tried to speak, but his lips were sticking to his gums again. 'A drink, please,' he whispered.

'Of course.' Duma rummaged in his cardboard box and brought out a litre bottle of Chivas Regal.

Felix shut his eyes.

'No ice, I'm afraid,' Duma joked. He produced two tin mugs. 'Will you have it neat or with Perrier?' Turning back, the emperor found the cave empty, and, in its mouth, a small cloud of dust.

thirteen

'You cannot be serious!' exclaimed Mr Mmalo, and then, remembering his manners, blinked several times and rephrased his statement: 'Pardon me, Felix, but you're joking, I presume. Yes – a joke?'

Instead of replying, Felix popped another chocolate-covered espresso bean between his lips, and prepared for the astounding rush from this, his latest treat. The crush of his teeth released a tiny explosion. A ball of energy – foaming chocolate goo and raw coffee grit – erupted in his mouth. As he swallowed, a second phantom bomb went off, the flavours more intense but fading fast. His tongue darted round his teeth, finding fragments. These were unbearably yummy. Surrendering, he reached for another of the little fat black bullets. They were an American invention apparently; Charlie had asked one of his circle to bring them back from a business trip to Denver, where they were known as buzz balls.

'Felix?' said Mr Mmalo.

'Mr Mmalo?' said Felix, thinking how odd it was that Mr Mmalo was called Mr Mmalo by everyone, even after years of acquaintance.

'You say the Cyclops scene won't be in the show?'

'Correct,' Felix answered in a brisk impatient tone – an echo of his old self – and moved on to the next item on his list.

Among the multitude sitting or sprawled around the stage, only one or two, like Kaz, noted the incident in all its detail: Felix's

surprising announcement, Mr Mmalo's uncharacteristically bold
challenge, Felix's brusque rebuttal. The majority were new to the
ways of this or any other theatre. Some five hundred in number,
they were an unruly throng of townspeople and *mki-mbizis*
recruited in the market-place to be the Chorus in the Creation scene.
As far as they were concerned, Felix's opening address on this, the
first day of rehearsals, was a long and tedious exposition of things
they didn't know or care about. But more mystifying than the director's chatter were his sudden silences, when his funny nude head
with its three-day growth on skull and chin, would lose its ferocious bunched scowl and, like a fist uncoiling, seem to be grasping
for something out of reach. And then there were the occasions –
twice in the last half-hour – when he slowly stopped speaking, turning bright red, as though embarrassed by the sound of his own
voice. Or other moments when he'd interrupt his speech to gobble
through a tub of ice-cream or light his umpteenth cigarette or
munch at small black pellets. He was clearly a very strange fellow,
confirming the Chorus's worst assumptions about the kind of
people who worked in places like these. Anyway, he was the boss,
sungura, the smart one, he was offering them a weekly wage –
minuscule but better than poverty – so they showed some respect
while he spoke, keeping their comments and yawns to a minimum,
while waiting for the first coffee break when, it was rumoured,
homebrew beer and palm wine would be available.

Meanwhile Mr Mmalo sat with a prim, downcast expression.
After the exchange with Felix, he had taken off his reading spectacles, popped them into his top pocket, and crossed his arms.
Another small act of defiance, of rebellion, it signalled that, con-
trary to his usual custom, he would not be taking copious notes
during Felix's speech. No, he needed a word with his director, and
although now was not the time and place, he was awaiting the very
first opportunity.

This came during the dance rehearsal later in the morning. The
Chorus, now much more exuberant than before – following refreshments in the coffee break – were being taught the first big *stomp* of
the Creation by Kaz, who doubled as company choreographer.
Some had picked up gourds, rattles and drums from the pile of

instruments at the back of the stage, and were playing them with gusto. Kaz had explained about the nudity required for the sequence when it came to performance, and although she had spoken in both English and KiSwahili, quite a few had misunderstood and thrown off their T-shirts and shorts straight away.

As God/Narrator in this sequence, Mr Mmalo wasn't required to dance, so he leaned on the proscenium arch, occasionally pinching two fingers into a bamboo snuff container, his attention fixed on his director.

Felix was standing in the auditorium, elbows on the front of the stage, head bowed over a full ashtray. He looked like a drunk at a bar. His stance was in fact designed to hold Kaz at bay. Since the revelation at the circus – that her son had been killed by a man called Popo-boy who was unlikely to be punished, or even identified – she had daubed her forehead with the traditional mark of mourning, white clay and ash, and gone on a permanent bender, inhabiting a state of loose-eyed, damp-skinned, nervy-fingered mania. This was fed into her work, mostly successfully, and when it wasn't, you challenged her at your peril. Although he should have known better – should have recalled the fate of those who once crossed his path – Felix made the mistake early in today's rehearsal. Questioning a particular dance-step, he was met not with outrage or stubbornness, but an acquiescent bow and a clearly voiced, 'Bwana.' With this one word she silenced him, humiliated him in front of the company, withdrew her complicity from the choreography and from the show itself. No, it was even worse. That word, that one little word made his whole career seem worthless: the fanciful pastime of one of those rich, spoilt non-Afs, those expat chappies with nothing better to do. Felix was furious, but dared not fight back. Except in his mind. Here he played out the scene, magnificently, again and again: pointing at the mottled paste on her forehead, and demanding, 'And what, pray, are you trying to prove? Perhaps I should roll up my trouser leg and walk round flashing my scar, proclaiming, "Look, look, I've been injured too!"' *Injured.* It was a favourite word. He'd used it several times in these rehearsals already, as he always did, urging the actors to find and work from that part of themselves, the *injured* part. It guaranteed truth. It's what made

supposed to be funny?

kaz pulling race

Kaz such a remarkable performer. Trouble was, she seemed too injured at the moment.

Felix balanced his cigarette on the rim of the ashtray and went for a stroll up the centre aisle, popping buzz balls into his mouth. Then, forgetting about the one in the ashtray, he lit another cigarette.

Hanging above stage and auditorium were the customary five light-bulbs. These suddenly spluttered like candles and went out. The Chorus sighed and mumbled: power cuts were familiar inconveniences these days.

'Oh, drat!' shouted Felix, then joked grimly, '"At least he made the trains run on time!"'

Kaz's mocking voice shot out of the darkness: '*Oyoyoyo*, if we all pray hard enough, ehh?, maybe he'll come back to us, ehh?'

'What d'you mean?' snapped Felix. 'Come back? What are you talking about?'

The bulbs flickered again and light returned. Felix went still. Everyone was staring at him. He closed his mouth. As work resumed onstage, he turned on his heel and hurried out of the auditorium, trying to look nonchalant, just after a breath of fresh air.

This was the moment Mr Mmalo was waiting for.

He caught up with Felix in the airlock between the two sets of double doors. Here there was a single blue bulb, just illuminating the bones of their heads. In this light, Mr Mmalo looked exactly like Emperor Duma to Felix, but for that matter, he thought, I probably do too.

'Felix,' said Mr Mmalo, 'I ask forgiveness for troubling you, but the Cyclops scene . . .'

Felix sighed. He was in no mood for this man, this church mouse with thespian airs. 'Yes?'

'How can you leave it out?'

Felix gave a hard laugh. 'Very easily.'

'But I mean . . .'

'Hasn't it got us into enough trouble?'

'Pardon?'

'When we did it before.'

Mr Mmalo hesitated. 'You mean all those years ago?'

'It might seem like that to you, chummy, but it's very fresh in my memory. But, then, it wasn't you who was dragged to the police station that night, was it?'

'Felix . . .'

'That's right – *Felix* – he was given the treatment. Did he ever get thanks?'

Mr Mmalo thought fast. He couldn't smell alcohol, but Felix was presumably drunk – he was certainly making no sense – and caution was advisable. 'But, but, pardon me, with all humility, but it was *your* concept, wasn't it? I mean, dear me, wasn't it? To play Cyclops like Emperor Duma.'

'To *hint* at a resemblance, yes, not to fucking go into all that fucking "I am Africa!" stuff!'

Mr Mmalo braced himself. The swearing, the swearing was starting. He gave a little laugh. 'But . . . you're the boss, dear boy, and you're always asking us to extemporise.'

Felix sensed the man's fear – of the old Felix – and now he felt it too, that presence, slouching and scowling, brilliant and cruel, here it was, here it came, erupting out of him, here came *Felixxxxxxx*: 'Extemporise? *Dear boy?* I'll extemporise on your fucking bollocks, you cu–!'

No, no, he mustn't, he mustn't say the word, the C-word, or the F-word, or even the B-word, he mustn't speak like that any more, think like that, be like that, mustn't, he mustn't.

Mr Mmalo watched, bewildered, as his employer staggered round the airlock with both hands clamped over his mouth, little mouse-like shrieks escaping from time to time. 'Felix, Felix,' Mr Mmalo said in a small, appalled voice, 'may the Saviour have mercy on you. This incident we're discussing, this was years ago!'

'Not to me!' roared Felix, and strode out of the airlock.

He charged across the foyer, and out into the street. Muttering to himself, he used his cigarette to light another. His hands were shaking.

If only he hadn't mentioned that Monday morning in the police cell! Images were forming, brushing across his nerve-ends. He shook his head. The images vanished, only to be replaced by others, other frights, the monstrous incidents of his life. Why, *why* was his brain always so eager to screen its stock of horror movies? Why was it forever waiting to ambush him? – to pop up and go boo! Why was he host to this never-ending tug-of-war between devils and angels? Why, *why*? Growling violently, he was about to kick an object in the gutter, when he looked again. A can of soup. Unopened. Strange – with so many starving people around. Campbell's soup, oxtail flavour.

fourteen

'Maa-may-mee-maw-moooooo.'

Walking down the oak-lined avenue, Felix practises not only his vocal exercises, but his *look*. For much of last year he'd been trying disdain, with brows arched high and eyes half lidded, peering down his nose, but a month or so ago he had started experimenting with something angrier, bunching his features. He likes the way it holds off people, at school, at family dos. It communicates that he has things on his mind, that he's serious, important, not to be mistaken for just another fourteen-year-old obsessed with sport, girls and other sillinesses. Like Charlie, for example, who has become a profound disappointment recently. It is doubtful whether the friendship will last.

The scowl isn't easy. It tires your face muscles. They yearn to spring open. But persist, and they yield little lines on the forehead and from the nostrils to the corners of the mouth, making you look older. When Felix rehearses it in front of the mirror, often for an hour or more, he is pleased with how the black thickness of his eyebrows complements the fascinating grey sheen on his chin – he is the first among his classmates to be shaving – how these two shadows, one descending, the other rising, close over his face like a hatch.

'Maa-may-mee-maw-mooooo.'

He turns off the avenue into Miss Rosewood's driveway, walking with the round-shouldered slouch that also takes some practice and determination – it is meeting a lot of opposition from his elders, at home and school. But these details are crucial: your look, your walk, your voice and, perhaps most of all, the thing that sums up the exercise, your written signature. Felix is not happy with that yet. If only he could draw better, he might achieve the fantastic leaping spider he has in mind. He wants people to take one look and declare, 'The boy's a genius!'

This is already Miss Rosewood's opinion. He has heard her say it to his parents – the auditor and his secretary wife – but as usual, when it comes to artistic matters, they didn't seem especially interested; and he's heard her say it to the other schoolteachers, who just smiled. Felix didn't take this personally. It wasn't him they were laughing at. People tend to disregard and mock Miss Rosewood. Felix cannot comprehend why. Although small in stature – straight-backed, the fulsome cherry-blonde wig gaining a few more precious inches – she is clearly a giant in thought and gesture. She talks so dramatically, describing even minor mishaps as an earthquake!, the atom bomb!, Hurricane Mary! Perhaps the problem is that her colleagues have a more timid approach to language.

'My little Feelie the genius,' is what she calls him and he is very comfortable with this label, this assessment of his talent. Now he simply has to construct a personality to match.

'Maa-may-mee-maw-moooooo,' he incants, heading for his first elocution lesson of the new year, slouching across Miss Rosewood's lawn. It needs cutting; the weather has been odd for January, more like before the Long Rains, with sweltering heat and quick, violent downpours, causing foliage to burgeon. No sign of old Milton, the garden boy, who always tips his hat nicely to young bwana Felix, or Betty the cook-maid, who is sulkier, with her slow, swaying walk, as though permanently dazed by sunstroke. Apparently they're not back from their holidays yet; Miss Rosewood explained that this year she was giving them ten days off, in place of a Christmas box, so that they could travel back to their villages and be with their families. She would 'fend for herself', she said bravely, as though talking about a spell in the jungle.

Evidence of her self-sufficiency is on display outside the back door. She has deposited rubbish in cardboard boxes on the red-brick patio – empty cans of Campbell's soup and Del Monte fruit pieces, a bottle of Gordon's gin, two boxes of chocolates – and stacked dirty crockery on the formica picnic table. Rather than let everything stink up the kitchen waiting for the staff to return, she took it outdoors. Birds and insects have done their own cleaning.

The pile of plates and cups is less than Felix would've expected; only three or four deep. Perhaps she did the washing-up for the first few days, then tired of it.

Now at the French windows, which overlook the rear lawn, Felix knocks, and waits for the familiar, 'Hil-lew-wooooo!' sung like an alpine call. When it fails to come, he turns the handle. Nobody locks their doors. Security is one of the luxuries which the new leader, Field Marshal Duma, has promised the non-Af community: 'Unlike some of our neighbouring countries, here you can live in a place where nobody steals. Nobody will *need* to steal, this is point number one, and those who steal merely for devilment – this is point number two – they will sorely regret it. Here you may live in one of the safest and most prosperous places in Africa.'

She's sitting just inside the French windows, the armchair positioned as though for an extemporisation lesson, when, framed by the doorway, she surveys his expressive adventures, each a little epic story, on the back lawn.

A shaft of morning sunshine falls on her lap, swimming with motes of dust.

She is asleep . . . French's Acting Edition playscripts and Hollywood magazines are scattered around . . . she has all the latest ones posted from London and America . . . probably reads the plays aloud, playing all the parts . . . another bottle of Gordon's is on the side-table, its flip-top hanging open, its green glassiness filled with nothing but air. Could she be drunk? Felix has never seen anyone drunk at ten o'clock in the morning, certainly not a white person.

His mind is working fast, trying to deny the evidence in his nostrils.

The smell is wet, active, and clustered round her head, which is invisible, slumped, the cherry-blonde wig at a funny angle, as though unsupported from beneath.

He doesn't look for very long. A fraction of a second. What he thought were motes of sunlit dust are, in fact, insects, tiny insects, thousands of them, millions. The focus of their activity is just below the wig. There is a quivering, running, dripping presence here; Felix sees it in one quick glance, and refuses to take another.

He swallows hard. His carefully practised scowl has vanished. It would be impossible to clench his features at the moment. They are smooth with fear.

His downcast gaze alights on a large buff envelope near her feet. It has British stamps and the familiar sticker of Union Castle Line sea-post. Presumably it contained the French's Acting Editions, sent by a London bookseller. But it is addressed to a Miss S. Rosenblatt. Can that be Miss Rosewood's real name? How queer. She has often said to Felix: 'You are part of the teensy-weensy Jewish group of the tiny expat community of this small African state – I've heard of minority groups, my darling, but this is too much! – try not to let us detect it in your parlance.' *You*, she says, not *we*. How queer.

He goes to the telephone and dials the number for emergencies. His parents have taught him this. They're keen on numbers; they're helpful with maths homework.

'Hillew,' he says, into the mouthpiece, pronouncing the word like Miss Rosewood does. 'I'm afraid there's been an accident of some sort here. I do wonder if you could send some assistance round, please.'

Although the operator is impressed by the composure of his call, he hears only the tinny shiver of his voice, and thinks how disappointed Miss Rosewood would be: it's not supported by much breath.

The police who arrive are a strange crowd. Black not white, as they would have been just a year or so ago. Nor are they as polite, nor as upright in stance and speech. Nevertheless, they were British-trained and they speak English, even some slang. Felix doesn't like all of what he overhears; nothing explicitly rude, but it's the way they make the incident sound so commonplace.

Yet this is Miss Rosewood, the one adult who believed in him passionately – '*Pashhhionately, my Feelie!*' – as she would put it, her fists shaking in the air, the bones of her knuckles gleaming like all the rings and bangles surrounding them – she was the one person who understood about his destiny.

'You can clear up the soup,' the sergeant says to one of his men.

Felix thinks he means the food on her tray, but no, he means *her*; it's police-talk for the state she's in. Seven days, they reckon, seven days since the stroke, seven days of sitting here, in this weather, and with that tear in the insect screen.

'Clear up the soup.'

When this is done, and everyone has gone, Felix remains alone, standing outside the house. British policemen would've taken him home, but this lot have a less sentimental approach to their work; it's routine what's happened; children see such sights all the time. Felix walks to the edge of the back lawn, where monstrous green-grey vegetation spills from the slopes of the Kwatokuu, meets a small rusting fence, and somehow stops in its tracks. Old Milton, the garden boy, might think this is his work, but Felix knows it is, *was*, Miss Rosewood. She would only have to say, 'Proceed no further, thank you very much!', and even a jungle would obey.

The muscles of Felix's face are neither scowling with disdain nor blank with shock. They're uncontrollable. They're quaking, jumping, and his panting is like a mad dog's. His diaphragm, about which she has talked so much, and which has remained something of a mystery, it's perfectly apparent at the moment, it's pummelling the bottom of his belly, it's a frantic paddle there, it's going to make him sick. He's crying – dry, wild crying – his parents don't like him crying, 'getting het up' as they put it – he must stop – he will in a moment. But something worse than tears threatens to come. A new emotion is being born, a kind of horror, laced with both dread and eagerness. It will mar his young life – and his schooling for almost a year – and introduce him to a new adult word, one which carries a curious status, there to be flaunted or hidden: 'breakdown'.

For the moment he holds on to the fence at the bottom of Miss Rosewood's garden, trying to control himself, sending little tremors along the wire this way and that, a tiny rattle, a blurred Morse code signalling help, help. The surrounding landscape remains impervious, ticking away to its own primitive pulse, dark with foliage, heavy with swelter. Miss Rosewood is right about this country.

Something's wrong here. It teems with multitudes, yet every horizon looks empty. He must leave, as she wants him to. But . . . overseas? . . . which way is it?

'I have such grand plans for you, my precious, such plans!'

Who will make them happen now?

Trapped
in Africa

fifteen

Insect screens, hot with sunshine . . . dingy light-sheets with fluttering pieces of shadow . . . perhaps the wings of giant moths . . .

Blowing his nose, Felix turned back to Emile. 'The odd thing is . . . to her, everything was a tidal wave, the atom bomb, Hurricane Mary – yet when disaster *actually* struck she never knew a thing about it. It was just the rest of us who . . .'

'Charlie saw this?' Emile asked quietly.

'No, no, Charlie had stopped coming to elocution by then.' Felix thought for a moment, then added in a hurt and sniping tone, 'I'm surprised you don't remember this story – I must've mentioned it before!' He hesitated again. On either side of Emile's wide schnozzle, that tortoise beak, which made the rest of his face seem so ancient and weary – on either side of this hard-nosed look, his small eyes had suddenly moistened. The emotion vanished as quickly as it had come, but Felix was surprised. It was unusual for Emile even to mention Charlie's name. 'Anyway,' Felix continued, 'Miss Rosewood never knew anything about it, what happened to her, so I still don't understand why she always had such a pronounced sense of horror. As . . . as I do.'

He wondered how much he could tell Emile. It was imperative to talk to someone about Duma. Charlie, shocked by his own brief encounter with the great dictator, had made the topic a no-go area. Kaz was . . . well, Kaz. Who else was there?

It didn't look promising. Emile was in a very distracted mood today, fanning himself with the sketch pad. Suddenly lowering it, he peered at the doodle Felix had done earlier. 'So, my dear, tell me what you see?'

Felix sighed. They'd been through this already. 'Well, it's the same image as last week, isn't it? A frightened face, arms wrapped round a frightened face. That's the eye, there's the nose, which you probably think is a vagina, and there's . . .'

'I had a client who always referred to the vagina as the wound. I suggested he stop. In this game, you can't *tell* people things, you can only *suggest*. No directives, no directives. *Des clous!* Anyhow, he just kept calling it the wound, the wound. So . . .'

Trying to signal that he didn't have patience for these digressions today, Felix scoffed a handful of buzz balls, and looked away. The fluttering shadows on the verandah's insect screens . . . they weren't giant moths . . . they were the silhouettes of hands. Perhaps the convent grounds were open to *mkı-mbızıs* now? The familiar buzzing, humming silence of the garden was lost to a new noise – human whispers and coughs.

'So, my dear, what you see?' Emile asked Felix, as if for the first time, pointing at today's doodle.

'A frightened face, wrapped in its own arms,' Felix replied tensely. 'This big, blind-looking eye makes me feel –'

Emile broke in urgently. 'This fellow who said wound for vagina, his turn-on was blind women. Could only get sexually aroused if they were blind. Jackie Rabinowitz. You remember him?'

Felix was amazed. Nice Mr Rabinowitz who used to run the gents' outfitters! Anyway, should Emile be naming names?

'He used to sojourn to outlying villages where no one knew him, and seek out women who were blind, y'know, from pestilence or famine, and he'd give them a coin or two to copulate with him. Was very guilty about it but, as I pointed out, the act was at least mutually beneficial to both sides. So, there we are. That was Jackie Rabinowitz. What a character, what a . . . No, no, *la barbe!* Rabinowitz was the transvestite. No, it was Shapiro, Jackie Shapiro.'

Nice Mr Shapiro – the dentist?!

'Where is he now, I wonder?' said Emile.

'The UK, I think.'

'Not so many blind people there,' mused Emile. 'He said his greatest-ever orgasm was with one villager who just had hollows for eyes – jeepers, creepers, did you see those peepers! – and she allowed him to –'

'Emile!'

'*Ouais?*'

'I don't really want to hear about Mr Shapiro's sex life.'

'It shocks you, my dear?'

'No, well, yes.' He stopped himself from saying, '*You* – you shock me, your indiscretion.' If Emile was spilling the beans about all his other patients, what was he saying about this one?!

'Last week,' Felix said timidly. 'Last week you said there was something I wanted to do . . . in the bedroom department . . . but was afraid to.'

Emile lit a cigarette. 'Yes.'

'That's preposterous.'

'Is it?'

'You're saying that *you* know about an urge in me, which I don't know about?'

'No, no, of course you know, you're simply suppressing the infor-mation. My dear, we can sometimes create our own police states – within ourselves – with the most violent censorship, torture cham-bers, all manner of absurd commandments – we sometimes do this until the thing called Truth is rendered quite invisible . . .' He faded out, eyes downcast, recalling his own passionate faith in Duma, that pioneer of African Marxism . . .

'So what is it?' Felix demanded, with the aggression of one who didn't really want an answer. 'What is this urge you think I'm sup-pressing?'

Emile proceeded gently. 'There's a little girl you often talk about. You know who I mean?'

Felix's mouth fell open.

'The daughter of some friends,' Emile prompted.

Felix found his voice. 'Yes, yes, I know who you . . . but this is . . . !'

Emile gave a sympathetic smile. 'You talk about her, my dear, in such a way. It's very tender, very touching. I'm not suggesting that –'

'You don't know what you're suggesting!' snapped Felix, turning icy cold. He rose. 'Forgive me for pointing this out, but you're not well.'

Emile laughed grimly. 'Not *well*? Who's well?'

'Yes, but, but – you're the doctor!'

It was Emile's turn to fix the other with a shocked look. Then he said, 'Compassion, my dear. If only you would develop some compassion for yourself, you would develop it for others.'

Develop. Emile's pronunciation of the word ricocheted round Felix's busy brain: *devil-up, devil-up, devil-up*. And earlier, when Emile used the word character, it came out as *corrector*. Were these just accidents, just the distortions of Emile's Belgian accent, or were they a form of Freudian slip, of code? Felix had always regarded Emile as the Great Corrector of his character, but maybe the old man was a less benign force. More Devil than Corrector . . . ?

A fly landed on Emile's face, near his eye, but he didn't seem aware of it, didn't brush it away. 'So, my dear,' he sighed, lifting Felix's sketch, and turning it in a clockwise direction, 'what have we got here today?'

Felix's V W Beetle stood at the far corner of the convent forecourt. As he pushed his way through the begging hands of *mki-mbizis* – yes, they weren't just receiving soup, they were resident here now – he was surprised to see a figure in the rear seat. A female figure. He could only see her back, but from the look of her old-fashioned hairdo she couldn't possibly be one of the refugees. No, more likely a resident of the hospital. Another old party, dazed with senility, had plonked herself in his car!

He quickened his step – and almost tripped on a shiny object in the dust. 'Tsk!' he said, before noticing that it was a Campbell's soup can. Green pea flavour. Unopened. Again? – with so many hungry people nearby? Felix frowned and rushed forward, his car key extended like a tiny lance.

Before slotting it into the door, he froze.

Hadn't he locked the car when he arrived here? And switched on the new alarm Charlie gave him? And double-checked it at least twice?

Yes, yes, yes, he had.

He was standing alongside the driver's door. He could see the figure's hands folded on her lap – *oh, those knuckles, those rings and bangles!* – and up as far as her bust. By just bending a fraction, he would be able to see her face, the wig. But he didn't want to.

He unlocked the car, slipped into the driver's seat, reached under the dashboard, and flicked off the alarm.

Avoiding the rear-view mirror, he kept his gaze low, fixed on the cubby hole, thinking of the can of tear gas there: also installed since the pack of child-muggers attacked his car a week or so ago.

'Felix,' a voice said, full of warmth.

'Is it *you*?' he asked, still avoiding the mirror.

'But of course. Who else?'

'Ehrm,' said Felix.

'And how have you been keeping?'

'Jolly well, thank you very much,' he answered. His voice sounded thin and unformed as a fourteen-year-old's. 'And yourself?'

'Oh, not marvellous, my darling, but it's not an earthquake. All things considered I'm a miracle, actually.'

The pronunciation of that last word. *Ek-tu-welly.* No one could fake that. Felix shook his head in wonder.

'And the career?' she asked.

'Oh tickety-boo . . . ish.'

'Didn't make it as an actor, then,' she asked, or rather told him.

'No, no, went into directing.'

'But *here*,' she said, as though making a correction. 'Not overseas.'

'No,' he said defiantly. '*Here.*'

'Hmn.'

Oh, that purr of disapproval, that sigh of criticism.

'I had such plans for you, Feelie,' she said.

'I run a theatre!' he protested. 'It got a mention in *Newsweek* once! I'm . . .'

'Such plans, such grand plans,' she repeated, voice laced with grief.

'Yes, well.'

'And now this marvellous opportunity is presenting itself, and yet you're turning it down.'

'What d'you mean?' he demanded.

'That marvellous character is offering to appear at your theatre, offering to restore your fortunes, and you're turning him down!'

'Which marv– You mean Emperor Duma?!'

'He's our leader, my precious, and leaders don't get where they are without exceptional qualities. He's done tremendous work for the common man in this country. And such a fine speaking voice too.'

'You're out of date!' Felix screeched, through gritted teeth. 'Three or four decades out of date! Most recently he was *wiping out* the common man in this country!'

Felix heard how hoarse he sounded, and braced himself. She would now lecture him on breath control, open throats, and how to rest on the vowels not the consonants. But she said nothing. 'You're suggesting I let Duma appear in my theatre, on my stage?!' Felix cried. 'Can you just picture it?!'

'I can,' she answered calmly. 'And I'll tell you something – it's not Hurricane Mary.'

sixteen

'Charlie, Charlie, what do we believe in, Charlie?'

'*We?*' Charlie observed, with amusement. 'Is this kinda . . . "Greater Power" we're talking here?'

'Well, yes, no, I don't know.'

'The ancient Romans,' said Charlie, 'they were constantly searching for a state of tranquillity. It comes up again and again in the stuff I read. And they find it – tranquillity – in religion, in philosophy, in all sorts of recreational treats, especially the Games . . . all these are their *tranquillisers*. Interesting word, yeah?'

Charlie's eyes radiated his brand of hippie wisdom, both piercing and soft, which Felix usually found captivating, but there was something odd about it today; a kind of sadness, a benign sadness. Felix scrubbed the itching week-old stubble on his chin and skull, and said, 'I mean, if the post is vacant, who is *my* Greater Power? As an artist, I've always believed it was me. The great creator. Me.' Charlie laughed gently. 'Well, yes, I know, ridiculous but true. As a director, in rehearsals, you can answer, "I don't know," or even "I must be wrong", but when it comes to the end product, the show itself, you can be neither puzzled nor mistaken. Everyone's relying on you so you have to be absolutely certain. And that's how I've always pictured God. Full of doubt yet not allowed the luxury. You know the old saying, "Man plans and God laughs"? Maybe that's all He's got left. His jokes.'

'Hang on, just go back a – you've always pictured God as you?'

'Oh! Oh!' huffed Felix. 'Is one to assume that doctors never play God?!'

Charlie shrugged, taking no offence. 'Dunno. But it's not what I believe in – God.'

'So what is?'

'Nature,' he replied, without hesitation. 'Doctors can try to play God, but Nature will only let them go so far. We can keep some-one's heart going, but not their soul. That's Nature's gift. So . . . yeah.' He lapsed into melancholic silence, smiling peacefully.

Felix's head fell back against the soft, dove-grey leather of the couch. They were in a glass room – the tip of a skyscraper that reached into blue cloud, puncturing it, making the afternoon storm seem more violent up here than down on the street. A regular after-noon occurrence at this time of year, the Short Rains, the tempest came and went in gusts of ferocity and calm, offering, in one moment, nothing but a close view of streaming darkness and, in the next, a distant patchwork of separate storms and blue skies – and rainbows, two, three at a time. All week Felix had been relishing the spectacle; often conjuring up the image of a cave, its mouth wide and dripping, and with a silhouette standing there, half man, half beast, magnificent, naked, trapped. When each rainfall was over, Felix climbed out onto the theatre's roof, cupped his palms in the water that poured down the side gutter, and watched as the fresh sunshine magicked up another rainbow in his hands, a tiny private one.

Such joys seemed out of reach today. He envied Charlie's buoyant doldrums – whatever their source – for his own despair felt like flu, raging through him, making his bones ache. Only one topic was trapped in his head: *Must save the theatre – the Golden Hits show won't do it – must have 'a last go' – but how?* He longed for the light-ness of spirit he'd known dancing on the roof the other morning, or his feelings at the board meeting itself: of powerlessness, of relief, of joy in failure. But he had still been so enfeebled then, barely able to stay awake, emotion spilling out of him, full of compassion for his enemies. Now, with the gradual return of his strength, came also the old demons: ambition and frustration, the two twisting together, lacing themselves into a whip, a scourge, lashing at his own back. Nothing helped – cigarettes, buzz balls, ice-cream – they just excited the sense of aloneness and panic. And as for the anti-depressant tablets from the Long Island clinic, he was thinking of suing!

'I had such dreams, Charlie,' he said, in a small voice. 'Such dreams.'

Charlie was surprised. 'You say that? *You?* But you've done well, you're –'

'Only *here*, not overseas! Oh, I had such plans, such grand . . . !' It was impossible to say more. How his ambition felt like a kind of illness, a kind of insanity. How it sometimes occurred to him that if he couldn't be famous, he'd be notorious. If he couldn't be an artist, he'd be a criminal, a mass-murderer, a tyrant, a Duma. Avoiding Charlie's eye, he said mournfully, 'My life isn't living up to my dreams.'

'Sure, sure, "coulda bin a contender", everyone's favourite movie scene.'

Felix rolled his head round to gaze at the man alongside him. Charlie hadn't sounded like Charlie then. Remembering the golden-haired boy who won all the prizes at school, Felix suddenly wanted to hug his friend, and wished, as he often did, that the bedroom department didn't exist.

Charlie shook his head slowly. '"A contender". It's amazing you feel that too.' He vacillated for a moment, then decided to confide in Felix. 'Y'know, yesterday, I got a delivery of new pharmaceuticals from my buddy in the States, my college buddy, Deany the chemist, and there's this incredible new painkiller, bit like Demerol, bit like Fentanyl, amazingly useful for childbirth and so on. And anyway, last night I was checking it out, just, y'know, twenty milligrams – and it's beautiful gear, beautiful, you sing quite a lot, and your mood keeps moving back 'n' forth, but always to a kinda sorrow. It really showed me my, like, my limitations. But it did it, y'know, in a tolerant, gentle way. I thought back to the day of my graduation from medical school. I remember popping into downtown LA that afternoon, had to get something at the pharmacy, and I looked up at the shelves, and I thought, *Holy fuck, it's a sweetshop! And I can have anything I want now!* I guess I knew there and then it was gonna be tough for me as a doctor.' He sighed. 'I mean, we students, we'd heard about "pad power", y'know, when you write yourself recreational prescriptions, or y'know, when you get sent samples from the pharmaceutical reps – "eating the mail". So OK, I'd heard about all those things, and now I've *done* all those things – but now what? Dead end. So, anyway, I was, like, understanding all this stuff last night, and feeling a bit low, and I still do, but I'm . . . I think I've got the answer.' He sat upright, and drew a notebook from his pocket. 'I've gotta start writing it all down.'

Felix frowned. 'Writing what down?'

'These tests I conduct when Deany sends me stuff.'

Felix's frown deepened. 'What, you mean . . . you'll still keep "eating the mail", but . . .'

'But I'll write down the results. You got it! 'Cause I don't eat the mail straight, I've been mixing and cooking up my own stuff for years . . . Well, tell the truth, I follow recipes that Deany sends over, but I can get off on it for hours, whiling away the long evenings. But now, let's start properly notating the results – "synthesis, dosage, duration"   let's start treating these as bona fide, kosher experiments. As Deany says, it's only a matter of time before the West decriminalises mind-altering potions 'n' powders. In twenty years or so you'll be able to see them on supermarket shelves, like booze, and then people will want the same variety, the same rows 'n' rows of colourful bottles, not just the present stuff, the party stuff. D'you see? I think Deany might be on to something here. I think I've gotta stop just messing around with this stuff, start treating it more like a scientific study. Who better than a doctor? As a kinda guinea pig. Who better than me?'

Felix sat thinking. 'What, sort of . . . mix work and play?'

'Why not?' smiled Charlie, noting his friend's tone. 'Like you. Your job. Work and play, both under the same umbrella. And there's superb opportunity for field work here too, different village societies, different tribes, already using different opiates and hallucinogens for spirit journeys, soul flight, to gain animal essence, natural wisdom, using the stuff not as a way of getting out of your mind, but *into* it. I dunno. Maybe this is all a crazy idea or maybe it's a bit of a brainwave. Maybe this could be . . .' He ducked his head shyly. 'Maybe it's the thing I've always been looking for.'

How many times? thought Felix. How many times have I heard

of these 'brainwaves', these cures for his boredom, these hectic love affairs with this or that, these rushes of energy and determination?

'What d'you reckon?' asked Charlie.

Felix smiled politely. 'When d'you plan to commence?'

'It's commenced.'

'Ah.'

'Before we came here, I tried upping last night's dosage. I'm trying twenty-five milligrams today. Last night it took two hours for the onset to occur. So, it should be round about . . .' He checked his watch, and nodded sagely. '. . . yup, any minute.' He sat waiting, pen poised above the notebook.

Now they heard footsteps hurrying through the outer office towards them. Charlie whispered jauntily, 'It's very gentle gear, but do lemme know if you notice anything out of the ordinary, right?'

'Right,' gulped Felix.

'Felix, Charlie, so, so sorry to keep you,' said a voice behind them, and they twisted round to see Lord Gomes, the theatre's British-Portuguese chairman. Felix attempted to rise, struggling with the leathery massiness of the couch, but failed. 'And thank you, particularly, Felix, for taking time from rehearsals to see me, I'm most flattered.'

'No, no, pshaw!' said Felix. 'It's a music and dance call this afternoon, so . . .'

'Excellent, excellent, and all going well, I trust?'

'Yes, I think there's –'

'Excellent, excellent,' said Lord Gomes, who was not in the habit of letting you finish your sentences. Felix had always put this down to the man's exceptionally hirsute ears. Hair also erupted from his cuffs, and would, you imagined, from his neck, arms and legs, if he were ever to wear anything less than the silk ties, shirts and suits that were his trademark even in the hottest weather.

'A little refreshment, gentlemen?' said Lord Gomes, opening a cupboard behind his desk.

Charlie nodded enthusiastically, while Felix gave a prissy shake of his head. Lord Gomes didn't notice, as he hadn't noticed Felix's abstinence at the board meeting last week.

While the drinks were being poured, Charlie whispered to Felix,

'Is there a really nice breeze in here?'

'No, not at all.'

'Interesting,' said Charlie, jotting a note.

Lord Gomes carried two huge goblets of Portuguese Piriquita towards them. 'I won't, thanks,' said Felix emphatically.

'Good Lord!' exclaimed Lord Gomes. 'What is it – tummy upset?'

'No, I –'

'Can this be the Felix we know and love?' laughed Lord Gomes.

Felix opened his mouth, then faltered. With his grip on the theatre feeling somewhat tenuous, now was probably not the moment to tell its chairman that for all these years he'd been dealing not just with a hard-drinker – good Lord, in Africa who *wasn't*? – but a fully qualified piss-artist.

Charlie came to the rescue. 'Felix isn't, like, drinking any more, Carlos.'

Lord Gomes did an exaggerated reaction of surprise, either from the news itself, or the fact that someone had finished a sentence in his presence.

'On my advice,' continued Charlie, 'I did some, y'know, liver-function tests and –'

'Ah, *medico maluco!*' laughed Lord Gomes. 'Well, all I say is let the doctors look to their own livers!'

'To our livers!' chirruped Charlie. He drank deeply, checked his watch, then added this information to his notes. Felix watched with trepidation.

'Now, gentlemen, down to business,' said Lord Gomes. 'Rehearsals are going well, Felix?'

Felix sighed: he'd answered this question once already. Why did nobody listen to him? 'Yes, they're –'

'Excellent, excellent, but trouble with one of the actors, yes?'

Felix narrowed his eyes. Lord Gomes didn't normally trouble himself with the day-to-day running of the theatre. Who had told him about Mr Mmalo?

'Well,' said Felix slowly, 'he's rather attached, alas, to a piece which I'm not going to include in the –'

'Excellent, but, Felix, I'm also attached to a certain piece which

I hope you *will* include, and that's why I've asked you here today.'

Felix tried to conceal his surprise. He stared at the dark skin around Lord Gomes' eyes – like the villain's make-up in silent movies.

'It's a little request item,' Lord Gomes explained. 'In an evening of this and that, it won't be a problem to slip it in, I presume.'

'Well, the show's not quite as haphaz–'

'Excellent. Let me show you.'

Lord Gomes whispered into an intercom, while Felix glanced at Charlie, wondering where he, as the middle man of this meeting, stood in all of this. But Charlie's face was inscrutable, vaguely trance-like now, and he had started to sing quietly.

The storm was passing. Felix watched it travel out to sea, the forks of lightning jagging to different points on the horizon, as if testing for a breaking point.

Just as thunder erupted, the door to Lord Gomes' outer office opened and a lion ran in.

Fully grown, female, with a dark yellow, almost greenish hide.

Felix's surprise was compounded by the sense that something had gone wrong. The animal was snarling, its ears flat, its body low and lithe. And Lord Gomes – who was, presumably, *expecting* a lion to enter – jumped backwards, clearing the couch. Meanwhile Charlie sat calmly, smiling with wonder, writing in his notebook. Felix was about to lean across and whisper, 'No, Charlie this is an *actual* lion!' when he heard a commanding voice: 'It's OK! Here, Simba, Simba . . .'

And now Felix saw the diminutive youth from the circus – the Great Zit? Zippo? – hurry into the room and, using a herdsman's long, peeled whip-branch, bustle the beast into one corner.

'It's the thunder, thu-thu-thuuundahh!' he explained in his gabbling way. 'They don't mind it in the wild, but indoors it freaks them, *ja-ja*, freaks 'em.'

The little fellow was wearing a second-hand pinstriped suit, with no shirt or tie, just a vest, and his hair hung greasily round his face, shading its corrugated skin. The fringe, the untidiness, the parody of adult dress, the black-metal-pierced eyebrows and lips . . . now he clearly looked his age, eighteen or nineteen. A mulatto, a *mongrel*, hunted and maimed by Duma's regime, driven into exile (with family in Germany, didn't he say, rich circus people?), and now back home, he gave the impression of having far outgrown the other entrepreneurial kids of the city, and their childish ambitions simply to run the contraband-market here.

'Felix, you know young Herr Zikkel, I think,' said Lord Gomes, from behind the couch.

'Zikki, please,' purred the teenager.

'Zikki,' repeated Lord Gomes, returning to the centre of the room and straightening his clothes.

'I've had the pleasure,' Felix replied quietly. He kept his eye on the lion.

She uncoiled from her snarling crouch, and shook herself down, her threat diminishing, her size doubling; the mustard-coloured hide, which had looked streamlined, with muscles tight to the surface, now seemed like an overlarge jumper, baggy in the neck and armpits. Zikki gradually lowered the whip-branch, and sat down. Lord Gomes waved the wine bottle at him. He gave a little sneer. The chairman obediently dived into his desk cupboard.

Felix was intrigued. There was something topsy-turvy about the relationship between the two. The teenager appeared to be calling the tune. Felix remembered Zikki's offer to buy the Alex – had that been more than a joke?

'Here's what the doctor ordered,' said Lord Gomes, with a wink to his other guests, and produced a bottle. Felix stifled a gasp. *Why was the whole world drinking Chivas Regal?* He glanced at Charlie, who was singing louder now, a looping snatch of 'Tequila Sunrise'. No one else seemed to find this strange. Things were closing in on Felix. He sat brooding: *How am I going to get through it, the dry world? . . . Things aren't looking good . . . My doctor's a junkie, my shrink is ga-ga, God's a joker, what chance have I got? . . . How am I going to get through it, how, how?* He shifted forward on the couch, trying to stop the panic without attracting attention, only to find the lion heading towards him, exploring her surroundings. He hated animals; he hated their power, their lack of reason, their different wavelength, their sublime, brutish unhumanness! People fantasised about extra-terrestrials arriving on earth, while Felix alone knew that they were already here.

The lioness stopped directly in front of Felix, and he found himself eye to eye with her unique glassy gaze – *both cold and warm, full of dangerous innocence* – and his nostrils filled with her scent – *why do beasts always smell so old?* – and he went cold as she aimed her great muzzle towards his crotch.

'Best to let her have a little sniff,' advised Zikki, as he saw Felix's colour change. '*Lass sie in Ruhe, lass sie los*, hmn? Just calm- calm, *ja?*'

'Ehrm,' whispered Felix. 'I'd actually prefer it if . . .'

Charlie came to the rescue, going onto all fours, swopping the tune of 'Tequila Sunrise' for a deep, throaty call: a slow, dragged-out, belching purr. The lion turned, dismissing Felix – her tail actually smacked his mouth softly – and approached Charlie. He became more submissive, going lower and lower to the floor. She put one paw on his back. He leaned rapturously into her embrace.

Zikki watched, impressed. 'Some of your best friends are lions, Charlie?' he asked.

'Mmm-mm-mmmmm,' Charlie answered, in the dry staccato rhythm of big-cat language.

'He's a brave man, *ja-ja?*' Zikki said, winking to the others. 'She hasn't eaten today.'

'It's all about food, that's right,' Charlie whispered, emerging from under the lion as she wandered away, and urgently taking up his notebook. 'Food rules the lives of velvet, sorry, of *animals*, food rules their lives, it all hinges on food, on appetite.'

'It does, it does,' said Zikki, looking at his watch. 'So we haven't got long!' He laughed raucously, then tickled the lioness under the chin. '*Ja . . . mein kleine babychen . . . jaaa.*' She flopped at his feet, looking bored.

'And so to business,' said Lord Gomes. 'I'll ask Zikki to explain the exact nature of this little item we thought it would be fun to include in our show. Zikki?'

'Thank you, your lordship, your honour,' the teenager replied, in the slightly jeering tone familiar to Felix from their previous encounter. With the weary look of a professional engaged in a familiar routine, Zikki reached into his jacket and removed a tightly rolled cape. As he shook it free, bits of pocket fluff, a feather or two and some cannabis leaves drifted to the floor. His well-rehearsed speech was delivered brightly, in a joke-German accent: 'Mein little friend Simba here iz the mother of a pride of Masai lions vich are mein pride and joy.' He nudged the lioness with his whip-branch, and she followed him to the far window. 'They are, oh, ja-ja, very special indeed since they are able to do something vich no other family of lions in the vorld can do.' Still retaining his deadpan expression, he went into a series of little twirls and passes with the cape, sometimes over the lion, who was yawning, and sometimes over his own diminutive frame. 'Is zis a bullfight? Am I Superman? Is it a bird, a plane? Or is it! – *Hoopla!* – ze disappearing Simba?'

Felix blinked. The lioness was gone.

How? Where? Had she been a hologram? Was it all these windows – this room of glass – runny with rain from the storm, sparkling with sunlight from the aftermath?

Charlie was rapturous, staring straight ahead, one hand scribbling notes in his book, spilling off the page.

'Oh, *mein Gott*, there she is!' said Zikki, pressing his nose against the window, and pointing urgently.

'Where, where?' cried Lord Gomes gleefully, running over to join him.

'Somewhere over zat rainbow!' answered Zikki in song. As Charlie started whistling along, Zikki turned to his audience, his dead gaze mocking them, and announced solemnly, 'Oh, ja, boys und girls, our furry, friendly little Lion has gone wiz Dorothy und the Tin Man und the Scarecrow to zat distant land of Oz, never to be seen again. Unless – *unless* – oh, mein little boys und girls, I've just had a notion. Maybe if ve call her name, maybe she vill come back to uz, from Oz to uz, shall ve try boys und girls? Oh, ja, please let's try, let's call wiz all our might – SIMBAAA . . .'

'SIMBAAAA!' called Lord Gomes, tickled pink.

'SIMBAAAAAA!' called Charlie, from the depth of his being.

Staring at the others with incredulity, Felix was starting to wonder if he was asleep in bed, when he felt the very real, very rough surface of Simba's tongue on his hand. She was standing next to the couch, her amber, cold-warm eyes locked on him.

Zikki's gaze was not dissimilar, observed Felix. Having acknowl-
edged the enthusiastic applause from the others, the teenager now
launched into a description of the rest of his act, which involved
lions flying, melting, being squashed, turning into tabby cats.

Summoning all his energy, Felix addressed Lord Gomes: 'But . . .
but . . . the show is to be a compilation of our past shows, a celebration of the Alex's past.'

'And its future,' beamed Lord Gomes, raising his glass in a toast.
'Its glorious future!'

'Hallelujah!' said Charlie.

Felix felt drowsy, flu-drowsy in the lift, travelling down twenty-two
floors with Charlie, Zikki and Simba.

She kept her nose close to Felix's inner leg, intrigued, a sixth
sense drawing her towards the old scar there; the wounded one in
the herd, the weak one.

Felix barely noticed.

They reached ground level and crossed the empty expanse of the
foyer. Lord Gomes' skyscraper, in rose-coloured glass, was one of
the few in town unoccupied by squatters. These were massed outside, though, and seeing the approach of Felix's party, they rose or
lifted their hands. The impression was of the whole pavement shuffling forward.

Noah was waiting at the entrance. He took up an aggressive
stance, rifle cocked, butt resting on his pot-belly. As Charlie and
Felix emerged through the door, he slipped alongside, and they hurried to the jeep, using a zigzagging route (some muggers operated as
snipers, from rooftops), Noah twirling as they went. We could be
dancing, thought Felix, imagining a Greater Power's view of them.
Charlie laughed and sang. Meanwhile Zikki, who required neither
vehicle nor bodyguard, mounted the lioness's back and, with a
brusque wave at the men, rode off into the sunset.

The day's last light, blood-orange and still vibrant, fell on the
puddles from the storm, and burned them up. The evening quavered
with heat.

Felix was surprised to find Alys dozing on the back seat of the car. Noah had collected her from a friend's birthday party *en route*. Looking down at the child, jelly-smeared and cake-sticky, Felix remembered Emile's disgusting comments and shivered. Banishing them from his mind, he stretched out at her side, feasting on her smell. She stirred, they curled into one another's arms, and fell asleep as one.

He woke. It was dark. They were still travelling, but slowing down. Coming up onto one elbow, he saw they were on an unlit road, and that a group of people was blocking their way. His first instinct was one of panic. Was this an ambush? But no – Charlie was happily scribbling notes, and Noah just looked fed up, as though their journey had been broken like this before.

The people in the road were awestruck, pointing to the sky.

'What is it?' asked Felix.

'The comet, Mr Felix,' said Noah. 'The name of him, I don't know.'

Felix squashed his face against the window, but couldn't see more than the customary spectacle of the night sky in these parts, with its uninterrupted view of half the universe.

'There's trouble with God,' said Kaz, as Felix arrived backstage. 'He's walked out.'

She looked genial – squatting in the wings, chewing on a wodge of *khat* leaf   and it seemed safe to approach. Her hair braids were held back by a soaking sweatband, her lilac leotard was wet too. 'We've called an early supper break,' she explained. 'I was trying to time the *stomp* to his narration, but no, the man said he had an urgent appointment – in heaven itself! – and hightailed the fuck outa here.'

'And we could really do with him at the moment,' added Frankie Hoong, the half-Chinese stage manager, with a timid laugh. 'To say, "Let there be light."'

'Indeed,' sighed Felix. Another power cut. The stage was lit like stages of old, with a row of floats – wicks in oil – along the footlights, and dozens of candles all around; some in screen boxes on the sides, others above, bedecking an old chandelier which someone had fetched from the props store. In this wavering brown light, members of the Chorus were ranged across the length and breadth of the floor, consuming their ration of liquor and cigarettes, having already emptied the cauldrons of fish, rice and fruit. A few went through the dance steps, lazily, just for their own pleasure, others played instruments, some slept. One woman sat on her own, eyes closed, head forward, singing a Swahili lullaby. A group of teenage lads, still unused to all the surrounding nudity, joked about their half-erections, and this in turn held the attention of a cluster of girls. The boy in Ray-Ban shades who was now Felix's appointed ice-cream 'dealer' – he'd dubbed him Mr Fixer – led a small gang of *magendo* kids, the bootleggers, darting here and there, taking orders for whatever anyone wanted, relieving them of their newly acquired wages. Whores were on the same mission, working the circles of men who sipped at reed pipes in calabashes of beer, while their wives, bruised old mamas, looked the other way and gossiped about the latest news from the distant villages where they were born.

Felix went for a brief stroll among the Chorus, mostly to give himself thinking time, partly to bask in their greetings, their thanks, their waves, the touchings of his clothes and ankles; '*Sungura . . . sungura mjanja . . .*'

Who needs the bedroom department, he asked himself, when the world loves you?

Refreshed, he returned to Kaz, and said, 'I'll find him.'

'Who?'

Felix stared at her, frowning. 'Mr Mmalo. I'll find Mr M.'

'*Ahm*, I thought you meant God.'

'Well, quite,' laughed Felix, and in this instant, while his guard was down, she added, 'Or Popo-boy.'

'Popo-boy?'

'Every time you go scurrying outa rehearsals – isn't that what you're doing? Looking for him? I mean, it's not just 'cause the work's so shitty, is it?'

'I beg your pardon?'

'The work,' she said, gesturing vaguely round the stage. 'The work's all a bit shitty and dumb, isn't it?'

Felix bristled. She was doing it again. Like when she used that word last week . . . the B-word . . . bwana. She kept sneering at his work. But it wasn't really that. It was *him*. She was hellbent on punishing him . . . him reborn, reformed, recovering . . . him as dry soul, her as old soak. Their friendship was in danger of disintegrating. How to talk about it? They couldn't. 'Look,' Felix mumbled, 'if you don't approve of this show, if you've stopped believing in the way I work, the way *we* work –'

She cut in roughly: 'You promised to help me find a man. You promised, – "to the finish", you promised. Have we even started?'

In his head, Felix shouted back, 'Yes we have, you stupid pisstank! We started and we finished! We found out that he's *gone*! If you weren't so bloody plastered you'd see there's nothing more to be – !'

Then it struck him.

There *was* something else to try. A possible route to Popo-boy. There was someone who knew where he was. Or . . . they certainly knew *who* he was. And in chasing these answers Felix could solve something else, make a choice, take a step that was tempting him remorselessly; it was like something boiling inside him, cooking up today's fever, driving him mad . . .

'Must dash,' he called to Kaz over his shoulder.

He found Mr Mmalo sitting on the roof of the theatre. Elbows on knees, a small pair of opera glasses held to his eyes, aimed upwards.

Quite unsurprised by Felix's arrival, as though expecting it, Mr Mmalo handed over the opera glasses, and helped locate the comet. 'See the Southern Cross . . . go a quarter down its spine . . . see the very bright star there, Acrux? . . . go left, down a bit . . . now there . . . see it! Do you?'

Felix said he did, though he couldn't be sure. The two peepholes slid across the dust of distant white worlds, making him dizzy, making his feet clench and grip the roof.

'We only get to view her once every two thousand years,' said Mr Mmalo. 'Just think of that! Think when the last time was! Ancient Rome ruled the world, our Saviour was about to be born! Think of the next time! Who'll be here then?'

'Gosh,' went Felix, echoing the other's tone of wonder while trying to plan his move.

'Now,' said Mr Mmalo, 'isn't that worth missing a rehearsal or two?'

'Apology accepted.'

The actor looked at him in surprise, and Felix smiled, saying, 'And *I* must apologise too. For our set-to the other day. And for, well, years of . . . one has said a lot of . . . I want to apologise for it all.'

Mr Mmalo's surprise grew. Felix had just said sorry. *Felix?!* 'Bless you for that,' Mr Mmalo replied quietly. 'Bless you.'

Handing back the opera glasses, Felix asked, 'How do you reconcile the two things?'

'Pardon?'

'Your belief in the Bible and your interest in science.'

Mr Mmalo cleared his throat, and then in his beautiful bass voice, which sounded remarkably like Emperor Duma's, he spoke the lines from rehearsals: '"And God made the stars also. And He set them in the firmament of heaven to give light upon the earth. And to rule over the – "'

'Yes, yes,' said Felix. 'But according to science, comets come from interstellar space, from outer planets, other worlds.'

Mr Mmalo smiled benignly, and pinched two fingers into his bamboo snuff container, every bit the village elder (and yet, mused Felix, so thoroughly *Christian*). 'One mustn't take science too literally.'

'People say the same of the Bible.'

'To each his own.'

'"You say ee-ther and I say eye-ther,"' Felix sang softly.

'Pardon?'

'The song, y'know.'

'No. Which one?'

'Nothing,' murmured Felix. He and Mr Mmalo had both been born here, yet they shared few reference points. One of them was a stranger. Which one? Felix had little doubt. His toes twitched again, clinging on, as the night sky swirled around him. 'What about a Greater Power?' he asked slowly. 'Where does that fit into your scheme of things, where does He, She or It . . .?'

'God,' Mr Mmalo said promptly. 'God resides in heaven. Some people say that science is a search for God. But for me . . . well, let me put it like this,' he continued, in that gently pedantic way which endeared him to some people and bored others. 'People make the mistake of thinking I am a Christian Scientist, but no, that is quite another kettle of fish, as they say. The Bible is my reality. Science is my fantasy world. My science-fiction world, one could say. All this . . .' he gestured to the night sky '. . . this is simply such stuff as dreams are made of.'

'Fine,' said Felix, sensing that things were falling into place. 'So the comet is simply – what? – a sort of shooting star.'

'Simply a shooting star,' said Mr Mmalo, beaming comfortably.

'Well, make a wish, Mr Mmalo, make a wish upon a star. Because, guess what? Tonight your wish is going to come true!'

Mr Mmalo turned to him, puzzled.

'So,' said Felix, 'why don't we tootle off downstairs and start work on the Cyclops scene?'

seventeen

Felix crawled along an air-duct in the basement of the theatre.

He was treating himself tonight.

The Alex's air-conditioning had packed up years ago, but even when it worked, Felix doubted whether anything other than stale draughts drifted down this particular tunnel of aluminium, with its squared-off, ribbed sides. A peculiar blend of grease and dust collected in the joints, a fluffy gunge both delicate and sticky to the touch. It was not worth thinking about what, other than time, had mixed this brew; it wasn't whole objects you feared finding; it was the before and after, the eggs or tiny bones; the soup of life, thought Felix. Whatever it was, his first-night clothes were becoming crumpled and messed. Never mind. No one would know he'd had them dry-cleaned for the evening, that he'd planned to present himself as a new man, the cleaned-up version, inside and out; they'd just assume everything was as per normal, with him in the customary drink-stained black suit.

Felix lit a new cigarette from the one before, and used its glow for illumination; a metallic half-light came and went with his inhalations.

Ahead, the darkness was broken by patches of speckled brightness: the grilles of two basement rooms.

Felix's excitement grew as he crawled forward and peered through the left-hand grille, saving the other, the best, for last.

In a large storeroom, its walls stacked with stage furniture and props, its centre cleared and lit by a single hanging bulb, were Simba

and six other lionesses. They paced around with muscular restless-
ness, a sharpness in their movements, in their eyes, very different
from Simba's torpor the other day. Felix glanced at his watch –
6.30 p.m. – and remembered Charlie's remark about animals being
governed by their appetites. Big cats came to life at night, their
feeding-time. How did circuses cope with this fact of life? he wondered. Were lion-tamers frustrated by sluggish performers at
matinées, and then terrorised during the evening show? Or did they
regulate it by creating false feeding times, and cheating the animals'
body clocks? Were circus lions in a constant state of jet-lag?

Even as he pondered these questions, the storeroom door half
opened and two short arms expertly discharged a basin of meat.
Felix watched a goat's bloody neck stick to the side of the
Ramayana throne, before sliding down into the jaws of a lioness.
The others were brawling over the rest of the food.

Felix observed that the feeding frenzy was not that different from
supper breaks upstairs, when steaming cauldrons were brought in
for the Chorus. *Ah, showbiz*, he thought, while preparing to turn to
the right-hand grille. He smiled to himself, deliberately delaying the
moment, teasing himself with the wait. Enough . . .

As though in bed, he slowly rolled over.

The chamber below was another props and furniture storeroom,
but darker. In a cleared space there was a seventeenth-century dressing-table (from the time-travel sequence in *The Odyssey*), with a
string of light-bulbs gaffer-taped round the mirror. Sitting in this
phosphorescent womb, stock-still, poised with concentration, perhaps meditating, utterly without agitation or hunger, and yet
nevertheless strangely similar to the beasts next door, was the thick
bald figure of Emperor Duma.

Felix gasped with pleasure. There he was. Here they were. All set.
Ready to go.

So long as everything went according to plan.

> 'You like to-may-to and I like to-mah-to,
> To-may-to, to-mah-to,
> Po-tay-to, po-tah-to . . .'

This was Felix's customary first-night mantra, sung under his breath, again and again, while his guts filled with a familiar cocktail of dread and eagerness.

'Let's call the whole thing off!'

Pushing through the doors to the foyer, he received a considerable shock from the metal handles. Charlie had once explained this was something to do with carpet-static. Maybe so, but the kick was swifter tonight, wilder, gleeful even. Felix began to slouch through the assembling audience, not mingling, never catching anyone's eye, ignoring all greetings. As expected, people weren't surprised by this, nor by his scruffy look. This was a first night so it was assumed he was tense and drunk; to be avoided at all costs.

Felix stopped in the centre of the foyer, lifted his mask-like scowl, and surveyed the scene.

Even though there was still twenty minutes to curtain-up, the crowd wasn't swelling fast enough to guarantee anything other than a half-full house. This was the one part of the plan he hadn't been able to solve. If people knew what was going on, they'd be queuing round the block – the board would see what he'd meant by 'a last go'! – but the whole point was for them *not* to know. It was frustrating. He watched the plump form of Mr Otiti, his administrator (also front-of-house manager, box-office chief, head of marketing, head of publicity, poster-designer and reserve barman), doing a tour of duty, chirping, 'Hi, hello, *hamjambo, hamjambo!*' to the thin groups of first-nighters in their jewellery and finery, some in tribal skins and robes, others wearing safari suits, or just T-shirts and shorts.

The trustees were there, refilling paper cups from the bottles of champagne they'd brought in leather cool-bags: Lord Gomes, Judge Okoth-Ofumbi, the cobalt heiress Muriel Slackforth-Carter and her husband, the lemur-faced Mrs Al-Qirib, old V. K. Bukherjee, and others. Charlie stood among them, bristling with bright-eyed, twitchy-jawed animation. This didn't stem, Felix felt sure, from assorted potions and powders the doctor had prescribed for himself this evening – there'd been no mention of his research project recently, thank God – no, if Charlie was buzzing at present, it's because he was in on the plan.

As soon as he heard it outlined by Felix – trembling with the audacity of it and expecting his friend, as the sensible one, the *doctor*, for God's sake, to tell him to pull himself together – as soon as Charlie heard it, he had begun to radiate that glow, that other side of himself, the far side of his planet, and he had whispered, 'Wild!'

They passed close now, smiled, winked, and, like the participants in a dangerous love affair, sang softly to one another: '"Let's call the whole thing off!"'

Pushing through the theatre's entrance doors – again, an electric current shot through his body – Felix walked onto the street, in need of fresh air.

Not easy to come by this evening. The whole afternoon had been heavy with heat; it hung over you, itchy and thick, a blanket of grey-green cloud; people sweated, the vegetation oozed, the tongues of dogs and lions drooped wetly.

Perfect, thought Felix, I couldn't have ordered better weather. In fact, he'd been studying the forecasts all week. The weather was a vital component of the plot.

Looking down towards the town and harbour, he saw the approach of a small motorcade from the newly formed Ministry of Technology and Culture. Smiling and waving to the pedestrians who were processing to the theatre – mostly relatives of the Chorus – the government officials were clearly under orders to present themselves as a symbol of the new free society . . . despite the presence of heavily armed bodyguards, and the fact that the motorcade bore an uncanny resemblance to other, less benevolent cortèges of the past.

Felix was in no mood for the polite banter required of him. Turning on his heel, he returned to the foyer, via the shock of its doors, only to bump into his least favourite first-night person, the local critic – a schoolteacher for most of the year – a sour Dutchman with an unhappy look in his eye and a bad back, which meant he sometimes sank from view during performances to ease himself in various ways. As the man opened his mouth, to utter some chilly greeting, no doubt, Felix shot away, alerted Mr Otiti to the arrival of the motorcade, then grabbed Charlie's elbow and steered him backstage.

A kind of chaos reigned in the great lightwell at the centre of the building, the terraces crammed with five hundred naked or semi-naked people, sitting, sleeping, eating, smoking, in the corridors, on the balconies and stairways, round every corner, in every doorway.

Perfect, thought Felix, nobody can move about too easily, nobody's quite sure what's going on, *perfect*.

He led Charlie to the dressing-rooms, and rapped his knuckles on one door, while calling, 'Knock-knock.'

'Come,' boomed Mr Mmalo from within, his voice much fuller and more actorish than normal. 'Yes – come.'

They found the man in agony. Dressed only in Y-fronts, he looked like a bucket of water had been poured over him. 'Lord have mercy, this heat!' he lamented, leaning his face towards a small electric fan screwed into one of the sockets for his mirror-bulbs. 'This heat and that load!'

Felix and Charlie turned to look at the Cyclops costume, which sat on the edge of the bed like a giant Humpty-Dumpty. As well as direct-ing and writing his shows, Felix designed them also, and had borrowed the Cyclops look from Alfred Jarry's sketches for his play *Ubu Roi*. Despite the surrealism of the egg-shaped padding, Felix was a stickler for realism so he had weighted it with ball-bearings to help Mr Mmalo with the character's dissipated waddle. The image was completed by a helmet, whose visor created the fearsome one-eyed gaze.

'Oh, come off it, Mr M,' Felix joshed affectionately. 'You'd be sweating like this if it was the middle of winter!' Inwardly, Felix gave thanks again for the weather. He knew that every performer has a point of physical tension, a point that no amount of experience or relaxation can fully eradicate, a point at which the unnatural busi-ness of making themselves the focus of attention finally comes home to roost. Some experience it in the sudden dryness of their tongues or stickiness of gums, others develop an oddly crooked finger or foot cramp, a fair proportion of male actors find that the stage has the same effect on their genitals as very cold water, while most females need to urinate frequently. For Mr Mmalo, the afflic-tion was in his sweat glands.

'It's ghastly,' he complained to Felix and Charlie. 'It gets so bad one can't concentrate properly, one can't *see* straight, literally!'

'Hey, y'know, I've got something that might help!' Charlie said, with what Felix judged an impressive display of spontaneity. 'Let me just pop out to the Cruiser and get my magic box.'

While he was gone, Felix made casual conversation with Mr Mmalo, admiring his first-night cards, chatting about various moments in the show, and then, to complete the illusion of normality, he suddenly said, 'Oh, by the by, I thought of a little something you could add to the Duma speech.'

'Oh, goody!' said Mr Mmalo, who prided himself on what he called his 'extemporisations'. While others were thrown by Felix's penchant for last-minute changes and topical references, Mr Mmalo always coped excellently, thanks to his ordered mind, his ability to create a methodology for everything, and his trust in a Greater Power.

A hologram-postcard of the Mother and Child was stuck above his mirror, their simpering eyes following you round the room.

Felix asked, 'Did you see the news last night?'

'I didn't alas,' replied Mr Mmalo, gesturing round the meagre belongings in his dwelling, where there was no evidence of a TV.

'Well, lend an ear. A news conference to announce that our drinking water is safe again, except that when one of the journalists filled a cup from the tap and offered it to the Minister he refused, declaring he wasn't thirsty. So I thought you could have Duma say something like, "No one would've caught me out like that. I had official tasters. Mind you, I did get through rather a lot of them. Three a day – one at breakfast, one at . . ."'

Together, nodding and chuckling, they bent over Mr Mmalo's script, and found the perfect place. The actor inscribed the new lines on the opposite page, via a meticulous system of asterisks and arrows, while Felix savoured the masterstroke of the plan. Mr Mmalo possessed the only copy of the mock-Duma oration. It had been cooked up by the director and the actor in private, as they used to do in the old days, the days of dodging the censor. Even at the dress-rehearsal, Felix had insisted that Mr Mmalo simply top and tail the speech, and both men relished the company's frustration and excitement.

A knock on the door now, and stage manager Frankie Hoong popped in. 'Oh, Felix, so sorry, didn't know you were here, sorry-sorry,' she said in that violently timid way of hers. Irritated, Felix gave a half-shrug, half-wave. She turned to Mr Mmalo. 'Sorry, but I wonder if I could just have the last line of your speech in the Cyclo–?'

'No, you couldn't,' interrupted Felix.

'Sorry, Felix, no, of course not, sorry-sorry.' Again she turned to Mr Mmalo. 'Perhaps just an indication of the length of – ?'

'No!' insisted Felix, wondering if these two had had some arrangement in the past whereby he had slipped her top-secret material. 'You get a *sense* of when any scene is coming to its natural end – an audience always does!'

'Yes, yes, of course, Felix, sorry, Felix,' said Frankie Hoong, who had heard this a thousand times. 'Sorry to have bothered you, Mr Mmalo, have a good show, sorry-sorry.' She withdrew, crashing into Charlie and then scurrying away, muttering another litany of apologies.

'Take two of these now,' Charlie advised Mr Mmalo, opening his case and producing a small bottle with four tablets, 'and the others just before the big scene.'

'One won't feel drowsy or anything, will one?' fretted Mr Mmalo. 'One can't afford to be anything less than one hundred per cent on the ball.'

'Nix side effects,' said Charlie. 'It's just sodium chloride, replacing all the stuff you're losing. You'll just sweat less, and feel less debilitated.'

'Oh, marvellous,' said Mr Mmalo. 'Just what one –'

He was interrupted by Frankie Hoong's voice on the tannoy: 'Five minutes, please. Full company – this is your five-minute call, please, thank you.'

'Is it really?' exclaimed Mr Mmalo, reaching for a body stocking slung over the chair; this was his first costume, as Narrator/God in the Creation.

When the Genesis show was first staged a year ago, the professional actors – with the exception of Kaz – had refused to appear nude for the Garden of Eden sequence. Felix was apoplectic with anger and confusion. (He devised nude scenes for all his shows, without ever being quite sure where aesthetic instincts ended and others crept in.) Eventually someone suggested a compromise: body stockings, dyed in shades of rose, olive or chocolate, depending on the actor's race, and with painted shadows to indicate pudenda. 'Don't you fucking understand?' Felix had shouted. 'Your lumps and bumps and bits look *worse* squashed into the cunting stockings than they do hanging free!' but this argument failed to win much support.

For Felix, the sight of Mr Mmalo struggling into his body stocking now, checking the leg seams with the diligence of a high-class tart, and yet oblivious to the corrugated outline of his Y-fronts, this was still like a red rag to a bull. 'Best get out of your way,' he said, lunging for the door.

Charlie stopped him with an anxious look, while saying calmly to Mr Mmalo, 'Lemme just give you the first dose.' He tipped all four tablets into his hand and pretended to select a couple at random. 'In case you forget in the rush.'

'Oh, bless you,' said Mr Mmalo, hurriedly popping the two into his mouth, turning on the tap in his sink and scooping up a palmful of water.

'Argh!' cried Felix in mock-horror. 'Tap water!'

'Oh, balderdash!' laughed Mr Mmalo.

Perfect, thought Felix, now we can blame the water.

'You *must* take the other two just before the Cyclops scene,' said Charlie. His concern sounded purely professional.

'Yes. That's right,' said Mr Mmalo, using one hand to hoist the body stocking over his large tummy, the other to scribble a reminder note in his script next to the new lines for the Duma speech.

Perfect, thought Felix, oh, thank God for this anally retentive pedant.

They left him dancing round his room, trying to stretch the layer of fake nudity over his own.

It began. Darkness, then light, then the flesh of people. An ear, some scalp, a second head, shoulders, breasts, thighs. Dozens of people, scores, hundreds, filling the space, its depth and width, and up, up, up: the air stacked with human beings, on ladders, platforms, hammocks, ropes, some upside down.

Smoke travelling among them, curling round a leg, wrapping a naked waist, draping over one arm like a scarf.

A drum played softly, feet shuffling in rhythm, rustling with anklets of sea shells, hands clapping gently, fingers clicking. Voices panted, purred, wept. A small choir of children sang a Swahili hymn about harvest time, while Kaz did a husky rendition of 'All By Myself'.

'And God saw that it was good,' said Mr Mmalo's Narrator. 'And the evening and the morning was the first day.'

It *is* good, thought Felix, in a rare acknowledgement of his worth. Any other director would've started with an empty stage to represent the first day of Creation, but I've filled it with people straight away, a multitude of Adams and Eves . . . they make sense of the light . . . Adam and Eve are everywhere, everything . . . there is only us . . . only each of us . . . my dreams only reveal their meaning when I view every character as myself . . . of course they do, there was only me making them up . . . me, the creator, the Greater Power . . . in life, too, things only make sense when they filter through me, my heartbeat, my passion, my vision of things, _my imagination . . ._ of course they do, I am the only thing I can feel.

Felix was sitting in the top level of the auditorium. It was too depressing in the stalls and dress circle, with their shoals of empty seats. He preferred sitting up here – in the gods – where there was no one at all.

The incredible, perilous height suited his mood. As on Charlie's sundeck, you didn't move around without holding on; the view was so steep, you had a constant sense of falling, or flying. It was as though you had died, or were from another planet, and were being granted an airborne vision of this peculiar human ritual called theatre. There it was, going on far below, on a bright rectangle, and aimed at a bowl of people somewhere underneath you – they were invisible, you just heard their noise – while your own eyeline was naturally drawn to the ceiling of the giant building, where the scale of things made you feel like Tom Thumb, and the massy plasterwork with its bright mounds and dust-dark shadows intensified the sense of being among the clouds, or in heaven, a romantic heaven adorned with garlands and ribbons and cherubs, cherubs, cherubs.

How beautiful, thought Felix, *I've never been happier, more excited, more alive.* He crossed and uncrossed his legs, sat forward then back, crunched buzz balls between his teeth, unwrapped chewing-gum, chain-smoked.

He lasted until the fifth day of Creation and then, holding on for dear life, climbed the steep stairs to the exit sign.

Down through the theatre he went, its doors electrifying him, the shocks growing in voltage each time, and into the darkened back-stage area with its limbo-land of black quick-change tents and white gaffer-tape arrows, its population hanging around like people in a red-light district, and through the vault door into his private stairwell, and down he went, down not up, through the door at the bottom, closing it tightly behind him.

He stopped. In front of him was a pride of lions. Zikki was nowhere to be seen. Nor the chain-leashes used in his act – attaching them to the stage floor. No leashes, no trainer. Just six fully grown lionesses loose in the corridor.

Simba, the mother of them all, came forward, recognising a familiar smell – the smell of the weak one, the wounded one – and aimed her nose at his inner leg, her whole muzzle seeming to sharpen, to point. She made a noise in her belly, not throat – not the low purring burp Charlie had mimicked so well, this was deeper, hungrier. Felix felt behind him for the door-handle. It gave a sharp shock, as though slapping away his hand. Simba growled, a definite *growl.* A veil of sweat slid over Felix's brows and stung his eyes. Not daring to raise his hand to clear his vision, he contorted his face wildly. Simba immediately dropped low, snarling. Had Felix accidentally given the signal for attack?

Then, through the blur, Felix saw the short figure of Zikki pop up from among the lionesses, a cheeky 'got-you!' twinkle in his eye.

He was dressed as Felix had first seen him at the circus, in animal-trainer costume, his face covered with blue make-up.

'Mein Direktor – *Heil*!' he said, clicking his heels and giving a stiff-arm salute. 'I am just moving ze panzer troops, or pussy troops, just moving zem to ze trap-lift, so no time for chit-chat, tomorrow von't vait, tomorrow belongs to me, so toodle-oo, ve'll meet again, don't know vere, don't know ven, *Heil*!' And he bustled the lions down the corridor, going, '*Rechts, links, rechts, links, rechts, links . . .*'

Felix pulled faces at the retreating figure, then hurried on, racing down passages and turning corners, until he reached *the* door.

He took a key from the inside pocket of his jacket, unlocked it quietly, and then knocked.

'Come,' called a voice, full and deep, eerily similar to the one several floors up, 'yes, come.'

Emperor Duma was sitting as before, wearing only charcoal-coloured shorts, his back rigid and his fists resting on his thighs. He was perhaps engaged in some form of meditation. His eyeline was directed at a high window on one wall, whose broken glass held a small picture of outside: a disused courtyard in the centre of the building.

From the dressing-table, the string of mirror-bulbs cast their glamorous light, softening the legendary head, dark and heavy as a buffalo, softening the power, softening the big boiled-egg stare.

On the dressing-table top, lay a pair of new, wire-rimmed spectacles. Charlie had arranged for these to be delivered a few days after his visit with the optometrist Mr Rosenblatt and, much to Duma's surprise, they suited his prescription perfectly.

'All well?' Felix asked now, trying to sound as if he was visiting just another actor, in just another dressing-room.

'Naturally,' Duma replied, in a low voice.

'Ready-*ish*?' Felix said, immediately giving himself away with a nervous laugh. He glanced at the dressing-table top again: he expected notes, a speech, something. 'We're about three-quarters through the first item, the Creation, and then there's a – a – a little fellow with a disappearing-lion act.' He faltered as Duma stared at him suspiciously, then continued: 'And he's supposed to have twenty minutes, but if I'm any judge of theatrical character, that little audience-milker will be there a tad longer, and then it's, ehrm, Cyclops. So – so, this is sort of your own half-hour call!' He ended with a short gasping laugh.

Duma nodded slowly, his mind elsewhere.

Felix endured the silence and stillness for about a minute before asking, 'Anything I can get you?'

'I'll need water on the platform.'

'We call it a stage.'

'What?'

'And I'm afraid there's no water in that scene, on that set, it's Cyclops' feast and he's drinking wine, well, we use Ribena, of course, so –'

'I'll need water,' Duma repeated quietly, in a way that made Felix reply instantly, 'But of course.'

He wanted to add, 'Will that be bottled water or water from the reservoir into which your death squads dumped their waste?' but just stood awkwardly, enduring another long, pin-drop silence.

Was now the time to raise the other issue? The one that had finally prompted – or, at any rate, legitimised – his decision to bring Duma here. Was now the time? How would one put it? A man who worked for you, a man called Popo-boy . . . Where is he? Who is he? Is he you? Are you now or have you ever been Po–?

No, no, no. This was not the right time. The evening was stacked with enough explosives.

Felix was about to leave, when Duma suddenly put on his spectacles, turned their flashing discs towards Felix, and rose. 'The water,' he said slowly, almost shyly. 'That was point number one on my agenda. Point number two is . . . thanks. I must thank you.'

'Oh, no, not at all.'

'You are risking a lot.'

Felix gave a vague, self-deprecating shrug, while both men thought back to the journey here last night, at 3 a.m.: Charlie driving his jeep, Noah-less, with Felix next to him, and Duma behind, covered from head to toe in a *bui-bui*, the black robes of a Muslim wife.

Duma was wrong. It hadn't felt risky. It felt easy, so easy. In fact, the accomplishment was magnified, made more fantastic, by the sheer *easiness* of the transfer. A short drive on to Bull Brak's land (the owner keeping well out of sight), and to the foot of the hill with the cave, a cloaked figure coming out of it, descending the slope, climbing into the car, a short drive back to the theatre and, hey presto, one dictator delivered to your door. Felix was still giddy with it. He was in charge of Duma now, he was his jailer in a way, his master. He *owned* Duma.

All his life Felix had liked to own the things he found most fascinating, most powerful. An art gallery became more interesting once he knew he could buy postcards of favourite paintings. A film's impact increased once he could acquire the video. A landscape was infinitely more beautiful once he could pick up a piece and carry it away in his pocket; he had pebbles from Ayers Rock, sand from the Sahara, a fragment of London brick, beach shells from Long Island. And human beings: his casts and companies, they all had to be photographed *by him* – his room was cluttered with boxes of snaps – they had to be possessed in some way, conquered. Promiscuous individuals like Charlie and Kaz talked of *having* people. Felix needed to *have* them as well, in his way.

And now he *had* Duma, who held the most intoxicating thrall for him. Duma . . . the Emperor Duma, with all his power and glory, all that horror and might, Duma the Great Dictator . . . Duma was *his*. What an incredible thing!

'We've had our differences in the past,' Duma said now. He shrugged slowly, then added, 'As my people say, "A stream meets another but does not cross over it."'

Felix waited for him to explain, but he went quiet, jaws locking. Setting aside the enigmatic dictum – he was famous for these – what had he meant about differences? Was it just a generalised comment – him as a Native African, Felix as a 'tourist', which is how Duma sometimes described the non-Afs? Or did he remember Felix *specifically* – did he remember the modest contribution to the liberation struggle made by the Alexandra Theatre? If so, it was strangely flattering. Felix struggled with his rising feelings, and squirmed in the heat of the room.

'Differences,' Felix echoed eventually. 'Differences, shmifferences. Y'know how it is. *"You say to-may-to and I say to-mah-to."'*

Duma's arms were crossed, wiping the sweat from his armpits. Every muscle froze. He stepped closer to Felix. Despite his short stature – he was a head lower than Felix – his bulk was formidable, his *density*; he seemed to be packed with more matter than other humans. 'What? What did you say? *Heh?'*

Felix swallowed hard. 'Nothing. Just a . . . it's just that song.'

'What did you say exactly?' Duma asked again. Behind the lenses, his eyes were bulging.

'Ehrm . . . "You say to-may-to and I say to-mah-to."'

'That's not the start.'

'Sorry? What?'

'"You say po-tay-to and I say po-tah-to,"' Duma half sang, half said, his voice starting to quiver with emotion, then cleared his throat briskly. 'That's how it starts.'

'Well . . . Actually, no, it starts with tomato.'

'No. Potato.'

'Tomato.'

'Potato.'

They faced one another, frowning, then Duma said, 'Y'know, I believe we are both incorrect.'

Felix blinked. Had he heard clearly? Was Duma admitting to being *wrong*?

'I think,' the dictator said slowly. 'I think it's ee-ther, eye-ther which starts it, and then we proceed to the vegetables.'

Felix thought hard, then said, 'You may be right.'

'I *am* right,' Duma replied, sounding more like himself again. 'It's ee-ther, eye-ther, then nee-ther, ny-ther, then po-tay-to, po-tah-to, and only *then* to-may-to, to-mah-to.'

'You seem very sure,' said Felix carefully, feeling he was on a tightrope.

Duma nodded, then sighed. 'A young lady. When I was at Sandhurst. An English rose. Her favourite song.' Closing his eyes, chin wavering like a snake charmer's, he slowly conjured up the memory:

> '"You say ee-ther
> And I say eye-ther
> You say nee-ther
> And I say ny-ther
> Ee-ther, eye-ther, nee-ther, ny-ther . . ."'

Felix joined in:

'"Let's call the whole thing off!"'

Duma's eyes opened joyfully. 'That's how it starts!' he exclaimed. 'That is definitely how it starts!'

'Goddammit, that's how the son-of-a-gun starts!' cried Felix, in an American accent, and then, improvising a little soft-shoe shuffle, began the next verse:

> '"You like po-tay-to and I like po-tah-to,
> You like to-may-to and I like to-mah-to . . ."'

He jumped as he felt Duma's hand clamp hold of his shoulder, but it was only the other falling in with the dance. It led them back and forwards past the dressing-table mirror with its string of light-bulbs, its crest of glamorous light, and so Felix was able to watch, in giddy exhilaration, as he and the Scourge of All Africa shimmied and swayed their way through the old Gershwin standard.

> '"And oh!
> If we ever part
> Then that might break my heart
> So if you like pa-jay-mas
> And I like pa-jah-mas . . ."'

As they approached the big finish, they steadied themselves in front of the mirror and, aglow in its light, beaming, sweating, arms outstretched, eyes fixed on one another in the most trusting way, sang loudly:

> '"So we better call the calling-off OFF!"'

The government officials had brought more than just goodwill to the Alex tonight. They had brought electricity. Their presence guaranteed no power cuts in this section of the city for the duration of the show, and thus removed at least one worry for Felix. Along with directing, writing and designing his shows, he lit them also, enjoying this skill almost more than the others. The Cyclops scene provided the kind of challenge he liked. He wanted the comic violence of the giant's island to surprise Odysseus, and the audience, wanted the atmosphere to be imbued at first with softness, a nostalgic beauty. So he used lateral fresnels and his beloved 'birdies' – adapted from shop-window mini-beams – to cast long, low yellow rays and create an impression of the bush at sunset. A generous spillage went into the wings, sliced by the side flats, and stretching to the back wall. The stage looked as though it was surrounded by tall boxes of late-afternoon light. The people in each – scene-shifters or performers waiting for entrances – they seemed small and still, almost posed, like pictures of themselves in this or another life. So close to the action onstage, yet disconnected from it, they went about their business peacefully, practising little routines, sipping water, whispering to one another, or just standing in repose.

The smell here was strong, of naked multitudes and lion piss, but Felix barely noticed.

He couldn't believe it. Here he was, standing on the side of his stage, in his theatre, next to the legendary, the infamous Emperor Duma, *and nobody knew*.

Duma was wrapped in the Muslim woman's *bui-bui* again, and people were passing within inches of him without realising how close they were to fame and fortune.

DUMA CAPTURED IN THEATRE WINGS . . . DICTATOR TRAPPED IN PROMPT CORNER . . . THE SCOURGE OF ALL AFRICA WHIPPED INTO A DRAMATIC FRENZY . . . EXIT THE EMPEROR.

Picturing these headlines, and glancing at the plastic cup of water in his hand, to put onstage for Duma, *as ordered!*, Felix wondered whether, instead of going through with the plan, he should rather trigger the discovery?

The choice was hair-raising, exquisite, unbearable.

Then he caught sight of Kaz nearby, dressed as Andromache, with hanging hair braids and bomber jacket. She was locked in her current mood: swollen-eyed with grief, yet calm, soothed by maize spirit and *bangi*, head constantly nodding, ticking to a drunk pulse – you never knew if she was about to topple over – with only two parts of her focus remaining clear: her work in the show and her determination to find Popo-boy. One of these had brought her into the wings.

Felix frowned. What was happening? It wasn't only Kaz . . . why were so many people suddenly gathering? Had there been a tip-off? Where was Charlie? They had arranged to meet at the end of the lion act. Why wasn't he here?

Calm down, Felix told himself. Mr Mmalo's Cyclops – that's what was drawing Kaz and the others. Everyone wanted to see the climax of the scene, when in the middle of the feast with Odysseus, Cyclops would spring up and, slowly metamorphosing into Emperor Duma, deliver the great oration. It had been withheld from them at the dress rehearsal, so now the whole company, pro's and Chorus alike, were collecting in the wings.

But witnesses at this point would spoil everything.

Abandoning Duma, the real one, hunched and docile under his *bui-bui*, Felix dashed over to Frankie Hoong, who was running the show from the prompt corner.

'Clear the wings!' he hissed. 'Too much noise, they're throwing Mr M, clear the wings!'

'Ah, righty-oh, Felix, sorry,' she whispered, lifting up one ear of her headset. 'I've just got a call coming up, sorry-sorry, and then –'

The words rose in his gullet – *You slit-eyed c–!* – but his hands flew to his mouth, clamping it shut. Evil little squeaks slipped out. He grasped his head and shook it as if it was a separate object. Then, with every face-muscle straining, he said, 'Please . . . I'd really appreciate . . . if you cleared the wings . . . now . . . please.'

Brow furrowed with surprise, Frankie Hoong obeyed, hurrying among the onlookers, whispering urgently to the pro's, shoving the Chorus roughly.

Felix dashed over just as she reached Duma.

'Not him – *her* – she's a guest of mine!'

'Sorry, Felix, sorry, I thought you meant everybo–'

'Look, just ffff–! Just please return to your corner, thanks.'

Frankie Hoong withdrew, while Felix closed his eyes, thinking, God, I hate being nice!

With the wings empty, and Frankie Hoong's sightline blocked by a flat, Felix took hold of the edge of Duma's *bui-bui* and waited, preparing for the next and most difficult stage of the plan.

Something was still wrong.

Mr Mmalo seemed in fine form, in full flow; he was reaching the transformation point in the scene and showing no signs of the symptoms Charlie had guaranteed.

Where was Charlie?

Maybe Mr Mmalo had forgotten to take the second dose of tablets.

Impossible. He'd written it down – Felix had seen him write it down – and this was a man with a clerk's brain trapped in an artist's body. If he wrote it down, he would *do* it.

Felix watched helplessly as Mr Mmalo rose from the feast table, and said to Odysseus, 'You ask why these rules exist on the island. You may as well ask why the island exists. Or why I exist. Because . . .'

He bent his knees, stretched his arms to the floor, and put back his head. Felix heard an extraordinary noise go through the audience – it was a silence, a sharp and tingling silence, as if each and every one of them had grabbed the auditorium's metal door-handles and been shot through with electricity.

'. . . because . . . because this island *is* me!'

The audience erupted with laughter.

Duma suddenly stirred under his *bui-bui*. He peeled away one corner, revealing a puzzled gaze.

'And I *am* this island!' roared Mr Mmalo – to thunderous applause.

'Wha'?' Duma murmured, as though stunned by a physical blow. 'Whass . . . ?'

'I warned you they'd laugh!' Felix cried, without separating his teeth, feeling a terrible panicky rage, feeling he really oughtn't talk to the Scourge in this way, feeling he didn't care.

'But, but,' whimpered Duma, 'he said "island" – that's why they're laughing – it should be "Africa".' He started towards the stage. Felix grabbed his robes. A swathe fell away, revealing a glimpse of the semi-naked dictator.

Onstage, Mr Mmalo had turned to the audience and, addressing them directly, boomed, 'People of Africa, I speak to you from my place of exile, wherever that is –'

'*What?*' roared Duma – drowned, luckily, by audience laughter – and then, suddenly, finally, it happened.

With no warning at all, Mr Mmalo toppled forward onto the banquet table. Plastic grapes and rubber chickens went flying, as well as the tureen of real goat mince on which Cyclops had been gorging.

The audience laughed and applauded again, thinking this was part of the act, and kept laughing for some time while nothing happened onstage.

Dhaba, the actor playing Odysseus, laughed also, thinking Mr Mmalo was extemporising, before realising he was genuinely unconscious.

This was his chance – *his* chance to extemporise, just like Felix was always telling them: 'There's no such thing as a mistake onstage in my theatre, *use it*. Use whatever happens!' Having started life as a market-place kid, busking for his supper, Dhaba now scooped up the fallen food and prepared to juggle.

Unfortunately his big moment came and went in the same instant, for the master was quicker than the disciple: Felix threw Duma's *bui-bui* over himself and charged onstage.

The audience greeted the arrival of the robed figure with delight, and watched, laughing and clapping, as it shouted instructions to Odysseus. Together they carried off the banquet table, with Cyclops atop.

'Oh, there you are!' Felix exclaimed, finding Charlie in the wings. They bustled Mr Mmalo into the nearest quick-change cubicle. 'Where the ruddy fuck have you been?'

'Yeah, sorry,' Charlie drawled, grinning. 'Met three fab naked people of all sexes . . .'

His pupils were dilated, his jawbone didn't seem to quite fit his mouth and, most peculiar of all, his voice was more than an octave lower. *The research project – he was still at it!* Felix glanced anxiously at Mr Mmalo's unconscious body. But no. However stoned Charlie became, he had never been known to harm a patient.

'Just help me!' Felix whispered, as he saw Frankie Hoong scurrying towards them.

'It's OK, I'm a doctor,' Charlie said slowly, in his curious bari-
tone – 'I'm a doctawww' – to no one in particular, while Felix did
three things simultaneously: with one hand he yanked Duma into
the cubicle, with the other he directed the Odysseus actor back
onstage, and with his nicest smile, he faced Frankie Hoong: 'You
can return to your corner, thank you, he's fine, it was the tap water,
he'll be back on in a tick, jolly lucky Dr Chabecq's here.'

'I'm a doctawww,' Charlie continued to boom, as if trying to
convince himself, while Frankie Hoong retreated, Dhaba entertained
the audience with juggling and backflips, and Felix transferred the
Cyclops helmet and costume from Mr Mmalo to Duma.

Within seconds all was ready. Leaving Charlie swaying over Mr
Mmalo, asking, 'Where doessss it huuuurt?', Felix pushed Duma,
now a waddling egg-shape, through the dark of the wings and into
the blazing light of the stage.

'Oh, drat!' Felix muttered as the dictator left his grasp. It wasn't
just that he'd forgotten to hand over the cup of water. *What had he
unleashed?*

There was no time to dwell on it. As the audience applauded
Cyclops's return, Felix frantically waved Dhaba offstage, punching the
air with a thumbs-up sign, praising the way he'd coped with the
emergency.

Now Cyclops was alone onstage, and the audience gradually
went quiet, bristling with anticipation.

Duma hesitated, his weight on one foot, the other slightly off the
ground, his egg-shape looking as if it might float away, and on his
face – what remained of it under the visor – an expression of slack-
jawed bafflement. He didn't seem to know where he was or what
was expected of him. Above his head, a hot light creaked.

The audience were dead silent now, waiting.

He waited also.

Someone coughed in the auditorium.

Duma's head jerked in that direction, like an orchestra conductor
whose prize pause had just been ruined, then his weight returned to
both feet, to his centre.

Now a giggle from the audience – now another – now a little
ripple – now silence again.

Felix's hands were clamped over his mouth, to stop himself from shrieking with mirth or terror. Someone slid into place alongside him. Assuming it was Charlie, he reached for his hand. But the skin was rougher. Kaz. He glanced at her. She stared back with a strange, calm look of gratitude. She wasn't in on the plan, yet it was as though she understood, and liked the way things were going. They held one another's hands and squeezed until all they could feel was bone, fragile bone.

Duma cleared his throat.

The sound of the house shifted: several hundred people leaning forward.

'My people,' said Duma in his quietest voice, yet effortlessly reaching the back of the upper circle, 'I speak to you from exile . . .'

Laughter – but more cautious than before, nervous even. They couldn't work it out. He looked the same, sounded the same, and yet his spirit made a different shape in the air.

'I speak from exile. Or so you think.'

Laughter – growing less.

'So *you* think . . . *you* . . . or *you*.' He was picking out the laughers one by one, freezing their smiles.

'*You* . . . and *you* . . . and *you* find the idea of exile entertaining. Explain this to me. Tell me some stories. Tell me about the birth of you, your parents or your parents' parents in Lisbon, Hamburg, London, Bombay . . . Describe the smells there, the first sounds you heard, the way the light fell on your faces. The English ones, or those from Germany, you knew grey light – was it like the light this afternoon? That was grey too, but different I think. Heh? The Indians, the Chinese, you knew heat, humidity. Did it smell like this afternoon? I don't believe so. Similar, but not quite, heh? The Portuguese, the Arabs, you heard cicadas in hot undergrowth. Was it like the side of a road here? Not quite, not quite. That good sound. Like a pulse, a heartbeat. Home. The sound of home, the smell of home, the light of home. Now talk to me about exile. Now laugh.'

He waited. Nobody took up his challenge. He smiled and waddled forward in his egg costume. 'Come on. I'll help you. Help you laugh.' He bent his knees, reached for the ground. 'Must I say it for you?'

Silence from the house.

'Must I? Or have you understood – finally – what I mean? About home. We are inseparable from it, and in the end that's not so funny, really. Really it is, in fact, the saddest and most beautiful thing we'll ever know. The first thing. Where we're from. And I don't just mean our generation, or the one before, or the one before that. I'm talking about a place where your forefathers' fathers . . . where their bones are mixed in with the dust that blows off the land on a fine morning, where their particles are the motes floating in the sunlight when you open your shutters, where you can't breathe without taking some of them back into you. I'm talking about home. I'm talking about a place where it and I are the same thing. And then I'm inviting you to laugh when I say . . .'

He leaned forward and whispered it like a lover:

'I am Africa, and Africa is me.'

where that leave the whites?

Africa as a bloody dictator – where he belongs, who he is.

PART III

Pembe Cove

eighteen

Felix saw it the next morning, when he went to sit in the empty auditorium, among the litter of the first night, the crushed paper cups, the roncocd programme sheets dusted with footprints, the sweet-stale whiff of clothes and perfume . . . There onstage, in the dim light of three hanging light-bulbs, he could still see Duma's outline. Not the comic-grotesque egg-shaped outline of the Cyclops disguise, but that of the man himself. It was impressive. Whenever Felix cast a professional eye on politicians abroad, in America and Britain, he found them lacking as performers, their style manufactured and passionless. They seemed only marginally more interested in what they were saying than you were. But see the great dictators, the great orator-dictators, and it's like seeing a great singer or actor; the technique is secondary, even the words are; first of all, they show you their soul. Call it a sense of heroic destiny, call it the energy of absolutism, but Duma had left it in the air like some supernatural signature, and nothing, not even time, would wipe it away.

dictators as actors

Felix smarted as he recalled the reactions after the show, epitomised by Lord Gomes: 'Weren't those lions jolly marvellous? Everyone loved the lions. And the Creation, of course, that's still very effective. But the Cyclops scene . . . I remember it being funnier before. And much more like Duma. He's lost the knack of it, that actor. I know he was feeling a little under the weather, but . . . well, I'm not an expert, of course, but I reckon his skit was a bit drawn out, a trifle tedious, and generally below par.'

If only they knew!

Felix had wanted them to know, and not to know. Even as Duma's speech was happening, Felix felt this tug, this irreconcilable tug, and knew that the dictator was feeling it too.

The theatre was closing for the festivities of the long weekend, Freedom Weekend, and when they resumed, Cyclops would be played solely by Mr Mmalo (who had recovered from his swooning fit after curtain-down: 'It was the tap water,' he was told), and then, no doubt, people would find the scene funnier again! Funnier than on the first night when the poor fellow was under the weather.

Meanwhile, Duma was still in the basement of the theatre, sharing a party wall with the lions. When his brief stage career ended last night, he made no mention of returning to his hillside cave, and Felix really didn't know what to do about that.

'It's a public holiday to celebrate the fact that you're no longer with us,' Felix said tersely, hoping to hurt. He felt muzzy with caffeine and tiredness. It had been a night of skim-sleeping, dominated by one of the relapse nightmares (*lifting a glass to the mouth, can't believe it!*), which now replaced the theatre nightmares (*a first rehearsal, forgot to prepare!*) as a recurrent fright in the small hours.

'To celebrate what?' asked Duma, rising from the floor, where he had just done a hundred press-ups.

'The first anniversary of the new government,' Felix replied, his courage dwindling.

'Is it a year?' Duma said, more to himself than Felix. 'Only a year.'

Felix finished stocking Duma's newly installed fridge with food. 'A long weekend, four days of festivities – of *sikukuu*. Town will be impossible. I'm going away. When I get back we must discuss your future.'

'Indeed,' replied Duma, who was in good spirits, refreshed by a long and untroubled sleep (Felix had watched from the air-duct for hours). He fetched a flywhisk from his cardboard box of belongings, and sat idly fanning the air. Felix was intrigued. Up until this point, dressed always in faded charcoal shorts, the man had looked more like Sub-lieutenant Cecil M. Duma of the King's African

Rifles rather than His Most Excellent and Revered Presence, et cetera. This was the first time Felix had seen any trappings of former glory: the flywhisk was clearly old and valuable, with heavy yellow ivory handle and black buffalo-tail switch. The potentate let it flop to and fro several times, then said, 'I'd like another shot. On the platform.'

'I don't think so.'

'Think on, then, think deeper. And next time we'll do it openly. We'll tell them it's me. Announce it beforehand.'

'Out of the question.'

'Think about it. Your theatre is in trouble, heh?'

Felix frowned. *Who had told him?*

'The attendance last night was poor. This is point number one,' he said, raising a little finger daintily. 'Point number two is that from the sound on the intercom –'

'We call it a tannoy!' Felix muttered irritably.

'From the sound of it, the little mongrel the little half-German half-caste – the lion-tamer, he sounds very popular. He has his eye on this building, I think. You can either abandon it to him, or contribute your own considerable imagination to saving it. Don't you owe it to yourself to try? To have . . . a last go?'

Felix froze. That phrase. Only the devil would know to use it.

Duma smiled. 'An interesting idea. If we told them it was me. Yes, I believe so. The lions on an open stage. The man so dangerous he has to be in a cage. Think about it. Think about your theatre packed to the rafters.'

'I'm thinking about it burned to the ground.'

Duma shrugged. 'Keep thinking. We'll talk again when you return. Have a good weekend.'

It was amazing: Felix had been dismissed by his prisoner. He started to hurry away, cursing the man's power, hating its pull.

'You've forgotten something,' Duma said quietly.

Turning back, Felix saw that the emperor was indicating his small, bright blue throne in the corner.

'Yes, sorry,' Felix mumbled, crossing to it. He opened the lid. Both men averted their eyes, from one another and from the inner container, which Felix now hoisted into the air. This discretion was an unspoken understanding between them, observed twice daily.

Out in the corridor, Felix still kept his gaze straight ahead and held his breath. One part of him was dying to take a peek, a sniff – you could make a fortune selling this stuff, to a local *féticheuse* or perhaps an overseas university – but another part resisted the temptation, out of pity for Duma, a kind of shame, an awareness of how the mighty hath fallen, reduced to the trusting helplessness of a patient, an inmate.

Returning the emptied and rinsed container to its bright blue shell, Felix said to Duma, 'One shan't, of course, be able to do this for the next few days while . . .'

'No,' Duma said, his manner brisk, untroubled.

Knowing him, thought Felix, he'll simply order his bowels to mark time, to go on to half rations, to observe a curfew.

'Or I could leave this with you,' Felix said nervously, holding up the key to the room.

'Thank you, no,' Duma replied instantly.

This was another unspoken understanding between them. The door would remain locked and Felix would take responsibility for opening and closing it. It was as though the dictator didn't trust himself with freedom. *Imagine if he walked out into the streets this weekend, walked into the Sikukuu!* Felix felt a kinship. To Duma, freedom was like drink. He dare not touch it.

Back upstairs, eager to leave the building now, Felix packed quickly – a carton of cigarettes, a shop-pack of chewing-gum, two kilos of buzz balls – then went to the fridge for a quick breakfast of Purple Passion Fruit ice-cream. (He'd cleared the contraband-market of their supplies of Chocolate Chip Cookie Dough, and was now experimenting with other flavours.)

As he poured himself a Coca-Cola, a small figure came to work alongside him; a boy-ghost aged eight.

A summer morning, the call of seagulls, sunlight falling across the kitchen table at home in Jamutiri Street, illuminating the mock-marble Formica, throwing huge shadows of his hands as they fix a cool drink, creating a magic light show. Long, child-big shadows – white, not black shadows – of fingers, glass and ice. A feeling of excitement. He will meet Charlie soon and spend today with him. The whole of today with Charlie! Charlie his best friend, Charlie the only person in his thoughts when he goes to sleep at night and when he wakes up in the morning, Charlie the love of his young life . . .

And now, many years later, he was going to meet Charlie's daughter, Alys, and spend not just today with her, but tomorrow and the day after, and the one after that, and the feeling was even more intense – it stopped the breath, it hurt slightly.

The plan was for Felix to stay with Alys up at the mansion, along with Noah and other staff, while Charlie went to the farm for the weekend.

It was one of *those* weekends, and Charlie was holding one of *those* parties.

It looked like he was master-minding a sporting event, or a rock festival, or a theme park!

Ground-plans and sketches covered the floor of Charlie's living-room, spilling out on to the sundeck. Wastebaskets and vases stood in for key locations, and paper arrows led to and fro, indicating a labyrinth of routes and chambers. Lists were attached to certain spots, lists of names, lists of supplies, as well as CDs, tapes, even old LPs of favourite film soundtracks: *Quo Vadis, Ben Hur, Spartacus, Satyricon*. Books were everywhere too, stacked or carefully isolated, the pages marked with coloured tags. Felix scanned the titles. *Dionysius and Bacchus, Erotic Treasures of Antiquity, Private Life In the Ancient World* – he'd noticed that one before – *A Complete History of the Orgy*, and Gibbon's *Decline and Fall*. A notepad lay across one volume – *Banquet of the Caesars* – showing that Charlie had copied out dozens of recipes; others were extracted from the satires of Horace and Persius. Museum catalogues and archaeology tomes displayed pictures of table settings, cutlery and drinking vessels, and sheaves of photocopies were piled alongside in plastic wallets.

The most extraordinary thing was that Charlie had done all this *on his own*. The evidence was everywhere: his handwriting, his extravagance, his nomadic untidiness – a job begun in a rush of enthusiasm, abandoned half-way through, another started nearby. These plans must have consumed him for months, and then, in the last few days, he had apparently assembled everything here, on the living-room floor, to survey the total picture. As Felix imagined his friend standing in the middle of it all, Charlie took shape, not as a figure of great power – impresario, playboy-host, emperor of revels – but someone littler, lonelier. If Emile were to see his son now, what would he make of it?

'Looks good, huhn?' Charlie asked, dashing through the door, freshly showered, wearing a towelling bathrobe. Flicking his hands dry, he began collecting the books and papers, piling them into the arms of a queue of servants who followed him round. 'This is gonna be the biggest and best of 'em all,' he said over his shoulder to Felix. The guest list at previous parties had been restricted to the non-Af community, with a few dozen good time gals 'n' guys to make up numbers. But this time the doors were open wide. Charlie's circle were allowed to invite whomever they pleased – associates were flying in from all over the country, from neighbouring states, even one or two from abroad – and Charlie's staff had spent the last few months recruiting an army of beautiful people, scouring the market-place and harbour, hunting like the slave traders of old. And, indeed, those who were selected had to submit to being stripped, washed and medically examined. But there the resemblance ended, for these slaves were to be paid and pampered. These slaves were to be free, free to dominate their partners in the games ahead, or not, if they chose; the whole party was to be a party of freedom, reflecting the national festivities.

'Oh, honey, come along,' purred Kaz, suddenly appearing at Felix's side.

'Not if you paid me,' he chuckled, covering his surprise at finding her here. He waved to Alys, who was playing on the sundeck. 'I'm cast as Nanny for the weekend.'

'Aw, c'mon,' Kaz said again, slowly drawing her fingernails down his spine. 'Come to our wicked ol' faaaaaarm.'

Our? Were Kaz and Charlie an item again? They'd certainly been up to something all night . . . Kaz, no doubt, helping Charlie with his pharmaceutical research – among other things! Their mouths were rubbed red and their stares were dull, the whites of their eyes turned fleshy. They reeked of it too. Not unwashed – Kaz was just out of the shower too – but giving off an over-warm smell, a sex smell, Felix presumed. Dear me, he thought, it's already in the air and the party hasn't even begun.

He felt a surge of anger. Kaz and Charlie. They both liked him, *loved* him they would probably say, yet not as much as they loved one another, loved whatever it was between them, whatever they did together, or enabled the other to do, *whatever it was*. Well, they were welcome to it.

While Charlie went to dress, Kaz drifted outside, towards the helipad, and Felix trailed after her. They walked along the mountain-top, gazing at the sea. 'This place . . . this morning . . .' Kaz said to Felix in her own voice, without the joky drawl she adopted with Charlie. 'Never thought I'd be here, in this part of the world, by now in my life. Home . . . it was so full of hate, I was sure I'd been born in the wrong place. It was a mistake, God had just made a mistake. So I'd go somewhere else, America, I suppose, and there, at the airport, coming to meet me, would be Kaz. Kaz at long last.' They stepped aside, to let a procession of servants pass, carrying supplies to the helicopter: boxes of Charlie's books, crates of food and drink, trunks with labels from overseas film costumiers and prop-makers. Kaz strayed off the path, closer to the cliff edge. Felix took hold of her arm – she was quite tipsy, he suspected. 'But then . . . like this morning . . . at least you know *where* you are. See what I'm saying? You might not know *who* you are, but you know *where* you are. And guess what? It's not so bad after all. Why did I want to get away in the first place? Y'know . . . smell it!'

Felix inhaled deeply. The air was exquisite up here, glittering sea air – so fresh and bright, it could have been through a filtering system; it was millionaire's air.

'You know why it smells so good?' Kaz asked.

Felix laughed. 'Yes! Because Charlie owns one of the best –'

'No, no,' she growled impatiently. '*Uhuru*. It's the smell of *uhuru*!' She peered at him intently, struck by a realisation, and now her tone grew more familiar and mocking. 'I guess, for you guys, nothing much has changed.'

'Pardon?'

'With or without Duma. Life's kinda the same for you.'

'To whom do you refer?' he asked icily.

'You. You honkies, you honky-tonks, you expat fat-cats, you *wasetla*, you *mzunye*, you non-niggers, you non-Afs, you, you, *you!*' She grinned at him dangerously. 'This weekend, brother, this weekend . . . Think about it. Think 'bout this time last year. This time *two years* ago . . .' She stopped. The tears had come as suddenly as the smiles. They weren't tears of celebration. She tried to control them, but the emotion was huge. She bent over, holding herself. 'It's here, Felix,' she gasped. 'Here, right in the middle of me . . . so sore, so sore.'

'Kaz . . .' he sighed, stroking her back. 'It happened a long time ago. You have to start getting over –'

'I know, but I can't, ehh?, I'll go mad, ehh?, I don't know what to do, it hurts so much now. Maybe before, maybe I didn't let myself feel it before. There was no point, no point in crying and shouting, it was too big, Duma was too big, it was like trying to shout at a mountain, and it was falling on everyone, the mountain, it was hurting everyone, not you people up here, but –'

'Stop saying that!'

'It's true! He was hurting *us* – his people – *us*! And you can feel as sorry as you like, but you'll never feel what I feel!' She shook her head slowly. 'Felix, I know you're my friend, OK, I know you're trying to help, but it's so sore, *so sore*. It's right in here, it's like birth, it's the worst pain you can know, but this time there's no joy at the other end, there *is* no other end.' She stayed bent over, rocking, hugging herself, knuckles white. 'My baby, my baby, so sore, so sore.'

Felix looked away. She was right. He had never known pain like this. Missing someone like this.

'I'm still on the case, y'know,' he said, in a dull voice. 'We'll still track him down.'

She leaned on her knees, nodding slowly, without conviction. Then she mopped her face with one hand, wiped it on the grass, and ran unsteadily towards the helicopter. Felix filled his cheeks, and blew out slowly. He was glad Charlie was taking Kaz out of town.

Now Charlie and Alys came charging from the house, racing one another to the helipad. Charlie pretended to trip, so she could win. Instead she came back and climbed on top of him, kissing goodbye. Felix watched. How they whispered and cuddled, how well they knew one another, every movement, every sound. There it was again – the thing Kaz was grieving for, a link that was phenomenal, unbreakable. And Felix would never experience it, never understand it fully. He scowled, mourning his own loss.

Then Alys ran to him, jumped into his arms, and buried her head, shrieking with excitement, while the helicopter, manned by her father, took off, blasting them with its down-draught.

It's Hurricane Mary, thought Felix.

As the aircraft rose into the sky, Alys became thoughtful, tilting her head all the way back, lolling it from side to side. Was she remembering her mother? Felix wondered. Was she remembering Isabeau, who died in a plane crash? Impossible. Alys was only a few months old when it happened. And yet, that look in her eyes now, as though something lived inside her, some small sense of it.

Alys reached towards the departing helicopter, then gasped as Felix threw her into the air. '*And* Lys is going too – *no*, she's not!' He caught her, threw again, threw and caught. '*And* she is – *no*, she's not . . .'

nineteen

As Noah reversed the Land Cruiser out of the mansion's driveway, taking them to the beach for the day, Felix gave Alys a goodnight-type kiss and began seeking a comfortable place to rest his head. *Injured with drink, injured with recovery,* he thought happily, surrendering to the rush of drowsiness. This sometimes came with such intensity that he wondered whether, since returning from America, he'd been bitten by a tsetse fly. But no, it was too pleasant, this feeling, particularly today, its brew thickened by the exhausting events of last night and the previous few weeks. Opening any new show was a feat in itself, but this one! *To have got the emperor onstage!* Ah, yes, here it came now, the delicious sleeping sickness . . . irresistible . . . a force rising from below, draining his strength, his will, excusing him from duty, freeing him utterly . . .

Noah turned down the steep mountainside. The angle of the road was incredible. As Felix fell gently against his window, his groggy vision was flooded by a tilting view of water, only it wasn't the ocean below, it was Lake Tidhamulala on a morning two decades earlier, the morning after his very first show at the Alex. He fell and kept falling, it seemed, both himself now and himself then, both sleep-struck, both felled by work, work, work, landing finally in long, soft grass on the lakeside, and lying there, a ghost easing in and out of his body with each slow breath . . .

The morning is beautiful, *oh, look at the morning.* One of those mornings when you shade your gaze not from the sun but a blueness of sky and water. The world seems fresh-washed.

And people, friends, look at them. Felix's viewpoint, with eyelids never quite closed, never quite open, is pleasantly familiar. It's like being a benevolent spy . . . it's how he spends a lot of time, at work and play, in the dark of the auditorium or the silvery gloom of the air-ducts.

Charlie is nearby, lounging on a deck-chair in front of his latest toy: an NEC portable television. Cube-shaped, militaristic-looking, it's become popular in the States since the end of the Vietnam war. Charlie's young chauffeur, Noah, stands on the roof of the Land Cruiser, angling a tall H-shaped aerial in different directions. They're trying to pick up a signal from the other side of the lake, which borders a neighbouring country. Over there they're showing coverage of the Olympic Games, currently in progress overseas. Duma's regime has been banned from participating in the Games, and has consequently banned them from State TV. Instead, a documentary is being shown this morning – about post-revolutionary Russian agriculture – and Noah can't seem to find anything else.

Charlie grimaces as yet another tractor thunders across the screen. 'Aw, man! There's only one person who'd enjoy this in the whole fucking shithole country and he's the one person not watching!' He indicates Emile, a distant figure swimming in the lake.

'Ah!' curses Isabeau, whose camera is trained on a group of men spear-fishing from a palm log raft. 'He's spoiling it. Call him back.'

'You call him back. He listens when you call.'

Isabeau is French-Canadian. In spite of her delicate looks – ginger-haired and fine-boned – she is one of those foreign women  whom Africa never succeeds in frightening. She currently spends long periods in the *bundu*, on foot or in a little ranch-hopper plane, photographing local tribes and wildlife for an American magazine. She and Charlie met and married as students at UCLA, and only returned to Africa a year ago.

'What an asshole,' Charlie comments now, watching Emile clamber aboard the fishermen's raft. 'What *is* he trying to prove?'

'Oh, no!' laments Isabeau, giving up on her shot.

'Asshole!'

a book about Africa for non africans?

A veil of sleep falls across Felix, and the next time he looks, Kaz has arrived. She's standing above him, being introduced to Isabeau:

'And she played Mary in the show last night,' Charlie explains. 'Twice. Madonna and Magdalene.' The second name brings a smile to his lips.

Awed by Isabeau's elegant, alien French presence, Kaz speaks quietly. 'I'm late, sorry.' She indicates a sleeping baby tied to her back. 'Had to fetch him from my mother,' she says, lying. Neighbours look after her baby when she performs. Since she joined the company at the Alex, her family have decided she is either a prostitute or a witch, and shun her.

'All the way from town – you walked?!' exclaims Isabeau, appraising the tall, dramatic figure before her, whose dark skin is 'blacked-up', so Charlie says, to disguise her tribal identity from Duma's policemen. 'You're not late, it's just a picnic,' adds Isabeau, gesturing towards the fishermen. 'We haven't even caught lunch yet.'

Kaz nudges Felix with her toe. 'And the boss?'

Charlie laughs. 'Zonked, drunk, happy.'

'Attaboy!' she says, joyfully slipping into Charlie's accent. She kneels next to Felix, then flops to one side. 'Ugh, still hasn't washed! That's like a fortnight's shit on him.' She thumps Felix lightly. 'You stink, mister, you stink!'

Felix doesn't stir. He is hoping that if he stays still enough they'll talk about him. Before long, his wish is granted . . .

'The show last night,' Isabeau says to Kaz. 'It was very courageous.'

'Courageous?' says Kaz.

'Ah, yes. I've been in this country only a little, uh?, but it's the best example of tenderness that I see. Unsentimental humanity. Always real. That actor who plays Christ . . .'

'Mr Mmalo.'

'. . . he's just an ordinary man. A bit fat, a bit bald. Felix even lets him wear glasses! Courageous. And the way he stages things! The multitudes. You know the photographs of Salgado? Your show makes pictures like Salgado! Multitudes, real people doing real work, in the air too, up and up! You see whole biblical cities. Abroad this would be a sensation!'

Kaz stares back steadily, unsure of Isabeau, then says, 'Glad you liked it.' She walks down to the lake's edge, untying the blanket from her middle. Squatting on the sand, which is yellow as butter, she dabs water on the baby's forehead, cooling him after the long walk, then opens her shirt to feed him.

On the television screen, the picture suddenly starts jumping, peeling away, coming and going. Charlie is about to praise Noah when he looks again. 'Aww, no, aww, shit,' he moans. 'Bring back the tractors!'

'*You*,' Duma says from the screen, 'I am hereby, herewith, and in person, informing *you* of an important new development affecting national security . . .'

'Asshole!' jeers Charlie, throwing a paper cup.

'Clown!' adds Isabeau. As Duma proceeds to outline a new commandment – this one makes it illegal to parp your car horn at traffic cops – Isabeau and Charlie turn away from the television, and watch Kaz feeding the baby. They are both thinking the same thing. When Duma interrupted programmes last week, it was to decree that all those of mixed race register their address at the nearest police station or army post.

'This one is *métisse*, uh?' Isabeau asks Charlie, indicating the child. 'The father was white, I think.'

'Looks so,' says Charlie. 'One of her Yankee boyfriends at the embassy, I guess. But it's not a problem anyway. If anyone starts hassling her, she just has to come to Felix, who comes to me, who goes to someone, who makes sure it's not a problem.' He cleans his sunglasses, squinting at Kaz's breasts as she lowers the baby.

Duma repeats his traffic-cop announcement in KiSwahili, then says stiffly, 'That is the end of this broadcast.' It takes a few moments before his image fades, during which the emperor sits forward, brow clenched, his gaze drilling into the camera lens, as though seeing into the home of each and every one of his subjects. Then the Russian tractors return, drawing another groaning laugh from the picnic party.

Isabeau sits on Charlie's lap, and they kiss deeply. Kaz notices, and stays at the water's edge. She strikes the surface gently with open palms, in rhythmic combinations, playing it like a drum. The lake is so silent that her soft percussion travels for miles, almost echoing, across the vast blue scene.

Felix listens, drifting, and when he surfaces again, Kaz is back among the group, now singing softly, rocking the baby, her forehead touching his: '*Msidhani mahaluti . . . Kabila sikusaliti.*' The baby half opens his eyes. They smile at one another. She sings: '*Ingawaje ni haiba . . . Mimi sina asiliye.*'

'These words,' says Isabeau, 'what do they mean?'

'They're from a poem, a Shaaban Robert poem,' answers Kaz. 'He's explaining the confusion of his crazy name – he's Swahili, ehh?, but his name is Muslim and Christian, ehh? He is saying, "Don't think I'm a mongrel." He is saying, "This is a privilege I can't claim."' She smiles. 'He is a good poet.'

'And this little guy, what's *his* name?' Isabeau asks, stretching out to take the baby. Her reach is open, long, eager. It is a distinctive gesture, which always touches Felix.

'Zach,' replies Kaz, handing him over.

'Zach,' Isabeau repeats softly. 'Ah, you're so good, Zach, look at you, you rest so peacefully.' Stroking his hair, she says to Kaz, 'We want to have children, we want this very much, but so far no luck.'

Embarrassed by her candour, Charlie gets up and walks away.

He paces restlessly. After a while he comes to a stop, and stands glaring at Emile in the lake.

'It's like having an X-ray machine for a father,' he often says to Felix. Home has come as a shock to Charlie after his overseas training, and he complains that Emile is watching his every step; 'My daddy the shrink!' And Emile is no ordinary psychotherapist. His passion for Freud is matched by one for Marx. Counselling needn't be the preserve of the privileged, he argues, and devotes half his time to working among the poor, helping them cope with the violence of their lives, distributing comfort, food, and generous portions of his wealth. He has been bullying Charlie to follow his example, and Charlie has tried, tried valiantly, but in his heart he knows that a different kind of doctor is needed for the disease and famine beyond the perimeters of the non-Af community. The fights with Emile leave Charlie with a maddening feeling of shame.

'"Mountains will heave in childbirth and a silly little mouse will be born."'

Felix's nostrils prickle . . . the rich, sour smell of local *bangi* . . .

Peering through his lids now, he sees that a big three-skinner joint is being passed from Isabeau to Kaz, and that Charlie is wandering around, reading from a book about the Roman poets. 'C'mon, try and guess who said that,' he asks the women. They stare back blankly. 'Horace! Y'know how we normally think, Horace just equals the happy medium? The golden mean. Well, this book portrays him as kinda . . . angrier. Says that, yeah, sure, we've gotta try and find a happy medium, but we've gotta fight ourselves to get there. Says that we're all mad, fatally flawed. Who would've thought it, huhn? Not Juvenal or Petronius. But good ol' Horace, good ol' flag-waving, wisecracking Horace. "Mountains will heave in childbirth and a silly little mouse will be born."'

'Oh, *Sharl*, stop,' says Isabeau, addressing her husband in a way that Felix will later adopt. She turns to Kaz. 'He is trying to show off, uh?, trying to cover up his real interest in that wicked old dame, ancient Rome. You know what I'm saying?'

Kaz ducks her head and draws on the joint. 'Dunno much about it at all.'

'Don't bother, please, take my advice. It's so male! The architecture, the statues, all so boom-boom-boom!, even the philosophy. You know what one of their dirty words is? *Softness*. Can you imagine a society that makes softness a bad thing?'

'They mean extravagance,' Charlie protests angrily. 'They mean *luxuria* –'

'Ah, no, no, my darling, you love the –'

'I love the grandeur. Life on such a scale! I love –'

'You love the sin,' chuckles Isabeau. She turns to Kaz. 'He finds it sexy, all the boom-boom-boom.'

'Yeah, sure, it *is* sexy,' concedes Charlie, reddening. 'I mean, the Romans tried everything under the sun. But the point is, they tried to fight against it, these appetites of theirs – of ours! *Excess* was as much a dirty word as *softness*.' He waves his book at the women. 'They tried to find the *golden mean*.'

Kaz leans forward to hand him the joint. 'But, sorry, what if there isn't one? This golden mean. Why is excess a dirty word?' She indicates Felix. 'This guy here, it's the only thing he knows. Excess. Works us so hard at the theatre that everyone hates his guts. Oh, sure they do,' she adds, noticing their expressions of surprise. 'He's like a maniac. He works like today is the last day of existence, and we gotta finish before the world does. No time for niceties, no time to be careful with people, we jus' gotta do it, do it! And then, when he's finished working, then he starts drinking, and he drinks like a maniac too –'

'And so?' interrupts Isabeau. 'What are you saying, please?'

Kaz raises her shoulders. 'I'm saying that last night the audience stood up and cheered. That's all I'm saying.'

The joint reaches Isabeau. She slowly wafts it over Felix's face. 'D'you think he's listening to us, really?' They all smile at Felix. Isabeau touches his mouth. 'When he greets you, he kisses like this . . .' She purses her lips tightly, making them into a wrinkled little bump. 'He kisses like an old man or a kid, saying, "Oh, I don't think I like this"!' They laugh. Isabeau smokes, scrutinising Felix's closed eyes. Then, speaking in a whisper, she asks Kaz, 'Is he straight or gay? *Sharl* and I are always discussing this issue. What d'you think?'

Kaz laughs, whispering back, 'I think he doesn't know.'

'Ah, then, he's gay! When a man says he doesn't know, he means he doesn't want to know. He's gay!'

'Maybe,' says Charlie, entering the game. 'Or . . .' He glances at Felix, then mouths to the others, 'weirder than gay.'

'*Weirder?*' they mouth back, giggling.

A sudden splash brings them round to the lake. Emile has either dived or fallen off the fishermen's raft. He swims away from it, then floats on his back, basking.

'*Now* I can get my picture!' exclaims Isabeau, and dashes away along the shoreline.

'See that little peninsula?' Charlie asks Kaz. 'See – there. It's where she's heading. She'll lie down, take her pictures right along the level of the water, the flat of the lake. I know her style. She'll click away for twenty minutes, lying like that.'

Kaz turns to him, the corner of her mouth flickering lightly. 'Twenty minutes?'

'At least.'

They sit in silence, a new, strange silence. Charlie puffs deeply on the joint then hands it over. Kaz inhales, eyes fixed on the lake. When she speaks now, it is without the American gloss. 'Wherever you see water, you are seeing a snake.'

'A snake?'

'*Ahm*, the movement of water . . . a snake.'

'OK, right.'

'My aunt used to tell us how a snake carried the great Creator around while he was making the world. Each night when they stopped, the snake shit got left and it grew into the mountains. So anyway, they travelled on and on, and eventually the Creator finished his work. But now he saw that there's too many mountains and trees and big animals for the earth to carry. So he thinks, How can I stop the land from sinking into all the water? He's picturing the earth, you must realise, like a flat thing, a kind of tray.' She glances at Charlie, checking his attention. 'So he asks the snake to coil itself, with its tail in its mouth, to support the earth. You know the *kata*, the rings, the padded head-rings we use to carry loads? The snake becomes like one of these, carrying the earth. And wherever you see water, this lake, or the sea, streams, pools, wherever you see it, you are seeing the coils of the snake slowly moving.'

Charlie nods. 'So to your people a snake is kinda . . . OK?'

She looks up at him, wrist on her forehead, hand drooping, a canopy of shade hiding her eyes. 'Mmm.'

'We see it differently.'

'Sure, oh, sure,' she says, touching a small wooden crucifix round her neck. 'I told Felix last night, I said now we must do some shows of the first part of the Bible.'

'Uh-huhn. And will you make the snake good or bad?'

She grins. 'Maybe we'll just make it a snake.'

'A snake in the grass,' he says, his voice very dry. She follows his eyeline to a dip behind them, where there's a tall screen of silvery grass.

'D'you think there're any snakes in there?' he asks.

'It would be a risk to find out,' she answers.

'It would,' he says, with a little laugh.

'I thought we agreed . . .'

'We did. But I must. Today. After last night. Watching you last night. You were mind-blowing. Please.'

She smiles to herself. He holds his breath. Suddenly Felix gasps in his sleep. They both start, then give jittery chuckles. Kaz finishes the joint, then nods towards the baby. 'And him?'

'Noah's here.' Charlie drops to his knees, takes the child from her arms, places it near Felix, and whispers, 'Let the two innocents sleep.' He crawls into the long grass, pauses at the last moment, and wags his arse like an animal. She laughs and follows.

Almost immediately the picture on the television starts jumping again, and now the muffled cheer of a mighty crowd is heard. Noah turns in delight. He is surprised to find Charlie gone. Carefully propping the aerial in place, he clambers down from the jeep's roof and peers at the screen. The sun is too bright now, he can't see much, but this doesn't stop him hopping from foot to foot with satisfaction. He turns up the volume. Another cheer – thousands upon thousands of voices united in excitement as some great feat of endurance is played out in the arena before them. Felix stirs and gasps again, this time in awe, seeing a vision in his sleep. Noah quickly returns the volume to its lower setting. He is about to settle down to watch the Games, when he hears a new sound. Above the lake a military helicopter has appeared, on a routine patrol of the district. Noah quickly bundles the television and its aerial into the jeep. Now he remembers something else. Kaz's baby asleep on the grass . . . its face, chest and hands are open to the sky, the skin a light brown colour. The helicopter approaches. Noah doesn't like it. It's like a human head. It tilts inquisitively, it appears to be thinking, it comes closer. Moving with a lazy, untroubled stride, Noah fetches Charlie's book from the deckchair, casually pushing the baby closer to Felix as he goes. Felix murmurs drowsily and collects the child in one arm. Lost in deep sleep, it responds, tiny fingers closing round a fold of Felix's shirt, face burying in the warmth. As Noah's pulse keeps time with its hammering noise, the helicopter hovers directly overhead. It looks down on a white man asleep with his child in his arms. It flies away. Noah mutters thanks.

Felix stares dreamily at nothing, farts slowly, shifts the thing in his arms a little higher, kisses it, and drifts on . . .

'*Jambo* Noah*, habari yako?*'

'*Sijambo*, Emile*, na wewe?*' replies Noah cheerfully, as Emile climbs out of the water. The old boy amuses him, with his attempts to talk KiSwahili, to fish with the men on the lake, to lecture anyone who'll listen on the merits of their mad emperor, as well as two great men called Fred and Mark, or squatting on his haunches like a native now, as he rummages for a pack of cigarettes among his clothes.

Suddenly Emile goes still. He has spotted Felix and the child. Noah wonders what he has done wrong, and moves away.

In fact, Emile is struck with wonderment. Before him is a symbol of everything that he teaches. He will often refer to it in years to come, when Felix becomes a client: 'I once saw you asleep with a baby in your arms, my dear. I can't remember now whose it was, but I didn't realise it was a baby – I thought it was *you*. It had the same thick black hair. When I went into the water you were alone on the grass, and when I came out there was this smaller you wrapped in your own arms. It was like an image of total peace, a man embracing his younger, vulnerable self, saying, "This is who I am, it is precious, I will protect it." And even though this interpretation was only in my head, you know something? I've never seen you looking happier.'

Emile is so moved by the sight that now, as Charlie pops out from the long silver grass, where, he explains, he was peeing, Emile goes forward to hug him. He hasn't held Charlie since childhood, a peculiar fact between them that goes against everything Emile believes. Reaching out his arms, he covers the awkwardness by asking, 'Where's Isabeau?'

The innocent question ignites Charlie's fear – *was he seen with Kaz?* – and he snaps, 'How the fuck should I know? She was trying to get a shot of the fishing, but you kept fucking spoiling it.' Charlie starts shouting now: 'What are you trying to prove? You're like a white Uncle Tom, you're ridiculous, you make a fool of yourself, a fool of me!'

He strides off. Emile is stunned. Over the next few hours his shock hardens. Charlie has never spoken to him like that before.

Nobody has. Although Emile stays for the picnic, he doesn't speak another word to Charlie that day. The day becomes a week, a year. By then neither party can remember when or why it started, but they have stopped speaking altogether.

As Felix dozes on by the lakeside, he dreams a strange dream in which a father and son meet after a long separation and fail to recognise one another. If it is a glimpse of the future, his dreams spare him the others: the fate of Kaz's baby, and of Charlie's wife – just months after they finally have a child, Alys.

'Look what they've caught!' someone cries. 'Look!'

Even Felix obeys, half lifting his head from the grass.

His friends are gathered on the shoreline, watching the fishermen haul a colossal, three-hundred-pound golden Nile perch from the lake; an African giant possessed of almost vulgar beauty, a goldfish-whale. In its first few moments on the land, with life only just leaving its body, and a radiance of sun and water on its astonishing orange and white skin, the creature's presence overwhelms the humans, who step back, the hair prickling on their arms.

'The cheeks are best, very sweet!' Noah informs the party as the fishermen prepare to barbecue the fish.

'The cheeks are a delicacy without parallel,' Emile agrees flamboyantly, addressing everyone except Charlie.

'Ah, then we must save them for the director,' says Isabeau, unaware that Felix has sat up behind them. 'As a final bravo for last night!'

twenty

.

'Look, look!'

Felix woke and looked. He saw Isabeau in goblin form . . . a miniature Isabeau tugging his arm . . .

'Look,' she said again. 'Look what I've brought.'

'Ah,' he said groggily, realising he was in the back seat of the Land Cruiser. He kissed the top of Alys's head, his eyes filling.

'No-o-o!' she said, pushing him away. '*Look!*'

'Thought there was a horrid stink,' he said, wrinkling his face as he saw one of the wild-dog pups among the beach towels.

'She's called Mimi, and – ask me what else she's called – ask me!'

'What else is she called?'

'She's called the runt. Daddy calls her the runt. And she's my baby.'

How can something so small and soft be so uncute? wondered Felix, as he stared at the pup's bat ears, its oily black snout, its coat with that sleek to slimy look, yellow and charcoal, sprinkled with feathery white spots like a disease. The pup's peculiar, distinctive odour permeated the back seat of the jeep, and stayed there, a blemish in the atmosphere.

In the distance, something similar hung over one section of town, where a pall of dirty smoke revealed that the festivities were already sparking out of control.

Then the jeep turned a corner, the town disappeared from view,

Felix wound down his window, and the day was perfect again.

Fulfilling all his predictions – and prayers – not another soul was to be seen on this stretch of the seaboard. The coast road was carved precariously between towering red cliffs on one side and, on the other, a steep drop to the ocean, where clear water showed white sand beds and apricot coral reefs, gradually sloping to turquoise depths further off, a peacock sea; the blue-green ripples fringed with purple and gold . . . the algae tides you get at this time of year, the algae bloom.

By the time the curving road brought Felix round to face his hometown again, it was far enough away not to show any carnival fires, or else these merged with the clouds that often draped the Kwatokuu. Pure white billows, they spilled through a cleft in the crater ridge, as though in imitation of the old volcano, but instead of lava, they cast luminous shadows onto the rock slopes, a travelling mirage, a vision, a mystery descending on the landmass, creating powerful depth there, and making you feel you were being offered a bowl, a colossal bowl. It was very primitive, it roared at you. Then, half-way down, and along a straight line, the cloud spectacle vanished. This had something to do with a change in air temperature or currents; Charlie had once explained the phenomenon to Felix, who hadn't listened, preferring to leave it as an enigma, a miracle.

Since returning from the Long Island clinic, Felix found himself viewing his birthplace as a visitor might. Seen through sober eyes, the crater and its weather were even more incredible, more gloriously mutable than it had seemed to a drunk. The locals moved around under the spectacle, the rolling, disappearing cloud act, without seeming to notice, or perhaps just giving it a passing glance. They saw it every day. Like the giant golden perches in the lake, the mountainscape was unremarkable, a common-or-garden miracle, a two-bit wonder of the world. Felix found himself watching it almost furtively, almost shamed by his astonishment. It stopped his breath, it touched his heart, it made him doubt his sanity. To think he'd been brought up here! No wonder he had read epic stories as a child, created epic theatre now, was racked by epic ambitions. No wonder Charlie was fixated on the Roman Empire. No wonder

Duma had delusions of grandeur, and believed that this land belonged to him. *How dare he?* thought Felix. *It's mine.*

He flinched. Looking down, he found Mimi, the wild-dog pup, wriggling into his lap. Checking that Alys wasn't watching, he bunched his fist and took aim . . .

'What did I tell you? Not another car here!' Felix boasted to Noah and Alys as they drew into the parking area above the beach.

Great shoulders of bush and palm trees, their trunks fixed in gale-force curves, leaned towards the sea, taking your eye there, making you want to run down the slope.

Known as Pembe Cove, this had been one of Felix's favourite retreats during his teenage years, when he felt he was losing Charlie to other, more powerful forces, like sports teams and girlfriends. Felix would often cycle here alone, and spend hours pacing up and down the perfect semicircle of spotless sand. With late Miss Rosewood's talk of overseas, overseas, ringing in his ears, he felt imprisoned by Africa. *Smack, shush, hiss*, went the surf, *smack, shush, hiss*. And then he would bathe naked, thrilled by a notion put in his head by Charlie's father – that strange man from the Belgian Congo, Emile – who once mentioned that when you enter an ocean, any ocean, you are instantly connected to the whole planet. Felix would eventually masturbate into the clear warm water, and watch his seed drift away towards the horizon.

Today, instead of running down to the beach, Felix led Alys along the cliff-top, where tall white dunes rose against a lovely, hard blue sky.

For his goddaughter's fifth birthday, Felix had commissioned the Alex's wardrobe mistress to copy the little frock and bonnet in Monet's painting, *The Artist's Garden at Vétheuil*. He'd dressed her in this outfit today, adding a small French parasol, another gift from another occasion. Processing along the path now, Alys sometimes displayed the parasol grandly, basking in the glowing shade, and sometimes grew bored and threw it aside. Noah was there to pick it up and carry it alongside his AK47. Mimi brought up the rear, struggling over the sand with a busy little run, her overlong white tail dragging behind. Felix glanced back now and then, hoping to find the pup lost or taken by one of the bigger seabirds.

'Where are we going?' Alys asked.

'To church,' laughed Felix.

'What's a church?'

'A Christian shul.'

'What's a shul?' asked Alys, the daughter of an atheist.

'A Jewish church.'

'What's a – ?'

'Ask your father.'

'Hm!' said Alys suspiciously, then stopped at a shrub that grew plentifully along the cliff-top, hung with closed pink flowers, globular and puffy. 'They look like Daddy's balls,' she observed: the daughter of a doctor and naturist.

It was Felix's turn to go 'Hm!' He led the expedition down a stone stairway, its treads lost in sand, then across the shoreline, where the rocks were padded with seaweed, and finally knelt at a hole in the cliff-face. Peering in, laughing with wonderment, he beckoned Alys.

Imitating his expression even before she'd seen anything, Alys walked upright through the hole. The men followed in a crouching waddle, Noah carrying Mimi.

Beyond, in wet green light, was a vast cavern. It resembled a cathedral, with a high domed ceiling and a level floor serrated in regular, smooth rows, like the remnants of pews. The far end was open to the sea, which swelled through the entrance, each wave heaving light into the gloom.

'We're being blessed, Lys,' said Felix. 'Blessed by your daddy's Greater Power – Nature. We're being blessed and we'll be happy for the rest of the day.'

Alys seemed less sure of the place. She thought she felt something drip on her, and decided she needed her parasol back. Retrieving it from Noah's arms, she noticed that Mimi was looking forlorn, and transported her onto the floor. The pup slipped around on the smooth rocks, then began its weird, bird-like twittering.

'She's hungry,' Alys declared. 'D'you want me to show you how she eats?' Before Felix could refuse, she said, 'Give me some food. Something for me.'

Felix dug around in his pockets, but could only find buzz balls. 'These'll be very bitter for you,' he said, handing one over reluctantly.

'Watch me, watch me!' she commanded. She chewed the chocolate, pulling a face, then went on all fours next to Mimi, and ballooned her cheeks. The pup's twittering became more frantic, and it went into a high-speed display, alternating between bowing submissively with flattened ears, and reaching up to lick the side of Alys's mouth. She let the masticated buzz ball dribble onto the floor, where it was gleefully consumed by Mimi.

'How charming,' said Felix grimly. 'Thanks, Lys.'

'Her real mummy does that with dead bucks.'

'Does she really? Rightio, onwards.'

As they crawled back through the hole, Felix said, 'I've just remembered, I think there's another route to the beach. Along the shoreline. There's a sort of rock path. Takes one all the way back.' Noah looked in the direction of Pembe Cove, hidden behind the bulge of the cliff, and frowned. 'It's fine,' Felix said. 'I did it a million times when I was a boy. You go back along the top, we'll go back this way, you take the high road, we'll take the low, see who gets there afore whom. Have a sort of race, what?'

'Yesss!' squealed Alys.

Noah protested, 'But Mr Charlie, he was saying I must never leave you for a single bloody second.'

'Mr Charlie will be told that we couldn't've been bloody safer,' replied Felix, touched by Noah's loyalty. 'And anyway you can keep watch as you go.' He pointed to the cliff path above. Noah sighed and shook his head, but nevertheless began to plod up the stone stairs. 'Wait, take the dog!' said Felix.

'No,' said Alys quietly, in a way that Felix recognised and feared.

'Darling, someone's going to have to carry it, and that someone is not going to be me.'

'Felix,' she said, directing her loveliest, long-lashed gaze at him, 'please.'

'Lys, I love you with all my heart, but I am not carrying that thing. It stinks!'

She hesitated, chin trembling, then decided that instead of crying, she would devise other punishments. 'C'mon, Mimi,' she said, lifting the pup. 'You don't stink, you're nice, you can come with me,' and she set off on the walk, whispering to the pup.

Felix rolled his eyes, then followed, thinking, If that fucking bat-dog-mutant spoils one more fucking thing today I'm going to fucking drown it!

Determined to enjoy himself, he lifted his face to the sunshine and fresh sea air. 'Clean, clean!' he whispered happily. He looked at Alys. From behind she could be Isabeau – a small Isabeau or Isabeau viewed from a distance. Quickening his step, Felix gently touched Alys's shoulder. Without looking up, she gave a kind of welcoming shrug, acknowledging the gesture, treating it like an apology. Then, reaching out with her free arm, the other carrying Mimi like a rolled-up beach towel, she took his hand. His heart soared.

The path led onto a rock shelf, which followed the line of the cliff like a second, lower lip, just above the ocean, a magical route shining with a film of water, and pitted with pretty tidal pools: clear undersea craters, Lilliputian-sized, populated by tiny transparent fish and luscious mauve anemones.

Noticing that they were now invisible to Noah – the head of the cliff overhung its foot – Felix wondered when last he and Alys had been so wonderfully, secretly alone.

'It's like we're pioneers, Lys,' he said quietly.

'What's it mean?'

'Like we're discovering this place, this country, for the first time, like we're the first people here.'

'Like Adam and Eve,' she remarked, half remembering her first visit to the theatre.

'That's right. The only people in the world. Would you like that?'

Alys didn't reply, but smiled to herself.

She's very wise, he thought, and very cruel, and very powerful.

Turning a corner, they were no longer alone. The rock-shelf path dipped down under a small sandy beach, where a boy lay on his back, flying a kite. A few years older than Alys, white-skinned, with long dark hair, he was completely absorbed in the kite, which an air current held suspended just a few feet above him. It was odd. He didn't seem to notice the arrival of Felix and Alys, nor their journey past him. He had a radiant expression, staring at the hovering toy as though it was something else, something less solid, an idea or dream. He spooled it out. Suddenly whipping in the breeze, it made a noise like an old man whistling through his gums.

Felix looked past the kite to Noah, who was visible again, and waved, while thinking, How stupid he looks, with his rifle held like that – it's only a boy!

But lowering his gaze again, Felix discovered that both the kite and its owner were gone. He chewed his lip. That was *very* fast.

'Who was that, Lys?' Felix asked.

'Noah,' she said.

'No, I mean . . .'

He faltered, eyes fixed on the trail the boy had left in the sand. The footprints were faint, with big bounding spaces in between, and on either side were smaller, deeper dash-marks, like from crutches. Felix glanced round. The atmosphere wasn't frightening, but it wasn't quite normal either. He decided not to dwell on his present train of thought.

The rock shelf resumed on the other side of the little beach, the cliff tilted forward again, Noah disappeared from view, and they walked on. But round the next corner, they were forced to stop again, abruptly.

The shelf was broken by a jagged gap. During the three decades since Felix had last taken this path, the sea had eaten away a short stretch of it.

'Oh, ffffiddlesticks!' muttered Felix.

'Fiddlesticks!' echoed Alys. She set down Mimi. The pup crouched back on its hindquarters, confused by the shadowy, wet atmosphere, scared to explore.

Felix considered the options. Alys was tiring. To go back, would probably mean carrying her *and* the bat-dog. To go forward, would mean negotiating a few yards of sea water.

Not too deep . . . no big waves . . . clear water, big boulders . . .

Best to say nothing, allow no discussion, no argument . . .

Removing his shirt and flip-flops, holding them above his head, he slipped into the water. It was warm and fresh, and his feet easily found the rocky surface below.

'C'mon!' he said jauntily, reaching back onto the shelf. He plopped the pup into Alys's arms, then hoisted them both onto his shoulders. 'It's lovely, oo, lovely, here we go,' and he started to cross the inlet, making splashy, putt-putt steamboat noises.

The sea was swelling in and out of the nook with more force than he had expected, and he had to struggle to keep his balance. But he had almost reached the other side – when it happened.

'Yeughh!' he yelled, as a foul liquid ran into his eyes, and kept coming, followed by the shocking realisation that Mimi was pissing on his head. One of his feet slipped. It quickly sought a new footing. Now something was cutting or stinging the flesh. He recoiled, and danced elsewhere, only to feel the same pain again, even sharper. He was toppling. His precious cargo and its demonic appendage were heading for the water. Alys shrieked. Mimi's four paws churned the air. With a surge of strength, Felix managed to heave them onto the rock shelf, just before salt water flooded his astonished face.

He surfaced, coughing and shaking his head, and then, roughly buffeted by a new swell from the ocean, finally managed to scrabble onto the rock shelf himself.

A few moments passed while he sat, breathing heavily, watching the water drip from his bowed head. His flip-flops were lost. And his shirt. With cigarettes, chewing-gum, buzz balls. His hands and arms were scratched and bleeding. And his feet . . . his feet were pin-cushioned with sea-urchin spines.

'I will butcher this creature of yours!' he snarled at Alys. 'I WILL BUTCHER IT!'

She burst into tears. He covered his face, suddenly remembering what it looked like in photographs – the eyebrows, the beard, the big black scowl, a storybook monster. 'No, Lys, it's all right,' he mumbled. 'I won't butcher her, I'm just hurt, just a little hurt, nothing serious, everything's fine, tickety-boo, we're safe, all is – AARGHH!' he screamed, as an armed figure suddenly sprang round the corner.

It was Noah. He'd reached the beach, and found his way back along the rock shelf.

'It's all right, it's all right,' Felix said to Alys – his scream had made her huddle into a ball. 'Darling, it's all right. Look who it is. Look who's won the race.'

twenty-one

As he limped round the last curve of the cliff, following Noah and Alys, and with Mimi in his arms (to show how much he liked her, really), Felix couldn't believe his eyes.

The beach at Pembe Cove was no longer white, but black, brown and a tiny bit pink. Every grain of sand was covered with human flesh: countless inhabitants from the outlying suburbs, shanty-towns and squatter-camps had chosen to celebrate here instead of town. Up in the parking area slack-bellied cars, stuffed with double their normal load, farting puffs of dark exhaust, were disgorging even more people, who poured over the top and down the sandy slopes, turning the scene into one of Felix's biblical compositions, with figures filling the vertical as well as horizontal planes, and populating the air itself.

A vast Asian family, with bearded men, robed women, plump children with pet dogs and goats on strings, everyone carrying rugs, umbrellas, chairs, crates of food and drink, streamed down from the ridge, alongside a group of near-naked *mki-mbizi* stick-people, who moved at a slower, ghostlier pace, waving away flies, many on sticks, yet smiling, sprinkled with rainbow dust. They passed a cluster of shaggy-haired rural teenagers whose faces were daubed with different-coloured clay mixtures – ochre, white, black, blue – worn like warpaint. A party of whores were spreading out across the beach: they had old, battered faces, the bruises making their features look Oriental, and were dressed like children; one wore bobby socks and a short, fanned skirt, and another was in Charlie Brown dungarees, while a third was baring her teeth, coated in leopardskin varnish. A yellow-haired white man drifted by in a floral-patterned frock. A fully clothed black woman sat in the surf, pushed around by it, filling milk bottles, a blue plastic bag round her head to ward off the sun. A naked old man moved past her, shuffling along on his hands, pushing through the little waves . . .

Felix narrowed his eyes. The old man . . . his legs were missing . . . you could see clearly now as he played in the water, diving, flipping himself around like a seal . . . he was the other half of the pair . . . the boy with crutches. Felix wondered why he kept seeing these two? And why, perhaps more surprisingly, their manifestations never troubled him? They possessed a special composure, particularly the old man.

He was remarkable in another way. Although legless in one sense, he was not in any other. Everyone else seemed drunk or drugged already, even the children, even the skeletal, fly-plagued *mki-mbizis*. The revellers who sprinkled them with rainbow dust had also shaken and sprayed beer into their midst, and just the taste of a few drops had sent them reeling. Nearby an old German non-Af tried to climb on top of a young black woman, then gave up, dragged his face to hers, and they kissed hungrily. One man, caught short, stood with drooping head and splayed legs, urine gushing through his cotton trousers. A group of bathers carried a limp, grinning woman out of the waves. In the water and on the sand, people fell over and stood up, swayed and staggered; some were perhaps dancing. A few tried to tap out tunes on bottles, cans and calabashes, but were drowned by the gargantuan ghetto-blasters and tiny transistors elsewhere, which gave out a dissonance of boom-boom rock and hazy-crazy jazz, gibbering DJs and high-speed sales-talk; this was a carnival without live bands, floats, costumes, religious rituals; here were the people just grabbing their new-found freedom in a delirium of make-it-up-as-you-go, smoke it, poke it, eat and be eaten, boozy woozy, non-stop happy hours; this was living for today, and today was only the first of the weekend.

'Mr Felix,' said Noah solemnly. 'This place, we must leave him, I think.'

Felix nodded vaguely, setting down Mimi so that he could lift Alys, then tutting as he noticed blood from his scratches mark her Monet frock. His gaze flitting around restlessly. Ever since his youth, he'd enjoyed watching drunk people on the local beaches. Long before he went into a job where he could bid people to take off their clothes, he relished the way breasts would fall out of bras and erections would burnish the fibres in men's bikinis. 'Yes, better go,' he said, without conviction, unsure of what he wanted, feeling itchy. Both the little accident in the water and the glorious walk with Alys beforehand, both had left him hungry for *something*.

'Eeeh, iss de mun!' said a voice next to him.

It was Mr Fixer, the boy in Ray-Ban shades, who was Felix's ice-cream dealer, and one of the Chorus in the show. Although aged only about ten, he was a wiry little character with several lifetimes of experience under his belt. He reminded Felix of Zikki. Both were midget-sized entrepreneurs, speaking English fast and furiously, despite their meagre vocabulary. Mr Fixer moved in a kind of hopping dance, circling you, offering his services, or himself, or whatever you wanted.

'Happy Liberation Day,' said Felix, shaking his hand and trying to move on.

'Happy cappy sappy, eeeh, no wuri, mun!' sang-said Mr Fixer, then did a cartwheel, landed alongside a black family group and pointed out Felix: 'Him iss de mun!' When he explained more fully, and in street patois, that this was the man from the theatre – the man who gave people employment, as well as free food, drink, and cigarettes, and all you had to do in return was take off your clothes, dance and sing – the group cheered. Bemused but flattered, Felix waved back graciously. 'Y'see? No danger, we're welcome here,' he said to Noah, half seriously. Mr Fixer was flipping and twirling himself across the beach, telling everyone that *de mun* was walking among them, celebrating the holiday not in some fancy mansion but here with only one bodyguard and what looked like his daughter; and people were standing to see Felix, lifting their children. Those closer by reached out to take his hand, or patted his leg, or touched the hem of his bathing trunks as he passed.

naive africans worshipping rich whites
sense of dislocation from the people?

It was like being at the theatre: he was a hero of the people; their *sungura*.

'Mr Felix, we *must* go,' said Noah, more worried than ever.

'Yes, yes,' said Felix, impatiently, reluctantly, sensing that the something he wanted, the enigmatic something, it was within reach, available here – *everything* was available here, and he was a king.

Noah tugged his arm. 'Mr Felix, it's not what you think. These people, they are saying funny things.'

'What things?'

Noah looked embarrassed. 'It cannot be, isn't it? What they're saying.'

Felix couldn't hold his stare, and didn't question him further. Then Alys suddenly spoke up: 'Where's Mimi?'

'Ohh, nnn– !' groaned Felix. The pup could be anywhere: among the crowds, or in the water. Or it could be that squashed shape on the sand, where a gang of about thirty men were playing a high-speed ball game. Each possession of the crudely sewn leather bladder caused a violent switch of direction, a chopping, changing wave of bone and sinew, with knees and elbows flailing around like weapons, the volatile stampede showing no regard for anything else on the shoreline. Yes, Mimi could easily be that squashed shape under their pounding feet.

'Where's Mimi?' repeated Alys.

'Yes, where is she?' said Felix, carrying her away from the game, thinking, I wanted to be rid of the smelly little bat-pup, but not like *that*. 'Let's look, let's see if we can see her.'

Now Mr Fixer was at his side again, arms laden with gifts. 'No Benninjerries,' he grinned, referring to Felix's favourite ice-cream, 'but yu don't wuri, take!' and he offered a couple of beers, a reefer, a plastic sachet of powder, a ripe mango. 'For de mun, de mun, eeeh – take, take!'

'No, thank you,' said Felix. 'Frightfully kind, but–'

'For de mun who is giving us back de Mun.' Felix slowed his step. Mr Fixer grinned, 'Giving us him back, de *Big Mun*!'

Had Felix heard right? Did it mean what he thought?

He turned to look at Mr Fixer, who scratched his neck with one finger. A beckoning gesture. Felix followed with his gaze. Under the boy's crucifix necklace, hung a tiny head woven in grass – a horned head. The African buffalo. Duma's emblem.

'No wuri, 's OK, mun,' Mister Fixer whispered, *''s good.'*

'What is?' asked Felix, angrily, hoarsely.

'He will be making de *mki-mbizi* be going away,' answered Mr Fixer, nodding towards some emaciated, fly-covered children begging from other people on the beach. 'He will be making us big, we are going big again, he will be doing this no wuri, de Big Mun will!' He pressed Felix's hand. 'Eeeh, bless you mun!'

How did he know? Had he stayed in the wings – secretly – when the rest were cleared away? Had he crept down to the basement? Or into an air-duct?

Felix felt more hands stroke him, and glanced at the admiring faces around him.

Earlier when Noah said that people were saying funny things, did he mean that they shared Mr Fixer's sentiments?

'We should go!' Felix said, suddenly, brightly, as though this was a new idea, steering Noah past Mr Fixer, and towards the parking area.

'Where's Mimi?' Alys said, becoming upset.

'Yes we're still looking, darling,' Felix answered, nuzzling her hair, trying to comfort himself. The sea-urchin spines were digging deeper with every step, and the sun was burning his bare torso and head, making everything worse, his thoughts, his cravings, his mounting panic. 'Noah thinks somebody saw her where the cars are,' he said to Alys. Unconvinced, she glared at him savagely. He swallowed hard. It was as if his lie, his betrayal, shocked her more than the loss of her pet.

Ahead on the slope, a small bony man, coated in sand, was having difficulty climbing. Drunk or malnourished or both, his limbs were uncoordinated and juddering; it was as though his skeleton threatened to tear through his skin and spill onto the dune like a game of pick-up-sticks. High above, on the edge of the parking area, where thin palm trees leaned forward, curving into mid-air like the girders of a wrecked roller-coaster, here a group of revellers watched, jeering and laughing: an audience at the Roman Games. The small man's companions tried to help him up the steep, slippery incline, but he pushed them off and tried to make it on his own, sometimes upright, sometimes on hands and knees. His precarious balance made the whole landscape seem to sway. Felix winced. The slope, the people on the edge, the leaning roller-coaster palm trees, the parked cars, everything was starting to topple along with the man. They would crush him, crush Alys.

Clutching her tightly, Felix shut his eyes and climbed blind till he felt the ground level out again.

He sighed with relief. There was the jeep. Charlie's silver Land Cruiser. Inside was every luxury. Cool air, soft music, clean towels to drape over his sunburned skin, fresh supplies of cigarettes and buzz balls, spacious leather seats on which to prop his injured feet. All was well.

But as they hurried towards their vehicle, another one, an old jalopy, crammed with laughing kids, came to a stop directly in front, blocking the way out.

Noah bolted forward, and tried to reason with the young driver, while the rest of the occupants spilled out, bottles and pipes in their hands. They surrounded Noah, prodding his pot-belly, making to snatch away his rifle, some holding up their arms in mock-surrender, some staggering around in comic death throes. Then they lost interest, and started to dance to the music that boomed from their car.

When Noah walked back to Felix and Alys now, his expression was odd: a white blush on his black skin, his lips dry and parted. 'Come,' he muttered to Felix, heading for the car-park exit.

'What? Why?' spluttered Felix, limping after him. 'Are we going to walk back?' Noah didn't reply, but led round a bend in the road. Here there was a couple of stylish wooden bungalows, non-Af holiday homes, each in a separate garden.

'Wait here,' Noah said gruffly. 'Safe here.'

'Where are you going?' Felix asked.

'To fetch the jeep,' Noah called over his shoulder, and vanished round the corner.

The sun was fierce. Felix took a few steps in one direction, then the other, his feet aching. The hobbling walk felt familiar . . . maybe from when his scar was healing after that Monday morning in the police cell? . . . or maybe earlier, during that strange time in his childhood, tagged with that strange adult word, 'breakdown'? . . . or all the years of lurching around as a drunk? . . . he couldn't remember. He carried Alys towards the nearest holiday home. On closer inspection, the house was boarded up, and what he thought was a water sprinkler in the garden turned out to be a swarm of midges. Crossing the lawn, Felix flinched and swore: the grass was thorn dry and sharp. He climbed onto the porch and flopped down on the top step. Alys immediately untangled herself from him, and strolled away along the shaded wooden platform, thoughtfully, like an adult. Felix hoisted one foot onto the other knee with a wheezing grunt – *Must lose weight, must stop eating ice-cream!* – and tried to remove the sea-urchin spines, pinching his fingernails together like tweezers. But the things were buried just under the skin, evil little black needles, just out of reach.

This isn't fair.

This is all too much.

There's only one solution.

He was beginning to understand that itch he'd felt on the beach. It wasn't the taste, which became more and more attractive with each passing second. It was the escape. The escape from thinking. The inside of his head was too bright, too noisy. He covered his mouth, appalled. It would be so easy to do it. Like those nightmares. You just lift the glass and it's all over – all the fighting, all the dos and don'ts – everything back to normal.

An insect on the lawn sounded like a playing-card caught in bicycle spokes – *tic tic tic* – otherwise everything was silent.

He struggled with his feelings, but everything seemed to be sinking. Some Lower Power, still more potent than any other, more effective, more familiar, this was arriving, coming to roost. He pictured it like a huge carrion crow, spreading dark wings, settling over him . . . and his head was lowered – cringing in fear or bowed with respect – and weighed down with the nest, a big fat nest . . . and dozens of starving mouths sprouted from it; hard, razor-edged mouths, crazy mouths, vicious in their need to be filled, mouths belonging to strange little creatures, part bird, part piranha fish. All these tiny things were in his mind, live things with minds of their own, or at any rate, *gullets* of their own, *bellies* of their own, tiny ministers of appetite.

'*Eeeeeiii, eeeeeiii, eeeeeiii!*'

This was their call. Felix couldn't get it out of his head – the image of these open mouths, the sound of their screaming, the noise of their need – he couldn't get rid of it.

'*Eeeeeiii, eeeeeiii, eeeeeiii!*'

He must feed them, poor little things, their need was very urgent indeed. Mr Fixer on the beach . . . Mr Fixer would be able to fix it. Felix rose to his feet, then sat again as he saw Alys coming back along the porch.

Thank God, he thought, thank God she's here. The need will pass now, please let it pass, please God, please Greater Power, please, anyone who's listening . . .

Alys had the grown-up air of one who has decided to confront a problem, not let it fester.

'Where's Mimi?' she asked. 'You said she's up here. She's not up here. Where is she?'

'I don't know,' he replied bravely. 'Lost, maybe. I saved her in the water – *I* saved her, that was *me* saving her, *me* getting hurt in the process – but then she got lost anyway. So. All one can say is, good thing you've got more.'

'What?'

'More. Five or six more of them back at the house.'

'But she was my baby, my runt.'

'Yes. Well.'

She stared at him with a hatred that stopped his breath. It was so naked, so pure. It was like her love.

'And where's Noah?' she asked.

Felix was about to confess that he couldn't answer that either, when they heard the automatic rifle fire.

'He's fetching the jeep,' Felix said, after a moment.

Alys began to cry. 'Oh, little one, little Lys,' said Felix, pulling her towards him. She resisted, but stayed within reach.

'I'll tell you a story, would you like that?' She didn't say no. 'Once upon a time there was . . . a little voice. A voice all on its own. And he talked to himself like baby voices do, *gla-gla-glomp, gloo-gloo-*

gloo, and he thought the rest of his life would sound like this, *boobity-bomble-floopity-floop*. But then he met another little voice, a golden angel of a voice, who you couldn't help but love, and together they talked like this, *"Hey, wow, gimme!"* And then they were sent to a witch, and she said, "I have a spell, I'll weave it in the air, and it'll bring you fame and fortune, and it's all to do with talking too, so now copy me . . . *Maa, may, mee, maw, moo."* And the voices laughed, but she was serious. *"Moo, mooo, moooo-o-o-oooooo*," went the witch like a cow, a lady cow, a cunt cow –!' He checked himself. But Alys didn't seem shocked, only disinterested. She'd heard this story before. Felix felt a rush of feelings, and wanted to hit her or hug her. 'And the one little voice, the golden angel of a voice, he said, "Bugger this for a lark I'm not talking like a cow!" and he ran away from the witch, and she cursed him, and for the rest of his life he could only ever say, *"Hey, wow, gimme."* And now the witch was happy, very happy, because now she had the first little voice all to herself, and together they held their secret ceremonies, going *maa, may, mee, maw, moo-o-o-ooooo!* And then she died. The fff . . . the dratted witch died. But her broom still worked, her magic broom, and so the little voice flew away over the seas and far away, to another world, and here they taught him to speak even more properly, *"Oh-la-di-dah, anon, anon 'tis so."* And he started to understand. In this faraway land they practised a strange, ancient ritual, a form of storytelling, where people sat in the dark and others climbed into a box of light and practised magic for them, making make-believe. And all the maa-may-moos and la-di-dahs, all the silliness, it was part of it, and . . . and it was incredible. What was in the magic box? Nothing. Light, smoke, stories. Nothing, really. Just air. Air in fancy-dress. Like a voice. Like an idea, like imagination. Nothing real, nothing solid. Yet it made you want to . . .' He stretched out his arms . . . like Alys on her first visit to the theatre . . . like Isabeau all those years ago, reaching for Kaz's baby . . .

'It was,' said Felix, 'it was . . . I presume . . . like love.' He felt the blood rushing to his ears, and dropped his gaze. 'You know there's nothing there, *actually there*, yet it's very powerful. I'm told. Very powerful. Love.'

'Love,' Alys said, recognising the sound of one of their games. 'Love-love-lub-lub-blub-blub.'

She climbed into his lap and stood there, one foot on his thigh, near the old scar, the other on the bottom of his stomach, but pushed away by its bulge, forced to slide down. She took his ear in her hand, and pressed its flushed colour, curiously, gently, to a rhythm, a little rhythm they had between them, and she chanted in a quiet, private voice, a playtime voice, empty of meaning, yet deeply preoccupied: 'Love-love-lub-lub-blub-blub.'

He tensed. Her foot would only have to slide a few more centimetres . . . no, not even that, he was coming up to meet her . . . and then she'd know. Her foot was innocent, like an animal's – the small toes just seeking a grip – but her mind was filled with her father's education. Had he explained – had Charlie explained that this thing meant nothing? – that it could be brought on by sleep, a car-ride, a child's foot? – it sometimes meant nothing! – had Charlie explained?!

A centimetre more and she'd know. She'd know, and either laugh or like it.

He wouldn't laugh. He might like it. He might fulfil Emile's prophecy in their session the other week. Here it was, the *something* he wanted to do, yet dare not . . . according to Emile. Old, wise, disgusting Emile, who knew him inside out, Emile who was the other witch in his life – the Great Corrector of characters – Emile whose mind was awash and overflowing with all the pain and love and filth of all his patients, his *clients* . . . the old pimp's clients . . . 'Go on, my dear, *mon petit chou*, just try this, just try that, be brave, experiment, I don't judge, I'm just here to help you *develop*, my dear, *devil-up* . . .' Emile was a devil!, a devil was grandfather to this beautiful, beautiful girl!

As Alys's foot slipped the last centimetre, Felix lifted her away, almost throwing her aside, then sprang up and ran. He was abandoning her at the deserted house – that wasn't very responsible – he didn't care. His pounding feet forced the sea-urchin spines in deeper, deeper, and the dry, spiky grass of the lawn made it worse. He didn't notice. He tore onto the road. He saw Noah approaching, driving the Land Cruiser. Felix bolted past, into the car-park, down onto the beach again, falling down its steep white slopes, wriggling, dancing, tripping through all the bodies below, heading for the water's edge.

The gang of men were still playing their ball game along the shoreline, thirty-odd of them moving as one, hurtling this way then that, turning at breakneck speed, churning through the surf, oblivious of anyone else.

To one side lay a little dark blob, flat-looking, puppy-shaped. Kicked away early on, it had landed beyond the perimeters of the mad game. But as Felix approached, a freak pass of the ball pulled everything in that direction.

Felix accelerated. He would be too late. He dived. The stampede crashed over him. Feet, knees and fists delivered terrible blows – they seemed to be raining punishment, yet without malice, like giant hailstones or a rough sea – and then they were gone.

He prised his face out of the sand. In the hollow below, he saw blood from his nose, and at least two teeth. He lifted himself higher. Under his chest, protected by the cradle which his arms had sustained throughout the assault, was the small ugly shape of Mimi, eyes closed, jaws arranged in a stupid smile, ribs rising and falling in what looked like sleep, peaceful sleep.

'I love you, Felix,' Alys said, when he returned the pup to her. 'I love you,' she said again, in a clear, purposeful way, meaning the words. 'I love you.'

'Love-lub-blub-blub,' he said, shying away, blushing in her presence again, this time happily.

'I love you,' she said, for the fourth time, even more tenderly.

Opening his eyes, he realised that although she was still saying it – 'Love you, love you' – she no longer meant him. He didn't exist for her any more. Every ounce of her being, her love, was directed towards the little bat-pup, the little devil stirring in her arms.

devils + angels.

twenty-two

Noah parked in front of the stage door without switching off the engine.

After Pembe Cove, they had tried driving up to Charlie's mansion, but the route was blocked with revellers, a mob like a flood, sweeping round the jeep, rocking and lifting, leaving it on the pavement, half overturned. When they were gone, Felix held Alys howling in his arms, while Noah managed to right the jeep. Finally they drove into this part of town, which was silent and deserted.

'And now?' Noah asked.

Felix glanced at him. The bodyguard's face was set and sullen, as it had been since he had retrieved the jeep back at the beach. Felix turned to Alys. She looked a mess: the Monet bonnet lost, the pretty frock crumpled, spotted with his blood. Overtired, and with a slight temperature from too much sun, she'd gone into a mood that Felix recognised and hated. When you addressed her, it was as though she didn't speak English, didn't know you, trust you. She'd stare back like an animal, like Mimi, wondering what you wanted.

Felix felt alone in the world. Emile could help, but Emile was on the other side of town. Sleep would help . . . sleep was a good idea . . . sleep was a safe way of disappearing for a while . . . sleep in his bed under the old family table, with the radio playing softly, and the jalousie shutters making the room look like it was in a black and white photograph.

But unless he could take Alys along – and that option was very complicated – sleep was out of the question too.

No. He would have to find some other way of comforting himself.

'Just going to fetch a T-shirt,' Felix muttered, and climbed out of the jeep. He heard a powerful *tshuk!* as Noah activated the door locks behind him.

Inside the stage door, the cement floor was cold on the soles of his feet, soothing to the tiny sea-urchin wounds.

The silence in the theatre was extraordinary. To think that such a huge, tall building – stretching all the way up the stairwell above him, and plunging downwards too – to think that such a vast place could hold itself so still. For five, ten, thirty seconds, a minute.

As far as he could remember, everybody had gone away for the weekend. Even the lions   they were back at the circus. The place was deserted. Except for Duma.

Duma in the basement. In the underworld.

Felix thought back to Mr Fixer on the beach. What had he said, how had he put it? Felix was 'de mun who's giving us back de Big Mun'.

Someone knew. Someone knew and liked it. How many more were there? Those people in Duma's palace – round an eternal flame – didn't Brak's officer call them 'a little cult'?

What have I done? Felix thought, then spoke it aloud, drawing out the vowels like an old ham – 'Wha-a-a-at have I do-o-one?' – starting to enjoy himself, imagining that this was his castle, and Duma was a monster locked in the dungeons.

Entering his room, he hurried to the fridge and lowered the flap of the freezer compartment. *Oh no.* He was out of Ben and Jerry's supplies. This wasn't like him – to be caught empty-handed. But he hadn't expected to be here for the weekend. There was a plentiful stash up at Charlie's place – quarts and quarts of the stuff – but what bloody use was that? Sweat coated his forehead. Reaching into the freezer, he scratched at the circular patch where one of the tubs had stood, then sucked the frost from under his fingernails. It just tasted like ice, vaguely dirty, vaguely metallic. Growling with disgust, he tried elsewhere. Yes, this yellowish cluster here, it held a hint of sweetness, of nuttiness . . . yes, some had spilled . . . here was a bit more, close to the front. He pushed his face against the freezer, licking greedily. The crystals held onto his tongue, sticking fast. With a gasp he pulled back – just in time. His eyes were wide. *What was he doing?* He'd almost glued his head to the fridge. And for what? *A scrap of Butter Pecan Surprise!*

'Don't care, don't care!' he snarled out loud, 'I *must* have some!'

And suddenly he knew – with certainty – that he no longer meant ice cream.

There was no point looking in his room. It had been systematically cleared. He had anticipated a day like this, and precautions had been taken. But there was still everywhere else. 'You can't honestly tell me,' he mumbled in his high, childish, private voice, 'not honestly saying, after all the years of hoarding, for that rainy day, not saying you're not going to find some *somewhere*.'

He peeked into this air-vent grille, felt behind that fire extinguisher, rattled the empty first-aid box, checked the general office, in the file-envelope third from the left on the second shelf, scoured the Green Room, especially among the stack of broken cooking pots.

His hands were beginning to shake. 'Shh, shh,' he comforted himself. 'Get it over quickly, just a quick one, a little one, doesn't mean a thing, it's medicinal, just for the cuts and bruises, don't think, you think too much, just *do*, shhhh.'

It was unbearable. The readiness to sin, the prickle in the skin, horror and hunger, his whole being pointed in one direction, ready to commit one unthinkable act, every muscle, every thought pointed like a blade . . . a murderer must know this moment . . . but nothing to be found, nothing to sin *with*.

'Cunt,' he began to hiss, faster and faster, the word sounding like hunt.

Then, just as he was about to give up, he saw him.

A man with a bottle, lurching along a corridor, everything in shadow except for the liquid, this lit like an advert: luscious honey-coloured hooch slopping to and fro.

Felix knew exactly who it was, and knew that his next gesture – reaching for the man's shoulder – was pointless. So he got a fright when his fingers contacted cloth, and the hunched mass of a shoulder. And the man's breath, and the breath of the bottle, two sharp, male smells . . . yes, this was real, or real enough.

'Beg pardon, but the need is urgent,' Felix said, trying to sound jocular, as he snatched at the bottle. The man, perhaps angered by this rudeness, or simply in a foul mood, or too drunk to know what was going on, growled incoherently and pulled the bottle free. Felix lunged again, and secured a vice-like grip. They began to tussle, snarling, 'Cunt!' at each other. Down a corridor they went, through a doorway, the rough bump of the lintel throwing a flop of liquid into the air, just past Felix's face – so near to his nostrils, his stretching tongue – and now they were in the wings, and now heading across the vast expanse of the stage. Felix was vaguely aware that the auditorium was full, every seat occupied, every level, the great slopes, each like an avalanche waiting to happen, the shadows heavy, gleaming with fleshy eagerness, a hundred, a thousand faces, and even though he couldn't stop to check, he knew they all looked like him or this man, a hundred thousand versions, young, old, bearded, smooth, fat, thin, sleeping, awake, bearing silent witness as the fighting couple reached the opposite wings, and tumbled away, out of sight again.

Felix came round in the basement, outside Duma's door.

His hands were splattered with blood, several of his knuckles were scraped raw, a fingernail was torn.

It had happened, the fight, it *had* happened, but the man had got away with the bottle – was that a victory or a defeat? – leaving him here. Why here? Because Duma had a bottle also. He'd offered it on the day in the cave, joshing about the lack of ice.

There was silence from inside the room. Strange. You would've expected the racket to bring Duma to the other side of the door, calling out.

Felix turned the key.

The room was in semi-darkness; the shabby gloom of a basement without direct sunshine or the lights on. The only illumination, grey and thin, filtered through the broken pane of the high window.

Was Duma gone? The door had been locked and the window was too tiny, but so what? The inside of Felix's television set was sealed and small too, but that hadn't stopped Duma. Yet Felix sensed the emperor was in here. Somewhere. Keeping as still as himself.

An incredible fear went through Felix, his nerve ends stroked this way and that by an attentive, ghostly hand. Why aren't you running? he asked himself. Is it just the promise of that bottle?

He turned on the lights.

'*Jinga!*' cursed Duma. There was stumbling, a flutter, and now, as the overhead bulb gave shape to things, a host of shadows seemed to topple away from one corner. The chaos intensified. Pieces of the ceiling were tearing off and falling through the room, shards and triangles, a legion of thin shapes, then with a whoosh they all swung to the window, went through in one draught, and the room calmed.

'I got one, I got one,' said Duma, emerging from the corner with a small cardboard box and his fly whisk. 'Been trying for days. They come in at dawn, and stay – if I keep the lights off. They used this place, I suspect, before I arrived. Believing, no doubt, it was a cave.'

He reached into the box. A frantic scratching within. Trying to secure a grip, Duma said to Felix, 'I'm glad you've come back,' his tone oddly hesitant and shy.

'Me too,' Felix replied hoarsely, suddenly excited. He'd said good-bye to Duma earlier; he wasn't expecting another visit for several days.

Duma lifted the bat from the box, its wings tangled in his fist. The animal's resemblance to Mimi was less than Felix expected, and only around its large veined ears. This tiny creature was uglier, quite fantastically so, its face dominated by a flat, sore-looking snout – as though it had flown into a wall at high speed – and its fur was a colour that had never been touched by sunlight; an opaque, foetal colour.

'No, we don't get the vampire ones here,' Duma remarked, noticing Felix's expression. 'But they can carry rabies.'

'Should you be holding it, then?' Felix asked.

Duma gave a small, vain smile, as though saying, You think my story ends with *rabies*?, then answered, 'No, no, of course I shouldn't.' He laid the bat on the dressing-table, and placed his shaving bag on top of it. The light weight was enough to restrain

sex w/ Duma

the creature. With wings spreadeagled and just its angry little face poking out, it looked like a squashed cartoon mouse.

'Ugh!' said Felix, giving an exaggerated shiver.

'Indeed,' concurred Duma. 'What was Our Maker thinking of?' Examining his hand carefully, for bites, and with his head lowered like this, he spoke gently again: 'Yes, glad you've come to me.'

Felix took a deep breath. 'I was wondering if I may ask you for a . . . ?'

'Have you known loneliness, Felix?'

Felix recoiled from this, Duma's first-ever use of his name. Covering his surprise, he answered, 'Through choice . . . one could say I had through choice, yes.'

'Interesting,' Duma commented quietly.

It seemed as if he wanted to say more, yet couldn't. He fell into a deep and peculiar silence. There was an edge to it. His eyes were downcast, but he kept stealing small, almost bashful looks at Felix.

Felix shifted from foot to foot, ignoring the evil prickle of the sea-urchins, his gaze fixed on the phenomenal presence in front of him. Uncertain of his own intimate needs, Felix invariably questioned everyone else's. The world was full of people waiting to pounce, to take more of him than he wanted to give. But . . . Duma? Surely not Duma? It was unimaginable. On the other hand, the man had been cooped up alone for months, a year, a year exactly – the anniversary was being celebrated, in fact – a year away from his twenty wives and countless concubines. His appetite was known to be voracious. It wouldn't be anything mutual or tender that he had in mind – if Felix was on the right track – it would be brutal, like in prison, Felix a mere receptacle. The prospect was terrifying, in a dozen different ways. He caught sight of the bat struggling beneath the shaving bag, and felt an urgent need to go to the toilet. Now spotting the emperor's little bright blue throne in the corner, he gulped, and dropped his gaze – only to realise that he was practically naked, in nothing but swimming trunks. And Duma just wore his charcoal black shorts.

'"You like po-tay-to and I like po-tah-to,"' Duma crooned sweetly.

Felix laughed loudly, to show he recognised the reference, and asked, 'What was her name?'

Duma raised his eyebrows.

'The girl, the girl who taught you the song, you said there was a girl, when you were at the military academy in England, an English rose, a, a, a *girl*.'

'Her name?' Duma said thoughtfully. 'No. No recollection. Too many names.'

'Pardon?'

'In the world. So many people, all with names.'

'Indeed,' said Felix, frowning to himself.

'But I will tell you this. She was strong.'

'Strong?'

Duma gave a bawdy chuckle, a locker-room noise that unnerved Felix even more, then said, 'Here things are very clear between men and women. But there . . . oh, she was strong.' He laughed again, but with less bravado. 'And love . . . this is a difficult thing, heh? Not in the family sense, in the sense of duty, but as a transaction between two free people, this is difficult. Heh? Love.'

Felix blinked in astonishment. 'You loved her?' he asked, thinking, You loved *anyone*?

Duma sighed, then spoke quietly, from his heart. 'It was like madness. She rose with the sun in my head each morning, she was the first and the last thing I knew every day, she filled my being. This was difficult for me.' He paused, holding something back, then continued with a vague look in his eyes: 'Difficult. The losing of yourself, the worshipping of the other. Difficult, Felix, difficult.'

Felix nodded slowly, thinking, If we're on first-name terms, what do I call him? *Cecil?* He decided not to risk it. 'What happened to her?'

Duma answered hoarsely, 'She disappeared.'

Felix stared at the dictator, while his mind began to race: the young Duma, alone in England, homesick, solitary, frightened, finding a girl, falling in love, frightened by this too, by her strength, as he put it, perhaps feeling his heroic future was challenged. She didn't fit into his story. Yes, she would need to disappear.

With a little *tsk* the light-bulb went out above their heads. A power cut. They were bound to happen this weekend, the holiday weekend. Felix held his breath. A needle of ice travelled round his body, all the way round. He could just discern Duma's form in the

shadows. Sitting very still. Was the man thinking, This never happened in my day – *at least I made the trains run on time* – or was his
mind on other matters? A long moment passed.

'I want to ask you something,' Duma said slowly. 'I've been wanting to ask it since you came in.'

'Really?' Felix said, with a nervy giggle.

'May I?'

'May you what?'

'Ask.'

'You can *ask*, but . . . ha-ha!' spluttered Felix.

Duma's silhouette shifted slightly. 'You laugh like an unmarried
woman,' he observed.

Felix began to gabble: 'Oh, is that a saying, a – a – an Igisha
saying? Don't suppose the bra-burners would approve but *c'est la
vie!*' He noticed that his voice, and indeed his leg-swinging stance,
had become more coy, girlish, even, and wondered if by some terrible coincidence, *and aided by the darkness,* he resembled the English
rose of Duma's youth? They had met at a military establishment,
after all, and she was apparently 'strong' – perhaps she was some
galumphing army lass with a light moustache?

He jumped as something hairy touched his hand. It was the
emperor's flywhisk.

'Felix?' said Duma, prodding him gently.

'Mmmn?' the other replied, through locked jaws.

'Have you known success, Felix?'

Felix hesitated, then understood, and laughed inwardly. How
naïve he'd been! The thing weighing on Duma's mind, the thing
inducing this odd, bashful behaviour, it wasn't as banal, as ordinary,
as *human* as lust. It was about destiny. Felix smiled. He and this
man . . . they really were rather similar. 'Success? Yes. I have,' he
answered.

'Tell me.'

'Oh,' said Felix, becoming the diffident one now. 'Oh, just . . . just
moments when one gets it right, y'know. Never the whole thing, the
whole show, but moments. And the feeling . . . well, it goes through
one, it's really rather overwhelming. Perhaps because of all the other
people involved, the people on the stage, people in the audience. The

mutual experience, the rush seems to be happening to a hundred, a thousand people as it's happening to you.'

As Felix spoke, Duma went, 'Mh-hmm, Mh-hmm,' a dry musical sound which you often heard in this country, a little harmony that people sang to one another.

The men paused together.

'And . . . when it doesn't work?' Duma enquired discreetly.

'Then the feeling is very low. Very low indeed.'

'Yes, yes!' Duma said, with passion.

'For oneself and, or so it seems, for –'

'The others, the hundreds, the thousands, the millions.' Duma sighed. 'As the Igisha chief says, "He who has people must expect to shed tears."'

They waited. As Felix's eyes grew accustomed to the gloom, he also became aware of the picture in the cellar: himself, bloodied, semi-stripped, standing here, almost to attention, in front of a seated man, a powerful man, in a gloomy, thick-walled room. The situation was familiar, yet there was one important difference. *He* was in charge.

'What was it like for you?' Felix asked in a hushed, excited tone. 'At the height of it all, what was it like?'

Duma answered in his lowest, richest voice: 'It was like thunder. It was like the great waves which people call tidal, but have nothing to do with the tides, or the moon – they're from the earth, the earth breaking. It was like when the Long Rains arrive, racing towards you, and you imagine it's just a dark blue shadow in the sky, until it hits you, and the water is like stone. *Kaaassshhh!* It was like –'

'Hurricane Mary?' suggested Felix, with a giggle.

'Heh?'

Felix shook his head, flushed. Duma went on: 'And so . . . living without it, this is hard, my friend, very difficult. A man's blood must never know such things – to have thunder and lightning in it – it's a poison, a beautiful poison – the blood must never know that. Becomes hard to be without it.'

Felix nodded. 'Mh-hmm. Mh-hmm.'

A rustle in shadows. The bat was struggling under the shaving bag. Duma collected it in his hands again.

'Ehrm . . .' said Felix. But Duma seemed totally unafraid of the tiny creature quivering in his grip. Turning it over in his hands, stretching out one of the wings, he fingered its substance, its span, and then held it up to the little window above, watching the light show inside the pinkish membrane. He pushed one of his fat fingers through, amazed by the elasticity: his digit went right round to touch another fingertip without ripping the skin-film.

The bat was panicking. Even in the dark, you could see the tiny flash of its eyes and teeth, straining for Duma's fingers.

'I really don't think you should play with that!' Felix said, in a high voice that reminded him of his mother's.

'No, you're right, you're right.' Duma chuckled, giving Felix an abashed glance – another tiny flash in the dark – touched by his concern. Then he twisted his finger through the bat's wing one last time, and placed it on the floor.

Felix frowned. Was that a little crack he'd heard? Had Duma broken the wing?

The bat tried to fly, but immediately crashed into the side of the dressing-table and fell into a patch of grey light on the floor. It tried to walk now, adopting the bat-posture Felix found most repellent: shoulders hunched, little muscles glimmering, the wings turned into stilts or crutches. One of these wasn't working. The creature grew more frenetic, its balance drunken, flipping across the floor, becoming enmeshed in its own limbs.

A memory came back to Felix – of himself lying in the police cell, incapacitated – and he felt a rush of pity for the repulsive creature. But as it skidded towards his naked feet, he could only dance backwards, crying, 'Ugh!'

'Stamp on it,' Duma advised. 'Put it out of its misery.'

There was something mocking in the remark. Felix recognised the tone, he'd heard it before: Africans laughing at him, an African, for his squeamishness. 'You do it,' Felix replied with a smile, taking on the emperor.

With surprising deftness, Duma was out of his chair, pursuing the creature through the shadows, and within seconds he had it trapped underfoot. But instead of crushing it, he leaned down and hooked his finger through the other, good wing – it looked like he was gripping a wishbone – and Felix heard a second little crack.

The bat took a few faltering steps: a meagre creature on broken stilts, its every fibre quivering with a kind of disbelief. Felix stared at Duma, appalled, then suddenly he remembered something. The KiSwahili word for bat – *popo*. He swallowed hard.

'Are you Popo-boy?'

Duma froze. 'What?'

'Popo-boy. Is it you?'

'Who's Popo-boy?'

'Oh, come now.'

'*Who is Popo-boy?*' Duma repeated, his voice different, cold, aimed at Felix like a gun.

'I don't know the details, but he was in your service, committed unspeakable deeds, they say, a sort of torturer . . . I don't honestly know the details.'

'Then why are you seeking this man?'

'He killed the son of a friend.'

'What was the deceased's name?'

Felix paused, grimacing. 'Ohh dear, Kaz told . . . Kaz said . . .'

'Kaz?'

'No, no, Kaz is the mother. Ehrm . . . Zik? . . . No . . . Zed, Biff, Buzz? . . . or were those her boyfriends at the American emba . . . ?'

'She's American?' Duma said ominously.

'What? No, no, she's . . .' He faltered, suddenly picturing Kaz in the old days, 'blacking-up' to disguise her race from Duma's mad laws, at other times putting on an American accent to comfort herself, except that was the wrong thing to do as well! He felt shame for her, and hatred for the man in front of him. 'Anyway, I can't remember the boy's name, but –'

'You can't remember his name and yet –'

'It doesn't matter, his name doesn't matter, I'm –'

'It doesn't matter?'

'No, of course it matters, but –'

'*It doesn't matter*, and yet you come here and accuse . . . ?!'

'You couldn't remember *her* name,' said Felix, with a little laugh, trying to decelerate the exchange, to calm his own spiralling passions.

'Whose name?' barked Duma.

'Your English rose.'

'What are you talking about?'

'The girl, the girl who disappeared.'

Felix hesitated. It was apparent that Duma had no recollection of their conversation, or of the girl's existence. Shaking with outrage, the emperor asked, 'Are you insane? All these crimes laid at my feet – are you all insane? Heh? You think I know about this Popo-thing, this Kaz-waz-whatsit, this English rose? This, that and the next thing going on all the time – and me busy trying to run the country, me on the seat, my finger on the button – you think I had time, you think I could've known?'

'"*I didn't know!*"' scoffed Felix, tempering it with jittery laughter. 'Beg pardon, but I do believe you're the only person in this country who can't hide behind that one!'

'Well, you think I *did*? Did know? In every police station, in every village, in fields and ditches – you think I could see it all going on? The face on the flags, the posters, your coins, your television screen, you think that was really me? Me really seeing?' He pounded his chest. '*This me?!*'

Felix swayed on his feet and wondered if he was going to fall . . . the sun at the beach, the sea-urchins in his feet, the stampede of the ball-players, the fight here in the theatre . . . and now this. It was too much, and he wasn't well . . .

Oh, that's right, he'd come in here because he needed some medicine, a bottle with honey-coloured liquid, a honey-coloured sphere see-sawing to and fro . . .

Felix turned towards Duma's box of supplies, peering through the gloom. The glint of curved objects, one on top of the other, all shaped the same. Cans, dozens, hundreds of cans . . . cans of soup, Campbell's soup. Stepping closer, he saw they were all chicken noodle flavour.

Duma was still shouting at him. 'You think it was *this* me?' The man's vocal power was extraordinary. Felix felt blasted by an explosion. If this is really happening, he reflected, I should probably, as Kaz might put it, hightail the fuck outa here.

'*This me, this me?*' Duma demanded.

'Not quite the point, old chap,' Felix mumbled. 'Authorised by you, even if you yourself were not – not –'

'Not guilty!' roared Duma. 'Not guilty, your honour, not guilty! You people will not make a sacrifice of me! So don't you dare come in here and –!'

Felix didn't hear the rest. The door wasn't that thick, but as Felix locked it behind him, Duma's voice distorted wildly, piercingly, on a high-pitched ascent, like a radio station sliding off its tuning, and there were tremendous bumps and crashes. Felix imagined what the bat must look like now, and his heart went out to it. Then he set off, groping his way down the pitch-black corridor, praying that Zikki had remembered to take away *all* the lions for the weekend.

Huddled in the Land Cruiser, he tried to quell his shivering.

Noah was staring at him, surprised that he had returned so fast – in less than a minute, according to the dashboard clock.

'You couldn't find a T-shirt, sir?' Noah asked again.

'Pardon?'

'You went for a T-shirt.'

'Couldn't find one, no,' said Felix, collecting his hairy tits in his hands and holding them tenderly. 'No, couldn't.' Twisting round to fetch a beach towel from the backseat, he saw Mimi asleep on the pile, and Alys in the other corner, crying. It was incredible. She had lost interest in the pup. He had risked life and limb to rescue it, not once but twice: from drowning and from the ball-players. For his pains, he now had sea-urchin spines embedded in his feet and two teeth less in his mouth. And after all that she'd simply lost interest! Felix surged with childish rage. She should thank him, love him! Instead she was crying in that hoarse, comfortless way: he knew it well – there was nothing you could say or do. It was mindless, it was like an imbecile's grief. You could shake her and ask, 'Why are you crying?', and she wouldn't know! You could ask, 'Why don't you love me?' and . . . !

He picked up the car phone and dialled.

Charlie answered immediately.

'Listen, old chap,' said Felix. ''Fraid there's been a spot of bother back here and –'

'Is Alys –?'

'No, no, tickety-boo. A little out of sorts, too much sun, but fine, fine.'

'What, then?'

As Felix listed their misfortunes, Charlie started to laugh, and this was instantly calming. Sea-urchins, an overcrowded beach, heavy traffic during a long weekend, these weren't serious things. And as for the other events: Felix hadn't *seen* Noah hurt anyone with the rifle fire . . . he probably just shot it into the air . . . and in the theatre . . . in the theatre, had anything happened at all?

'It's holiday time, ol' buddy!' laughed Charlie. 'It's just the *Sikukuu*!'

'Yes.'

'Look, why don't you and Alys come and join us here?'

'Yes.'

Charlie paused, surprised by Felix's acquiescence, then continued: 'There's a last bunch of guests flying out in a couple of hours. Get to the airfield and join them.'

'Yes,' said Felix, his eyes narrowing.

Coming down the other side of the street, dwarfed by the great wall of bougainvillaea, was a thin man in pyjamas. Felix thought it was another ghost, or an image from his library of horror books – the one on concentration camps – before realising it was Emile. . . Emile, away from the convent hospital, heading for the theatre . . . Emile coming to find him.

'I may want to bring a friend,' Felix heard himself say into the phone.

'Bring who you like,' Charlie answered, with a whoop of laughter. 'Hey, man, the party's just beginning!'

PART IV

a Farm in Africa

twenty-three

'Hi, hi – I'm Charlie's neighbour.'

This was the only apology offered.

Everyone had been waiting on the small hot aircraft for close to an hour. Then an armoured police vehicle drove on to the runway, the back doors opened, and a big old man, dressed in Hawaiian shirt, khaki shorts and flip-flops, slowly climbed out and heaved himself onto the plane, changing its weight, sending a light tremor through every seat.

'Charlie's neighbour, hi, hi,' he kept saying, as he made his way down the aisle, before eventually strapping himself into the last empty place – the one next to Felix.

The plane immediately taxied to the other end of the airfield, turned abruptly, accelerated and took off.

Felix flexed his jaw, trying to unpop his ears, as the tremendous yet routine sensations of flying mingled with similar feelings about the man alongside.

I'm sitting next to him . . . look at his hands, his fingernails . . . smell his smell . . . his bare kneecap's almost touching mine . . . he's like just another person, and yet, and yet this is a legend! . . . saint or sinner? . . . army man, mercenary, freedom fighter, traitor, spy, Duma's right-hand man . . . which of these? all of these! . . . now Inspector-General of Police . . . Africa's own free-ranging cowboy, Africa's very own Dook!

'Hi – nice to see you again,' said Bull Brak, shaking Felix's hand.

He knows who I am – he remembers this time!

'Ah, yes, we met at Charlie's,' Felix replied meekly. 'Hello.'

'And once before,' Brak said incisively, as though to warn the other that although he might look old and comical, with his beach clothes, his thin, dyed hair and his face ablaze with veins, his mind was still razor sharp. If called upon, he would have no trouble recalling his rescue of Felix in the police cell that Monday morning six years earlier, relating every detail, fabricating a few others, and remaining crystal clear about which was which.

'Oh, that's right,' Felix mumbled, now embarrassed by a vivid image of himself naked, bleeding, helpless, upturned like a tortoise.

But Brak just smiled back wearily, through hooded eyes. He made Emile's hard-nosed, seen-it-all-before gaze look positively innocent.

Sitting in the aisle seat across the way, Emile was still wearing his pyjamas, but with Noah's pinstriped jacket over them.

Felix had borrowed the bodyguard's shirt, which was sour with sweat and much too large for him.

(Noah himself was driving away from the airfield at that moment dressed only in vest and boxer shorts, trying to keep Mimi from crawling under the foot pedals.)

Bull Brak appraised the odd garb of his fellow travellers, as well as the little girl with the French parasol and old-fashioned frock, but thought nothing amiss; this was one of *those* weekends, after all.

The rest of the plane passengers, one dozen male and one dozen female, were all young and beautiful, all perfect people; already medically examined, deloused, showered and freshly dressed by Charlie's staff. Yesterday they were fishery workers, waitresses, herd-boys, street-kids, market-place vendors selling this, that or themselves. Today they looked like fashion models, bristling with vanity and expertise. Already, on this small and crowded plane, they were too close for comfort. And Felix had overheard one of them telling the pilot that they were 'the last load', which meant there were more at the farm. As many as two hundred more, someone said. *Two hundred* perfect people? What a ghastly thought.

The infamous excesses of the party – was one expected to

participate? – would people take no for an answer? – where did the
excesses actually take place? – were there other rooms, quiet rooms,
reading rooms?

The weekend was so full of peril for Felix, it was hardly worth
worrying about.

The reunions, the family reunions . . . !

Felix hadn't introduced Emile and Alys to one another, except by
name, and since neither knew of the other's existence, these meant
nothing. So the long-awaited moment, the moment Felix had cherished in his imagination, of overseeing the first meeting of
grandfather and granddaughter, this passed unremarkably: a dazed
old man and an overtired little girl nodding suspiciously at one
another.

But since then the two had surprised Felix. Alys was normally
shy with strangers, hostile, even, and Emile was renownedly irritable with children. Yet he had sought her hand when they arrived at
the airfield, and she took it eagerly, then allowed him to carry her
onto the plane. She was presently asleep on his lap.

Watching them, a prickle of envy went through Felix. Like
Mimi, he wasn't of much interest to Alys at the moment.
Childhood was so mysterious. Felix hated the way he didn't understand its rules . . . rules he must have mastered once. He had never
fully lost his own innocence, yet he couldn't always contact Alys'.
Important things happened inside her, secretly, without explaining
themselves, making her seem fickle, even ruthless. Their encoun-
ters often left Felix feeling betrayed. Now there was a kind of
fear, too, or shame – shame for what might have happened at
Pembe Cove.

He longed to talk to Emile about these matters, but Emile was
out of reach too, his mood peculiarly quiet and still. Other than a
brief reference to 'bad dreams', he had offered no explanation for
his departure from the convent hospice. Some shock had occurred.
It was perhaps not physical, although he did look different now,
transformed from venerable old prophet to wilderness man, hermit,
tramp. Felix didn't like to stare at him too closely; he felt he might
see the man ageing, wasting, as in speeded-up film, to the sound of
a low, folding rustle.

What on earth was going to happen at the other end of this flight, when father and son meet? Would there be a terrible confrontation? Would Felix be blamed?

Never mind, he thought, I'm the man who's keeping the Scourge of All Africa as a pet in my basement, I'll think of something, or events will take their own course . . . 'Man plans, God laughs' . . . time and our underselves doodle in the dark, sometimes in unison, sometimes not.

Lifting a steady supply of buzz balls to his mouth, he turned to the window.

They were already over wild Africa. The harbour and city, its shanty-towns and refugee camps, reservoirs and plantations, these were already far behind, and below was mile upon mile of short-grass plains, with thorn thickets, cacti and dwarf shrubs, greened from a plentiful rainfall recently, and patched with small cloud shadows.

This was not among Felix's favourite views. He was in love with his homeland, completely hooked, but, as with his other enslavements, he liked to be boss. The more his body yearned for something, the more urgent his need to rule it, to make it a drug of *choice*, to become fussy, to select, to say when, where and how he liked it. So, as for the type of landscape below, it was too flat, regular and crowded. All those short, wide-branching mimosa trees, they scratched at his taste, they held him away.

But now the plane skimmed over the edge of the Vundwawe Crater, another extinct volcano, thousands of times larger than the Kwatokuu – you could fly for an hour before seeing the western rim – and Felix caught his first glimpse of the bowl within. Here it was, *his* Africa. The savannahs. The great game country, the grasslands. Their greenness was tinged with yellow, glowing yellow, as though soaked with light, yet not sunlight, rather a source within the land; there was a sense of something else shining through, old Africa perhaps, for the landscape played tricks with your sense of past and present. It was like a cross-section of the earth, laid out flat, and with time, not geology, on display: planes of existence, plains of grass, each with its huge herds of animals, those ancient processions, the vast grazing fields divided by boundaries of mauve

mist or rock kopjes with brilliant green fringes, one giant lawn after
the other, some dry and unoccupied, some hosting a solitary white
whirlwind, God's bored finger drawing in the dust, and then
stretches of heavy damp shadows looking like they belonged to a
different day – that's yesterday's weather, you think – and then eventually mountains again, cool and blue, more like ice floes, from
much longer ago.

There were several other aircraft on the tarmac, parked at the far
end; a flock of ranch-hoppers and helicopters, two hot-air balloons
and, dwarfing them all, a military troop-carrier. This belonged to an
army chief, Brak explained, who'd been allowed to bring all the
officers, even non-commissioned ranks, from his division. 'A pal of
mine, another survivor from the old guard,' Brak added, in a confi-
dential tone which unnerved Felix. 'In fact, the general's actually a
third cuz of the old emperor himself!'
    Felix was relieved to see that Charlie wasn't at the airstrip.
Instead they were met by one of his rangers, a sullen man with
blue-black skin and a safari suit who surprisingly, introduced himself as Elvis and then never spoke another word.
    The plane's passengers divided themselves into three jeeploads,
and Felix was pleased that Bull Brak went with a group of the perfect people. (The policeman had spent the flight either chatting
them up, or sitting back to grind his small teeth and readjust the
folds of his khaki shorts, whispering, 'Oooh, Jesus, man!') So now
Felix, Emile and Alys had a jeep to themselves: a big, dusty old
bush-banger with open sides, a tarpaulin stretched over the top and
Elvis at the wheel.
    As they travelled, Felix stretched out one arm and played with
the buffeting air currents, letting the light gently hurt the sunburn
from his morning on the beach. He rejoiced in this different, thick,
dry heat.
    The noise of the vehicle, grating, bashing, squeaking, and the
buzz of the bush, made for a harsh but stirring cacophony, and, at
one point, a mixed herd of zebra and wildebeest added to it with
their running hoofs, and Felix marvelled at how easily this land
gives off a drumbeat.

The farm was only a few miles further, coming into view suddenly as you crested a rise. Charlie enjoyed the way that this first sight of it always made newcomers snigger and redden. Situated in a small lush valley, a feminine arrangement of folding, velvety foothills led down to the Nguza river, and, in a saddle between one end of its banks, opened to the savannahs again, except that the first and dominant feature of the panorama was a cluster of erect red stone columns.

'What are those things called?' asked Alys, as she always did upon arrival, testing whichever adult she was with.

'Buttes,' Felix replied primly.

Rousing himself, Emile peered at the precarious, free-standing rocks, and said, 'Look more like *iffs* to me.'

Laughing together, all of them, even Elvis, they drove down into the valley, crossing the security checkpoints, where armed guards opened the barriers hurriedly, comically, sitting on them like seesaws, and waved as the visitors sped through, shouting affectionate greetings to their boss's daughter, and down the long drive, past a large parking-field crammed with guests' vehicles – jeeps, combis, several coaches, a battered grey bus – and finally into a large, circular yard.

With a fountain in the middle, it was surrounded by eucalyptus trees, the main farmhouse, the *boma* for outdoor banquets – a tall, lashed-bamboo stockade – and the first ring of guest bungalows. These were shaped and coloured like honeycombs, built from mud bricks, with regular gaps – a cooling system – and topped with grey thatch.

Felix helped Alys and Emile down from the jeep, his eyes skimming round the yard, wondering when Charlie would appear.

But he didn't. No one did. Apart from a scruffy brown goat, a chicken, and a plastic bucket – the ubiquitous features of any local scene, urban or rural – the place was strangely deserted and quiet; the foliage ticking with insects, the trees sweating gum. Perhaps all the other guests were resting. *Did guests rest during these weekends?* It was two-thirty, and the heat of the afternoon was incredible.

Felix held his breath. Here he was at last, on the farm, Charlie's wicked farm.

Elvis went off to summon the staff as the other jeeps arrived and their passengers dismounted. The yard filled with figures stretching, stamping, brushing the dust off their holiday clothes. Felix added a seventh slice of chewing-gum to the wodge in his mouth, careful to put the wrapping into his pocket and not litter the land, then strolled over to the fountain.

This was, so far, the only evidence of Charlie's infatuation with ancient Rome on his very African farm. In creamy brown marble, it consisted of a stack of reliefs, each depicting hectic scenes from the Games: beasts eating criminals, gladiatorial combat, chariot circuits with horses and riders, some winged and triumphant, some trampled underfoot.

'Is this original, d'you think?' Felix asked, as a figure joined him. 'Can it be?'

'Yup, sure is.'

Felix saw who he was talking to — Bull Brak — and came to attention. The policeman unplucked his shorts from the massy cleft of his buttocks, and then submerged his head into the basin of water. 'Oooh – nice!' he cried, shaking off cascades of drops like an old hound. Indicating the fountain he said, 'One and a quarter mill apparently. Yankee bucks.'

'Goodness me!' said Felix, who was constantly surprised at how rich Charlie really was.

'And he got it cheap!' Brak added. 'From a museum in one of our neighbour states. It was closing down.'

'The museum or the state?' Felix asked, with a nervy laugh.

Brak stared back blankly. 'Charlie got a tip-off, grabbed it before it went to auction. It's how he gets a lot of his Roman stuff. Museums in war-torn countries, Third World or Commie, countries changing hands, countries fighting, countries falling, so on and so forth. The centre of gravity goes – and then what? Nobody ever thinks of the museums, hey?, with all these masterpieces or whatever you want to call them. They're in a safe home, a secure environment one minute, and the next they're swimming in shit. So our friend gets in fast, he grabs 'em.'

'Is that legal?' Felix asked, then wished he hadn't. It sounded critical of Charlie, testing of Brak.

But the man just gave his lazy, cowboyish, *Big Dook* smile. 'He pays good money. Why not?' Felix shrugged, choosing not to engage this man in a debate about the antiquities of history and our global heritage. Brak offered a Camel untipped, and then, as he leaned forward to light it, changed the subject: 'I appreciate your help with our friend, by the way.' He gave his distinctive laugh – '*Haw!* Just wanted to say that before we get too pissed.'

Felix's eyes widened; more shocked by the first of the two statements. Brak's gaze was unreadable, but he was presumably referring to Duma.

'Appreciate it,' Brak said again, lighting his own cigarette. 'Think it's terrific what you're doing.'

What did he mean? Like Mr Fixer on the beach, did he imagine that Felix was masterminding some kind of plan – some restoration of Duma to power?

Am I doing this? Felix wondered. Maybe even without realising. His underself – the part of him drawn to Duma, drawn to his horror and his might, drawn to the idea of the Jew and the great dictator, the former in charge for once – was his underself up to something, without, in a way, the rest of him *knowing*?

'Dr Chabecq sends apologies, gentlemen,' a heavily accented voice said behind them. They turned to see the arrival of a round old woman carrying a clipboard. Her huge eyes were outlined with kohl, she had yellowish makeup, and black hair oiled back into a luscious bun. She wore a purple yashmak, and now, as she spoke again, Felix recognised the sounds – the rolled r's, the gargled h's – as Arab. 'He has been unavoidably delayed, ah me.'

'The madam of the joint,' Brak whispered to Felix with a chuckle. 'Anything you want, and I mean *anything*, she'll get it for you.' Raising his voice, he said, 'Bi Mirza, nice to see you again, how you doing, sweetie?'

'I'm well, my big Bull, and you?'

As they kissed on both cheeks, the woman took the opportunity to whisper some news in Brak's ear. Felix only caught snatches of the bulletin – 'We've got . . . it's here . . . for you' – but he saw Brak fill his cheeks and blow out weakly, blissfully, like someone extinguishing the last candle on a cake after they'd made the wish of a lifetime.

Unable to contain his excitement, Brak confided in Felix again: 'Oooh, Jesus, this place, hey? It can give a bloke a stroke!'

'That is, alas, what has happened to one of our early arrivals,' said Bi Mirza, overhearing, as she jotted a note on her clipboard, 'which is why Dr Chabecq is otherwise engaged at present.' She smiled wearily at Felix. 'As you theatre practitioners know, it is *so* useful having a doctor in the house!'

'Will the patient live?' Felix asked, with an uneasy laugh.

'Let us hope so, please,' she replied.

'And if not,' added Brak. 'At least they'll've gone out with a bang. *Haw!*'

'Oh, my Bull!' said Bi Mirza, unable to stop herself from sharing his raucous laughter. 'I'll come back for you,' she said, brushing her hand under his chin and winking one huge eyelid slowly, almost creakily – then said to Felix, 'Follow me, ah please.'

They rejoined the others. Alys was overjoyed to see Bi Mirza, rushing into her arms, abandoning Emile as she had abandoned Felix, and Mimi before. But her trust in Bi Mirza reassured Felix: it meant she wasn't misused in any way here, as he secretly feared – and it meant that, if there was any truth to Brak's crude joke about Bi Mirza's position here, she clearly also doubled as housekeeper and nursemaid. Addressing Alys as 'my little sovereign', she handed her over to a maid with instructions to take her to 'her little palace', adding promises that she would join them soon. As a team of servants began herding the perfect people to their barracks elsewhere on the farm, Bi Mirza led Felix and Emile across the yard, through the outer circle of guest bungalows, to one beyond, which overlooked lawns, the river bank, and a stretch of jungle on the other side.

'We are a little short of space this weekend,' she said, as she ushered them towards one of the doors. 'And most of the rooms were, ah me, occupied by the time you telephoned, but we did our best to jiggle and juggle so I hope this is satisfactory.'

'I'm sure it's tickety-boo,' said Felix, as they entered the room, a sitting area. He savoured its shadowiness: the iciness of the air-conditioning, a circular fan at work as well, purring away overhead, the tinted, sliding French window across one wall, with insect screen beyond. 'Oh, yes, this is . . .' he started to say, then, poking his head through an arch, froze. In the next area, there was only one bed, a double. '*I can't sleep with my shrink!*' a voice within him screamed, while he heard himself finish his sentence: '. . . just tickety-boo, thank you.'

'We find people spend so little time in their own rooms anyway,' Bi Mirza added mysteriously, smiling in that odd, sexy way, and slowly winking one big eyelid.

'Well, quite,' commented Felix, trying to sound knowing, while his other voice continued to rage: '*Shouldn't Charlie have briefed her better? Shouldn't he have explained that his friend, late arrival or not, would not be sleeping with his travelling companion? – or, in fact, with anyone!*'

Felix glanced to Emile, but the old boy was unaware of anything, his eyes open but sightless, a light snore in his throat.

'Day or night, you'll find me at the other end of this,' Bi Mirza explained, touching the wall-phone. 'I have the only office job here!' She gave a throaty laugh, and then added, 'So anything you want – and I mean *anything* – just ask.' Felix smiled back numbly. Bi Mirza bowed her head and withdrew, saying, 'Have a lie-down or what-ever, please, I've no doubt Dr Chabecq will be along to say hello in a while.'

And find me in bed with his father?! Whom he hasn't seen for twenty years!

'Right,' Felix called after her cheerfully. 'Good. Thanks.'

He helped the half-dozing Emile onto the bed, holding apart the insect net. As the old man turned away, rolling into sleep, one fore-finger caught on the mesh. Suspended in mid-air, the gesture seemed to say, Wait, or Why?

Felix surveyed the bed. Oh, the idea of sharing it with Emile – their dreams, their night-time excitements, all the involuntary shiftings of flesh and thought, a mingling of their underselves – *unthinkable*.

The prospect was so alarming, that Felix had to leave the bunga-low and catch his breath outside the door. He was struck by the tremendous heat again, and by the red spectacle of fireball lilies rooted in the wall opposite; both things lay heavily, exquisitely on his senses.

Then Charlie bounded round the corner, looking clean, fresh, and euphoric – whether this was chemically induced or not, Felix couldn't tell – and fell upon him. They hugged and kissed.

'Welcome, ol' buddy, welcome,' Charlie said. 'I am *so* pleased you're here at last.'

'Me too. But you realise I'm not here for, for . . .' Charlie waited, amused, while Felix floundered. '. . . for *the* weekend, sort of thing.'

'No,' said Charlie.

'No! I'm here for, for . . .'

'*A* weekend.'

'*A* weekend, yes.'

'Good. Whatever you like. It's all here.'

'That's what I'm scared of.'

'Don't be. Experiment. Or don't. Everything, anything, and nothing. It is all here.'

Felix buried his head in his hands, groaning with mock-disapproval, while he felt a prickle of excitement.

'Who's your pal?' Charlie asked, reaching for the bungalow door.

'Oh, no one,' said Felix blocking his way. 'One of the Chorus from the show, an old man, poor, homeless, I decided to give him a treat, a holiday, you know what a softie I am.' They laughed, and Felix steered Charlie away. 'He's asleep. Probably sleep all weekend. Now, show me round, give me a grand tour of – Ow!'

'Wha'?'

Felix pointed down. 'Told you on the phone. Sea-urchins.'

'Sea-urchins,' Charlie echoed slowly, kneeling to examine Felix's feet. 'Nice, nice word – "sea-urchins".' A peacock walked by. Charlie made its mewing call. The bird allowed him to reach out and stroke its neck, his fingers tightening and intensifying the psychedelic sheen of the feathers. 'This happened with some wood I was touching,' Charlie told Felix. 'Everything's very soft at the moment, very nice.' Catching the look in his friend's eye, Charlie snapped out of it and laughed. He gave the peacock a last caress, and smiled up at Felix, 'Say hi to tomorrow's lunch.'

twenty-four

Emile woke with a moan. After a moment, Felix heard little cough-like noises – little gasps of emotion.

'Are you all right?' he called through the arch. He'd spent a sleep-less night in the sitting-room, on the cane settee.

'Yes, thank you, my dear, yes.' Emile's voice was clear and calm. 'Just a dream of water again. So beautiful. Will you bring me some?'

'Water?'

'Water.'

Felix swung his feet onto the floor, and, as though testing them, stood slowly. Yes, the sea-urchin spines were gone, carefully removed by Charlie after the peacock encounter. Felix felt his way across the dark room to the fridge. It was installed next to the TV like a hotel mini-bar, and stacked like one, except that the bottles of champagne, wine and spirits were full-sized, and the ledge above was arranged not just with glasses, corkscrew and peanuts but also bowls of white powder, clingfilm stretched over their rims, sweet-jars of tablets, containers with the finest hashish, hand-crafted Oriental pipes, disposable syringes and other equipment, everything laid out neatly, with printed instruction cards, explaining all side effects, and outlining the history of each substance, emphasising its positive aspects. Prominently displayed was a printed sign with a jaunty, burlesque tone:

ARE YOU BORED WITH E. AND CLASS-A? THE SAME OLD BUZZZZZZ? WANNA TRY SOMETHING NEW? WANNA EXPERIMENT THIS WEEKEND? FIND ME. CH.

Yesterday afternoon, having lost courage during the tour of the farm – after approximately five minutes – Felix had fled back to the bungalow and, needing a cool drink, discovered the fridge and its supplies. He was furious. Surely Charlie could have thought to clear them from *this* room. The narcotics weren't of interest – Felix was too squeamish to entertain the idea of shooting or snorting things into his blood – but the bottles! He wasn't at all happy about being near all those bottles. What if he sleepwalked? His underself going for a stroll, a midnight feast. Surely Charlie could've thought! But then Charlie could've thought about a lot of things. It was obvious that Charlie didn't spend these weekends thinking at all!

His anger provided the perfect excuse to miss dinner. He assured himself that it wasn't from any reticence to meet the other guests and *join in*, whatever that entailed! He rang through to Bi Mirza, and requested sandwiches and ice-cream in the room for two. She was speechless. In all her years of offering guests 'anything, and I mean *anything*', she'd never been asked for this. Nevertheless the tray-supper was duly provided, and Felix spent the evening watching television with Emile. A large part of the news bulletin was devoted to extracts from the Freedom Weekend speech that John C. Guwedekko had made earlier in the day. While Felix absently studied the face of the new leader (he really *did* look like Africa's Guevara), comparing it with that of the old one, which he knew rather better, Emile fidgeted and heckled: 'American aid?! *La foutaise!* – aid for trade, you mean, you stupid child!' Turning to Felix, he complained energetically, 'But he doesn't mention the elections, you notice that? Hello, Mr President . . . some elections, please? Ah, no, no, no, he's stopped mentioning elections! So – we're still a one-party state – so, explain to me, please, *what has changed*?' Felix nodded and tutted, crunched buzz balls and smoked.

Using the light of the fridge, Felix now poured a glass of Perrier, sniffed it to make sure it *was* Perrier, then closed the door, returning the room to darkness, and found his way through the arch to the area beyond, with the bed. Sitting in a chair alongside it, he helped Emile lean up and drink.

As the old man settled back again, Felix smiled to himself – they were now in the classic therapy position – then said, 'Tell me about it, your dream.'

'Ah, it was so beautiful,' said Emile. 'I was processing with all my male relatives down this rocky slope, like a cliff, very steep . . .'

'You've dreamed about them before,' commented Felix, 'all your male relatives.'

'Have I? *Alors, là!* And we're all helping one another down this slope. Particularly my late father. He was a rather brutish and overpowering fellow, y'know, a mine-owner in the Congo, but in the dream, he's very old and frail, and yet he's trying to help me and I'm helping him. It's very tender.' He paused, giving a small cough of emotion. 'At the bottom is the ocean, but not shallow like on a shore. Massive deep swelling water . . .'

'You've dreamed of that before too.'

'Have I? As it swells, it is so vast and heavy it can swamp us all, yet we're not afraid, we keep heading down to it, it's so beautiful.' He reached for Felix's hand. 'What you think it means?'

Felix smiled again. 'Well, you know the form. Make everyone in the dream *you*.'

'Yes. So I'm making my way down a steep cliff with a host of my selves, my male selves, and we're all helping one another, especially my dominant male self who used to be overpowering but is now frail, and I'm helping him and he's helping me, and it's very tender . . .' He paused again. 'And at the bottom there's this massive force which I should fear but I don't – in fact, it's beautiful.'

Felix heard a rustle as Emile's hands went to his head. 'Our imagination!' he whispered. 'It's the human gift. Or, rather, the reward for being human. The rest of it is such a violent, sorrowful affair, but there is this one marvellous reward. The imagination.'

'I heard a joke in America,' Felix said. 'God talking to Adam. He says I've got good news and I've got bad news. The good news is that I've given you both a brain and a penis. The bad news is that you can't use both at the same time.' Emile didn't laugh. Felix stared at the pitch darkness in front of him, feeling he was in outer space, sitting on a chair in outer space, his guru floating horizontally at his side, then asked, 'So . . . what do you make of your dream?'

'Oh, I think it's fairly clear,' said Emile with weary impatience, more like his old self. 'Don't you, my dear?'

'Yes.'

'Water. Our first sensation. Water. Probably the last as well.'

They remained in silence for a long while. Felix could sense something altering between them. Then Emile said, 'Felix?'

'Hmn?'

'Would you mind if I say something?'

'Do,' Felix replied without enthusiasm; he always hated it when people prepared a conversation in this way.

'You have been,' Emile said slowly, 'you have been something of a let-down to me.'

'Join the queue,' Felix replied instantly, covering his shock.

'The work is hard, y'know. All day we must listen to your obsessions with your pee-pee and your poo-poo.'

'I've never had either.'

'I don't mean *you*.'

'Oh, beg pardon,' Felix said sharply, 'I thought you said *I* was the let-down.'

'You are. Listen. You are not a listener. It's a flaw. You're not the director now, not in charge of this scene, so hush and *listen*. What I'm explaining is that we are swamped by our clients' neuroses, compulsions, illnesses, sins, crimes, lies, let's not quibble about terminology, they drag this baggage into our rooms, this hysteria, like great nets of fish, great twitching heaps and humps of living, dying matter, all slimy, all reeking – *pouah!* – spilling all over our rugs and floors . . . messing, messing!'

'An ocean image again,' interjected Felix, trying to regain ground. 'Interesting.'

'Manuel Dias, who shits with a hand mirror, Clementine Balfour who comes to my sessions with pleasure balls up *la chatte*, Fatima Ismail who shoplifts lingerie and pisses on it, Milton Hertzberg who must achieve orgasm whenever he's in a car-park, Kennon Jabavu who's busy finger-fucking his youngest . . .'

'*You know what you need?*' Felix shouted at Emile in his head. '*You need censorship! The artist must never practise censorship, the shrink always.*'

'. . . and the only thing that makes it bearable,' continued Emile, the words tumbling out with rapid-fire precision, '– is one's own selfish quest for what we call the well-timed interpretation. The elusive and instinctive moment, comment, suggestion or silent understanding that gives the client an opportunity to change. Winicott says it can be recognised in only one way. It will create a *response*. If the client responds in any way, by speaking, by falling silent, by becoming enraged, by laughing, by changing their lives, then it has been a well-timed interpretation, and *then* you can start, *then* you can develop the work.'

Devil-up. Despite himself, Felix smiled at Emile's pronunciation . . . and this brought a memory of Miss Rosewood and her elocution classes, and her ambition for him – *such plans, Feelie, such grand plans!* – and her disappointment in him too. Glancing round in the darkness, Felix shifted closer to Emile.

'Well, Felix, you have never given me this satisfaction,' said Emile, his voice slowing. 'Sorry to tell you this. But I'm afraid I can't waste time with the bullshit any more. No time left. Do you see? No time left, and so much time wasted. Oh, it drives me to distraction. Hint, suggest, imply, plant, but never just say what needs to be said!' He clicked his tongue. 'Anyhow. Say it now. A profound, profound letdown.'

'You can feel as let down as you want, dear boy,' Felix replied, voice quavering with hurt. 'One has, in fact, changed one's life, *drastically* changed it, but you won't recognise that because it wasn't following your directives, it wasn't your idea! It was Charlie's. Your son. With whom you're incapable of having a relationship! And then you dare to lecture other people on how to lead their lives, to alter their characters, their –' He mimicked Emile's accent: '– *correctors*. You, the Great Corrector of characters?! Tosh! You are a selfish, stubborn, arrogant old –!'

Emile cut in: 'You mean the drink – this drastic change?'

'Yes, of course I mean the drink!'

Emile blew the air, 'Phfff!', and said, 'The Pleasure Principle, the Reality Principle, creaky old stuff, devised by a little Yiddisher shyster. No, no, no, you've just lit a time-bomb, my dear, a time-bomb. I'm not saying abstinence can't work and isn't necessary for some people, but *you*. Phfff! It's just another way of staying in control. It's like you and sex. "Can't use my brain and penis at the same time, so I won't use one of them *ever*!"'

'That was just a –'

'"I don't engage in sex, I don't touch drink, I'm in control."'

'Quite the opposite,' protested Felix. 'In confronting one's addiction one must surrender to one's powerlessness in all its –'

'Oich veich, please don't wheel out that twelve-step, Bible-thumping, all-American crap! Where is the change – in *you*? You still bring your black scowl into my presence – those eyebrows, that beard! "Stand off!" they say. "Be warned, be frightened of me!" – and your drawings still produce face after face of screaming terror, *patati patata*. Where is this change?'

Felix couldn't answer. He leaned forward, hugging himself, grateful for the darkness, alarmed by it as well. It was outer space. He was all alone. The only other person – guru, priest, teacher, *Daddy* – the one person he could trust, that person was floating away . . .

'Need some air,' Felix muttered, standing abruptly. 'Many thanks for the chat. Appreciate it hugely.'

'You're angry, my dear.'

'Course I'm fucking angry.'

'Well, don't be. Or no, do. Be angry. It's very bracing. Who knows – maybe we've hit on a well-timed interpretation, *finally*. But think on this. I speak out of concern. Out of love.' Felix groaned. 'Yes, well,' sighed Emile. 'Love is not something that comes easily to you. But when you find it, find love, starting with yourself . . . starting with the little boy in you, because he's the one you're scowling at, holding off, he's the one whose face comes up through the drawings, gasping for air, crying with terror . . . until you take him in your arms, until you love *him* . . . ! Y'know, I once saw you asleep with a baby in your arms, and I thought –'

'Yes, yes, I've heard the story!'

'With your ears you've heard it, not with your heart!' Emile sighed again. 'Well, well, you've still got some way to go, my dear, and until you get there, you might as well go to the fridge, open one of those bottles, and – *Salut!* – have one on me.'

'Fuck off!' Felix snarled. 'I know you're not well, I know you don't mean every word you're –'

'Oh, but I do.'

'Well, then, fuck off, you old cu–! *Fuck off!*'

Felix stumbled across the dark room, pushed through the curtains, slid open the big French window, crashed into the insect screen beyond, pulled it aside, and fell into the open air.

With eyes tightly shut, he breathed deeply, slowly.

Devil-up, devil-up, the devil mustn't get up, mustn't get the upper hand.

He opened his eyes.

It came as a shock to remember where he was. On a patio. Outside a bungalow. Overlooking a sloping lawn, a riverbank, and a jungle. Charlie's wicked farm.

The air was a steamy, brightening grey colour – just before sunrise – and filled with birdsong: trillings and whistles, a wuk-wuk call, another like a drop falling into a pool, doves with their incongruous urban cooing. There was a wet smell. Rain had fallen during the night and the patio was shining and insect free. Everything out here seemed cleansed and settled.

From the opposite bank of the river, Felix heard sudden movement through the undergrowth, then an animal's voice – *baa-hoo! baa-hoo!* – big teeth wrapped round the sound – *baa-hoo!* – perhaps a baboon or hyena, one giving a signal to the rest, the pack on some kind of manoeuvre, arrival or flight, maybe an ambush? The crashing noise grew, travelling, a chase, small panicky yelps, the *baa-hoo!*s more frequent, hoarser, then a cry of fear, quite human, and suddenly the drama disappeared or resolved itself, leaving just the dawn chorus again, and vervet monkeys going through nearby trees – *shush, plop* – safe from the dangers across the river.

Felix inhaled deeply, sensuously, angrily. *This is why I've changed, and I have changed!* He relished the way that the pink, coppery sky

Africa - both innocent + corrupt. Not bad - but problematically Eurocentrically understood? Africa, the heat of Darkness.

looked new and old at the same time, virginal and experienced, blushing and wise, and the way the wet smell was both rotting and fresh; all the death of the night, all the life of the new day was held in it, along with a peculiar excitement, like the promise of a drink or some forbidden fruit, a wildness, a danger. Africa, Africa. Under the choir of birds, monkeys, bushbabies and flying squirrels, there was a ringing and buzzing, a pulse of insects and frogs, like a long quiet drumroll, a roll of cymbals, tying knots of eagerness in his belly . . . the show was starting . . . Africa, Africa.

Felix started to walk down to the river, down across the wet lawn, when the slope lowered abruptly to reveal several large animal shapes in front of him. For a moment he thought they were garden sculptures. But no, they were waterbuck, big, solid, grey. Harmless-looking. Yet it was disquieting to be so close to wildlife. Equally startled, they trotted off briskly. Except for one, a male. He appeared to be tethered to a stick in the ground . . . or maybe his horns were caught on it.

Intrigued but nervous, Felix hurried past. He reached a bamboo grove at the water's edge. Now there was a new sound from across the river. A lion's purring, panting call. *Mmmm, mmmmaa, mmm-maaaa.*

Suddenly the bamboo stalks creaked. Felix stiffened. The lion's call had come from across the river . . . hadn't it? He glanced back to the lawn. The waterbuck did seem tethered. Was it a pet, or some kind of bait? The bamboo shifted again, clearly this time – you could see the tops moving, describing the progress of a journey within, heading towards him.

It'll be guineafowl, he thought, it'll be something small and charming . . .

The charge was abrupt. The last few bamboo rattled like the bars of a cage, then sprang apart, and a dark mane burst into view. Felix stumbled back, as confused as he was frightened. It was too small for a lion, it was too devilish . . !

'Scared you!' cried a familiar voice. 'Didn't I, ehh?'

Kaz! – shaking with laughter. He pushed her away roughly. Although she was naked, her coxcomb and braids were elaborately adorned with parrot feathers, dyed leather thongs, cubes of bronze, cobalt and mirror, making her head seem strangely and indecently clothed. She carried a wrapped towel in one hand.

'Hey, hon, 'm so happy to see y',' she said, struggling to speak clearly. 'So, so, *so* happy you's here, hey, *yaiy!*, here he is!'

'Kaz, good morrow,' he said primly. She reeked of indoor odours, late-night odours – ashtrays, bottles, strangers – odours that polluted this lovely riverbank at dawn.

''m so happy,' she kept repeating, flopping on the grass and rolling from side to side. 'Awww, look, he's here, he's here!' She reached up and held his knees, cupping them in her palms. Wishing he'd put on trousers before storming out of the bungalow, he pulled his T-shirt lower.

'Isn't thiss place b't'f'l?'

'Very beautiful, yes.'

'So happy!'

'Good,' he said – finally recovered from the fright, and now softening his tone, 'One doesn't often hear you saying that these days. It's good.'

Her rolling came to a stop at the water's edge, and she stared at it upside down, head thrown back. Dawn was brief in these parts, the air without real light or temperature yet, just filled with promise, and this rested in the river more than anywhere else, on shelves of red-brown rock under the crystal surface. Kaz seemed to enter the trick of its substance – her skin was the same colour as the rock – and she looked translucent. Now she started to hum, buzzing in the back of her throat, snapping her fingers slowly, picking up some languid beat in the ground, then opened her mouth and allowed sounds to form. Her voice, too drunk for speech, was perfectly placed for song. Why is that? Felix wondered, smiling as he saw her make that face, that singing face; lazy frowns and flinches, comic expressions of disbelief as this thing, this spirit, rose out of her. Air, water, land, it shoved aside these petty divisions, it was all of them, none of them, it spoke English, KiSwahili and a language called the blues, *zaa-zo-yojeeee-yeah*, it took you by the hand, it invited you to climb, it made you ring with joy and pain, and then it finished, leaving you in mid-air, calm, amazed, longing for more.

She chuckled, stretched herself, and said, 'Giss a smoke.'

'Seems such a shame,' he said, inhaling the fresh air. But he *was* clutching a pack; he *had* thought to bring them along. Lighting two, he sat beside her, the lush dew washing his legs. They smoked, saying nothing. She fell asleep. His gaze wandered over her naked, long-limbed body, back and forth. He thought about touching. Not like when they groomed one another . . . massaging one another's scalp or feet . . . not touching like that. Maybe some time this weekend . . .

'We're gonna get hitched,' she said suddenly.

'Pardon?'

'Hitched. Us.'

'Who?'

'Me 'n' Charlie.'

Felix laughed. She opened one eye. ''s the truth. He proposed last nigh'.'

Felix laughed louder. '*Last night?!*'

She came up on one elbow. 'Yeah, wass the madda wi' last nigh'?'

'How could you be sure he was talking to you?' asked Felix, feeling his cheeks redden, his smile going cold.

'Wha'?'

'Weren't you here last night?' he scoffed on, floundering. 'I mean, you all. Weren't you all here? All of you up to all sorts?'

'Yeah.' She thought about it, then asked quietly, 'Wha' . . . you think maybe he diddin mean it? Tha' maybe he was too outa his head?'

'I don't know, darling, *I* wasn't here!' he snapped, and then gave little puffs of embarrassed outrage. A strange hurt went through him. Kaz and Charlie marrying! It was impossible. *His* Charlie marrying *his* Kaz. Impossible. They were pissed, high, joking.

'Bedda get going,' Kaz mumbled, struggling up. 'Bedda go, ehh? As they say . . . "It remains tomorrow."'

'As who says?'

'Huhn? My aunt, she always used to say it . . . "I must go, it remains tomorrow" . . . always said it if she stayed late. I think, y'know, after long feast nights, in villages . . .' she gestured vaguely towards the surrounding land '. . . people used to say it.'

She gave up trying to stand, and leaned on all fours, with breasts and belly sagging. '*Oyoyoyo*, I'm happy,' she said. 'Are you happy?' She raised her head slowly and frowned at him in that way of hers, that way which belonged to her aunt and her ancestors, that *African way; eyes* creased and bloodshot, as though squinting across an immense distance. Felix held her gaze. Her boozy breath repulsed him. In turn, she hated his new timidity. They stayed silent, peering at one another. *What is it like to be you?* they both wondered. *I used to know.*

Then suddenly Kaz noticed the rolled-up towel in her hand. 'Hey – thissis why I came to find you. Charlie had it done f' me. It can help you. Here.'

Unwrapping the towel, Felix found a piece of ancient Roman jewellery: a pendant that filled the palm of his hand. The surround was made of gold, in the shape of ivy leaves, alternating with emerald crystals and small creamy pearls. The sardonyx cameo, which had originally been set into its centre, was missing, fallen or prised out, and in its place was a portrait of Kaz's son. A black-and-white photograph, slightly out of focus, cut from the background of a larger composition. Possibly a production shot of *The Iliad*, Felix thought; the boy had been one of the Chorus. Whoever sliced this fragment from the main picture and glued it into the pendant – Charlie probably, in stoned and generous mood – had done it crudely, hurriedly, creating an ugly thing, drawing your attention to the contrast between the chopped photograph and its exquisite setting, and insulting both. For all his star treatment, the boy still looked insignificant, smudged, a face in a crowd, absurdly framed by jewels. It reminded Felix of the plushly mounted Instamatic shot of Isabeau in Charlie's living-room. They were both wrong somehow, offensive somehow. Felix felt a rush of anger. The idea of Charlie rifling through the old production photos at the theatre, cobbling together this piece of barbarism, and then offering it as a kind of love token – *his* Charlie doing this to *his* Kaz – it was awful. And, worst of all, it had *worked*, this gift, this gesture, it had brought her solace. Last time Felix had seen Kaz she was bent double, hugging herself with grief. Now she was smiling.

'It's very nice,' Felix said, in a dull voice.

''s for you,' she said, knotting a reed from the riverbank and slipping it through the pendant's loop. 'T' help wi' your search.'

Felix sighed. It wasn't even *our* search any more. 'Kaz, Kaz,' he said gently.

She slipped the ornament over his neck, then leaned forward and kissed the small, blurred face in it. 'He's here,' she said, sitting back and sniffing the morning air. 'I think he's here.'

'He's everywhere,' said Felix, touching the little face as well. 'Think of it like that.'

She frowned, then spoke with weary patience, as to a drunk. 'I mean Popo-boy.'

twenty-five

Where is everyone? Felix wondered, standing alongside the Roman fountain in the main yard. Apart from Elvis, wiping the dew off the seats of the big jeep, the farm still looked completely deserted. Where was Charlie? He had promised a dawn game drive – he promised yesterday when Felix excused himself from the tour of the farm. Fleeing back to his bungalow, he heard Charlie call after him: 'OK, but come and look at some of my animals in the morning, they're less scary – they're just predators and giants! I wanna show you myself. Don't forget, early, at six, see you then.'

Now Bi Mirza arrived, with Alys riding on one plump hip . . . Alys, transformed from the weeping, hot child of yesterday . . . Alys, radiant and sweet, and overjoyed to see Felix. As much as she had dismissed him yesterday, she worshipped him today. She showed it by stretching out her arms towards him – that trusting, yearning gesture – like her mother used to do.

Hugging her, kissing her hair, Felix addressed Bi Mirza: 'Charlie said he wanted to come along on this drive.'

Bi Mirza looked astonished. She checked her watch.

'I know it's early,' spluttered Felix, 'but he said . . .'

'It is not early and nor is it late,' the Arab woman replied, in her thick but lyrical way. 'However, the festivities are in progress, well under way, already a moon old, with all the feasts and rituals, and it would be most unusual, not to say unthinkable, for the host to absent himself at this stage.'

Felix felt mixed, tugging emotions; a child excluded from a game he'd refused to play. 'But Charlie wanted to –'

'Dr Chabecq wants you to have a good time, sir, he told me specifically. You are to do whatever you desire. And a game drive now . . .' She looked at the sunrise. 'Why, it will be enchanting!'

Felix turned towards the open jeep. The tarpaulin was rolled back this morning. 'Is it safe?'

'Perfectly,' she replied. Following Felix's gaze to Elvis's rifle, slotted into a clamp on the dashboard, she chuckled. 'He hardly ever has cause to use it.' Then, moving closer to Felix, she said, 'The only danger is from the sun. You're not wearing any block. Please put some on. I've coated my little highness.'

Alys was handed back to Bi Mirza, while Felix, feeling even more like a child, a scolded child now, scuffed his heels through the dust and trailed back to the bungalow.

Emile was sitting on the cane settee, his back to Felix, smoking a cigarette, watching early-morning television.

Felix crept past, collected a tube of sunblock from the bathroom (the bungalow's cupboards were stocked with everything a guest might need), and was tiptoeing out again, when he heard: '*And another thing!*'

He swung round, ready to resume the fight with Emile. But it wasn't the old man who'd spoken. It was a figure on the television screen. Duma. In the basement back at the Alex. Filmed, it seemed, by a security camera on the ceiling. The emperor was a distorted small figure far below, one hand raised and hectoring: 'When you accuse me of these crimes,' he said, his voice coming and going, as if across long-distance airwaves; '. . . disappearance of . . . and Kazwaz-whatsit, and the English rose . . . you are forgetting that . . . being point number one! . . . and that . . . point number two! . . . but, most importantly, let me bring your attention to point number three . . . concerning not my crimes, but crimes against me . . .'

His voice was becoming clearer. Felix watched – through fingers locked over his nose – as Duma walked closer to the camera. 'Let us talk not of my murders, but of my murderer. I have often stated that I dream the truth. I know how I will die, when and where, and who my assassin will be. The time has come to impart the latter information. It is a matter of utmost national security. So I hereby, herewith, name the name. I appoint the man.' He aimed one finger. 'It is . . .'

Felix dived for the door.

Outside, he saw his face, white with shock, in the window of the bungalow opposite. Rushing over, he said to himself, 'Oh, no, not this again, no please.' Speaking in his small, private voice, he continued, 'It's all right, shh, shh, far away, can't hurt you, shh, it's all right.' Now he tried a different tack, smiling: 'Come on, *come on*, you're not really bothered, are you?' Next he gave himself a stern talking-to: 'Now listen, we are *not* going to start this nonsense again! Charlie may have put a camera in there, to protect us, or to, to, Lord knows!, but let's just . . . !'

He stopped. Bi Mirza and Alys were standing behind him, frowning.

Bi Mirza cleared her throat. 'Are you ready to go, please? If you hope to see any game, you must . . .'

'Yes, yes,' said Felix, pretending to tidy his hair in the reflection. 'Yes indeed . . .'

'What's the matter?' Alys asked, noticing tears on her godfather's face for the first time. Felix tried to wipe his cheeks and mumble an excuse, but his fingers and voice were quavering badly. With a little kick, Alys signalled to Bi Mirza that she wished to dismount. She crossed to Felix and beckoned him to lean forward. Using an adult tone, guaranteeing confidentiality, she asked again, 'What is it?'

'There's a big bad man in there,' he whispered back, nodding towards his bungalow.

'Come, let's look,' she said, taking his hand.

Bi Mirza stepped forward. 'Unless you depart before sunrise, the game won't –'

'Shush!' commanded Alys, and led Felix into the bungalow.

Duma's face was filling the television screen now – perhaps he had climbed onto a box under the camera – but, strangely, his voice had diminished. It was fuzzy and inaudible.

'*That* man?' asked Alys.

'That man,' sniffled Felix.

Alys picked up the remote control. 'This is what you have to do,' she explained. 'Watch me, watch me.' With one press of her tiny finger, Duma was gone. 'You see?' she said proudly.

'Yes,' Felix replied, in a hushed tone.

'It's easy.'

'It is.'

She tried to reactivate the television. 'D'you want me to show you again?'

'No, no,' he said, snatching the remote control from her. 'Let's go on our game drive now.'

'Does he want to come?' she asked, nodding towards Emile, now asleep in the cane settee.

'No, we'll leave him.'

'But he's not a big bad man?' she checked cautiously.

Felix hesitated, then said, 'No. No, he isn't.'

'OK,' she whispered. 'Then I'll give him good dreams.' She kissed the old man's hand.

'He'll appreciate that,' Felix said. 'He needs good dreams. Now, come on . . .'

He's here, Felix thought, as they hurried back to the main yard, *Duma's here. And Popo-boy. Kaz said she thought Popo-boy was here too. They're both here, Duma and Popo-boy. There goes a quiet weekend.*

When at last they were alone in the back of the jeep, and had set off, and the rush of air was like a soundproofed partition between them and their driver, Felix confided in Alys: 'Thank you.'

She smiled slowly, as one amused by another's childish fears, yet touched also, and realising that it completes a picture of them. She said, 'I love you.' And then again, holding his face in both her small hands and looking directly into his eyes: 'I love you!'

Felix nodded, knowing a response was required, an echo, yet scared of the words today. He avoided the issue by using a gruff, joky voice: 'That's tremendously sweet of you, Lys, love you too.' They passed a cluster of whitewashed buildings. He glanced over – *Is this where it goes on, the revels?* – then asked, 'Are you all right, have you seen Daddy?'

She shrugged, snuggled deeper into his embrace, and did her favourite thing: holding the lobe of his ear, enjoying its small cool plumpness, squeezing slightly now and then.

'Love-love-lub . . .' she said in a way that invited him to join in.

'Ooh, look out,' he cried. 'Hold on!' The jeep thumped over a dip in the road, lifting them off the seat and plonking them down again. Alys squealed excitedly. 'Ooo-weeee!' he said, imitating her. 'Did you feel the butterflies?'

'What?' she called above the noise.

'Butterflies!' he shouted, rubbing his tummy. 'Lots of butterflies. Must've had them for breakfast. A butterfly breakfast.'

She found this very funny. He hugged her tightly. She held his ear-lobe and squeezed it gently.

'Is this nice?' he asked, as the jeep raced off the road and onto a vast savannah, the noise subsiding, rushing softly like water.

Her expression was extraordinary, pulled tight with joy, little teeth bared, eyes glinting, almost demonic, but in a fairy-tale way: a sprite, a goblin. 'It *is* nice!' she answered.

'Just the two of us,' he said.

'The two of us,' she repeated, making his heart soar.

It was a big open morning, and as they travelled they saw galloping giraffe, an eagle in flight, a herd of elephants stripping trees, a mother cheetah and cubs sunning themselves on the tarmac of the airstrip. Sometimes they drove close enough to touch and sometimes they kept their distance, Elvis always knowing when to do which. And they saw a swirl of vultures in the blue, and caught a smell of something stinking to high heaven, and both airborne clues led to a two-day-old buffalo carcass lying on an immense dark patch, more like ink than blood by now, its emptied rib-cage home to a thick, trembling soup of blowfly larvae (this stirred Felix, who shook his head briskly); the scene completed by a pride of bloated, sleeping lions. And they saw more lion and more cheetah, elephant and giraffe, so many more that they became blasé, like people do about the cloudscapes out of plane windows or the old volcano back home, fast-food wonders, junk miracles, and eventually they just stopped looking, and put their heads back, cuddling one another and thinking their separate thoughts.

I'm safe out here, Felix decided, completely safe. The great grasslands were so vast he felt he was being granted a view across the whole country, the whole continent, and so wide that the horizon seemed to dip at each far end, curving into the shape of the earth itself. Here there was nowhere for even a ghost to hide. The sky was clear; tremendously high and peaceful. Heaven is empty, Felix thought, smiling to himself – the Greater Power is out to lunch. Then, cresting a rise, there was a cloudbank shaped like a gigantic old man, furious, bearded, with a shock of white hair, and Felix laughed in his face. Hey, O Blessed Jester, why so glum? look at me, look at me . . .

I'm grinning, I can't stop grinning, I'm grinning inside, I'm singing in there too, I'm yawning with joy, my shirt is blowing, filling, my lungs too, filling with the smell of air, dust, land – it's intoxicating! – my head's a kite, I'm high and I'm clean, I'm drunk and I'm sober, I'm hooked on my own chemicals, I'm delirious with Felix-fever, I'm suffering delusions of grandeur, I'm imagining that I am Africa, and, even crazier, even better, *I am me*!

twenty-six

Felix adjusted the sleeve of his black toga, and gingerly appraised the meal before him – a black stew served in a glass bowl coated with black lead – while the storyteller, black-robed and hooded, continued to address the other banquet guests, all dressed in black.

'. . . So when the room was finished, hung with black, on the walls, ceiling and floor, and furnished with black benches, Domitian's guests were shown in, at night, and without attendants. The place settings were marked by black stone slabs, like tombstones, lit by little black lamps, like those hung on tombs . . .'

Everyone glanced to the slabs at their elbows and murmured appreciatively.

'And then there appeared beautiful boys, naked and painted black like spectres, and they moved round the guests in an uncanny dance . . .'

As he spoke, the curtains parted at one end of the chamber, and the aforementioned boys stood there in the flesh. Even the black-skinned ones were painted black. To the driving rhythms of double oboe and tambourine, they began to gyrate and stamp, their movements aggressive, thrusting, lewd, mournful.

'. . . finally ending at the feet of the guests, one for each of them.'

Felix twisted round to look at his. The return gaze was unnerving: contrasted against the black body-paint, the youth's eyes looked completely white and vacant.

'. . . The food and drink was, as you can see, the banquet of the dead, all in black. The guests shook with terror. The room was silent as the grave. Only Domitian spoke, and he talked only of murder and sudden death. At last he dismissed them. When they returned to their biers and carriages, they found their own servants missing. So they were taken home by strangers. Finally, just when they were starting to recover, a messenger from Domitian was announced. Every guest thought their last hour had come. But instead, they each received their gravestone, which was actually made of silver, and all the valuable dishes which had been set before them, and finally, even the boy who had stood at their feet, now washed, clean, and beautifully dressed.'

Felix glanced round again, even more uneasily, at the half-moons of pure white eye staring back at him.

'. . . And such were the feasts of the Emperor Domitian, given to celebrate his victories.'

Everyone applauded. The large crowd included Bull Brak, Lord Gomes, and other trustees. As they began to eat, the women, and some of the men, wriggled down the eating couches and stretched out their toes to make first contact with the nude, blacked-up figures standing behind.

So far so good, thought Felix, as he retracted his feet, making sure they weren't even touching the edge of the couch. So far nothing too obscene or threatening.

Following the game drive, feeling that his confidence had never been stronger, his recovery never more secure, and fearful of only one thing – returning to his bungalow, and the television set there – Felix had taken Alys back to her playroom, and then asked Bi Mirza to lead him to this section of the farm. 'Only to *see*,' he warned Charlie, who was amazed by his arrival. He was just in time for the Black Brunch, which heralded the beginning of what Charlie called the serious phase of the party.

Charlie flopped at Felix's side now, throwing aside his storyteller's hood – and voice. To relate the tale of Domitian's feasts, he had assumed a honeyed and wonderstruck tone, which brought a smile to Felix's lips: it sounded like the narration in American documentaries. Only half listening as Charlie now began comparing Roman and Greek revelry, Felix cast a professional eye over the room's props and set. To his surprise, it was all slightly amateur. You could detect this just at the edge of things – where that drape didn't quite close or that platter was chipped – the lurking presence of cardboard and plaster, of staples and sticky-tape.

'. . . I guess it was more a kinda religious thing for the Greeks,' Charlie was saying. 'It brought them to a state of theolepsy, a kinda mind-fuck with the gods, who approved of hedonism, gratification, the whole bag.'

'In *The Odyssey*,' said Felix, eager to be on familiar territory, 'Aphrodite sleeps with the Ares, the sun-god, and when her husband, Hephaestus, gets upset and summons all the other gods to see what's going on, there's no moral reprobation, no criticism. They delight in it. Fidelity in marriage is being mocked by the goddess of love herself!'

'There y' go,' said Charlie. 'For the Greeks, excess is blessed, cathartic, a safety-valve, it's healthy, it's prescribed by the gods and your doctor.' He gave his shy-naughty smile. 'For the Romans, their brand of *la dolce vita* is . . . well.'

'What?'

'As Domitian's little prank shows, something else is at work.'

'What?'

'Cruelty.'

'Cruelty,' Felix echoed slowly.

'Yeah, his guests are put through this evening of gloom, doom and terror *before* they get rewarded with the silver slab, the fancy tableware, the boy-fuck. Their pleasure is gift-wrapped with cruelty. C'mon, I mean, look at the Games. Give the people *panem et circenses* and you have a happy population, all appetites sated.' Seeing Felix's grimace of disapproval, Charlie grinned. 'St Augustine tells the story of a young student who avoids going to the Games. Then at last he gets taken there by some pals. He says, "OK, you can drag my body there but not my soul." So at first he sits there with his eyes closed. Then some noise, some God-almighty shout from the crowd, makes him look. And then he can't turn away. He gets drunk. Drunk on blood. The blood out there in the arena. It gets into his own blood. As the man tells it, "He looked, his blood burned, and he took away with him a madness which goaded him to return."'

Felix gave a half-laugh. 'Well, if anything round here is habit-forming, I'd better give it a miss. As Kaz says, "It remains tomorrow, so I must go."'

He didn't move.

Charlie watched, amused, then said, 'Do you know the worst thing about habit-forming habits?'

'Wouldn't have a clue.' Felix chuckled grimly. 'Do tell me.'

'Monotony,' replied Charlie. 'Everyone keeps talking about the problem of *monotony* at the Games. The audiences got so fucking bored so fucking quickly. Kept coming back, hooked on it, but needing something more, something different. Had to keep changing the show, keep devising new acts. Blind gladiators, women gladiators, children gladiators, children fighting small animals, animals fighting tied-down birds, something else fighting fish. On and on. And . . .' He lost his track, looked round vaguely. 'I mean, take this weekend. No, OK, take this banquet. Took hours to set up, prepare the menu, arrange for all this gear, and now . . . now I'm already ready for something else.' Sighing, he nodded towards the meal before them. 'You gonna partake? "The Shield of Minerva", favourite dish of Vitellius, bit of a gastronome. That peacock you met yesterday – his brains are in there. Also the livers of parrot-fish, the tongues of flamingos, and the entrails of lampreys. We've added the black sauce.'

'I think I'll give it a miss.'

'Stroll with me?'

Squeezing politely past his naked blackamore, Felix followed Charlie. Their faces were brushed by several layers of curtains infused with the chamber's smells of candles and food, and then suddenly they were in the whitewashed entrance hall, where a host of different sensations made them blink and sniff. Bright daylight from outside clashed with the neon signs over serving hatches and doorways: changing rooms, a check-in counter for coats and umbrellas, a cocktail-and-narcotics bar, and a pharmaceutical kiosk. Here some wag had scrawled a large piece of graffito – THANK THE GODS THERE'S A DOCTOR IN THE HOUSE – obviously the favourite joke of the establishment.

Charlie beckoned Felix into the pharmaceutical kiosk. At the

far table, festooned with test-tubes, steam- and ice-baths, burners
and filters, stood a tall, stooping American. He had long plaited
silver hair and a Zapata moustache, and was dressed in a white
coat. Waiting alongside, licking his lips, was a chubby young man in
full Roman armour.

'Well, friend,' said the American, in a languorous, husky voice, 'it
kinda depends whether you want mescaline's flowing visuals or the
warm earth world of peyote.'

'I think I'd like something in between please,' the Roman soldier
said, in an impeccable British accent.

'Right, right,' replied the other, and began work, murmuring to
himself; 'Let's try this . . . but add a lil' . . . anhydrous Et_2O . . .
mmn, take away a lil' . . . mmn . . . propylthiophenethylamine . . .'

'Excuse me,' said the party-guest. 'I definitely don't want any jitters, you will make sure there's no –'

'No jitters,' the tall man drawled reassuringly. 'No nausea, no
cramps, no frequent urination, no neck-ache, no motor co-ordina-
tion problems, maybe just a touch of vertigo – but only when your
eyes are open.'

'No hangover?' the other checked fussily.

'No negative price to pay whatsoever. Here ya go, friend.'

As the satisfied customer was handed a beaker to drink, Charlie
indicated the American to Felix, whispering, 'This is Deany, my
college buddy, the pharmacist who sends in my medical supplies.
This time he's flown over in person to have him a lil' ol' African
holiday.'

'Oh, I see, gosh, yes,' said Felix. It was hard to believe that this
round-shouldered, silver-haired wizard was Charlie's contempo-
rary.

Before the Roman soldier left, Charlie gave him a green questionnaire from a stack on the counter, and explained about his
research project. How – with Deany's assistance – he was exploring a new range of party drugs, and hoped to publish the results;
half scientific study, half recipe book. 'It's only a matter of time,'
Charlie said, his eyes bright, 'before the West gets as laid-back
about drugs as it is about booze, and then we'll see them on our
supermarket shelves, with all the sales-devices, all the sexy bottles 'n'

labels . . . it's only a matter of time. And me and Deany here, we'd
love to have your help.'

The soldier went off happily. Now Felix and Deany shook hands,
both saying how much they'd heard about one another. The
American went quiet, his long fingers retaining their hold on Felix's,
locking his gaze too. Deany's pupils were very pale: a thin grey with
pink showing through, like old jeans. Felix imagined that the man's
eyes were originally blue, but, along with his hoarse voice, they'd
become ghosts of their former selves during the long years of pharmaceutical research. Deany leaned closer: 'I reckon I've got the
very thing for you, Felix-friend. This juice I'm thinking of grants
great awareness, great Sunday-afternoon feeling, and your dreams
walk side by side with real life.'

'Oh, I'm on that already,' Felix replied perkily.

Deany's eyes registered surprise, and then, as Felix explained
about the Long Island clinic, they filled with a kind of horror, and
finally, like their former colour, all interest drained. Turning to
Charlie, Deany said, 'And what can I get you, fine friend o' mine?'

Charlie grinned. 'Aw, Deany-boy, gimme somethin' . . . sexy!'

'Somethin' sexy,' the other echoed lazily, with a smile. 'That's
what everyone's asking for. But I'm not gonna give to you what I
gave to them, I'm gonna give to you the house special, the *crème de
la crème*, the vintage blend. Man, just breathing's gonna make you
shoot. And shoot, and shoot. Hush now,' he cooed, as Charlie
opened his mouth in enquiry. 'Just trust me. Just take it and fill in
the form, please, sir.'

As Charlie accepted the green questionnaire, laughing, it
occurred to Felix that, next to Deany, his friend was a novice.
Charlie's suntanned limbs and blond locks showed flatteringly
against his black toga; he looked centuries old, yet clean and pure,
more Greek than Roman. But all innocence vanished as Deany
handed over a beaker of colourless liquid. Felix watched Charlie
drinking it with an intense, impatient greediness, which he knew
well. Charlie was also given booster supplies in mini-phials, and
he hoarded these in a satchel strapped under the folds of his
garment.

Another guest came in with a list of request-orders for Deany.

Making way for him, Charlie fetched a pre-packed satchel from behind the counter, and said to Felix, 'This's for you.'

'Charlie!' huffed Felix.

'Just look.'

Felix's satchel was stocked with chewing-gum, buzz balls and cigarettes. 'And this?' he enquired, digging deeper and uncovering condoms and lubricants, Elastoplast, New Skin, antiseptic wipes, and a little spray of breath-freshener.

'Just in case,' smiled Charlie. 'Does no harm just to carry the gear. You don't have to use it.' As Felix started to protest again, he added, 'You don't have to *do* anything. You don't have to come any further. You can turn round and walk out that door. Go and swim this afternoon, tell Alys stories, read, snooze, whatever.'

Felix thought for a long while, scowling at Charlie – his old black scowl, his keep-away scowl – then he strapped on the satchel, put hands on hips, and, feeling like an explorer, said, 'Lead on!'

twenty-seven

The design was masterly.

Once you'd left the entrance hall with its side chambers and booths, you followed a sloping stone floor under a dark vaulted ceiling, into a courtyard where daylight burned again, then through a small moist orchard of nectarine trees, and finally out onto a terrace. Here you surveyed a most unexpected vista.

It was either the ruins of a whole small city or just those of its huge amphitheatre. The scale was difficult to grasp. The area was scattered with half-collapsed archways and broken columns, exposed interiors, roofless basements and underground passageways, stairways ending in mid-air, floors with beautiful fragments of mosaics, and marble rubble among long grass. Some of the weather-beaten stonework supported awnings and particoloured sails, and here and there were semi-transparent silk tents and reed-work hovels.

The sun, fire torches and concealed pools of water threw surprising patterns of light – on ceilings or in far corners – sometimes sharing shadows, which grew fluid and multi-layered, leading the eye into mysterious recesses and caverns; while bluish smoke from incense burners and coal braziers mixed with red dust-clouds blowing in from the surrounding landscape, creating a travelling mist reminiscent of one of Felix's stage effects; it curled round the heaviest pillars and seemed to lift them fractionally off the ground.

The smells were of roasting meat and animal dung, of perfumes and oils, of wood gum and wine casks, of nuts, salt and flowers, of cinnamon, vetiver and pomander.

Soft noises were also carried on the air: moans of human pleasure, the bleating of animals, splashing of water, and strange music played on rare instruments; ancient bagpipes, the sarrousophone – a chilly, barbaric sound – or the kythara, a Roman version of the lyre.

Felix shook his head slowly. 'Did you import it all from a real site?'

'No, no.' Charlie was whispering with pride. 'It's all artificially weathered, and . . .' He searched for the word.

'Distressed,' said Felix.

'Beautifully distressed, huhn? Designed by an archaeologist pal of mine. Specialises in Carthage, Volubilis, Alexandria, *et al*, Roman Africa.' Charlie's eyes grew dreamy. 'Y'know, the Romans did a lotta hunting in Africa. Elephant, lion, leopard. Well, it wasn't hunting actually, it was tracking, catching, more like modern zoo or conservation pick-ups, but without the dope-darts, choppers and big rigs. Can you imagine! – the bravery – just imagine! This was all for the Games. Needed game for the Games, needed hundreds of wild beasts, thousands . . . Suetonius says *five thousand* were once paraded in a single day. So the animal-catchers, they combed Egypt, Morocco, Tunisia, further, deeper, some say they got down as far as Senegal. Anyway, me and this archaeologist pal, we had this fantasy. What if they got down as far as *here*? And what if they, like, built an outpost here, a little home from home, and how would they fill in the long nights before the next test of strength, the next safari, their own Games?'

Felix marvelled at Charlie's imagination – the idea of drug-supermarkets, or this game-for-the-Games scenario – if only he could cook up something that brought him peace.

Grinning, Charlie spread his arms across the view. 'So that was our brief for all this. My archaeologist, he's into the ol' poppy pipe . . . I gave him a six-month supply and asked him to doodle.'

Doodle. Felix noted the word, the magic word, and immediately thought of Emile – Emile back in the bungalow. Was now the right time to tell Charlie? Would there ever be a right time? Did it matter?

The weekend was starting to make its own aimless, purposeful shapes and loops.

Charlie smiled. 'You still with me?'

Instead of replying Felix just reached for his buzz balls.

'What's he doing?'

'Which one?'

'Him.'

'Which him?'

'The one whispering, moving around whispering,' said Felix. 'There – *him.*'

As they watched, the man in question crossed to a wall of veils and drew one, peeling away another layer of darkness from the shadowy chamber, where assorted couples were just discernible: in various stages of undress and sexual activity. Now the man moved to the nearest couple, bent over their kissing heads, and said something.

'He's teaching them the rules as they go,' Charlie explained. Along with a few other spectators, he and Felix were seated above the action in a little tiered gallery, like at a squash court; the audience communicating in discreet murmurs, out of respect for the players. 'He's a historian pal of mine from Morocco,' Charlie continued. 'Abdul, another expert in Roman Africa . . . he's written one of those *The Private Life of* books.'

'He's doing it again,' Felix observed, as the man called Abdul drew another veil.

'Yeah. He's teasing them. He's explained that only newly weds could make love before nightfall, and only libertines did it without darkness, so now he's gradually taking theirs away, the darkness . . . see how it's affecting them . . .' The exertions of each couple grew with each new spill of light. 'It's the naughtiness, y'see,' continued Charlie, in a low excited voice close to Felix's ear. 'At the start, Abdul told them to just get stuck in however they wanted. With one proviso – the women must keep some of their clothes on. Now they're learning the rules, the Roman rituals of love-making, and they're . . . Look there!'

Felix tried to pay attention, but he wasn't at all comfortable. If only Charlie wasn't here. Or the other spectators. If only he could watch from a more concealed viewpoint, like an air-duct, for example, if only he could curtail the free space around him, behind his neck, if only he could stop people arriving and departing, if only he could organise the scene to his exact requirements.

'Whoops, they're asking for trouble,' laughed Charlie, directing Felix's attention to a male couple: one sitting, the other kneeling in front of him.

'Not allowed?' Felix asked Charlie.

'Oh, sure. But it's got to be done to *you*. If you're a sucker you're a slave – as it were.'

The two men received a telling-off from Abdul, laughed, and immediately adopted the 69 position. 'But – but – I don't follow,' said Felix. 'They've doubled the disgrace!'

'It's the naughtiness,' Charlie whispered into Felix's ear, and then kissed it lightly.

Felix froze. 'Uh, sorry,' Charlie said, but nuzzled closer. Felix stared straight ahead. He half wanted to respond, but how? 'Just lean in,' said a voice inside him, 'it's simple.' 'No, it isn't,' a second voice said, 'it's the most complicated manoeuvre you'll ever make, that little lean-in.' 'Talk,' a third voice advised, 'talk your way out – or *in* – demand an explanation, an end to these enigmatic codes and rules and games, which everyone else seems to understand except you! Say to him, "Now listen, old sport, what exactly are you? Kaz says you're marrying her. I know that's preposterous, but where would she get such an idea? *What are you?*"' The silence was stretching, it was lasting too long, meaning too much.

'Sorry,' Charlie said again, but genuinely. He added cheerfully, 'Blame pal Deany-boy.' Taking the green questionnaire from inside his toga, he consulted his watch, then filled in the first line, writing fast, stopping now and then to check his pulse, his forehead, his neck glands.

Meanwhile, trembling from the little encounter – *should he have done something different?* – Felix turned back to view the spectacle below. The couples were all engaged in a flurry of new activity. 'And now? What's happening now?'

Charlie glanced up from his work. 'Oh. Yeah. Abdul's just

children

revealed the reason why he asked the women to keep something on. It was the Roman way. Chicks had to wear *some* layer of clothing. Not even whores would do it without a stitch.' They watched the women tearing off their remaining clothes and the rhythm of everyone's passion swell. Charlie clapped his hands and laughed. 'Good old Abdul!'

Now the viewing station was on a little bridge spanning a clear rockpool, its water alive with the sunlight that found its way through a surround of broken colonnades.

'This is modelled on Tiberius' Blue Grotto,' said Charlie, who was becoming more animated with every passing moment; scratching his hair, flicking his wrists, tweaking the seat and crotch of his garments like an overheated child. 'And, yeah, what we're gonna see here is, uhh, one of his inventions in old age, to, y'know, revive his powers.'

The door from a changing area opened, and Felix watched as two attendants led out an elderly Asian man, his sagging skin like waterlogged cloth. The attendants steered him down a series of ledges into the pool. Once afloat, the old boy became more chipper, doing a slow crawl. Now a dozen children scampered out from behind the pillars and weed-bushes, and flew through the air, plopping into the water like a herd of pink and brown seals. Felix's fellow spectators on the bridge began oohing and aahing . . . these were either just the sounds which adults make when children swim, or something hungrier. Felix went still, frowning.

The children were diving, long deep dives, pearl-fisher dives, which took them along or between the swimmer's legs, and the water churned and foamed as he was assailed by various submarine activities. He started to smile. His smile grew mightily. Wreathed in glistening wrinkles, his face could have been a type of seaweed. Narrowing his eyes, Felix suddenly recognised him – V. K. Bukherjee, the theatre trustee, the one who had demolished Felix's career so eloquently at the board meeting.

'If he didn't look so happy, it could be piranha at work, huhn?' Charlie observed. 'Tiberius called himself the old shark and the kids his little fishes. And when –'

He stopped, mouth open. He was addressing fresh air. Felix had marched off the bridge.

'Say, what's the score?' asked Charlie, catching up in a tunnel leading out of the grotto. 'Is it 'cause of old V. K.? I know he's not your favourite person since –'

'No. It's not V. K.'

'What, then?'

'Where's Alys?' Felix asked.

Charlie replied instantly: 'She wasn't among them.'

'Why not? If you're letting those other children . . .'

'Buddy, am I about to be lectured?' The warning was light, and Charlie was smiling – or at any rate his jaws had begun to twitch in a loose, involuntary way, which still looked friendly. He paused, battling the exhilarating waves of feeling mounting inside him, then tried to explain calmly, 'I'm not here to judge. A lot of what goes on here ain't my particular bag, but it ain't my business either. Folk can do what they please. I'm –'

Felix cut in hotly. 'So? Anything? Does *anything* go?'

Charlie gave a small, careful shrug. 'In the cult of the bacchanalia, the holiest article of faith was to think nothing a crime.'

'I don't care about the cult of the ruddy . . . !' Turning away, Felix leaned his forehead against the cool stone of the wall. He felt baffled and frightened. Watching the spectacle in the pool was like being in there himself: beset from below, by hidden things, little mouths and fingers, now nipping, now caressing, little demons, little temptations. *The incident at Pembe Cove yesterday . . . on the bungalow porch . . . Alys's little feet clambering on him, slipping down, slipping . . .* The more Felix thought about it, the more he panicked, and the more enraged he became. Wheeling on Charlie, he demanded, 'How old were those children?'

'OK fine, yeah, yeah, yeah, let's hear it from Felix!' exploded Charlie, eyes blinking rapidly. 'The rest of us muddle along as best we can, wanna bit, gimme bit, touch me, help me, hold me, love me, but not Felix, so let's hear it from him. I mean, y'know, in village societies all round us, kids sleep in the same huts as their folks, hearing them screw, seeing them screw, an' uhh . . . wha' were we talking abou'? . . . no, OK, OK, what I'm saying is that they witness, like, their parents' *love*, and, and, and . . . what? Huhn? Is there village after village of jittering sex fiends or, or – or *forty-six-year-old virgins*?! I don't think so! Don't think so, don't think so, don't think so . . .'

Charlie kept repeating this phrase, as if hoping to wind himself down, then suddenly said, 'Uh, 'scuse me,' and started writing on the questionnaire at high speed. Peering over his shoulder, Felix read: '*At 2 hr point after consumption, trying to keep a clear conversation going but pretty sure there* are *problems.*'

As suddenly as he'd begun, Charlie stopped writing, took hold of Felix and hugged him. 'Love you, ol' buddy, I do, I really do, with all my heart I do, love you with my heart and in any other way you want, and OK, OK, I know that's not cool for you, and it's just Deany-boy's juice talking anyway, and 's OK. Your innocence, I love your innocence, you're more innocent than old V. K. back there in the pool, and I don't want to scar it. Go back to the farm, go swim, sunbathe, this place isn't for you. It gets much heavier from here on . . .' His gaze roamed down to Felix's chest, where the toga had opened to reveal Kaz's pendant. Peering at the little portrait, Charlie worked the muscles round his eyes, as if unable to establish whether the blur was in the photo or his sight. 'Why are you carrying round a picture of my kid?'

'Your kid?'

'Sure.'

'But,' said Felix slowly, 'Kaz has never . . .'

'No, she didn't even tell *me* at first,' said Charlie, still speaking rapidly, though his balance grew calmer. 'Then . . . a picnic by the lake one day . . . were you there?, loaded probably . . . we were barbecuing this amazing fish some men had caught, and I took Kaz aside . . . Duma had just brought in the law about "mongrels", and she had this kid . . . so I was saying, y'know, I'd help if there were problems, and she said, "That's good to know 'cause he's *yours*." Jesus, Jesus. Man, I nearly . . . ! I mean, Isabeau was there that day . . . outa earshot . . . but there!' He covered his face. 'Difficult to talk about. Y'know, I ended up helping as much as I could, paying for him to have a decent education, to go on to university – it's where he was arrested, right? – but really, and I don't want this to sound bad, but Kaz should've told me earlier, and then she needn't've . . . I could easily've done a termination myself . . . y'know.'

Felix nodded ponderously, eyes glazed, trying to absorb the news. He half remembered the day that Charlie had mentioned; a beautiful blue day. And Isabeau. Beautiful Isabeau. Canadian but thoroughly French, delicate-boned but tough as old boots, armed with cameras, tramping across Africa like it was her backyard. She and Charlie couldn't have children. It took them another fifteen years from that day, and several trips to overseas clinics, before they were finally blessed with Alys. Then, just months later – their Greater Power now laughing up His sleeve – Isabeau was in the middle of an aerial shoot when her small plane crashed. The family lost more than its wife and mother that day. Isabeau had been the restraining presence in Charlie's life, allowing him a certain amount of recreational activities, but always keeping him in check, keeping the doctor well, helping to maintain that golden mean prescribed by the Roman poet.

'I miss her so much,' Charlie said suddenly. He stared at his friend with a big, open, hopeless expression. Felix dropped his gaze, hushed as always by this subject, this *missing* of loved ones, which afflicted everyone else. Charlie touched the photo in the pendant. 'And then this kid went and died too,' he said, rubbing the face gently, as though trying to bring it into sharper focus. 'He was kinda "terminated" after all. And we *won't* find the guy who did it, he's gone, the bird has flown. Kaz knows that an' I know that, but we're scared to talk about it. It's sad man, *sad*. Anyway, I'm gonna make it up to Kaz, gonna do that one of these days, but . . .' He scrubbed his fingers over his forehead. 'OK, sorry, I'm just a bit out of it right now, sorry we just picked the wrong time, sorry . . .'

He wandered away, down the tunnel, jotting notes on his questionnaire, and then, reaching the other end, ran into the daylight, picking up two perfect people as he went, one in each arm.

Felix stared at the portrait in the pendant. Despite the grainy edges and dark blocks of shadow, a new clarity was emerging. The sweep of the cheekbones, the shy-naughty turn of the mouth, these were Charlie's features . . . the hair braids, the raunchy puffy eyes, these were Kaz's . . . Charlie and Kaz together, that's what you could see in this face.

Why hadn't they told him before? It needed to be kept a secret, he could see that, but why from *him* . . .?! How strange that something had happened . . . something so important . . . so close by . . . and he hadn't caught the tiniest glimpse of it.

Felix blew out a stream of air, steadying himself, thinking hard. He understood Kaz's grief differently now . . . she'd had the baby without its father knowing . . . she'd risked his displeasure . . . she was already shunned by her family . . . this child was *everything*.

'And Popo-boy?' he asked himself aloud. That was the one part of the boy's portrait that hadn't become clearer: the identity of his killer. Charlie remained certain that he had fled. Kaz believed he was here, at the party. *Charlie's friend . . . whatsisname . . . Dee . . . Danny . . . didn't Charlie call him something like Danny-boy? That strange wizard . . . could he be Popo-boy?*

Felix slipped the pendant under his toga, and set off slowly. As he left the tunnel, he noticed a lone figure among broken colonnades. It was the youth he had seen before, the youth with waist-length hair, dirty, naked; the youth on crutches. *Who was this figure?* He looked white skinned, but could he be mulatto? Was he perhaps the ghost of Kaz's son . . . Charlie and Kaz's son . . . ?

Felix glanced round, searching for the boy's companion, the old legless man, but he was nowhere to be seen. Not yet. As at Pembe Cove, Felix felt sure that if he spotted one, the other would appear before long. Their visitations were always rather reassuring. It was another mystery. Felix took a deep breath, then headed further into the ruins, and not back as recommended by Charlie.

twenty-eight

'What are you on?' . . . 'When did you take it?' . . . 'How do you feel now (think about eyes, neck, fingers, toes, think inside too, think about breathing, belly, think even deeper)?' . . . 'What do you *feel?*'

Felix chuckled to himself. He quite fancied filling in the green questionnaire; a blank one, found on the floor with a footprint across it. Having no pen, he traced one fingertip along the dotted line, answering, *I feel good.*

He puffed at his cigarette. Modern accoutrements seemed permissible in these areas of the ruins. The meticulous Roman rituals, and everyone's delight in them – these things had gone by the wayside: they required too much concentration and discipline. The party had reached a stage where people were more than drunk, more than high. Some were still endeavouring to fill in their questionnaires, writing against walls or low ceilings or on one another's backs; dutiful students in an exam of pleasure. This one told of seeing Modigliani faces in the people passing by, that one described the voluptuous hands of the music, a third spoke of delightful tooth-rubberiness, another reported a brief but fascinating spiritual emergency. Their unbroken focus on themselves suited Felix perfectly. With a length of toga pulled over his head like a hood, its visage hazy with cigarette smoke, he felt like an invisible sleuth or avenger, he wasn't quite sure which, but the photo-pendant was like a badge, licensing him to explore. He'd been enjoying the sensation for some time now as he drifted through all the interleading rooms and corridors, courtyards and alleyways. Somewhere in the labyrinth he'd happened across Muriel Slackforth-Carter and other trustees queuing in front of a peephole, and they never realised it was him. In turn, it was becoming harder and harder to distinguish regulars from newcomers among the party-goers, pillars of society from refugees, masters from servants. Status had slipped off with clothes, barriers of language and race had been swept away by the great wash of alcohol and chemicals, and, in the greedy tenderness of love-making, millionaires held the faces of street-kids and whispered, 'Are you OK?'

I also feel wise, Felix notified his questionnaire. *All-seeing, all-knowing.* Oh, it was so charmingly silly what people were doing to one another, making such a fuss about it all. He alone could see that this adult business of love-making was simply a return to babyhood – the closed eyes, the full mouth, the reassuring hand on the feeding head.

And the games, the child-like games. In one chamber couples were using low tables – like coffee tables with the glass removed – as pleasure aids. One partner lay underneath and made hectic L noises with their tongues (reminding Felix of Miss Rosewood's elocution lessons), while the other squatted above, feet quivering, tummy squeezing hard. Intrigued by the activities here, Felix would've stayed longer if it were not for the smell – the overpowering scent of air-fresheners. Elsewhere he found a same-sex zone, and was diverted for a while by its ambience, where humour and lust vied for dominance. Here was a muscleman frotting another's pecs and promising to give him a pearl necklace; there was a woman feeding different-coloured berries into her lover and whispering sweet nothings; and there a tall boy, with a dextrous, dancer's body, attempted to simultaneously mount three men fanned out below him like a Busby Berkeley formation. But further on, where roof and walls narrowed into a dark tunnel, Felix grew cautious. He could only dimly perceive the scrums of bodies, but they looked potentially aggressive – hands might reach out to grab him – and the floor was perilous, rolling with dildos, and slippery with condoms, these wriggling and glimmering underfoot with lives of their own. Felix thought of sea-urchins and turned back.

'In a little known encounter between Oscar Fingall O'Flahertie Wills Wilde and Friedrich Wilhelm Nietzsche,' a lone bearded man with an exceptionally high voice said to Felix as he passed, 'Wilde kicked off with, "One must either be a work of art or wear a work of art." "No, no," said Nietzsche, "Remain faithful to the earth." "On the other hand," Wilde retorted, "Give a man a mask and he will tell the truth."'

I'm with Wilde, Felix thought merrily, pulling his hood further over his face.

Round the next corner, the atmosphere was suddenly different. What looked like rays of black sunshine found their way through the roof, lighting the activities below clearly enough, yet leaving plenty of shadows for a black-robed figure to creep through. There was a special energy here. It was as though everyone had just been given a fresh dose of pharmaceuticals, all at the same time, and the wave of their hit, their rush, somehow swept over Felix, lifting his senses too.

I feel . . . I feel . . . ?

The place was heavy with people. They were on the floor, in hollows up the walls, on ceiling shelves and in hammocks. It was as if he was inside one of his own stage compositions, one of the biblical numbers, as if he was stealing through the thick of it without anyone knowing. To sit in a dark auditorium creating such spectacles, shaping them, lighting them, watching them, this was pleasurable enough, but there was always a constraint, a sense of having to behave yourself. Crawling through the air-ducts in the old days, that was better, you could express yourself more, you could murmur and squirm. But here, now, this was a new treat, actually to pass among all these bodies, peeking and prying as close as you liked – *nobody seemed to notice or mind* – it was like tiptoeing through paradise. Nakedness. Was anything else quite so natural and so shocking? Violence, perhaps. Similar in a way. Nakedness jumps at the eye like blood. The darkness of secret hair and flesh, the sudden appearance of new information, new features – breast-cheeks, nipple-eyes – a whole new face between a man's thighs. And now, to examine nakedness, not in repose, but in full arousal, full flow. Ah. Such intimate rawness – who called these things genitalia? Oh, no, no, sexual organs!, these are organs, definitely organs. To peer at them now, shifting a limb perhaps to get a closer view – *oo, oo, look at me looking, look at her letting me look* – to see them so near, you feel you've crept into the owner's body, and you're inspecting the flaps and tubes and valves of very hidden things – *ooo, look at him peeling that slice of her, fold by fold, finger, thumb, tongue* – you're in a butcher's shop at midnight, playing among the shine and scent and slap of meat, meat, meat, oh, it's a delicious, vicious thing, *nakedness*!

Felix reeled from the place.

He found himself outside again, in a walled garden, empty of people, half open to the sky. The weird light he had seen, the black sunshine, it was perhaps moonlight, or pre-dawn light, or dusk . . . difficult to tell. He must have been wandering around for hours, maybe longer, maybe a day. His muscles were aching, weighed down with a welter of strange excitements as much as tiredness. He hadn't sat down for ages – to do so would be to miss something, surely – his feet were swollen, his walk a hobble. He liked it – it felt familiar, he wasn't sure why.

He could hear sounds coming from the furthest reaches of the ruins – drumming, the pitty-pat of straps, the lowing of beasts – while on the garden wall, a trail of graffiti drawn in human substances with care and artistry, invited him to proceed . . .

Oh, this place was incredible, it was everything he wanted, here he could just look and look to his heart's content. Here he could even reach out and touch if he chose. Who would know? . . . *what* he touched, *why* he touched. He could go that far. Why not? He could even . . .

It suddenly hit him. What he was up to. All this searching and spying . . . it was just preparation for something else. Somehow, somewhere, at this party. This was it. The time, the place. Noticing the crumpled green sheet of paper in his hand, he stared at its insistent question, 'What do you *feel*?', and blushed, alone in the garden he blushed. Then he drew the breath-freshener spray from the supplies Charlie had packed in his satchel, and aimed it at his mouth. The nozzle gave a little gasp. Smiling, he whispered, 'I know. Shocking, isn't it?'

twenty-nine

'Whatever you want – think about it – we're gonna grant it you.
We're gonna honour you, we're gonna thank you.'

Bull Brak finished whispering again into Felix's ear, then straightened up, and swung back into his agitated prowl, a boxer limbering
up, rolling his shoulders, flexing his arms, stamping and skipping.
He receded down the cavern, half vanishing in the strips of steam,
which whipped out of his way as though scared to make contact.
The humans had no such choice. Lined along the walls, it was their
task to apply more grease as he passed, to scourge with branches, to
receive an extended arm, stretching the muscles.

Brak had been pacing the long cavern for a while now, and, each
time he came down to the audience end, he loomed down to whisper in Felix's ear: 'We're gonna grant you anything you want, we're
gonna honour you, yes we are, yes siree.'

Felix didn't know what on earth he was talking about, except
that it almost certainly concerned Duma.

Big-boned, slack-muscled, Brak's body was yellow and hairless,
daubed with liver spots, scrawled with thick blue veins. Every inch
of him glistened with sweat and grease smears – clear little waves
with brown crests – and the grease smearers gleamed also, and the
walls were clammy and dripping, a drum played, steam hissed,
throats panted, Felix was soaked with excitement.

Who might it be, the one for me? he mused, scanning the bodies of
Brak's slaves. *Will it be you or you . . . her or him?* Pretending to

cough, he covered his mouth and had another quick shot of breath-freshener.

'C'mon – get me started!' Brak commanded his minions. 'C'mon – let's go!'

The women reached lower as he passed, and the men leaned forward, clicking their tongues, as though encouraging an animal, the drumbeat increased, people panted faster, shaping their lips and breath – *Hoo-hoo-hoo! hi-hi-hi!* – and now a woman disengaged herself from the rest and waddled alongside him, bent double. Others crowded round, joining in, while Brak processed, blowing his lips, shaking his head – sending sprays of sweat this way and that – slapping the hunched backs of his pleasurers, taking one or two by the neck and jerking them into a faster rhythm.

'Thass good, yup, yup – not too much, careful, careful! OK, OK, start bringing it in!'

The drumming grew loud, deep and slow as, from the steamy recesses of the cavern, two teams of men, ropes tied round them like harnesses, dragged an adult rhinoceros, rear-first, down the slippery channel of the floor.

'It's too doped!' roared Brak, as he leaned towards the monster. 'Hit the bloody thing! Wake it up a bit! Hit it, hit it!' People pummelled the thick hide, hammered the plate-like folds, creating another kind of drumbeat and releasing puffs of dust and dried mud, while the rhino stirred slightly and half lifted its great log of a head, the horn strapped with padding. Now Brak disappeared from view as the crowd surged round, and all Felix knew of what followed was a final triumphant bellow from the man and a sleepy fart from the beast.

'Is Popo-boy here? At this party?'

Brak's bloodshot eyes didn't seem to register anything, so Felix spoke again: 'Popo-boy. D'you know that name? D'you know who I mean?'

Brak sighed, slowly, thoughtfully, took a swig from his bottle of Chivas Regal, then helped himself to another of Felix's cigarettes, and finally answered: 'Yes, of course I know who Popo-boy is.'

'Well, then – that's it.'

'Whass wha'?'

'You said you'd grant anything I asked. *That*'s what I want. *That* name.'

Brak nodded, more to himself than Felix, smiled in the same way, drank and smoked.

They were still in the steam cavern, but alone now, the people and animals gone, a rhino turd on the floor the only evidence of what had transpired earlier: a flat, dry, whitish turd, patterned with undigested grasses and leaves, a twig, some pebbles. Felix liked the smell it gave off; it reminded him of circuses and childhood car drives into the *bundu*; it took him back; it carried a whiff of the future as well. The sensation passed, and he shifted restlessly. He wanted this to be over quickly – this chance encounter with Brak, this unexpected opportunity to solve the mystery – he wanted it to be over, so that he could pursue his own private quest, his new goal for the weekend.

'Why d'you want to know?' Brak asked eventually.

Felix wondered how to phrase it. 'To settle a score.'

'For yourself?'

'Someone else.'

'Always the best way to settle scores.' Brak rearranged his drenched towels and lay back on the ledge, blowing cigarette smoke towards the moist, dripping ceiling. 'So what if I was to tell you it's *me*?' he asked.

Felix wavered, unsure whether this was a confession or a test. The man had deliberately made himself vulnerable, lying down, facing away. There were loose rocks about. It would be easy to threaten him, to gain the advantage. And Felix's mood was just itchy enough . . .

'It isn't me,' Brak said lazily. 'But d'you see what I mean?'

'No.'

'Well, what if it's someone you can't take on?' He gave his laugh. '*Haw!*'

'Look,' Felix said carefully, 'it's information for a friend, as I said. Two friends, actually. They lost their son to your . . . in, in police custody. They want justice.'

'Justice,' Brak echoed with a melancholy chuckle. 'Me too. I want justice.'

'Oh, really?' smiled Felix, taken with the man's sense of humour. 'You've been treated unfairly – *you*? In what way?'

Brak raised himself onto one elbow, and swivelled round, eyes suddenly full of passion. 'I'll tell you! I've trekked all round this bloody continent, I've served this regime and that, and every bloody time I've landed in the shit! D'you think that's fair? I was born in Northern Rhodesia, went into the regular army, loyally served my country, and what happens? They move the fucking centre of gravity! All of a sudden the goodie's a baddie, the friend's an enemy. Is that fair? I go walkabout for a bit. Become one of the dogs of war. OK, it's cash-not-commitment now, anything goes. Hire myself out in the Congo, Sierra Leone, bit later to the MPLA crowd in Angola. I'm working for the blacks now, the real *Africans*, I've got to be on the right side now, the winning side. No. Wrong again. I'm caught by the South Africans and deemed a fucking war criminal. Is that fair? About to be put up against a wall and shot when I offer a deal. Any classified info about my ex-masters is theirs for the asking. A few years later I'm one of the big brasses in South Africa's special security forces. I've got to be OK now, I'm part of the military might of white South Africa, the strongest bloody army in Africa. Wrong again. Some dickhead throws it all away for a mention in the history books and I'm on the fucking run again. And what happens then? I end up here – as Duma's right-hand man! D'you still want to keep talking to me about fair?' He took a quick drink. 'You – what's your job again?'

'Ehrm,' answered Felix. 'I'm a theatre director.'

'Jesus-fuck. Anyhow. OK, are there any centres of gravity in the job?'

'Centres of gravity?'

'A play, gimme a play everyone thinks is good.'

'*King Lear*.'

'OK, *King Lear*, so let's say you decide to put this *King Lear* on at your theatre, and let's say you put it on well, to the best of your capabilities, and then let's say everyone comes to see it and they say, "But this play is a dud, the story is a load of bullshit, this King Lear character can go fuck himself." Now how would you feel, hey? They've moved the centre of gravity. You've served up something honourably and then they change the fucking rules! My friend, we're in Africa. It's a big, rough place. You can fuck round with it today but tomorrow it's gonna fuck you. So don't talk to me about *fair*!'

'No, all right,' said Felix, liking the man despite everything. 'So who's Popo-boy?'

Brak heaved himself onto his feet. 'When you've delivered what we're hoping you'll deliver, then I'll tell you.'

'Deliver? What are you hoping for? Who's we?'

Ignoring these questions, Bull Brak made his way down the cavern, running his thick fingers through the hot moisture on the rocks. 'In the meantime,' he said, over his shoulder, 'keep on trucking as the young people say, keep on moving, keep going forward, that's the secret . . .'

thirty

offers all kinds of love
sexuality + love
are just not OK.

Afs and non-Afs, mused Felix, stepping through another doorway, *the party's splitting into Afs and non-Afs.* In spite of the wide choice on offer, the Afs favoured straight booze and straight humpy-pumpy, while the non-Afs seemed determined to try everything else under the sun. Afs weren't in evidence at all in this new room. The atmosphere was very wild here, and Felix doubted whether he would find what he was looking for. He needed a gentle touch – whether from man or woman he wasn't certain, or perhaps even a child (*maybe Emile was right?*) or even a friendly goat wasn't out of the question, but whoever, whatever, it surely wasn't here. Every eyeful made him wrinkle his face squeamishly, and this wasn't going down well with those who noticed.

So this was the inner circle, thought Felix, this was what Charlie described as the Roman idea of *la dolce vita*. Here it was, not the Games but a place with a similar draw, a place you thought you wanted to avoid and yet, once glimpsed, where you return again and again, happily, hungrily, seeking sanctuary – here it was, the den of cruelty.

Everywhere you looked on this crowded dance floor – thumping to acoustic rock versions of Charlie's favourite Roman movie themes, and chaotically lit by modern disco spots as well as burning lime and sulphur torches – everywhere you saw different experiments with human nudity: its gentle gleam was either studded with metallic stars and pins, or dulled with body-paint and tattoos, or coarsened with homemade scarification – whip-weal and flea-bump shapes – or glossed with fresh blood. A couple whose organs were pierced, and linked by thin chains, did a tugging, clashing, flinching jig. A man, his nipples impaled by hooks from which hung animal jawbones, stood swaying to the music while being slowly penetrated by a woman with a pointed dildo; her bra, fingernails and high heels were spiked too. A white woman, her lower lip vastly extended by a wooden plate, in the Ethiopian style, and her neck stretched by brass hoops, squatted rhythmically on the tongue of an Oriental man whose scrotal sac was elongated by a similar system of rings. A pack of yelping teenage girls bounced a bier on which lay a fat man bringing himself off with rolled-up sandpaper. 'Look, look, look!' cried a man who'd had his pecker surgically split, and was proudly lifting the two heads with twine jiggers. 'And-and-and!' panted a team of young men who were passing round a limbless woman like a rugby ball, this way and that, with feints and fancy spins, plea-suring her on each catch. 'Hugga hugga thuck thuck,' another group chanted goonishly, their parts bumpy with pearl implants, their flesh bristling with staples, blades, weights, barbed wire and clothes pegs. 'Nnn, mmm, nnn,' was the muffled call of those whose mouths were taped; they sat, bound, knees up, in stirruped chairs, they were strapped onto operating tables, they hung, rocking, in leather-and-chain cradles. 'Oh! – oh! – oh!' grunted people as they suffocated, shaved and sliced themselves or one another, spat, kicked and flogged, kissing all the time, kissing, kissing, everyone was kissing all the time.

'There is no snuff session!' a voice snarled, as Felix rotated slowly, bewildered and tired. 'I thought there'd be snuff sessions!'

It was the diminutive circus teenager whom Felix thought of as the Great Zit, but who called himself Zikki. He was dressed in a leather bondage outfit, not much more than child-sized, with torso-straps, pouch and long boots, with which he presently kicked at his bad luck. 'I heard they had it at previous parties!' he complained loudly. 'Why not this one?'

'Dear me, no idea,' said Felix, collapsing onto one of the divans that lined the walls. The reverberating thunder of the music filled his chest, making him wonder if he was having a heart-attack.

Zikki sat next to him and shouted into his ear, 'I swear they promised, it's not just my dum-dum-dreams, *ja*? – they promised!' He poured another glass of Chivas Regal and threw it back in one, like schnapps, fuelling his tantrum. 'Nobody fucks with me like that! The fukken . . . *scheisser*! . . . *arschloche*! Look at me – look at me dressed like a fukken clown, a fukken trapeze clown, a, a, a . . . !' He tore at his bondage straps, almost tipping his little body off the divan. Suddenly he began weeping. Felix stared at him in amazement. His distress was real, huge, total, like one of Alys's upsets; the world had come to an end. Zikki's streetwise swagger, his dark jokes, it was just precociousness, a cover-up – Felix had travelled down similar roads himself. Here was a small and ugly teenager, his skin the wrong colour, and badly scarred because of it, a 'mongrel', a child unable to hold his drink, to have what he wanted, to be the centre of attention at this mad party. Felix put his arm round the little fellow's shoulders and rocked gently while the other continued to sob and rant incoherently.

Might Zikki be the one? Felix mused wearily, reaching for his breath-freshener. Probably not. He left the spray where it was. What time of the day or night was it now? he wondered. His feet were burning, his lower back aching. Walking or standing, that's all his body knew, hour after hour, walking or standing. He tried tempting himself with thoughts of bed, or food, or just fresh air, but his other side whispered, 'No, no, keep searching, this is it – this party – this is where it's going to happen.' '*Oh, but how?*' he replied angrily. The choice was too vast, the risk too horrible – what if people said no, or laughed – and, anyway, everyone was too busy, busy, busy; the pharmaceutical experiments had spiralled into complete bloody lunacy; people were making paper darts out of their questionnaires or using them as mopping-up pads.

A couple pushed through the throng of dancers. It was the woman with the spiked bra and dildo, and the man with animal jawbones hanging from his chest. He disengaged these, so that he could climb onto one of the divans and huddle into a ball, face down, apparently in considerable pain. They were in their late thirties. She had a cultured American accent, he the pukka tones of a British non-Af. Felix heard only snatches as they yelped at one another over the music:

'Told you to be careful!'

''S the point of being careful?'

'Point is to hurt, not to harm!'

'No, point is to wake up, to dispel hypocri–!'

They were interrupted by the arrival of Charlie, ushered to their side by a concerned friend. This person boomed, '*Good thing there's a . . .*' then paused, as if in a song, and the rowing couple, not wishing to appear rude, joined in, '*. . . doctor in the house!*'

Charlie shook his cheeks, making wuggle-wuggle noises, slapped his face a few times, bounced his eyebrows, needing to clear his head, and finally set about examining the patient.

'Ouch,' went Charlie, seeing the damage.

'Is it ghastly?' the man called – still topping the music – and began to weep.

'Oh, Rupert, I'm sorry,' shouted the woman. 'Dammit, I wish I had my specs.' She turned to Charlie. '*Is* it ghastly?'

'He'll survive,' bellowed Charlie, fetching a syringe from a cabinet on the wall. 'And, in the meantime, I am gonna make him feel so, so good.'

'Me too,' hallooed the woman. 'Make me feel so, so good too.'

'Say hi to Special K,' grinned Charlie, injecting him, then fetched a second needle for her. 'Takes away pain, brings bright dreams, Special K, alias Ketamine, this mother, she was big in Vietnam, and, oh, man, I mean BIG!'

'Goooooood morning, Special K!' the couple chanted. Charlie laughed, waved, and turned to go.

'Charlie!' Zikki shrieked, through his tears, as the doctor lurched about trying to rearrange his toga, which was unwinding like a bandage.

'Yessir?' answered Charlie.

'I was promised snuff sessions if I came here! You said that they –'

'Not me, wait, wait, whoah, not me!'

'OK, Carlos then, he promised that –'

'Well, if his lordship promiscd . . .' replied Charlie, tumbling around the area with his unravelling toga, '. . . let his lordship deliver.' His spinning dance brought him close to Felix, and he sang out cheerfully, 'Oh, hi, ol' buddy, didn't see you there.' Finally giving up on his toga, he extricated himself from it, slowly, gracefully, a frown of concentration on his face, as though engaged in a piece of performance art, and then, stark naked, ploughed back into the heaving mob.

The man named Rupert suddenly called across to Zikki, 'I say, you're right! There *were* those sessions here.'

'See!' Zikki cried triumphantly to Felix, as though he had been arguing against the fact.

'Who were they?' Felix yelled back, his curiosity aroused. 'The people who were, ehrm . . . the . . . the snuffees.'

Rupert's American partner answered – despite the volume, her tone was intense and sentimental, 'Lost souls, incurables, suicides, junkies, those haunted by crimes, the poor, the homeless. Their families were well paid. That was the deal, the attraction.' She added quickly, 'Or so I'm told – I never participated myself.'

She suddenly slumped onto Rupert, and they began kissing dreamily. Zikki sucked at his bottle like an infant, breathing through his nose. Felix touched his toga. The folds were drenched with sweat. Icy sweat. Like he found on his pillow most mornings. He rose slowly, unsteadily. 'It's just because you haven't eaten,' he reassured himself, unafraid to talk aloud, the music drowning everything. 'If you've been here as long as I think you have, then Feelie just needs some foodie-woodie . . .'

He trudged up some stairs. Here was a narrow stone balcony just below the low ceiling, almost no more than a pelmet, curving all the way round the dance-floor. The place seemed to have a different atmosphere from up here, less raucous, the movements of everything more sluggish, the swaying dancers, the roving lights, the music – now the big syrupy love themes of Hollywood's Rome. Felix spotted Charlie down below, naked, touching and being touched, moving among the slowly heaving knots of people like a high priest, a master of ceremonies, a candyseller at the movies, for he was dispensing powders and potions from a tray round his neck; Charlie in his element – Charlie not looking bored – Charlie without the shy smile that always moved Felix. A woman slipped a horned leather mask over Charlie's face – which suddenly made him seem clownish, Felix thought, like a suburban fetishist – and then he danced away, quickly engulfed by the bacchanal.

Trying to locate him again, scanning the crowd, Felix saw a new figure. A figure in pyjamas, with thin grey hair. Felix narrowed his eyes. Yes . . . it was.

Someone had put cardboard sunglasses on Emile, and a studded muzzle. Dazed but unfrightened, he was stroking the passing, dancing bodies. Because of the sunglasses, he seemed blind, relying on his sense of touch, savouring it. Becoming bolder, he ventured towards the centre of the dance-floor, and now Felix saw – over the heads of the revellers – the naked, hooded figure of Charlie reappear out of a smoky group, and move, unknowingly, towards his father.

They were going to meet. Here, now, in *this* of all places.

A space cleared, and the two men wandered towards one another, both shakily, one with age, one with chemicals, and neither showing any emotion, for they didn't recognise the other. Nevertheless they hugged, briefly, half sexually, with a joky kiss through hood and muzzle, then danced a slow, exhausted foxtrot for a moment or two. Finally they stumbled away again, in opposite directions.

Felix breathed again. He stood still, not knowing what to do. One hand went to his mouth. He panted slowly, stifling a sob. Then he turned, hurried to the stairs, reached for the banister, and missed. Watching the dance-floor rise slowly to meet him, he wondered what medication it was on.

thirty-one

'Sozzled,' said a voice. 'You're sozzled, aren't you?'

He opened one eye. There she was again, peering down at him, like at the airport on the day he returned – the woman in the turquoise wraparound – Mrs Al-Qirib, the trustee. Given the nature of her question, she was presumably the only other sober person at this party. She must be lonely. Maybe they could talk. Maybe more than talk. Time could be running out for him and his quest. Daybreak might suddenly come sunlight bursting into these rooms and halls, making everyone dive for cover. He mustn't be left alone then, on the floor among all the debris, his mission unaccomplished. So why not Mrs Al-Qirib? She was rather ugly – the flyaway specs, the light moustache – but people said looks don't matter. It was tenderness that counted. He groped for his breath-freshener spray.

'Sozzled!' she said, seeing it. 'You're disgusting!' He thought he saw her giggling into her hand as she scurried away. Perhaps she wasn't sober after all.

He struggled into a sitting position. There was a strange underwater atmosphere here, the music quiet and bubbly, the light playing on the surface of chests and forearms above him, the middle air murky with a sour fug of feet and arses, the floor a bed of squelching, crunching waste matter. And questionnaires. Scores of abandoned questionnaires. He spoke to the nearest one: 'How do I feel? you ask. Well, oh dear, I don't feel at all well.' It was his own fault – the lack of food, the lack of sleep – he should've been more careful, should've remembered he was still ill, 'in recovery'. Now anything could happen . . . the melting of walls between this and that, the backward ticking of clocks . . . and the ghosts, the ghosts could come . . .

He began to panic. Each intake of breath grew like a balloon within him; it felt like he had helium inside, or laughing gas without the laughs, and he wondered if, like passive smoking, there was passive drugging. Everywhere you went at this party, your nostrils prickled with the stuff . . . it was like chemistry class at school . . . that whiff of old rubber tubing and bad eggs, strange oils cooking, icy fumes . . .

'Your face!' said a voice, and he saw Kaz crawling over to him, her body gleaming, her hair matted, one eye closed by a bruise, but as happy as before, on the riverbank at dawn. 'Poor baby.' She laughed affectionately. 'Your face – I've been watching you. This be open house, honey, everything is permitted here. Here you can be Felix the *dirty* cat. Hmn? Isn't there someone, *something* you like here?'

'Don't know,' mumbled Felix, reaching for her like a child.

'He doesn't know, he does not know,' she repeated, taking him in her arms. She found a smouldering cigarette stub on the floor and puffed on it, putting back her head. Her eyes were shut. As Felix watched tears of stoned joy slipping out of them, he remembered her other tears, and her saying, 'It just rolls on and on,' and he wondered if she enjoyed *that* in a way too, gloried in it. He wanted to say, 'I've found someone who knows who Popo-boy is, and I know about your son being Charlie's as well . . .' but there seemed no point in saying anything at the moment. He felt angry with her. He wanted her to be hurting again, for real, in this room of comic-grotesque hurt, this temple of hurt. He wanted her to need him, need his news, he wanted to be strong and important, in charge, not feeble, inexperienced, sprawled on the floor, listening to slow dance music, whips, blows, and moans of pleasure.

Close to emotion, light, fluttery, stinging, he tried kissing her shoulder, her arm, tried touching her breasts, tried reaching into her lap. She allowed it, eyes still closed, head lolling back, signalling compliance, ready to join, to help if this was genuine, yet suspecting it would peter out as it always had when they tried it before: many times before when they were drunk. 'I'm gonna make it my mission to make you!' she used to say regularly, a few years ago.

Sensing her lack of conviction, fearing it, his hands fumbled aimlessly, his tongue lolled. Oh, what to do?, how to do it? A picture came to mind. An infant, her infant, the one whose name he could never remember but whose killer they were hunting . . . that infant in her arms long ago – and in his own arms too – didn't he hold it once? – didn't something like that happen?

'It's OK,' Kaz whispered tenderly as Felix wept. 'It's OK.' She moved his lips to one of her nipples. It tasted of blood. She rocked him for a while, singing a lullaby, '*Msidhani mahaluti . . . Kabila sikusaliti.*' He liked doing it here, sucking her breast, here just below the sea of people, in the good, sour, human fug of feet and arses, a smell that he knew from the Alex, from backstage during the Chorus scenes, a smell that was warm and safe; and he liked the sense of eyes, eyes up there, just above all the forearms and breasts, eyes that were glancing down occasionally, peeping at him like he had peeped at others, seeing him with this remarkable woman, this powerful actress and singer, this bluesy brown creature, this chestnut-coloured Afro-American dame, this chick, this broad, *Charlie's broad*, beautiful Charlie's beautiful broad . . . and here he was, Felix, the scowling, plain one, the inexpert, green one, here he was – with her – kissing in rude places, touching, able to *have*. It was incredible. He was on his way.

Doing the coughing-trick, he covered his mouth, had two blasts of breath-freshener, inhaled on them deeply, like he'd seen people do with reefers, then prepared for lift-off. Meanwhile her hands, which had been on his chest, moved onto his belly, gently, smoothly, like a masseur, or mother, signalling it's all right, just relax, this is good, and then, with infinite sensitivity, she reached down again.

Puzzled not to feel any contact, Felix squinted through the gloom, and saw that someone else's hand had met Kaz's above his crotch, and was handing over something.

'Want one?' Kaz asked, showing Felix a greyish tablet already dissolving on the sweat of her fingers.

'Nnnnn thnnksss,' he replied through gritted teeth, but it was already too late, the excitement was subsiding. More furious with her dealer than her, he swung round, but whoever it was had gone. Instead, a lone, pale form was hopping through the forest of legs towards him. As it got closer, he saw that it wasn't a large rabbit as he first thought, but the old legless man with white hair and beard, swinging along on his fists. As this character moved past, he smiled with such kindness that Felix's whole being was warmed. He had no intention of following the old man, but others around him did, it seemed; the whole crowd, the whole room was beginning to incline in that direction. It was odd. Despite refusing Kaz's offer of the tablet, Felix felt he was experiencing the first wave of its effect. Kaz slid away now, as though on a slow-tilting floor. Felix reached for her and started to topple, falling with her. He shut his eyes.

When he looked again, he and Kaz were on a bare mattress in a gloomy room. There was something intensely familiar about the atmosphere: the mix of weak electricity and thin sunshine. Felix whimpered softly, recognising it. The light of Monday morning fil-tering into a police cell: the one at the end of the corridor. And there he was, the man in the cheap suit, his back to them, bent over his attaché case, rummaging through its contents, listlessly, his manner gloomy and bored, back at work after the weekend.

It's all right, Felix told himself, you're all right, Kaz is here, this isn't how it happened, nothing will actually hurt this time.

The man turned. It was Duma.

'Oh dear,' Felix said quietly.

Duma nodded towards a chair. It was the same one as before, an orange plastic one, the bucket seat easy to clean, with strips of rubber tubing hanging loosely round the legs. Duma was going to resume where the other man left off. '*Keti hapo!*' he said firmly.

'No, please, please,' Felix cried, in a tiny voice, wetting himself instantly as before – or was it a rush of sweat he could feel there? – or blood? – was the scissor wound open? – were they already at that stage? He tried to scrabble away across the floor. There was a terrible, hopeless slowness to his limbs, and he couldn't say the word no, it was too provocative, only, 'Nnn–! nnn–!'

'Not you,' Duma said in a kindly tone. 'Her.'

Kaz obeyed without hesitation. It must be the drug she's just taken, Felix decided, watching her sleepwalk to the chair, her eyes open but glassy, smiling slightly, nervous yet brave, as one volunteering to help a magician.

Duma tied her to the chair, then leaned onto his knees, so that their heads were level. He wasn't wearing his glasses. These were still a sign of weakness, not to be worn in public, not even here. His big boiled eyes looked sore. They shifted slowly, roaming over her face and body.

'What tribe?' he asked.

'Tribe?' She laughed. 'Oh, man, I'm a city girl, my mom she cleaned at the American embassy, my dad he –'

Duma cut in fiercely. '*What tribe?*'

She gave a calm smile, then replied fearlessly, 'Tao.'

He sighed, as though wishing she had answered anything but that. 'A low, *very* low form of life,' he commented quietly. He touched her skin. Felix remembering him examining the little bat before he broke its wing.

But Kaz remained untroubled, smiling in Duma's face. 'If you think so, honey, 's up to you. "You say to-may-to and I'll say to-mah-to."'

Duma's expression hardened. 'Why d'you talk to me in that way?'

'Huhn?' Kaz asked, head lolling.

'*Unatoka wapi? Mwamerika?*'

'American?' Kaz laughed. 'No, man, you didn' understand, my mom she just worked there. At the embassy. I'm born 'n' bred right here, brother, right in –'

'Then why d'you talk in this way? Like something you aren't.'

'Huhn? Wha'?'

'Our voices come from deep inside, from our bellies, our hearts. You've forgotten who you are.'

Kaz stopped smiling, stopped playing. 'You're wrong,' she said, gazing steadily at the man, as though suddenly realising who he was, what he'd done to her. 'Here's from my inside, from my belly, my heart . . .' She spat in his face.

'Kaz . . .' gasped Felix. Duma went still. Felix had never seen him as still. A boulder with dynamite under it.

Duma wiped his face in an odd, laconic way. Then he said to Kaz. 'Are you CIA?'

Felix frowned – had he heard right? – then broke into a slow smile. This was past history! Duma's fear of the CIA, of an American plot to dethrone him. This didn't apply any more. Duma *was* dethroned. He was disgraced, his power broken. No one needed fear him any more. You could spit in his face, do anything you wanted. The man was powerless to retaliate, he was an insignificant *nebbish*, a little fantasist, a short-arse with a big mouth. There was no danger here. Hundreds of people were close by, near this room – wherever it was in relation to the dance-floor – Felix needed only to call out and Duma would sorely regret finding his way to the farm, and risking freedom again. Felix rose to his feet, ready to explain all this, when he felt hands grip his arms, several pairs of hands. He tried to turn, to identify these people behind and around him, but they held his head fast, forcing him to watch the scene in front of him.

'You probably understand that I'm going to hurt you now,' Duma said to Kaz, speaking with a new, grim lifelessness, 'but do you know how easy it is?' His hand strayed over her, without lasciviousness; just a kind of curiosity. 'You've heard about instruments, electrodes, complicated processes. Unnecessary. One needs so little. Just a match, a splinter, a few drops of glue, industrial glue . . . your imagination will do most of the work. It's a worse beast than I am. And it's already inside you. So my job is simple . . .'

As Duma expanded on his theme, Felix began fighting with his captors, and was effortlessly restrained. He tried again, and again failed. The battle continued, growing slower, almost rhythmic, almost obliging, both sides rocking together, and now an extraordinary thought rose in Felix's mind – *Thank God it's her, not me* – to be followed by an even more extraordinary sensation in his flesh. If the questionnaire was put in front of him now, he would have to lie to it. Answering truthfully at the moment would be impossible. Impossible! To report his helplessness, and the strength of others around him, and the horror about to unfold, to report these things and then to say, 'I feel curious' – no, no, he could never, must never, admit that! But it was as if there was a hand in his chest now, a small fluttering hand, waving, beckoning, urging, *c'mon, c'mon, c'mon.*

'. . . so it's not difficult,' Duma said, finishing his discourse, 'breaking a person.' Kaz stared back calmly, close to a smile, a dare. Duma suddenly pointed to Felix. 'Ask him.'

Felix tried to keep his voice level – he mustn't reveal any excitement. 'Was it you in the cell that Monday morning? Was it? It couldn't've been.'

Duma replied with precision: 'I do not know to what you are referring. So, no, it was not I.'

Felix swallowed hard – gleeful, horrified – then forced himself to say it. 'But you are Popo-boy. Yes?'

Duma thought for a long time, then answered. 'All right. Yes.'

'Wha'?' said Kaz, as one waking. 'He is . . . wha' . . . *Mungueeh!* . . . *this* is Popo-boy?'

All the terror that had been absent so far flooded through her now, and anger too; both surging together. 'Where is he? What did you do with him? Give him me, give him back!'

'Who is she talking about?' Duma asked Felix.

'Show him!' Kaz cried. 'Show him the picture!'

Duma nodded to the people holding Felix, and they released one of his hands. Yet even as he reached through the folds of his garment, he knew the pendant wasn't there, wasn't touching his chest any more. Somehow – on the dance-floor, or in any one of the chambers, alleyways and halls before that – somehow, somewhere it had slipped off. The necklace was only a piece of knotted reed, hastily improvised on the riverbank that morning.

He had lost it, the picture of . . . what was the boy's name again? . . . Kaz's son, Kaz and Charlie's son . . . he had lost the picture just when they most needed it, at a moment they had all dreamed of, the moment of finally confronting his killer.

'Give him back!' Kaz shouted again, now to Felix as much as Duma. 'Give me my son!'

The cry came from her belly. Felix had heard this sound before, seen this thing rise through her; it was like a force from the earth. She managed to rock forward onto her feet, still tied to the chair, and began swinging it, swinging herself at Duma. He stumbled back. One of her leg fastenings came loose. Her grip on the floor was better now. Roaring, she shook the chair. It had held her like stocks – now it would be her weapon. A hand was free. She grabbed at Duma.

Pandemonium had broken out round Felix. One of his guards lurched into view at last. Felix blinked. This man was Duma also. And the man on the other side. And the one behind. And even more gathered around them. A crowd of Dumas.

As Felix battled to make sense of it, a figure pushed through and rushed to help Kaz. Charlie. He helped untie her. Strangely enough, the first Duma allowed this, standing aside meekly. Kaz was free to attack him now. But the whole scene was calming, not accelerating. Felix couldn't work it out.

'Shouldn't have brought Popo-boy into it,' Kaz panted.

'No, shouldn't've,' Charlie agreed angrily, sluggishly.

'Shouldn't've done that!'

Charlie rounded slowly on Felix. 'Should not have done that!'

'*Me?*' said Felix.

'Well, it was, with respect, *you* who brought it up,' said the first Duma, whom Felix now recognised as Mr Mmalo.

'It was you, ehh?' Kaz said, mopping her face. Like Charlie, her voice seemed to be slipping through different emotions, half real, half acted. 'You spoiled it, he spoiled it, spoiled it . . .'

'Spoiled . . .' echoed Charlie, feeding a capsule into Kaz's mouth. ''s OK, 's'll help.'

Now that he was no longer encased in a role, it became apparent that Mr Mmalo was pie-eyed as well. The actor had probably abstained from pharmaceutical experiments – these were unholy – but he certainly liked his drink. 'Didn' know wha' on earth to do,' he complained to Felix, as if they were in a rehearsal room. 'Popo-boy wasn't supposed to come into it. I'm all for extemp'r's'tion, as you know, but . . .'

Felix wheeled away sharply and left them all to it: Mr Mmalo protesting his innocence, Charlie comforting Kaz, some of the others starting to argue, jostle, or make love. They were both men and women, the host of Dumas in the room, old and young, Afs and non-Afs, their faces daubed with clay or greasepaint, or wearing masks – wooden tribal masks, plasticky joke-shop masks, plaster half-masks – or just Duma noses, Duma bald-caps, Duma moustache-and-beards, some drawn on felt-tip pen. Perhaps it was a game, some ultimate kick at the party, dressing up as the ex-leader . . .? Felix didn't want clarification, he didn't care, he was hot with fury.

Reaching the door of the cell, he saw that the dark passageway was jammed with more people, drawn by the commotion, packed into every available space. Finding his way blocked was the final straw. His rage changed into a new emotion, one he had never felt in his blood before, and couldn't begin to explain. He threw himself at the first row and tried scrambling over them, onto the mass of heads beyond, tried exiting like this, ready to kick or punch anyone who protested. Instead they were pliant under his hands and knees, this crowd, they yielded, dipped and rose with his exertions, cushioning him, helping him, unwinding his toga when it became tangled, a hindrance . . . they unwrapped him like a gift, passing the long bolt of cloth one way, him the other, stroking his flesh, whispering and touching . . . and finally, in the darkest part of the corridor, a she or he guided him into themselves, while someone else kissed his mouth, others caressed and fondled. 'No, no,' he moaned, when his lips were free. 'Let me see what . . . how . . . *who*!' The person near his face, a young woman, smiled sympathetically, but those further down didn't even hear. He battled to tilt his head down, to identify something, anything, of the connection gripping him – despite everything, it was good – but there were too many hunched necks and shoulders, there was a sameness, like when animals group. He knew a moistness, a friction, and heard a hoarse, angry cry which barely sounded like him. People lost interest immediately afterwards, almost dropping him to the floor. Within moments he was the only one left in the passageway.

He stood motionless for a long time, wondering how much of it had actually happened. Too much, he decided. Here he was: his body naked, his heart hurting. The hurt felt foolish. He brushed himself down, and saw to his astonishment that someone had fitted on a condom. He flung it away. Groping through the shadows, finding his things, the toga, cigarettes and sweeties, the little breath-freshener spray, he grimaced to himself. So that was it. The earth-moving, life-changing *it*. People said you grew wiser afterwards, you grew up, instantly, in front of your own eyes. But he had a sense of being younger, a teenage boy, *a girl*, his worth devalued. Which was absurd. The whole thing had been absurd. A little joke, courtesy of The Great Prankster. Felix should see the funny side, and laugh. I will, he told himself – in a moment or two I'll laugh.

thirty-two

Emerging into the outdoors, showered and changed back into his own clothes, Felix was stunned when he asked a passing servant the time, and the woman, who was carrying a live coal in a small wire basket, told him it was almost five-thirty – on *Sunday*, not Saturday afternoon.

He did some quick calculations. Thursday was the first day of the long weekend. It began with him going to Pembe Cove and ended with him here at the farm. Early the next morning he went on a game drive, and then asked the way to the ruins . . .

He'd spent about sixty hours in there . . . almost three days.

His feet were hugely swollen, and his spine ached with every movement. Stretching it slowly, he put back his head and gulped at the fresh, warm air, with the good smells of the farm – bananas and milk and woodsmoke – and, from the savannahs beyond, the fragrance of wild grasses just before sundown.

The sky was filled with big clouds and different blues: hard blue and powder blue and deep blue and a faded yellowing blue on the horizon, like in a romantic painting. As Felix watched, with hands on hips and a you-old-devil smile on his face, the sun began setting – with blinding whiteness this evening – a peaceful, slow explosion going off at one end of the view, the rest growing vast and soft, everything sprouting long shadows.

There was a golden end, and then darkness came fast.

Felix found Alys in her playroom, on the floor, with Bi Mirza at the window, a radio in her hands, trying to tune it to a particular programme, the Overseas Service, perhaps. It looked like a familiar Sunday-evening ritual. She gracefully rotated the little machine this way and that, catching the programme, feeling it slip away, catching it again, all with a fisherman's patience.

'I'm very sad,' Alys confided as Felix, groaning and flinching, lowered himself onto his knees.

'Why's that, darling?'

'No one's been here. All day.'

'What, not even – ?' whispered Felix, indicating Bi Mirza.

'Yes, *her*,' said Alys listlessly. 'But no one. Not today. And not yesterday, and not . . .' She searched for a way to describe her week-end. 'Is there more here?'

'What?'

'Here at the farm. Is it more than at home?'

'I don't understand. Is what more?'

'Each time it's morning. D'you get more here? Before it's lunch-time. And before it's supper-time. Is there more here?'

'No,' he said sheepishly. 'It's my fault . . . you've just had a rotten weekend. I'm sorry.'

She looked at him closely, wondering if he meant it, wondering why he'd betrayed her so badly. She expected it of her father – he was always disappearing – but not Felix. 'I'm very sad,' she told him solemnly.

'Oh, darling,' he said, kissing her hair, smelling the wonderful ordinary smell of the day: its dust and sun. And her smells too – her clean smells – her purity – he feasted on it. He couldn't stop. He inhaled her scent as if it were a drug, trying not to snuffle or gurgle, not to sound filthy. But she was like a cure, an antidote, to the last few days.

She tolerated it for a while, then pushed him away. 'Where've you been?' she asked plaintively. 'Where's Daddy?'

'Oh, darling,' he said again, lifting her. 'I'm here now, I'm here. Let's play, we'll do whatever you want. What d'you want?' He rocked her. 'Little Lys, little one.'

'A story.'

'Yes.' He took a deep breath. 'Once upon a time, there was a farm in Africa . . .'

'A farm like this?' she asked.

'Good gracious, no. With a moo-moo here, and a maa-maa there, here a moo, there a maa . . . *that* sort of farm!'

As he talked now, making up an adventure, following its aimless twists and loops, but determined to keep it funny, no scary bits, determined to make it end happily, he tried not to think of the party. Especially not the final incident – the one of whose substance he was most sure – no, he mustn't dwell on it, or it would find its way into the fiction he was weaving . . . he would start inventing sub-plots about rugby scrums and spilt milk . . . no, he must think of other things. He gazed round the room. Alys had sent for the Scarecrows, the big African-style cushion-dolls, and these lay around in positions of comic collapse, among other scattered toys. The electric light was on, making the room very bright, almost garish. This brightness – the way you could see into every corner – this was familiar. From childhood or the dry world? Hard to say, they seemed to occupy the same place within him these days. The brightness at night . . . a radio playing . . . a feeling of safety. It reminded him of something specific, a specific memory, but he couldn't place it. Like trying to remember a dream, you feel what it's like, you have a clue, its theme is sounding, and then it fades abruptly, completely, just before the little story starts.

Bi Mirza let out a little cry of pleasure. Now hanging half out the window, she had caught it perfectly, her radio programme. It was an Overseas Service, but not from London . . . the announcer spoke a chopping, guttural language, probably Arab. Felix wondered which country she was from. Misreading his expression, she replied, 'A cookery talk – a recipe from home.' Her eyes shone, there was a sweetness to them. 'Home,' she murmured. 'Oh, to be there now, I'd – I'd –'

'– live happily ever after?' suggested Felix.

'Happily ever after!' Bi Mirza echoed passionately.

'Ever, ever after!' concluded Alys.

All three broke into smiles, and stayed like this for a while, silent and still, as though between them they'd solved a great mystery.

thirty-three

Felix lay in Emile's arms, unafraid of the intimacy now, grateful for it, enjoying the other's coarse, sleeping breath, his dry bony embrace. Felix imagined he was Charlie or even Alys, being held by a good father.

This aside, Felix's night was racked with sleeplessness. After all those hours, no *days*, at the party, this was the last thing he expected. Perhaps he was too tired to sleep. Perhaps he *was* sleeping some of the time, skimming in and out, while all sorts of notions, discoveries and story-fragments journeyed alongside, like tiny fish hitching a ride on a large one.

A cage, a wall, a wall, a cage . . . will I remember? . . . is it worth remembering? . . . is it inspiration? . . . is it small-hour flotsam? . . . a cage, a wall, a wall, a cage.

Emile woke once, with a little gasp.

'Just a dream,' Felix reassured him.

'Yes, yes,' he answered, in that peaceful, haunted tone people use when they're half asleep.

'Tell me.'

'A familiar shore, a wave comes on to it, wraps round a rock I know well, pulls back into the sea.'

'Doesn't sound alarming,' said Felix, rocking the old man gently. 'Explain it. Decode it. Make yourself everything, make everything you.'

(It occurred to Felix that even Duma's famous catchphrase made sense this way.)

'A familiar part of me, a wave of me comes on to me, wraps round a rock of me, pulls back into me,' he murmured contentedly. 'Yes. It's explained.'

'Good,' said Felix. 'Now explain something else.'

'Hh?'

'It's something I've always wanted to ask you.' He paused, staring into the darkness, seeing a picture of two figures slowly foxtrotting on the dance-floor. 'Explain about you and Charlie.'

It had taken Felix twenty years to ask the question, but Emile didn't respond as expected – as Felix had always heard in his head whenever he pre-rehearsed the scene. In that version, Emile would answer, 'None of your business, my dear.' Instead, he now said, 'But you were there when it happened.'

'Where? When what happened?'

'At the lake. The picnic. The barbecue . . . with that magnificent golden perch.'

Felix frowned to himself. This picnic. Someone else had mentioned it recently . . . who? . . . it didn't matter. He proceeded cautiously. 'Remind me . . . what happened?'

Emile was silent for a long time, then he said in a shocked voice, 'I don't recall. But that's when it happened.'

'When *what* happened?'

'When we parted. We never said another word to one another after that day. I know that. I just can't recall the actual . . . *aie!* . . . you were there! Why can't you remember?! Anyway, whatever it was, it was only – as these things always are – only the trigger. Insignificant in itself. *Nullissime!*' He paused, thinking hard, then said, 'Anyway, my dear, it's not your business.'

Felix grinned in the dark. 'Well, that's debatable. You're two of the people that I'm closest to. Charlie is certainly my oldest –'

'Be careful of him.'

'Pardon?'

'Beware.'

Felix gave a small laugh. 'Beware, beware, the Ides of March.'

'Joke if you want, my dear, but joke carefully. I know him well and I don't know him at all.' He hesitated, then went a step further. 'I don't trust him.'

Felix suddenly felt uneasy. 'I'm sorry about that,' he said, content to leave it.

But Emile was opened up now. In a clear, flat voice, he explained: 'He's growing up, you love him, more than your partner, his mother, and once again Freud is wrong, you're happy for him to fuck her, kill you, as long as he keeps going, keeps walking, for he is your future, your living ghost, your immortal self, your *all*. And yet . . . and yet. There's something not right, something in his look. And you know it. Because you're trained to know. And you wouldn't have minded him being deformed or maybe blind, your Oedipus, but not this. A sense that there's . . . something empty in him, something missing. And instead, there's . . . I don't know, it's the words we mustn't use . . . a badness? . . . a madness? Something I've always feared in myself.' He cleared his throat, then added, 'I wish he hadn't gone into medicine. Ah! . . . *un toubib*! It is such holy territory. Our flesh. *Us*. I wish he had stayed away from *us . . .*'

'Maybe you're wrong,' Felix said brusquely, not wanting any more.

'Hh?'

'You're wrong about many things. You were wrong about Duma . . . Duma and his plans for this country! Maybe you're wrong about this too.'

'Maybe,' said Emile, in a strange tone, not sounding his usual all-knowing self, but hushed and frightened. He hugged Felix tightly. 'Where am I, by the way?' he asked slowly. 'What is this place . . . ?' Before Felix could answer, the old man was snoring quietly again.

Felix lay awake for another hour or so, eyes drilling into the darkness, wishing he hadn't asked Emile about Charlie. Maybe he hadn't, he decided eventually, maybe he would wake up in the morning and realise he hadn't. A kind of peace washed over him with this, and he was finally falling asleep himself, properly, deeply, when it happened.

A tremendous thump on the window, breaking it – instantly, cleanly – one huge shard falling into the room, falling through the curtains with a rush of bright blue moonlight. Then stillness again . . . that side of the room now a black-and-blue tangle of curtain, glass and light.

Felix was off the bed and standing upright even before it had finished settling, and Emile was sitting up on his elbows.

Venturing closer, Felix couldn't work it out.

The impact had dented the insect screen. Although immensely tough (made to keep out more than insects), the screen was pliant, so it had broken the glass without tearing away itself. Instead it bulged through the gap, a huge rippled bulge – the eye of a giant fly.

Beyond, in the night, on the lawn, there was a fast, low, almost soundless race in progress, going this way and that.

A race of champions, thought Felix: just speed and technique, no grunts and groans, no effort at all.

Then a large shape loomed back into view, back into the dent of the insect screen – cracking off another piece of window, making Felix jump back – a large grey shape, with other shapes around it.

Everything settled again.

A blurred massiness now filled the belly of the screen, contained by it, blocking out most of the moonlight. It was peculiar. A sense of a fierce but inanimate struggle . . . the only sound being short, snatched breaths.

Gradually, Felix's disbelieving eyes pieced it together.

The main shape was a waterbuck, its horns tethered to an uprooted stake . . . a second shape was a lion with jaws fastened over its windpipe, performing the asphyxiation with stillness and patience . . . a third and fourth shape were other lions with teeth fixed in the buck's spine and lower belly, not eating yet, just holding it steady for the executioner.

Felix saw a flashlight on the bedside table, set there in case the farm generator failed. The animals didn't seem to notice as the dazzling beam came on. For Felix, it was like looking through a peephole. The fantastic tumble of bodies, frozen with all the grace of acrobats or dancers, the ferocious intensity of mouths clamped on flesh, the quiet preoccupied breathing . . . it could have been one of the groupings at Charlie's party.

Then, with no final gasp or signal, it was over, the buck was finished. Any trace of calm and order vanished, with four, five, six more lion heads diving into view, matriarchs, young adults, and cubs, all launching into the meal.

Ripping, blowing sounds, moaning full mouths, nostrils fighting
for air, heads down, eyes closed, shoulders bent, straining; the buck
seemed to come alive again and struggle as the pride found better
places for themselves, clambering, slipping over one another, paws
already slimy with fat and fluid; everything growing lustier now –
mmm, aaaa – pink muzzles appearing in the flashlight beam, red
faces, red foreheads; now a sudden blaze of colour from the centre-
piece, the buck itself – a bright cavity of ribs – down it goes again,
down into the suffocating feast, where the diners can't breathe, can't
eat fast enough; the crack of buck-bone, hollow bellows of pleasure,
busy eructing noises, snorts and snarls of anger; there's terrible
aggression, terrible rivalry, desperate unsparing greed, they're feeding and fighting at the same time, no allowances made for the young
ones, while more and more lions try to reach from the outside; a
squabble, a tug-of-war, a resolution, a moment of quiet, of con-
tentment; the rows of chewing faces turning black with blood.

Felix had no time to absorb the shock of it, or even exchange a
word with Emile, before he heard voices outside the bungalow.

'Which way? . . . which one? . . . where did they end up?'

Without warning, the door crashed open and a dozen or more
people piled through the archway and into the bedroom.

'It's here, it's here!'

More people arrived, swarming around and over the bed, blocking Emile's view, bunching towards the window, gasping,
whispering.

'Jesus, look at that!'

'Wow!'

'Careful, there's glass here!'

'Good! Step on it!'

(Giggles, shushings.)

'Jesus, Jesus!'

'Put on the main light!'

'It'll frighten them!'

'No, it won't!'

'Put on the light, put on the light!'

The light, which now flooded the scene – to a further chorus of
'Jesus! – Fuck! – Look at that!' – revealed scores of people crowded

theatre

into the bedroom, some standing on the furniture, some carried piggy-back, all eyes on the fourth wall, a few brave fingers reaching there too, where tiny bubbles of animal hide and hair were pressed through the bulging, straining insect screen. Heavy with feasting lions, a top corner of the mesh had already ripped from the frame, and the rest was slowly coming away, threatening to spill its awesome load among the spectators.

The lions themselves remained indifferent to their audience, occasionally glancing up with those demonic glassy stares, or making strange noises deep inside themselves, more like resonance than sound, a kind of thunder.

Through the hole in the insect screen, big bugs began to dive-bomb the crowd, seeking the light or a feast of their own; moths and flying beetles shooting through the air; dark thudding shapes, they clipped you round the face, shockingly, suddenly, again and again, making Felix think of a biblical stoning, while someone else laughed and chanted, 'A hard rain, a hard rain is gonna fall!'

With a prickling, pulling tear, more of the screen shuddered free.

'It'll break!'

'Let it, let it!'

'Oh, man, oh, oh, oh!'

What an end this would be, thought Felix, as some instinct urged him to lunge at the open corner of the screen – its edge was curled like a handle   and help it collapse, and take the first falling animal full on, in his arms . . .

The lions' meal was going fast – a dirty chunk of it appeared and vanished. Now more of the carcass came apart, causing more vicious arguments and tuggings . . . members of the pride running off with leg-bones or just rags of skin.

As the bulge in the screen lightened, the pressure in the room eased too. People started drifting away, one woman whispering, 'That was my first kill!'

The last of the lions, their faces just greasy now, the fur flattened and greyish, all the blood licked away, heaved themselves up and climbed out of the screen, leaving two-dimensional outlines here and there, but no trace of the buck. In twenty minutes, the animal had disappeared completely.

As the spectators filed out of the bedroom, Felix saw Zikki standing next to the window. The teenager ran his small fingers over the magnificent warps in the insect screen, as though these were works of modern art, then discovered a sticky patch of something caught in the mesh, and carried a trace of it to his nose, curiously. Now Miss Rosewood stepped from behind the half-collapsed curtain – Miss Rosewood, unconcealed by shadows or the back seats of cars, but clear, solid, *there*. Zikki held out his fingers for her to sniff, and they conferred in low whispers.

Felix shook his head slowly. A phrase was looping round and round his mind:

A cage, a wall, a wall, a cage, a wall, a wall, a cage . . .

Felix sat on the bed for the next few hours, motionless, staring at the wreckage, while Emile slept at his side. Seeing daybreak come, Felix swung his legs to the floor – then flinched. His feet were still swollen thick. Maybe it wasn't all those days of traipsing through the party. Maybe it was still the sea-urchins. Maybe nothing else had happened since then, and the weekend was just starting. Hearing Emile stir, he twisted round, let out a yelp – *oh, his spine, oh, that wasn't from sea-urchins!* – and sat puffing, a weak smile on his face. Emile's eyes were dull. With any luck he'd have no recollection of the night, neither the conversation about Charlie nor even the lions. Felix stroked the old man's shoulder. 'Come for a swim.'

'No, thank you, my dear, *je suis crevé*, I'll just sleep a little more.'

'You're sleeping too much.'

Emile smiled. 'It takes practice. The big sleep.'

Felix smiled also. 'That was a good film.'

Emile fell silent, gazing intently at the hollow of beams and thatch above him. He reached for Felix's arm. 'Help me sleep, my dear.'

Felix stretched and yawned. 'Hmmmm . . . ?'

'Tell me a story.'

Smiling, Felix sat alongside the old man on the bed, as he'd often done with the old man's granddaughter, and said, 'Once upon a time . . .' He hesitated, searching for inspiration.

'Yes?' said Emile.

'Once upon a time there was a wave, it came onto a shore, it wrapped round a rock, it pulled back into the sea, and they lived happily ever after.'

'That's it?'

'That's it.'

Emile chuckled warmly. 'Ah. Beautiful. Tell me another.'

'Once upon a time a man and all his relatives, his male relatives, were descending a steep cliff down to the sea, and they all helped one another, even the man's father who was sometimes brutish, even he helped, and the man and his father were tender towards one another, and down the cliff they went to the sea, and they lived happily ever after.'

'The sea again,' observed Emile.

'Indeed,' said Felix.

'And that's because why, I wonder?'

'Because it's beautiful.'

'Mysterious,' said Emile.

'Magnificent, dangerous, it can hurt you, soothe you, drown you, transport you, it's the stuff of dreams.'

'And, and, *and*, my dear, you must always remember, when you enter it, when you go into that blueness, you're connected to the whole planet, the whole universe. *Ah, sensas!* What lovely stories.' He grew sleepy. 'Tell me another.'

Now the sea - fish - rockpools - dreams become emblematic of the self.

Too much going on here?

thirty-four

Felix found Charlie alone in the swimming-pool.

Situated in the private section of the main farmhouse, at the very end of the garden, and with no fence round it, the lipless smoky black pool was out of bounds to Alys – and even adults approached with circumspection. There was an element of optical illusion to the design; your eye went across the flat lawn, the silvery water, and straight into mid-air. Swim to the far side, however, and you realised that the overflow slopped lusciously down a precipice, and onto the wilderness below. At this end of the pool there was a shelf under the surface, where you could sit, sprawl, sunbathe, make love, hold secret conversations, or, like Charlie at the moment, simply contemplate the view. He looked forlorn; not like himself at all.

It was a few minutes after 6 a.m. To a chorus of birds, monkeys and insects, the colours of sunrise were fading into the humid white of the day.

As Felix paddled across, the back of Charlie's head jerked abruptly as though startled out of sleep or melancholy, then he quickly ducked under the water to revive himself, and turned to see who it was.

'Oh, fine, thanks, ol' buddy, hi! and you? yeah, good,' he said in a jumble. His eyes were puffy, his skin yellowish, the birthmark on his neck, that divine lovebite, engulfed by a greedy surplus of the real thing.

Felix had never seen his friend like this. He thought about his list of questions, and wondered whether Charlie was in any state to answer them. Reaching the underwater shelf Felix stayed silent, taking in the view: the river, the saddle of hills, and the red rock formations . . . the buttes and iffs they had laughed about on the day of arrival. At last he cleared his throat: 'There was a lion kill outside my room during the night, well, practically *in* my room.'

'So that's where it was.'

'The buck tethered to the lawn each night – is that why it's there?'

'Uh-huhn.' Different feelings and ideas seemed to be flickering through Charlie's head . . . they were half visible in his eyes, here one moment, gone the next . . . tiny fish in a rockpool.

'Isn't it dangerous?' Felix persisted. 'Attracting the lions? That close to the house? I mean, with people around.'

'Yeah.'

'Yeah, what?'

'Yeah, it is dangerous. Did you enjoy it?'

Felix wavered, then answered, 'It is one of the . . . it is the most exciting thing I've ever seen.' Blinking, feeling a rush of giddiness, he added vaguely, 'Dear God.'

They leaned on the shelf, elbows propped, legs swimming slowly, going nowhere. Then Charlie reached for something on the edge of the lawn. To Felix's astonishment, it was a green questionnaire. Charlie's original one. He'd somehow managed to carry it through all the convolutions of the party, from its distant beginning to its recent end, observing his behaviour along the way, treating it as one prolonged pharmaceutical experiment. Creased and dog-eared, blotched and softened with God-knows-what, the paper was covered in small handwriting, back and front, upside-down, in every corner and margin, often overlapping into spider-nests of grey scribbles. This was Emile's doodle-exercise done by a Martian. Lifting it to his nose now – wetting it, ruining it further – Charlie's eyes searched for a millimetre of clean space on which to make another note.

Felix looked away, embarrassed for his friend. Easing forward over the edge of the pool, he realised that the location of the party – Charlie's small city of broken halls, alleys and stairways – was just visible below. A lone figure was wandering around. He was so pale from head to foot that Felix was convinced that he was seeing a storybook ghost at last; a ghost looking like ghosts should. And even when his tired eyes slowly separated the figure's paleness into its different components – long, plaited silver hair, long white chemist's coat – even then he still held to his first impression; this was a ghost roaming a deserted battlefield, guarding it through eternity. The party had, in a way, belonged to this phantom, this wizard, more than Charlie, and its site was now his to haunt.

'What's his name again?' Felix asked.

Charlie leaned forward. 'Hey, look at him down . . . that's Deany!'

'Don't you call him "Deany-boy"?'

'Uhh . . . yeah, sometimes.'

'"Deany-boy". Sounds a bit like . . .' He left it in mid-air.

Charlie laughed. 'Oh, Jesus, man, it's not *him*! This's his first trip to Africa. Well, physically. That man's mind-trips could take him anywh– '

'It's – sorry – it's not *who*?'

'Popo-boy. Deany isn't Popo-boy.'

'Are you?'

Charlie smiled woozily, thinking this was a game. He replaced the questionnaire on the lawn. 'Duma is Popo-boy, isn't he?'

'No, I don't believe so. Nor Mr Mmalo.'

'Nor Deany. Nor me.'

'D'you know who it is?'

'Nope.'

'Bull Brak does.'

'Then ask him.'

'I have. I will again.'

'There ya go.'

'But it isn't you? It definitely isn't you?'

Charlie turned to look at him, rolling his head in the water, resting it on the surface, nuzzlingly, as on a pillow.

'You're serious, aren't you?'

'Yes.'

'What, I killed my own kid? Is that what you reckon?'

'Well . . . you said you wished . . . when Kaz was pregnant with him . . . didn't you say, if she'd told you, you could've . . . ?'

'Yeah, I did say that. I play around a lot. When things go wrong, I make them right. Normal procedure. 'S what I explained, 's what I meant.' He stared at Felix for a long time, in complete silence, and when he spoke it was in a lucid voice. 'What's the matter with you? This is *me*. You've known me since we were kids. We've seen one another every day. When did you see me change into this other guy, Popo-boy? When did that happen?'

Felix looked deep into his friend's eyes and knew he was talking from his heart. After a lifetime together, Felix could vouch for one unchanging fact about Charlie: he told the truth.

'It didn't,' Felix replied. 'It didn't happen.'

'My sin,' Charlie continued, 'when it comes to the day of atonement, my sin is that I've, like, never known how to get through the long nights. And I see it, y'know, I see it in others too. So I've made myself available to help. In, y'know, whatever way I could . . . cash, feel-good stuff, whatever. And sometimes people have gone crazy with what I make available to them. But . . . anyway . . . ain't my place to judge.' He shrugged and stared at the view, his chin on the water. The sky had gone from white to grey, showing vividly against the dense, dewy green of the hills; it was going to be one of those grey-green days, those sticky days. Charlie stayed silent for a while, then said, 'Remember when we were kids, and a school holiday came to an end? Or a Jewish festival or just a long weekend . . . remember that feeling? On that Sunday night?'

'Dear me, yes,' Felix answered.

''S how I feel now.' Charlie went still, thinking deeply. He half reached for the questionnaire, needing to write something down, then decided to discuss it instead. 'It's funny you mentioning Jewish holidays.'

Felix looked at him. 'I didn't.'

'Huhn? No, it's funny 'cause I sometimes wish I still believed. Y'know. Still had religion. I think people who have that are lucky. Or dumb. But happy anyhow. Don't you reckon?'

Felix didn't answer. He felt a vague sensation of yearning. And yet for what? . . . the memory was of tedium . . . those days, those Saturday mornings in the small, hot shul – now a second-hand bicycle store – the thin congregation, barely enough for a *minyan* even then, people fanning themselves and gossiping, just slowly marking through the rituals . . . *stand, sit, turn the page, duven, mutter along with the rabbi* . . . nobody really paying attention, nobody remembering to pray from the heart, and yet, and yet . . . Charlie was right . . . it had been the answer to absolutely everything.

Charlie reached for the other's hand. 'Buddy?'

Felix replied gently, 'Yes. I'm here. You're not alone.'

'Buddy . . . make tomorrow and the next day as good as this weekend.'

'All right,' joked Felix, and hugged the other's shoulder, allowing Charlie's body, which was naked, to roll against his own. He felt unafraid of these chance moments now. He stroked Charlie's hair, gazing at him . . . his strong, straight profile . . . that, at least, was undamaged by the revels. Felix smiled, wondering if he'd expected to find it chipped like a marble bust.

Charlie turned to face him. Felix thought they were going to kiss. Instead, the other asked plaintively, 'Why have you stopped trusting me?'

Felix blushed. 'I haven't. Perhaps your father . . . y'know, over the years . . . perhaps he's brainwashed me a tidge. He doesn't hold a very high opinion of you, I fear.'

Charlie gave a grim laugh. 'Hey, tell me about it! Fathers!'

'Well, quite,' smiled Felix. 'You know what I hate most about them? There are times . . . it's usually when I'm falling asleep in a chair, and you know how you start to feel heavier? . . . your hands . . . and in your face, heavy, sort of thick, a bit stupid, and you're tipping forward and . . . for a moment I'm him. I've turned into him. The little auditor from Salford, Lancs, in the Admin Dept, Colonial Services . . . the little king in Africa. It's such a fright it always wakes me up. D'you ever get that?'

Charlie was silent. Then, as if Felix hadn't spoken, he grinned sluggishly and said again, 'Tell me all about fathers! I mean, if Alys could've chosen, she'd have asked for you, right?'

'Oh, would she?, no, no,' Felix mumbled, and untangled the embrace.

He peered down at the party-site again, the party-ruins, and at the pale figure drifting through them. 'I wonder where our friend

Deany spent the last few days,' he remarked to Charlie. 'Which of
the rooms was his idea of heaven?'

'I bet he never left his little kiosk,' said Charlie affectionately.
'Everything he wants is in there. We've all gotta, y'know, go out and
find things, search through this 'n' that, grabbing at the world, but
Deany-boy . . . he just sits there, and it comes to him!'

Charlie's voice was laced with something like envy. Felix suppressed the urge to scoff. Charlie reached for his battered green
questionnaire again, and began turning it this way and that, determined to find space for just one more note. He stopped – suddenly
aware of Felix's incredulous gaze. 'Don't laugh at me!' he growled,
striking the water with his fist.

'I wasn't. I'm– '

'Don't laugh! This is important . . . this is my art! There's beauty
here . . . 'm gonna publish this . . . me and Deany.' He smoothed a
corner of the wrecked paper. 'Just the act of writing . . . the way the
paper dents under me . . . or the displays in flames, in ceilings, in
tree bark . . . they're as strong as anything you'll see in galleries . . .
's a gift . . . and one of the other compounds makes you invisible,
invisible . . . and in other material, other gifts, other feelings . . .
slow-on-slow, or wind-on-skin, standing to the side of things, heart-
push, solid music, the flooding of, the finding of cum, the
four-o'clockness of moments, an out-of-the-blue window   oh,
c'mon! This stuff comes with grace in it. How can you laugh?' Felix
stared at him, open-mouthed. Charlie stayed silent for a minute or
two, then said quietly, 'Jesus . . . I don't feel so good.'

Felix chewed his lip, then asked cautiously, 'Haven't you got anything you can take?'

'Huhn?'

'For your . . . well, what is it? A hangover. Isn't it just a . . . ?' Felix
paused – a note of scorn was creeping into his voice – he must be
careful. 'Y'know, for your . . .'

Charlie smiled coldly. 'Yeah, sure, there's something to take, I can
get myself straight-line-mellow no problem, thanks for your concern.' As Felix started to reply, Charlie said, 'Must make a move,'
and hoisted himself out of the pool, causing a big flop of water
onto the rocks below. He sat in the overflow, looking dazed. 'Must

make a move,' he murmured again, fingering the disintegrating questionnaire. His body was pale and skinny – he hadn't eaten for three or four days. Staring up at him, Felix thought he fitted perfectly into the picture of this hot, grey, early Monday morning.

Charlie's mobile rang. As he collected it from the lawn, he also hauled over his doctor's case, and a tray neatly laid with breakfast. Felix felt overcome with drowsiness, and floated heavily, only half listening to the conversation.

'. . . Will do,' Charlie said, winding up. 'We're on our way back anyway, thanks, *ciao*.' Tossing the machine back onto the grass, he said to Felix, 'That was about the Alex.'

'What?' said Felix, jolting awake, and sitting upright on the shelf.

Charlie took a moment to answer, first swallowing three tablets with mouthfuls of mango juice. He put back his head, breathed the air, basked in the light. 'The cops, a contact of mine . . . they're trying to sort out a . . . a kinda riot, I guess . . . the *sikukuu* crowd getting out of hand.'

'A riot? At the theatre? *A riot?*'

Charlie drained his glass, then said, 'People seem to know Duma's in there.'

'I see,' Felix heard himself say.

'They seem to, y'know . . . want him.'

Both men kept still, and then Felix asked: 'To lynch? Or to follow?'

Charlie frowned. 'To *follow*? Why would anyone want to follow him again?' Felix didn't answer. Charlie waited, then said, 'We're gonna have to do something about– '

Felix cut in, 'Indeed.'

'Aren't we?'

'We are.'

Charlie stared at Felix closely, then they both smiled, yelled madly, plunged under the water, and raced to the other end.

PART V

the Greatest
Show on Earth

thirty-five

Felix thought at first it was a queue for the box office. The biggest, best queue they'd ever had; three, four, five queues thick, and a hundred queues long; a fantastical creature with its tail at the harbour, its body wrapping through town, through the market-place, up the main roads, limbs spilling into all side-streets, alleys, doorways, and its head pointed firmly, tenaciously at the theatre.

Charlie leaned next to Felix, pressing his face against the curved glass of the helicopter. 'People have been arriving from all over the interior. Holy shit, hey? Hot diggedy-do!'

Although the queue was still fairly orderly, its outskirts were flanked by riot squads on standby: mixed groups of police and soldiers. It was difficult to tell which was which. The new regime had been so bent on demilitarising Duma's state, they had granted only meagre funding to the forces, and the men below were dressed in a rag-bag selection of camouflage fatigues, dress uniforms and PT wear, with or without helmets – some had baseball caps or builders' hard hats – and on their feet were boots, sandshoes or green wellingtons. Their shields, into which they hammered batons and sticks, trying to menace the queue, looked like trashcan lids. Sections of the queue returned the threats, yelling and singing, armed with petrol bombs, flaming torches, every weapon imaginable, legitimate and makeshift. Early casualties were evident: half a dozen *mkimbizi* figures lying in an alleyway, wounded or worse, flung there like broken puppets. Clearly some factions of the queue – little Mr

Fixer among them, no doubt – were grabbing this opportunity to address a few social grievances. Other factions looked more peaceful, more celebratory, waving palm fronds, hand-made banners, cardboard placards.

Unable, from this height, to read any slogans, or decipher the different chants, Felix said quietly, 'What do they all want?'

'You keep asking that,' Charlie commented. 'They're a lynch mob. Aren't they? What else could they be?'

Felix didn't answer. The ride in the helicopter, the massing throngs below, the queue and the riot squads . . . it was all inducing a familiar, giddy mixture of eagerness and dread – *This is showbiz! this is politics!* Reaching for his buzz balls, he saw Alys – a golden angel flying through the sky with him – surrounded by her toys from the weekend. She wore a strange expression of concern. It disturbed more than comforted – a child shouldn't look so wise and sad, so experienced – and put the oddest thoughts in Felix's mind. The helicopter . . . it was a kamikaze plane . . . someone needed to call it back.

Down they went, aiming for the theatre.

Felix could now see that his beloved building was wound tight with human beings: they swathed each corner with the thick, difficult flexibility of ship-rope, an interweaving solidity, fastening every doorway and the lower windows. The place was impenetrable, except from the sky.

He ran both hands over his head, collecting sweat by the palmful. It was lush – and cold – in the back of his hair, the spot that soaked his pillow every night. Suddenly he remembered something . . . in the urgency to leave the farm, with Charlie summoning his helicopter and manning it himself, in this rush, somebody had been overlooked. Felix turned to Charlie. 'The chap I brought along for the weekend, any idea where he is?'

'Be in one of the other planeloads, I guess, with Deany-boy and all the others. Tell the truth, I forgot there was anyone with you. Why did you never introduce us?'

Felix shrugged – remembering father and son on the dance-floor, their joky kiss through mask and muzzle – then said, 'I don't know. Everything was so . . . so . . .'

'Yeah, wasn't it?' Charlie hovered, checked his sights, and landed on the theatre roof.

There were two other helicopters already parked here. Issuing instructions for Alys to be flown home, Charlie clambered out. Felix kissed her goodbye, and followed. As the aircraft took off again, he saw her small face pressed to the glass. That odd look in her eye . . . oh, it was Isabeau's look! . . . that's why it was so wise, so experienced, so disquieting . . . her mother was present. Felix felt something rise in his chest. It was as though his soul was trying to leave with the helicopter, rather than go through what was to follow. A kind of ache, a kind of weariness, fell over him.

Climbing through the window into his room, his most private room, Felix saw that it was occupied. Even his chair was taken. Bull Brak sat there, with legs spread under the table, his big yellow feet on the bedding. Lord Gomes was pacing around, browsing and touching. Still dressed in their weekend outfits – Brak in beach-wear, Gomes in silk safari suit – they were drinking whisky from a familiar, fat honey-jar of a bottle.

Oh, to see it again, thought Felix, in this room, and to smell its . . . no, to *feel* its fumes here again.

He wanted to crawl straight into bed under the table. Would that be very rude? he wondered.

'Hi, guys,' said Brak.

'Gentlemen,' said Lord Gomes.

Neither looked particularly concerned. 'Bit of a major situation out there, hey?' Brak said lustily.

He heaved himself out of the chair. Felix immediately claimed it – then had second thoughts. The three men were now standing in front of him, looking down. Did it seem like he was taking charge? They had expectant expressions on their faces, slightly amused. It was odd. Why weren't they more troubled?

Charlie strolled to the window and turned his back, needing to pop, sip or snort something and not having enough to offer round. Beyond his silhouette, the picture looked normal: the old jalousie shutters framing a simple view of green-grey sky and palm tree. A seagull even flew by. But rising through this same normal picture came the noise of the giant, multi-headed, multi-limbed queue on *queue at the ~~theatre~~ theatre is also a lynch mob/political gathering.*

the lions?

the streets thirteen floors below. It was so loud, on every side, a sort of moan, both angry and ecstatic, that you felt utterly enveloped; you were inside the throat of the crowd.

Felix slouched in his chair, eyeing the raffia mat and pillows below. It was very inviting. He could just keep slipping down. Checking himself, he said, 'Well?'

'Well?' echoed Bull Brak and Lord Gomes.

'What are we going to do?'

Everyone looked philosophical.

'Ah,' said Lord Gomes.

'Yup,' said Bull Brak.

'The million-dollar question,' said Charlie.

'I mean,' spluttered Felix, 'what do they want?'

'Ah,' said Lord Gomes.

'Yup,' said Bull Brak.

'Another million-dollar –' Charlie started to say, then snapped out of the rhythm. 'You're doing it again! Isn't it obvious what they want?'

'Not exactly,' said Brak, replying for Felix. 'Duma didn't stay in power for all those years just through terror.'

'What d'you mean?' asked Charlie.

'Well,' said Brak, casually examining the objects on Felix's table until he found what he was looking for – a pack of cigarettes, 'Let's put it like this. He has his supporters.'

Are you one of them? Felix wondered, peering at the old warhorse.

'Lots of supporters, yup,' added Brak, hitching up his shorts, and then standing there, thumbs on hips, big fingers lolling, cigarette in the side of his mouth, the full *Dook*-look. 'Yessiree. Maybe as many as fifty-fifty in that crowd. Which makes the next step hard.'

'What is the next step?' Felix asked.

'We don't know.'

'That's why it's hard,' added Lord Gomes, with a suave chuckle.

Felix studied them through half-closed lids. They were lying. They did have a next step. But they were waiting for *him* to take it. Why? To keep their hands clean probably. They were both clean-hand experts. For years and years Lord Gomes had demonstrated his consummate skills here at the theatre, being semi-supportive, semi-critical of every decision Felix took, so that, whatever the outcome, he could claim the credit. And Bull Brak had been doing the same thing, but *all over Africa*, for goodness sake!

No, these two old pro's were playing some kind of game with him.

Not Charlie, though. Charlie seemed as innocent as he was.

Felix rose and walked away from the chair, vacating it.

No one moved. Below, the crowd moaned.

Now Zikki came running in. 'Here you all are!' he cried. His voice had the same furious, blaming edge that Felix had heard at the party when he was longing for things he couldn't have. As then, the streetwise swagger and fairground sparkle were gone – he was a child, a teenager unable to cope with a complicated predicament. 'We've got one big major fukken problem here!' he whimpered.

The others laughed.

'Please!' rebuked Zikki. 'My babies haven't been fed!' Everyone frowned, working it out. 'They were supposed to go back to the circus for the weekend, I left some dick-headed beastman to do it, *ja?*, but he got *sikukuu*-happy, one-two-three, and then this fukken mad fukken situation blew up here, four-five-six, so he couldn't get them out, and couldn't get food in, and now my *babychens* are fuk-of-a-hungry, fuk-of-a-angry. It's not good.'

'There's a butcher just across the street,' Felix said helpfully, with a vague memory of the day, wasn't it recently?, when he saw two monkeys or dogs in the window, one still half alive. 'Over there – straight over the street.'

'Then try and cross it please!' snarled Zikki. 'Be my ga-ga-guest!' He burst into tears. 'My *babychens* are starving! It's evil to see, to hear! *Meine babychens, meine kleinen babychens*! They're starving and they won't let me near them! What must I do? *Meine armen Kleine, meine kleinen babyleins, meine lieblingsbabykins!*'

'Please calm yourself, my friend,' said Lord Gomes gently – they had, as Felix had noted before, a curiously sympathetic relationship. 'Help is at hand. My helicopter is on the roof. I will instruct my pilot to fly to my property, where the deep freezes will be emptied, the contents will be conveyed back here, and within the hour your *babychens* will be feasting on the finest Argentinian steaks and French gigots of lamb.'

'Thank you,' said Zikki, wiping his eyes, blowing his little nose.

Lord Gomes addressed the room: 'There we are gentlemen – the first of our problems is solved – *muito bem*!' With stylish grace he stepped onto the chair, onto the table, and, hip hop hup, climbed out of the window.

thirty-six

They were audible now, despite the much louder noise of the mob outside. The moans of the lions possessed an echoing resonance, full of deep, almost pleasurable agony. It was as though the underworld itself was calling out to be fed.

Descending his private stairwell, Felix peered round the door on the ground floor – soldiers, policemen and theatre staff were building barricades everywhere – then he continued down to the basement. He passed the storeroom where the lions were locked. Smelling him, they threw themselves at the door. He heard nostrils, claws. Hurrying on, turning a corner, he finally reached *the* door.

Without knocking, he unlocked it and entered.

In contrast to the animals in the adjoining room, the Emperor Duma looked calm and well fed after his weekend alone. Empty soup cans, foil trays and paper cups were tidily piled in a cardboard box next to his fridge.

'What is happening out there?' he asked. The high window in the room looked out onto an internal yard, so for several days he had listened, with growing mystification, to the baying of the mob and the moaning of the lions. His tone was calm. 'Outside – what is going on?'

'I don't know,' Felix mumbled in reply.

'Untrue.'

'I'm sorry?'

'Of course you know what's going on. Or, at least, you know

more than me. You can see out of the upstairs windows. So even if you don't *understand* what is going on, you are nevertheless able to answer my question to some extent. So. I will ask it again. What is going on?'

Felix remained still. On second thoughts, Duma wasn't at all calm. This was his version of screaming panic.

'Don't call me a liar,' Felix said, surprised by his own boldness.

'No. My apologies.'

They faced one another, both aware that Felix still hadn't answered Duma.

'How was your weekend?' Felix asked.

'Quite pleasant, thank you,' replied Duma, agreeing to change the subject for now. 'Got some writing done.'

Felix glanced to the dressing-table with its soft crest of makeup lights. An almighty ream of paper was neatly stacked here, the potentate's flywhisk laid across the top. What was this? His own *Mein Kampf? The Thoughts of Emperor Duma*? Or was it his last will and testament? Felix recalled Duma's most recent TV appearance – in the bungalow at the farm – and him saying, 'I know how I will die, when and where.' Charlie had once proposed that Duma was eager for death; as long as it could be heroic. He didn't want to be torn apart by a mob. He wanted something else, something nobler.

'And yours?' Duma asked.

'Sorry?'

'Your weekend?'

'Yes. Tickety-boo. Went into the interior.'

'Aaaha,' murmured Duma, with yearning. 'Tell me. Be my eyes. What did you see?'

Felix blinked away images of grease and tongues, horns and muzzles, and then said, 'Game . . . y'know . . . birds, animals.'

'Mh-hmm, Mh-hmm,' Duma purred warmly as Felix spoke, then asked 'Were they African animals?'

'Of course African animals,' laughed Felix.

'I used to collect unAfrican animals.'

'Oh. Yes.'

'Llamas, kangaroos, polar bears.'

'Yes.'

'Do you know *why* I collected only unAfrican animals?'

'I don't,' replied Felix. 'Tell me.'

'Because I would never cage an African animal. Never!'

As Felix nodded slowly, pondering the logic of this, a sudden bestial moan came through the wall. The men looked towards it, lifting their heads together, heavily, lazily, like grazing wildebeest, then Felix said, 'Is it true you killed a lion once? With your bare hands?'

Duma smiled wearily. It was a look Felix recognised from his stay in America, and the endless celebrity chat-shows on their TV channels; that tired, smug look when the *is-it-true* question comes up.

Duma gave a long sigh. 'Yes, it is true.'

'And how does one do that, then? How does one kill a lion with bare hands?'

'You get your fist down its throat.'

'Pardon?'

'Your one hand must be down the throat, the other must grip the tongue. It can't close its jaws, it can't breathe properly, it starts to choke. You gain the advantage.'

'Are you serious?' Felix asked – then bit his lip. He was addressing the most serious man in the world.

'Try it,' Duma said, with a serious smile. 'I assure you it works.'

'But how do you get your fist past the teeth?'

'Yes, that's the tricky bit,' Duma conceded solemnly. 'It is the moment of reckoning. It requires inspiration and courage and something else – call it blessing, if you will – the extra thing which separates some men, whether engaged in lion-wrestling or not, from their fellows.'

'Heroic destiny,' prompted Felix.

Duma went quiet, unsure if he was being mocked. He smiled slowly, testing Felix: 'Something we share.'

'Along with Gillette Lemon Lime Foamy,' Felix parried, returning the smile.

'Oh – once upon a time, heh?' chuckled Duma, nodding towards Felix's skull and chin, where dense, ferociously black hair had sprouted since his performance as Mr Rosenblatt the optometrist.

'And is it true,' Felix asked again – making the dictator laugh – 'is it true that you kept crocodiles in your swimming-pool?' Duma's smile froze. 'I only ask,' continued Felix, 'because they're very African animals, and to them a swimming-pool must feel like a kind of cage.'

He waited. Duma was silent. The lions pined and moaned through the wall.

'Even if they were being properly fed. These crocodiles.'

Duma still made no comment, just flexed his chin, while his glasses – the glasses which had brought them together – collected some light from the dressing-table mirror and flashed it at Felix, gently; a wink, a warning.

'Are you Popo-boy?' Felix asked suddenly.

Duma's expression didn't change; if anything, the light in the glasses steadied.

'Did you . . . ? The son of my friends, a student . . . did you dispatch him in your swimming-pool? Was it a name for you – Popo-boy – or maybe the crocodiles? Was it? Hm? Are you Popo-boy?'

Duma was completely motionless. In the tone of a prisoner-of-war, giving only name and number, he said: 'I am Gomgom the hermit.'

Felix sat back sighing, feeling that round one was over, and not knowing who had won.

They listened to the lions and the crowd.

'Do you, excuse me, have a cigarette?' Duma asked.

'Of course,' said Felix, handing one over. As he flicked open his lighter, and leaned forward, he noticed Duma's fingers on the filter-tip. There was slight, almost imperceptible movement . . . they were trembling. Not from the interrogation, not from fear or anger – no, no, Felix recognised the tiny shiver – it was desire. Duma was desperate for this cigarette. Felix wondered how, if the man was a smoker, he had endured the last few days? Why hadn't he asked for a supply? Did he practise abstinence as an exercise in self-discipline? 'Appetite,' whispered Felix – abruptly withdrawing his lighter before Duma could suck on the flame.

'Heh?'

Felix grinned. 'Appetite. That's what it's all about. Life. I've solved it – The Mystery Of. You grope around for Greater Powers, Lower Powers. Is it . . . the Gods, Yourself, Nature, Art? Well, none of these. It's just a thing called Appetite. It's just about being fed, being sated, getting what you need. Or *want*. Which is which? That cigarette, say, do you want it or need it? Ah, trying to work out the difference, there's the rub!' He paused, listening to the low thunder in the walls and the ceiling, then said it again, slowly, relishing the melodrama: 'Appetite.'

'And imagination,' added Duma, brightly, studying his unlit cigarette like a rare and wonderful object; a trophy of his will-power. Speaking in a full, rich voice, a voice that set the phrase in stone, he said, 'Appetite *and* imagination.'

'Goodness.'

'I've surprised you?'

'You've quoted me.'

Duma looked at him quizzically.

Felix collected the sweat in handfuls from his face and hair. 'Appetite *and* imagination. Of course you've got to include the other. The contrast makes it sublime. Makes us such marvellous creatures. Makes us capable of art. Conflict . . . conflict is the melting-pot of art. I tell my actors all the time . . . use both sides of yourself all the time, your male and female sides, your adult and child sides, animal and intellect, earth and air, et cetera, use *complication*! Your characters are complicated. Pain and beauty live side by side, horror and tenderness, et cetera, cetera. This double thing – this is what lies in all great art. And this is the undoing of all politics, d'you see? Forgive me for trying to teach my grandmother to suck eggs, as 'twere, but y'see . . . politics seeks to reduce everything, to make it black *or* white. Politics is thoroughly and fatally confused by the glorious, dangerous, love-hate, comi-tragic muddle of our existence!'

Duma nodded slowly, with amusement, then sang sweetly, '"You like po-tay-to and I like po-tah-to."'

Felix joined in: '"Po-tay-to, po-tah-to, to-may-to, to-mah-to . . ."'

'"Let's call the whole thing off!"' they sang together – then immediately went silent, and eyed one another again. The only movement came from the unlit cigarette bobbing up and down in

Duma's fingers, still keeping time to some tune in his head, a little pulse, a little gauge.

'So,' he said, after a while. 'The mystery of life is solved.'

Felix gave an embarrassed half-laugh. His outburst on Life and Art was echoing round his skull now, in that sober bright space, with every corner lit up, exposing it harshly. He said, 'Well, for today it is. Tomorrow, maybe something different, what?'

Duma didn't mirror his jocularity. In a grave tone, with no trace of irony, he said, 'No, no. We have solved the mystery of life. This is good. Do you mind if I mention it in my speech?'

Felix furrowed his brow, watching as Duma levered the huge stack of papers off the dressing-table and onto his lap – having first set the cigarette aside, carefully – then searched through, found the appropriate place, and inscribed an addition.

These papers were a speech? *One* speech?

Felix swallowed slowly. A familiar flutter had started up inside him, making him giddy, exciting his nerve ends. 'Speech?' he asked Duma. 'What speech?'

'In tonight's presentation,' was the reply.

'Tonight's presentation,' murmured Felix,

Hearing his tone, Duma looked up from his papers. 'We are doing a presentation tonight, I presume?'

'D'you mean a show?'

'That sounds flippant but yes.' He replaced the papers on the table. 'There is, it seems, quite an assembly out there.' Felix didn't comment. A look of fear went through Duma's eyes for the first time, a tiny, private look. It was quickly banished. Then he lifted the cigarette, aimed his gaze at the lighter still in Felix's hand, and raised his eyebrows.

Felix feigned confusion. 'Ehrm . . . ?'

Duma signalled with his eyebrows again, more explicitly.

'Isn't there a little word?' said Felix.

'Heh?'

'And doesn't the little word begin with P?'

A thick and dangerous silence fell. Felix gave a small laugh, both scoffing and jittery. Duma dropped the cigarette onto the floor and ground it underfoot in a restrained but thorough way, until it was powder. Felix thought of the bat. Now Duma sat back.

'What *is* going on, Felix – outside?'

The sound of his name on that tongue – Felix had only heard it once before – it brought a strange mix of sensations. He sat, savouring these, and considering his options. He thought for a long time. Then he rose to leave.

'HAVE I FINISHED?' Duma roared suddenly. 'No! Did I say this meeting was over? I DID NOT!'

Felix's body halted at a twisted angle. If it had been a volcano erupting instead of just a man – and at that instant, Felix honestly wasn't sure – and if molten lava was to petrify him for ever in this position, future archaeologists would puzzle over his position. The limbs leading away in a brisk stride, half departure, half flight, the head twisted back, half furious, half shocked.

'You have no right,' Duma said, struggling to control himself. 'No right to censor this information.'

'Oh, that's jolly good,' said Felix, catching his breath and unlocking his muscles. 'You're lecturing me on censorship. You. On the subject of censorship. Well . . . that's quite amusing, really.'

'Good. If you find it so, then . . .'

'Do you know that every time I did a show I had to report, in person, to your Public Information Office, with the material, and justify my reasons for wanting to do, say, *The Iliad*, to someone who'd never heard of it, and only wanted to know if it contained pro-American propaganda? Do you know that your police arrested me once? For including, in one of my shows, a scene you know quite well now, a scene about the one-eyed giant called Cyclo–'

'Yes, yes,' said Duma impatiently. 'They arrested *everybody* at one point or another, they were a little over-zealous. Clearly they didn't harm you. You look perfectly–'

It was Duma's turn to freeze with shock – as Felix flew at him, arriving nose to nose, and screaming: 'I am not perfectly anything! I am not unharmed! I was cut open from here to here, my leg was cut open like a sack of sugar. I bled, I pissed myself! I have never been so terrified in my life! Do you understand what I'm saying? Terror! D'you understand terror? From this side of the fence! Do you, do you?' His screeching face was touching Duma's now, brushing it, twisting first this way, then that, as if trying to find a place to bite, or a way in, trying to enter Duma's head. 'Do you, huh, do you?' His arms and fists stayed fixed at his side – curiously distanced from his snarling, snapping mouth – as if bound, shaking with rage and impotence, dying to touch the great man, but scared to, scared of what he might do to Duma, of what Duma might do back. 'Do you, huh, do you? Yes! Bigshot, huh? Big bad Duma? Not so fucking brave now, are you? *Emperor* sir, your royal majesty sir, your fucking fuckface sir, your cunting cuntship!'

Felix backed off, shuddering with emotion. Duma was splashed with spit. They looked at one another. Duma opened his mouth to speak. Felix rushed at him again: 'So I will let you know about tonight! *I – Me!* The one you arrested, tried to silence. I will let you know about tonight's *show*! You will say *show* – not *presentation*! This is point number one. You will say *stage* – not *platform*! That is point number two. And this, this is point number fucking three!' He leaped at the furniture, scattering Duma's papers: 'This is a makeup table, not a writing desk!, these are makeup lights, not reading lamps!, so get some slap on, ducky, throw on your cossie, stand by, and if you're lucky, *if you are lucky*, you will be told whether you're going on, when and where to enter and exit, and what, if anything, we want you to say in between!'

'We?' said Duma calmly. 'Who is "we", please?'

'I don't know!' shouted Felix, even louder, as he felt the ground slip from under him. 'But be that as it may, you will be told, you will be told!'

Duma nodded – to himself – then bent over to gather his strewn papers.

'So you won't need these!' yelled Felix, marching across them with a high goose-step, smashing his feet down. 'Won't-need-these! Will-not-need! No-need-for! Fucky-fucky-cunt!'

Duma went very still, a contained, private expression on his face, and his slow, heavy breathing was the only sign of implosions that might be occurring. He looked up. Felix swallowed hard. Those round spectacles, they were like holes of light . . . lion's eyes . . . the lens of an X-ray camera.

'I don't think we should fight,' Duma said lightly. 'Do you?'

director directing the dictator

'Don't mind, don't care,' chirruped Felix, bouncing on the balls of his feet.

'As we Igisha say –'

'I'm not interested in what you fucking Igisha say!'

'We say, "When two elephants fight, it is the grass that dies."'

'Oo-oo!' sang out Felix. 'How profound, oo-oo!'

'We also say –'

'Don't care, not interested, shuddup!'

'"Shuddup"?' repeated Duma, smiling. 'But isn't "shuddup", forgive me, a command of censorship?'

'No, wrong term again, chummy,' replied Felix, smiling back. 'We call it cutting.'

'Cutting?'

'Cutting, yes, cutting.' He grabbed handfuls of Duma's speech. 'Much too long, dear boy, needs cutting, cutting. Probably packed with stuff about mongrels, twins, inferior tribes . . . oh, yawn-yawn. I recommend you lose all that, and discourse instead on your love of African fauna and the songs of George Gershwin. And if there's any stuff about not smiling in public, not touching soldiers, not –'

Duma clapped his hands in delight. 'The artist! The artist with a conscience!'

'Yes, that's it, yes!'

'Are we quite sure?'

'Yes, yes, yes!' chanted Felix, trying to drown him out, to deflect his cunning (he could *feel* its approach). 'Yes, yes, yes!'

'Is that why you curtailed freedom of speech among your workers here at the theatre? Among your people?'

'Never did that,' retorted Felix – *he must keep smiling, must keep on his toes*. 'Everyone was free to speak their minds. I usually told them to bugger off, but they were free to try.'

'I think you did more than tell them to –'

Felix began to laugh. 'Yes, I did. I often called them cunts, tits and wankers. Oo, wasn't that tyrannical!'

'I think it was, yes,' said Duma. 'I think it caused a great deal of suffering. After your first visit to me, I asked Colonel Brak to do some homework, and according to him, we had frequent and serious complaints about you.'

'Oh, don't be ridiculous!' Felix cried gleefully – he'd overestimated Duma's cunning, the man was clutching at straws. 'I was just a piss-artist, a little thespian lush, a little drunken diva, a poisoned dwarf, used to be two-a-penny overseas, in Shaftesbury Avenue or Broadway, with swirling capes and monocles, but I was here, so, *c'est la vie*, behold the little king in Africa!' He faltered, realising that he'd just described his father.

'According to our information,' said Duma; 'There was an incident here, for example, on the thirteenth of February 1987, when you told one of your workers . . .'

Felix listened in amazement. Brak must have dug out the theatre's old security file, and Duma had memorised sections of it! 'Listen, sunshine,' shouted Felix, 'I'm not going to be called to judgement by *you*!'

'Why not?' Duma parried lightly. 'Since when did violence exist only in deeds, not in words, even thoughts? On what scale must we judge the terror you caused among your workers?'

'Are you seriously comparing that with . . . ?'

'No, I'm not. I'm simply asking you not to sit in judgement either, that is all.'

Felix swayed on his feet, remembering all the people upstairs, in his office, waiting. *Waiting for what?*

Duma leaned forward to collect the papers from Felix's hand. 'I'm also asking that you allow –'

'It's cut!' Felix said, swatting away his hand. 'Told you. This speech is cut. Look . . .' He tore up the pages. 'Gone.'

'Not so,' smiled Duma. 'It came from my heart. I'll find it there again. I don't need the paper.'

'Oh, good, well, then . . . !' Felix began tearing other pages into shreds and hurling them round the room, skipping and laughing. 'Cut, cut!' Duma laughed along, and echoed the word, holding out his arms, letting pieces of paper land like snowflakes. Catching a larger fragment, he paused to examine it. Felix danced over to him. 'Oh, look, here's someone wearing glasses – too studious – let's cut the glasses!' He snatched the spectacles from Duma's nose, and jumped up and down on them. 'Cut, cut!' Duma guffawed, openly mocking. Spotting the emperor's flywhisk, his ivory-and-buffalo-tail sceptre, Felix seized it – 'Cut the props!' – and smacked it on the floor. It bounced in his grip, unbroken, ricocheting through his arms. 'Cut, cut!' he yelled, trying again, smashing it harder. It didn't even chip. Duma applauded. *'Cut, cut!'* panted Felix, lifting it above Duma's head. *'Cut you!'*

'Me? But you worship me.'

Felix stopped, his club in mid-air.

The emperor smiled up at him. 'You can't take your eyes off me. My voice is music to your ears. You're intoxicated by my smell. You thrill to my touch. You're a lost cause. You're in love.'

Felix stayed still. The silence lasted for a minute or more. He licked his lips. A drink would be nice now. He didn't dare glance at the emperor's box of supplies. 'Be careful,' he said to Duma, in a hoarse voice. 'Like the saying goes, I tend to kill the things I love.'

Duma gave a tiny smile. 'Then I was right.'

'Sorry?'

'When we first met. I felt I was shaking hands with the one who would do it. I was right.' He paused. 'I'm always right,' he added quietly, with a touch of regret.

thirty-seven

The meat had arrived and was coming in through his window.

Great chunks of frozen meat – sides of beef, whole lambs, pig legs – all melting in the hot African afternoon, melting on his floor, where people were stacking them . . . little pools of meat-flavoured water . . . little trickles running towards his bed under the table.

He crouched there, within the insect net. The others didn't seem to notice or mind. Sometimes he was bent double with waves of terror, at other times he sat calmly, cross-legged, listening to them talking above; they sounded like parents playing poker, having meals, making decisions.

Many people were present. The theatre company had come to work, to do tonight's show, finding their way across other roofs, troopers that they were, and dallying up here now, awaiting developments, abuzz with it all: Frankie Hoong, Mr Mmalo, Dhaba the Odysseus actor, and Kaz, who was singing a husky, bluesy rendition of 'Oh Mah Man Ah Love Him So'. The Alex's administrator, Mr Otiti, was there, and several of the trustees. One of them looked especially troubled. Judge Okoth-Ofumbi. He'd been sitting with head in hands ever since Mrs Al-Qirib referred to the board meeting six weeks previously, and his own proposal to use the theatre as a courthouse for show-trials. Had fate come home to roost? Would the present situation be resolved by some hastily arranged hearing, with him presiding? – and the place packed to the rafters with that mob out there? He shuddered with horror. Meanwhile the board's chairman, Lord Gomes, paced to and fro, in a chic kind of way, his smooth but sudden changes of direction making it look like he was on a catwalk. Charlie was at the window, his back to the room, his hands lifting something to his face. The crowd around him included the boy with long hair and crutches, the old legless man, and Miss Rosewood. Zikki was presently missing.

Bull Brak finished talking on his mobile, receiving instructions from his superiors. He addressed the room: 'Situation's difficult to monitor, but it seems to be worsening. Very volatile, very unstable. There's looting everywhere, an incendiary device has gone off, all sorts of weaponry's coming out of hiding, *mki-mbizis* are being picked off like crows on a fence, one of the famine camps has been razed to the ground, an office block too. So. It looks like they want us to do something.'

A ripple of laughter passed round the room.

'*Huw!*' went Brak, joining in. 'But, no, they *are* trying to be more specific this time. They're saying they don't want him handed over to . . .' He nodded towards the open window, and the noise beyond.

The laughter faded.

'Apparently some of his supporters are more powerful than anyone thought, and there's no guarantee that handing him over would end in . . . a way that would stabilise the operation.' From his upside-down view under the table, Felix saw the exchanged glances between some people: Bull Brak, Lord Gomes, and one or two of the trustees. '. . . So that option is now closed,' Brak concluded, in clumsy code to his associates.

'Leaving us with what?' someone asked.

'Ah,' said Lord Gomes.

'The million-buck question,' said Charlie.

'Yup,' said Bull Brak.

There was silence for a while. then somebody else said, 'Where's Felix?'

'He stepped out for a mo',' Lord Gomes replied quickly, almost too quickly, then sat in Felix's chair, and wiggled one of his crocodile-skin slip-ons under the table. Felix frowned at it. A moment later, Lord Gomes passed down a note: *Must make a move a.s.a.p.* As Felix sat, mystified and pondering, Lord Gomes' hand appeared again, this time depositing the bottle of Chivas Regal on the floor.

Never having learned of Felix's abstinence, Lord Gomes was trying to be helpful, trying to calm the other's turmoil, trying to lubricate some decision.

Felix collected the bottle, feeling its weight, its realness. Oh, it was so smooth, so elegant, so dangerous, this lump of glass between his fingers. He pulled out the fancy cork, listening to its little flirting pop. It was as though the whisky had been holding its breath and released it now, blowing a kiss, letting Felix smell the smell, the smell of a most intimate partner.

This isn't fair, he thought.

As his right hand lifted the bottle to his mouth, his left hand intercepted it. He arm-wrestled himself, rocking from side to side under the table, trying to conceal his exertions from the people above. Silent tumbles and tugs-of-war now ensued, his movements slowed down and exaggerated like a mime artist, with accompanying grimaces and mouthed expletives. His right hand proved the stronger. The whisky rose joltingly towards his face. Abandoning its grip on the bottle, Felix's left hand clamped itself over his lips. The right hand unlocked three of its fingers from the bottle's neck, and prised through the fleshy barrier, their nails digging cruelly. At last they secured a big enough opening for the bottle's mouth to work its way in, and meet Felix's own. It levered his lips apart. His teeth were still clamped shut, a last line of defence. The bottle withdrew a fraction then rammed them lightly. His skull rang. In that instant the bottle was through, home, and tilting. Liquid filled his mouth. The bottle withdrew. Felix's cheeks were bulging, his eyes watering, his tastebuds in chaos. Refusing to swallow, unable to breathe, he started to turn red.

Beyond the insect net, the conversation started up again. A voice said, 'What's needed is a gesture.' Felix swayed forward to see who the speaker was. Mr Mmalo. Dressed in jacket and bow-tie as usual, with his attaché case on his lap, and the bamboo snuff container in one hand.

MR MMALO: . . . A symbol. A symbolic gesture. I am devoted to both Christianity and Science, though I am not, as people sometimes mistakenly think, a Christian Scientist, who believe, unlike yours truly, that . . .

LORD GOMES: Oh, do get on with it.

MR MMALO: Yes, so sorry, just meant to say that it is perhaps the Bible that we must turn to, rather than the manual or textbook. A symbolic gesture. The crowd must be appeased with something.

LORD GOMES: Perhaps that could be *you*. You do a fair imitation of the emperor. We could throw you to them.
(*Laughter*.)

LORD GOMES: . . . Barabbas instead of Christ.

MR MMALO: (*tetchily*) I think you've got that the wrong way round.

LORD GOMES: Don't you use that tone to me! *Por amor de Deus!* I'm the chairman of this bloody theatre, you're only – !

BULL BRAK: Guys, gents, please, let's keep it sweet and easy. Now the trouble is, what's needed here is something that has dogged my whole fucking life, pardon my French, but I've trekked the length and breadth of this great continent of ours, searching for the very thing that this operation requires . . . a centre of gravity! One of the hardest commodities to come by in Africa. A centre of gravity. The crowd does need appeasing, our actor friend here is right, but trouble is, there are *two sides* to this crowd. The lynch mob and the supporters. And *both* need appeasing.

A VOICE: That's impossible.

ANOTHER VOICE: *Both* sides appeased?

EVERYONE: (*ad lib*) Impossible, can't be done, etc.
(*Pause. Through the window, the noise of the crowd grows ever more ominous.*)

FELIX: (*Blue in the face; thinks*) Appease both sides . . . *Eureka*!

A VOICE: This meat's starting to stink.

ANOTHER VOICE: Where is the little fella?

EVERYONE: The little fella, where's that little fella?

(*On cue, Zikki rushes in.*)

ZIKKI: The meat! *Meine vleis! Danke Hemel!*

(*He lifts half a cow – proving considerable strength – and moves to the door. Under the table, Felix spits out the whisky . . .*)

FELIX: WAIT!

thirty-eight

It felt like a first night.

Other people must only know this feeling at Christmas time, reflected Felix, as he buttoned his black shirt; your workplace turned into a party place, everyone dressed up, exchanging presents and cards, the corridors packed, a charge in the air, a strange charge . . . nobody behaving normally, shy colleagues blossoming, veins running with adrenaline or other addictive chemicals and, at the end of the day, some conquests and some disappointments, and the building shaken to its foundations.

And this evening . . . this wasn't going to be just an ordinary first night, or even a gala . . . this was going to be, in the words of Zikki, the greatest show on earth.

The light of sunset lay in the slats of the jalousie blinds. All seemed peaceful outside. The great oceanic soughings of the crowd had subsided. Three thousand of them were sitting in the auditorium downstairs, another thousand standing at the back, down the aisles, on the stairs, in the doorways, and those who couldn't fit would listen to the proceedings on loudspeakers specially installed round the foyers; three thousand more were assembled there. The building was heavy with people.

When Felix looked out earlier, to watch the audience enter (first checking in all weapons at the stalls manned by Brak's men), he saw several camera crews securing vantage points. Apparently the airport was besieged with arrivals of the international media. The phones in

the theatre hadn't stopped ringing, and were now switched off. Everyone was under instructions not to grant interviews until it was over.

Felix pulled on his old black jacket, veteran of a hundred first
nights, and hummed 'Let's Call The Whole Thing Off'.

Now Charlie entered in a white linen suit, also singing happily. In
the mirror, Felix noticed himself blushing. Earlier, during a little
crawl through the air-ducts, he had watched Charlie and Kaz
making love in her room. And it was 'making love', not mere copu-
lation, and all the ruder for it. To spy on such intimacy . . . !

Charlie beamed at him now. 'How you feeling, ol' bud?'

'Oh, yes, tickety-boo. Fortune, or good stars, or whatever . . .
something good is beaming down at last.'

'Like your namesake.'

'Sorry?'

'The Roman dictator – I must have told you – when we were kids
probably, when I was reading it all for the first time.'

'A dictator? A dictator called *Felix*? Tell me again.'

Charlie grinned, and took a deep breath; 'Real name Sulla, 138
to 78 BC, captured Rome twice, ruled as emperor, had all his enemies
slaughtered, amassed great wealth, managed to retire peacefully,
thus becoming one of history's only dictators to die of old age!'

'And why Felix?' asked Felix.

'Took it from the goddess of good fortune, Felicitas . . . Felix . . .
's Latin for auspicious, lucky . . . you can also say Faustus. Which
was what he called one of his twins . . .'

'Faustus? Like the play?'

'Yeah, now listen, fortune is shining on me too, and I want you to
know straight off. Me and Kaz, we've been talking and . . . we're
gonna get hitched.'

Felix blinked. Kaz had told him the same thing on the riverbank.
He'd assumed it was drunken nonsense. Now Charlie was talking
about it seriously.

'The way we look at it is this . . . we've been together so long now,
sometimes just as friends, sometimes lovers, and we're good at both.
And we can't just be lifelong ravers, we're both getting too old, and,
y'know, it's time Alys had some proper parents instead of, like,
y'know, just me . . .'

And me! thought Felix, his senses reeling. It had happened again. He, who prided himself as the great spy, the great peeper, operating from the dark of the auditorium, or within silvery air-ducts, or half asleep on a lakeside knoll, watching, learning, knowing everything . . . he had missed this coming, he'd missed this completely!

'. . . and it'll be good for Kaz as well, to be a mother again, help her stop obsessing about our lost one, so – that's it, ol' bud, that's the first piece of good news!'

'It's splendid,' said Felix, wishing he meant it. It *was* good news . . . wasn't it? Alys *did* need proper parents, or even, bless them, Charlie and Kaz. 'Yes, splendid, don't know what to say.'

'Well, just wait, just hold on to your hat, buddy, because the other thing is . . .' Charlie danced round the room, laughing with joy. 'We're gonna give it up!'

'Give what . . . ?'

'This, this,' he cried gleefully, emptying his pockets of potions and powders, tablets and phials, and heaping them on the table. 'And this, and this – everything!'

'Gosh,' said Felix quietly.

'It's incredible . . . this idea,' said Charlie, trying to catch his breath. 'We both got to it at the same moment. It was fucking incredible, man, it was seriously freaky. I mean, d'you see what it means? It means it is *meant to be!*' Felix narrowed his eyes, wondering how many potions and powders were on the table and how many inside Charlie. 'I mean, we just can't do it any more,' said Charlie happily, his eyes wide and bright, his gaze spinning. 'I mean, OK, take this weekend right? We're really wasted man, really wrecked. Pharmaceutical? Schmarmatitical! It's crap, it's shit! Can't do it any more, jus' can't do it, and that's great, isn't it? – that is Nature, that is our Greater Power, saying chill out, grow up, put your feet up, relax, become responsible, just love, just love the people you love, and be loved, and, and . . . and that's great, isn't it?'

'Yes, it is,' said Felix, starting to laugh, catching Charlie's delirium.

'We're gonna clean up our act!' whooped Charlie. 'Get clean, get dry. We're gonna fly to the States, go to that place you went to on Long Island, we're gonna do it together, it won't be easy but we'll help one another, we'll get through it!' Suddenly emotional, he knelt in front of Felix and hugged him. 'And it's all thanks to you, buddy. We've been inspired by your example. It's wonderful how you've changed, fucking wonderful! We've both noticed it, both noticed the same thing. There's a beautiful spirit in you now.'

'As opposed to blended whisky,' laughed Felix.

'A beautiful spirit,' repeated Charlie, his eyes sparkling. 'And we want some of that too. And we wanna pass it on to Alys. And thank you, buddy, thank you.'

Touched, Felix kissed the top of his head. 'You've saved my life twice, so if I can return the favour . . . well, that makes me very happy.'

As Charlie turned away now, to take a tablet and strengthen his resolve, Felix decided that the idea was growing on him. The idea of Charlie, Kaz and Alys becoming linked – the three people he loved most – and linked by his example, he liked this. Perhaps he could even bring Emile into the equation. Perhaps he, Felix, could live with them too. Then life would be totally safe.

At that moment, a helicopter landed on the roof above them. Plaster sprinkled from the ceiling, the jalousie shutters rattled – wings clapping, slats winking – and Felix felt a tingle of fear.

Bull Brak loomed into view, climbing through the window dressed in a battered DJ. His skin gave off a distinctive sheen, one that Felix recognised: nothing shines quite so raffishly as a drinker's face after a hot shower and a patting of aftershave.

'Guys – all set?' said the huge man, digging inside his clothes, round the shoulders, like a blowsy dame, trying to rearrange his braces. 'The President sends his blessing – which means, yes, we have electricity for the evening – *Haw!* – and also his apologies. Can't make it in person.'

'Previous engagement?' Felix asked harshly, feeling bold.

'Yup.'

'Probably wouldn't do for him to be here tonight.'

'Probably not,' replied Brak, smiling and untroubled. 'Probably a recommendation from the powers that be.'

'His Greater Power.'

'He *is* the Greater Power,' giggled Charlie.

'Actually not,' said Brak. 'There would've been phone calls to make. Overseas calls.'

Felix turned away, as though in scorn, while his heart pounded. *Overseas calls? To the President of the United States of America maybe? The Prime Minister of Great Britain? Them being told, 'There's this theatre in Africa . . .'* This was exceeding his wildest dreams.

'Jesus-fuck, gents, these last few hours!' said Brak, extracting another whisky bottle from where he had hidden it earlier, behind a stack of Felix's books. 'It takes a helluva lot to rock my centre of gravity, but I don't mind admitting that this operation . . . Jesus-fuck! I tell you, Charlie, when tonight's over we'll all be ready for another of your parties.'

'There won't be any more,' Charlie announced cheerfully.

Brak paused in the middle of a glassful, finished it, then gave his laugh: '*Haw!* Good one.'

'I'm serious, Brakkie.'

Felix looked at his friend lovingly. Stoned out of his head, maybe, but at this point in time he *meant* it. And who knows? He might still feel the same way tomorrow morning.

Brak was also studying Charlie closely, and coming to the same conclusion – *he meant it* – but this was less welcome news. It wasn't serious, simply irritating. Brak's day had been exhausting. The task of standing on a tightrope and juggling, thereby keeping all balls in the air and, more importantly, your hands clean, had left him in a mean mood, a drinking, slugging, rutting mood. It showed in his jocularity: rougher than usual. Associates knew the signs and avoided him at times like these. If Charlie had been more focused, he might have done the same, and changed the subject. Instead, he said: 'I'm cleaning up, Brakkie. I'm going on the long clean road, the long, dry drive. I'm –'

Brak cut in: 'Y'know, I love those parties of yours. I'm no trick-cyclist, but I've studied human nature in my own way, and I reckon that, y'know, most people harbour a secret urge or two. Funny things in us. It's like our imagination gone bad. At your parties we can get rid of them in a nice, clean, healthy environment with medical assistance standing by. Otherwise we're just gonna get rid of them elsewhere. And, believe me, I've seen the "elsewheres". Both as a cop and as a soldier, I've been to "elsewhere".'

Charlie laughed, still not noticing the man's mood. 'Well, sorry, pal, you're all just gonna have to find another Charlie and he's gonna have to fix you some other parties.'

'No,' said Brak quietly.

Charlie didn't hear. 'But I'm delighted to have been of service.' He turned to Felix, 'I'll go get Kaz, bring her in, she wanted me to tell you first.'

He was almost through the door when Brak called after him: 'Popo-boy!'

Charlie stopped. 'What did you just say?'

'Popo-boy.'

'That's not my name.'

'It's not, no. It's your code-name.'

Charlie and Felix stared at Brak, neither of them breathing.

'Our name for you,' Brak continued. 'When prisoners pissed us off beyond the call of duty. Then we had this little saying among ourselves, "OK, send him to Popo-boy."'

'You sent them to me?' asked Charlie, dazed. 'Where?'

'At the farm.'

'The farm. Where? Where at the farm?'

'At your parties. Bound, gagged and having fun.'

Felix saw the colour drain from Charlie's face.

'Tranquillised and masked by your staff,' Brak said to him. 'And muffed by your friends.'

'Muffed?' Charlie repeated faintly.

'Isn't that the word? A modern word.'

'Snuffed,' said Felix, thinking the word didn't sound at all modern.

'Yup, well, I wouldn't know,' Brak commented. 'I never went in for those sessions. Reminded me too much of work. When I'm at a party, I'm at a party, I don't want a work environment. I need other things. And actually, Charlie, you didn't go in for those sessions either, did you? But lots did. His lordship did, and also –'

Felix broke in: 'Kaz? Did Kaz take part?'

'No,' Charlie replied instantly.

Felix glared at him. 'How do you *know*? You don't seem to know about –'

'Because we would've talked about it. We talk about everything.' Charlie's voice was calm, his eyes blank. 'She knew nothing about it. Like me.'

'Then who on earth was arranging . . . ?!'

'The same person who arranges everything else,' Brak explained helpfully. 'Bi Mirza. When that old girl says, "I can get you anything and I mean *anything*," she's not bullshitting.'

Felix sat down, feeling sick. Bi Mirza . . . that dewy-eyed auntie listening to cookery programmes from home! Alys's nursemaid! Yet whatever else she'd done, the Arab woman had, for some reason, respected Alys – Felix felt certain of this. The farm didn't alarm Alys, it just bored her. He slowly worked out the rest. 'But . . . I mean, if these people in the sessions . . . if they weren't people with incurable diseases, or suicides or whatever, if they weren't *volunteers* . . .'

'Yeah,' said Charlie, ahead of him.

'If, instead, they were from police cells . . .'

'Yeah.'

Felix paused, his blood running cold. 'Then Kaz's son . . . your son . . .'

'Yeah.'

'Zach,' said Felix, suddenly remembering not only the boy's name, but the sensation of holding him once, as a baby, at the lakeside, one morning long ago.

'Zach,' Charlie echoed quietly, painfully. His legs suddenly gave way, and he sat with a thump. 'Zach . . . arriving for one of our parties. Masked, tied, doped. Probably even happy. It's not hard to make people happy.' He patted his pockets. Remembering that everything was on the table, he heaved himself up again and selected a tablet. There was a numb look on his face. 'Yeah . . .' he said slowly.

They heard another helicopter coming in to land. Its downdraught blew through the window, making the shutters jiggle, wave and wink again, and another sprinkle of plaster fell from the ceiling. A light dust collected on the heads and shoulders of the men, who were all sitting thoughtfully like dummies in a museum.

'Ah, gentlemen!' chirped Lord Gomes, climbing in through the window, dressed in stylish tie and tails, with a winged collar. 'Ready for the off?'

'Yup,' replied Bull Brak, standing, hoisting up his trousers, downing a tumbler of whisky. 'Yup, let's go see if the little Kraut half-breed needs a hand.'

'Charlie, are you joining . . . ?' Lord Gomes started to say, then noticed the colour of Charlie's face.

Bull Brak explained: 'I've told him about Popo-boy.'

'Thought you knew,' Lord Gomes said breezily.

Charlie stayed still. Everyone waited for a moment, then Lord Gomes turned to Brak, discreetly mouthing, '*Shall we uhm . . . ?*'

Brak answered, 'Yup, time to hit the trail,' and they exited.

The friends sat quietly. A seagull flew by the window. It looked odd against the darkness. Night was falling rapidly. A glow came from below, from down on the street. Produced by the lights of the television crews.

Felix felt furious. He wasn't sure why, or with whom. Brak and Gomes, of course . . . Duma, of course . . . even Emile . . .

He hated the fact that Emile's paternal, shrink-like view of his son had proved right. He hated the fact that he himself had doubted Charlie and been proved right. He hated the fact that Charlie had been the only one who hadn't known.

Charlie hadn't known about Charlie!

Looking up now, Felix saw a strange thing . . . Charlie mutating in fast-motion . . . the doctor had swallowed his magic potion and was changing into a monstrous creature . . . the golden, sun-kissed head was growing warts and tusks, the love-bitten birthmark was spreading and bubbling like a burn . . . Felix watched this idly for a while, and then, flicking his head, said: 'Kaz.'

'Yeah,' Charlie answered, in a small voice.

'D'you want me to . . . ?'

'No, no, I'll do it.'

thirty-nine

Felix beat Charlie to Kaz's room.

He was installed above it, in the air-duct – panting, his knees and palms grazed from the frantic crawl – just before Charlie entered.

Kaz's ghetto-blaster, playing 'American Pie', was positioned on top of something near the air-vent, so Felix witnessed the scene in dumbshow, eyes glued to the rusted grille.

Kaz was at her dressing-table, making-up as Andromache, dipping her fingers into a plastic basin of grey clay. It dried into white streaks, leaving moist dark patches here and there. Worn by everyone in the *Iliad* scenes, it helped to create the dusty, battered look of the long siege.

She was pleased to see Charlie enter, and smiled. He went over and put his lips to the back of her head. She reached up and held his neck.

Then, with his hands on her shoulders, steadying them both, he met her eyes in the mirror and started speaking.

Felix wondered how he was putting it.

Our son . . . we've found out what happened to him . . . he was brought to one of the parties . . . tied, masked, tranquillised . . .

Kaz stayed very still. When Charlie finished speaking, she said something. Perhaps asking him to leave her alone. Both looked strangely composed. They could have been talking about small matters.

Charlie exited.

Kaz stood, accidentally knocking over her chair. Andromache's bomber jacket was over the back. She righted the chair and retrieved the jacket.

Felix thought about Andromache in the story. She says to the body of her loved one: To me, most of all, you've left the horror.

Now Kaz bent over slowly, arms wrapped round her middle, aching in a way that Felix had seen before. He remembered her saying that the pain of grief is like birth, beyond anything you can imagine. And he remembered thinking, I will never know this, never long for anyone as much as this.

As Kaz stayed bent, rocking herself, the door opened and a figure came in. Felix was expecting it to be Charlie again, so when he saw who it was he turned cold.

The young man . . . the one whose portrait was in the pendant . . . Zach.

His face is as indistinct as in that little photograph, except that now it's grey clay obscuring his features. He is one of the Chorus. Pulling off his T-shirt, he helps himself to more of his mother's makeup: the wet mixture in the basin. He slaps this on his torso, half dancing to the music from her ghetto-blaster. Kaz doesn't notice him. They stay at the mirror, she bent double, rocking back and forth, he jigging and swaying, almost in the same rhythm, almost making contact, just missing each time.

forty

To the beat of African percussion – calabash, *dundun*, and talking drums – to the wail of the ancient sarrousophone, to a tape of Ol' Blue Eyes singing 'My Way' and another of the dawn chorus over the savannahs, to the steady clap and stamp of the crowd, and to Felix's private, barely audible rendition of 'Let's Call The Whole Thing Off', the greatest show on earth began.

The place was packed to the rafters, to the gods.

Squeezing his way through the dense multitude in the side aisle, Felix saw all the trustees crammed into one stalls box, and smiled to himself. this was their idea of roughing it. Lord Gomes beckoned him, and, leaning over the edge, confided, 'You've done it! We were all just saying, "He's done it!" When you asked for "a last go" at the board meeting, we thought, well . . . thought you were *finito*. But you aren't, you aren't. You've done it! "Last go" indeed! *Não sabia que eras tão esperto*, you clever old bugger! We must talk. Here, take this . . .'

Felix waved, declining the cup of champagne, and pressed on through the spectators.

Now, despite the surrounding hubbub, he heard something. A distinctive tinkle of jewellery. He remembered that sound! . . . half cowbell, half jailer's keys. Then he saw a woman's hand, knuckly, beringed and braceleted, come rattling into view from between two oblivious strangers. It reached out and waited, fingers open, both inviting and commanding, a mother cuing a child. Felix wondered whether to stand fast, to defy the order, but he saw that his right arm was already yielding. He gripped the woman's hand, all bone and jewels, and she pulled him to her. She was sitting on one of the little flap-seats against the wall, used by usherettes in the old days. Despite the vigour of her summons, her expression was soft and thoughtful. He knelt before her. She stroked his hair, and spoke tenderly: 'Now that you're about to enjoy the most enormous success, everything we dreamed of, how d'you feel?' Before he could answer, she continued, 'I feel almost . . . nervous. I've dreamed of this for so long, Feelie, of fame and fortune for one of my pupils, and it seemed so unlikely, so preposterous, *here* where we lived, so now that it's actually happening . . .' (Ah, the way she pronounced that word – *ek-tu-welly*.) She chuckled: 'Listen to me! Everything going so well, and there's me sniffing Hurricane Mary round the next corner!' With eyes filling, she took his hands – *how strange to touch hers again* – and said, 'My darling, I wish you everything you wish yourself . . . success and happiness and, most of all, health.'

Odd – that order of priority. Not like her at all. But it was already too late to question her. Without warning, she'd risen and danced off into the crowd, bony wrists held high, rattling her bracelets like music hoops.

Climbing to his feet, Felix found himself next to Bull Brak. The colonel was briefing a plain-clothes policeman, who carried a small, hi-tech cam-corder. 'We're not allowing the foreign media inside,' Brak explained to Felix. 'Our friend here is gonna catch the only footage of what happens and then we can distribute it as we see fit. Any tips?'

'Tips?'

'The best filming angles and so on. You're the director, the expert here.'

Felix thought for a moment. 'Well . . . doesn't actually matter where you shoot from or what kind of results you get. The shakier it is, the more it misses the main moments, or half catches them round people's heads, the more blurred it is, the further away from the action . . . it's all for the better. Then the footage becomes mystical. Blown-up, slowed-down, played over and over. Y'know, think of Kennedy's ride through Dallas, or Sadat at his last military parade, or . . . you know the kind of thing.'

Brak nodded with amusement, then said to his cameraman, 'Got it? Film as badly as you can. Good thing we checked with an expert, hey? *Haw!*'

Felix moved on and, heeding his own advice, caught only glimpses of the stage, where the first item in the programme – the Creation – had started. While most of the company's professionals had found a way of reaching work today, most of the Chorus for the Garden of Eden hadn't, either because of the mob, or because they had recast themselves as Mob instead of Chorus. So the great piece of staging, Felix's masterpiece, the wall of naked people, this was a paltry affair tonight, with scaffolding bars revealed in between a few dozen bodies.

The audience watched in a relatively ordered way, both restless and rapt, half enjoying the delay, the holding back of what was to come.

They didn't have to wait long. Felix had rescheduled the running order so that the Cyclops scene came next.

First there was a short speech by Mr Mmalo (wearing the egg costume, but with the helmet in his hand, so that they could see it was *him*), in which he politely explained that if people remained calm, they would get what they wanted.

But would they? wondered Felix. Would it work? Would both sides be appeased? He crossed his fingers.

The Cyclops scene started, and the audience endured the first half of it – the banquet in the cave, the topical jokes and references (once such a hilarious device) – endured it with the same shuffling, excited impatience with which they'd viewed the Garden of Eden.

Then, at the point when Mr Mmalo rose and said, 'You ask why these rules exist on this island, but you may as well ask why the island exists or why I exist,' then the audience started to go quiet, very quiet, almost as though they knew the script, knew the whole plan.

They didn't laugh or jeer when Mr Mmalo cried, 'This island is me, and I *am* this island!' They knew this was only a trailer, a teaser.

And they had spotted the new figure lurking in the background, waiting there . . . a figure who now started to move into the light.

He kept coming forward, masked by Mr Mmalo's padded and gesticulating bulk, kept coming till he was directly behind. Then, like a gentleman in a ballroom, he tapped Mr Mmalo on the shoulder. The actor gave a gracious bow of the head and left the stage.

The Odysseus actor, Dhaba, exited as well – almost running, almost breaking the spell, almost spoiling the incredible tension within the theatre. Everything here . . . all the people, the thousands and thousands of them, and the building itself, its insides . . . the breath of the humans and the air of the place . . . everything was united in this event. It was like a cathedral.

'My people, my citizens, good citizens of Africa, I salute you.'

Duma, who was dressed in plain trousers and open-necked white shirt, waited, stock-still, listening to the silence, then continued: 'I salute you . . . not from exile, as some of you might have expected, nor from beyond the grave, as others thought, but from here. Here. My homeland, and yours. The place where we exchanged our love.'

A tiny murmur of dissent began in the house.

'All of you,' said Duma, overriding it, 'all of you gave me your love. At one time or another. Whether out of conviction, whether out of indifference, or whether, and let us be frank, out of fear, all of you, at one time or another, gave me your love.'

He had effortlessly upped the temperature, Felix noted. The Master Orator had, in that fractional moment when the murmuring began, climbed onto a slightly higher pitch, accelerated his speech that little bit, and sent a charge of energy through the air; just enough for now, holding huge volumes in reserve.

'You . . . and you . . . and you,' said Duma, using another of his favourite techniques: picking out individuals, robbing the audience of its huge anonymity, its single mountain-like presence. Scanning the plains of the stalls, the great slopes of the circle and the gods, he singled out a few, the weaker-looking ones; a predator making its selection from a herd of prey. '*You* liked what I said . . . *you* liked my strength . . . my army, my police force . . . *you* liked my style . . . my policies, my trade links, my meetings with world leaders . . . they made *you* feel good, important, *you* became me . . . we were in it together, you and me, God and the Land, we were all in it together – *it* – the thing we called Dumanism.'

He paused, and checked the silence again – it was still intact, almost palpable, there in the air, like a temperature.

Now, flopping one shoulder forward in an odd, louche way, and smiling, Duma began changing the mood, flirting with the audience, as though bored with the safety of it all.

'And then you – and you – and you – you changed your minds, or at any rate changed your direction, for like chickens or goats it wasn't so much a question of mind or of body, but of one of you going a different way and the others following. There is little thought behind it.'

The words chickens and goats, the audience hadn't liked these; a murmur grew again; this time Duma didn't quell it; instead, like a champion surfer, he climbed aboard and rode it, still smiling, still magnificently in charge.

'*You* changed,' he said loudly, to the whole audience, his gestures, lungs and voice suddenly swelling to encompass everyone inside the auditorium and those in the foyers, all seven thousand of them. 'You changed, not me, you altered, shifted, and, how shall we put it?, you *weakened*.'

A cry from the house.

'Oh, yes, yes,' he said, relishing the start of a two-way exchange. 'You got soft and sick, like children, women and old people, you lost heart, you had no balls, you became a nation of the blind, and the blind were leading the blind, and the lame were limping on ahead and covering your arses, or were they your faces?, which way were you pointed?, who knows, who cares, you thought because you were moving it must be good, it must be right, it must be *change*, and a change must be a change for the better, and so when your blind leaders, your lame guard, your chicken wives and goat children, when they started going that way, away from me, you just said, "Let's follow, let's always follow, follow!"'

The audience was answering in a bizarre manner: screams of protest, yells of approval, but all suppressed, all emitted through gritted teeth, jutting jaws, trying not to drown Duma, desperate to hear the next thing. Their voice was like an approaching gale, or tidal wave. Duma was fearless, both facing these mighty elements and riding them at the same time, buffeted and shuddering, grinning, arms spread wide – athlete, conqueror, or rock star, come on, love me, desire me, worship me – prancing and taunting the audience.

People started throwing things – soft things – caps and fruit.

Felix thought fast: Was now the time? – the moment to move to the next phase? – maybe not yet, not quite yet – Duma was still in control, still coping, coping well – he derided the missiles, deflecting one with a cheeky twist of the elbow, kicking another.

Now, without warning, by suddenly going still, and thus stilling them – he continued, 'We are in it together. You and me, we are in my offices, in my council chambers, in my army posts. You . . . and you . . . and you . . . and me . . . our appetites and our imagination, they're in it too, making sense of it, giving meaning to everything. Creating, in fact, the meaning of life. Our lives.'

Felix swayed slightly, assaulted by the familiar words.

Now, with a fast bend of the knees and intake of breath, as if collecting something from the earth, Duma changed tack again, and cried, full of passion: 'You betrayed me, but I forgive you! Why? Because I love you! You loved me once! And I love you . . . but more, much more' – he turned the last word into a howl of yearning, *mawwwww*, while tears filled his eyes – 'a million times more, I love you. I love you because you are Africans. Africans like me, most of you are this, not the "tourists". Let me explain. Point number one. There are those who came on a visit from Europe or Asia years and years ago, they or their fathers, or their fathers' fathers, and they live here and they call themselves Africans, yet they remain *tourists*! – you know the type, every time there's trouble here or in our neighbouring states, you see them gathering at the big hotel in town and being airlifted to safety – well, we are happy for these tourists to fly away, they are like flies, we swat them off our flanks like the buffalo with his tail. Point number two. There are those who come looking for their roots. American Negroes. They come on sentimental journeys, on package tours, to see the slave houses, or maybe they're posted here by the *Washington Post*, or the Foreign Department, or the CIA. They take one look, these American Negroes, and say, "This place is unhygienic, it's dirty, it's savage, get me out of here!" Well, we take their insults, their expressions of disgust or pity, and we blow them away too, we blow them into the sea like a great wind. We remain indifferent to all tourists. Why? This is point number three. Because there will come a time when people will line up in their thousands, their millions, waving application forms, asking to come in, begging to come in, buying and bribing their way in. Not far from where I'm standing, across our borders – these meaningless patterns which little Europeans drew in the dust – there, in 1959, you all know the story, there were found two large teeth and a piece of skull . . . the oldest human remains on earth. Africa is the cradle of mankind. Africa is where man began, and Africa is where man will come back to in the end. As the rest of the world becomes more and more crowded with uncontrolled breeding, where will everyone turn? Before, it was to America. Now it will be our turn. We will become the New World. We, the Oldest World. Africa is the future. Why? This is point number four. Africa is a huge, empty, rich continent . . . *rich*, most importantly, it is rich. Gold, silver, diamonds, copper, our own cobalt reserves – our blue gold – and cotton, sisal, tea, coffee, fruit, maize, bread, bread, bread for all the people – there will be no famine! – but bread for all, and meat too, and fish, water, rain, growth, plenty. We have it all, we have merely to tap our resources, we have barely started, we are one of the richest swathes of this planet, and man shall feast freely here. Point number five. To make it work, to make Africa work, will take special imagination and courage. It must become united, the United States of Africa, with petty tribalism eradicated, the troublemakers dispatched, and those who remain must unite behind one ideology. Capitalism, communism, these are mere building blocks. We must forge a new social order. Call it Africanism, call it Dumanism, the word is unimportant for now, but in forging it, we must risk the displeasure of the United Nations, the World Bank, and suchlike organisations. It doesn't matter, for, in the end, the US, the European Union, everyone will be at our doorstep, not we at theirs, we will be like Arabia with its oil, and we have something even richer than oil, we have *earth*, we have Africa, the beautiful dark land, old as time, old as the planet, new as the future, and it is ours . . . Come, my people, come, say it with me, WE ARE AFRICA AND AFRICA IS US!'

It was as though the whole audience stumbled: all seven thousand of them, all stumbling, all caught out by his twisting of the famous phrase. They had been ready to bellow it with him, in mockery or devotion, but at the last moment he confounded them, and, like a choir, suddenly finding, at the very climax of the most familiar chorus, something changed, their voices and allegiances went spilling in different directions, all at once.

The tidal wave was breaking.

Duma's balance rocked. One arm flinched, the hand jerking slightly, as though seeking a grip in the air, and he began blinking rapidly. He straightened like a soldier coming to attention, or someone trying to see over a crowd. He no longer seemed exhilarated.

Charlie was wrong. This wasn't a man who knew that the end had come, and accepted it, and was simply seeking a noble and fitting death. This was a man trying to save his skin. The speech, with all its techniques, all the sudden changes of subject, all the surprises and mood swings, these were calculated to win the house, to restore him to power. But they were dangerous games to play with seven thousand people. When you didn't have armed troops surrounding them – or you – when you couldn't guarantee crowd control. It was a question of focus. If you trip up a multitude, how do you regain the focus? You only have a moment, a split second, to do it, or all can be lost.

Duma's split second was almost over.

Felix decided not to wait any longer. Slipping out of the back of the auditorium, he went into the sound and lighting box. In this black chamber, with its big window overlooking the stalls and stage, two operators worked an ancient bank of control panels bristling with small levers, buttons and dials. Frankie Hoong sat alongside, running the show from here tonight instead of the wings. Felix said to her, 'All right – now!'

Speaking into her microphone, she issued an instruction. Felix looked to the stage. Almost instantly, from the flies behind the proscenium arch, a unique curtain began to descend, a semi-transparent curtain, a curtain of bars . . . *a cage, a wall, a wall, a wall, a cage* . . . a fourth side, to complete the box.

Felix slid open the big window above the control panels and leaned forward, so he could see and hear to the full.

Duma watched the curtain of bars descend with a look of relief. People were throwing bigger, harder things now, shoes and stones, and people were standing, and people were slowly swarming towards the stage. The sound was thunderous. Duma had begun to fear that he'd lost the moment. He couldn't be *heard* – this was the crucial thing – without his voice, that magnificent umber instrument, without being able to offer up his arguments, threats and love, he was in danger of losing all dignity, and becoming just a little clown in a silent film, dodging flying objects. So when he saw the curtain of bars descend, he thought he was saved; he thought it was arriving to hold violence at bay – it was difficult to hurl things through bars, and grasping hands couldn't reach him. Once the mob realised that, they would quieten.

But now, when they did, there was a new, low noise to be heard, growing steadily. It spilled from those who knew what was coming (Brak's messengers had infiltrated the crowd): a *chut-chut-chut* of teeth, the clickings and snapping of fingerbones, the jigging of heels; a drum joined in from somewhere, *ufff, ufff, ufff,* and the ancient sarrousophone wailed, *iiiyyyeee, iiiyyyeee.*

'All members of the company be advised that the stage is now out of bounds,' Frankie Hoong said into her microphone. 'Do *not* enter the stage area, I repeat, do *not* try to come on stage or into the wings until further notice. Remain backstage, behind the pass doors, keep all pass doors closed, for your own safety. I repeat again . . .'

The cage front was securely in place, and full lights came up, revealing the entire stage. The Creation scaffolding had been flown out, quietly, while Duma was in his spot. Now, behind the dictator, a bright wooden playing field took shape; you could see into every corner; it reminded Felix of childhood, safe rooms at night, all lit up, the darkness elsewhere.

The first one came up through the trap in an odd, comical way – it flew, it bounced – like a rodent flushed out of a hole; it seemed rodent-sized too, against the vast brightness of the wooden playing field; it didn't look threatening; if anything it looked hurt – hurt by whatever prod or firebrand Zikki had used to encourage it out of the tunnel below – and it looked confused, confused by the light, the noise, and the man sharing its space.

Duma didn't notice that he had company. He was holding the bars, gaze fixed on the crowd, puzzled by the atmosphere.

Now, with an odd cock of the head, like a cartoon cat – *Wait a cotton pickin' minute here, I'm hungry and there's food!* – the shape of the animal changed dramatically. It fell into a low squat, a flat-eared, rolling-shouldered, long-limbed squat, with head aimed like a spear, and the tail giving a peculiar, sexy, itching flick. Old instincts – calculations about wind direction, grass height, distance of the final sprint – these went through the body. You could see them in the travelling ripples of lean muscle, and in the fluttering pulse of its breathing. It took a few paces in this low, long, crouching pose. Then it realised there was no wind, no grass, no cover and no obstacles – nothing but a short distance to be crossed. Then it attacked.

Duma turned in time to see the sudden acceleration – that unhuman speed. He was hit with such force that he fell over, rolled, and returned to his feet in one movement – the lion elsewhere for a second. Then they came together, as if by mutual desire – Duma had known to go into the attack, not run from it – and staggered around; the beast on its hind legs, the man with his hands at its throat, the two swinging around, half breaking their grip, searching for another, the perfect one, the right one, caught in a deadly, high-speed dance.

He's trying to get his fist down its throat, thought Felix . . . maybe it works, maybe he could still win . . . *Where are the others?*

In between the audience's gusts of breath, Felix could just hear a tiny voice screeching in German, and he saw a little curl of smoke rising from the trap – either hide or timber smouldering – evidence of some frantic battle below, a battle with the animals, crazed with hunger and bewilderment, trapped perhaps by the hastily constructed tunnel; a battle to get them out into the light.

Meanwhile Duma managed to land a tremendous double-fisted punch on the brow of his opponent. It backed off and stood there, shaking its head, a dumb, curious look on its face – a pussycat after a scare. Duma swung towards the audience and began shouting. For an instant they went silent, and to Felix's astonishment he heard the dictator say: 'Felix – stop this!'

'"Let's call the whole thing off,"' Felix sang under his breath – '"You say to-may-to, I say to-mah-to,"' – feverishly, eyes glued on the stage '"Da-dum the whole thing off!"'

'Felix . . . !' cried Duma.

'The wonderful, wonderful cat,' chanted Felix, flexing his fingers. 'Whenever he gets into a fix, he reaches into his bag of tricks!'

The lion sprang again, and Duma went down. In one move, the lion secured its jaws round his windpipe, and it was all over. Now just a matter of time, of patience, of waiting while the prey went through its customary struggle to kick, to push away, to catch its breath, catch just one breath, open the vice, do the impossible, while every convulsion wasted breath, wasted strength, wasted the life.

Duma gave no final sign at the end, no last thrust, not even a shiver from dying nerves, nothing, and his contribution to the next part of the coupling – after the ravenous beast lifted its head from the stranglehold, freeing its teeth – this was loose and flopping, his body jumping around, shuddering to each greedy, snogging punch of the lion's muzzle, while his huge and formidable spirit no longer took part.

The smell of the feast reached the other members of the pride. Untangling themselves from below-stage obstacles, they came hurtling through the trap, and fell on Duma.

The audience watched, motionless. Silence. Except for that ripping, blowing sound, which Felix recognised from last night at the farm, the animals barely able to eat fast enough, to eat and breathe at the same time.

There would be approximately twenty minutes of this, thought Felix, professional instincts alerted. It had transfixed the spectators in his bedroom at the farm, but twenty minutes was a long time for a full-sized audience to watch so little. The lions were huddled round the man, and unless you were Brak's cameraman, presently using his zoom lens, you could see nothing of Duma, nothing of the gore, nothing very interesting at all.

Felix leaned past the sound technician, to the computer that Charlie had donated to the theatre a couple of years ago, and began calling up cues from the rest of the show: tapes of classical and popular music. He dipped in and out of these, mixing from one to other, humming to himself. Then he moved over to the lighting board and did the same. The technicians stood aside, familiar with Felix's penchant for mid-show improvisations like these. Hijacking Frankie Hoong's headset as well, Felix gave a sequence of instructions to the smoke-machine operators, and those in the flies with cracked-oil atomisers and autumn-leaf bundles. Now he began to jam like a musician, playing the different boards like synthisizers, dancing around the booth, singing along to the tapes. Onstage, the air grew hazy and romantic, and leaves fell, and now it was flooded with sunset oranges, now foresty greens, moon-splashed blues, ghoulish reds . . . the colours drifting on flying carpets of smoke, slowly rising and diving to the tunes of 'The Pearl-fishers Duet', 'All That Jazz', 'Strawberry Fields Forever', Mozart's Concerto for Clarinet in A, and other Felix favourites. The emotion of music and light worked its spell on both factions within the audience, offering catharsis to each, a chance to grieve or celebrate, as there before them Duma's great boast became reality: changing from man to food, he would become dung, he would be cast onto the land as sustenance, and finally he and Africa would become one.

The twenty minutes were almost over, the lions arguing over the last remains with ferocious tugs-of-war, when an astonishing piece of luck befell them – a second meal arrived.

She came running through the pass door at the back of the stage, through the mad smoke and light and music, wailing like Andromache in grief . . . that long, terrible, beautiful, open noise.

Both the lions and the audience froze.

Felix's whole being went heavy . . . it felt like sudden fever.

The woman was his friend. She was in a cage with lions. He must get her out. He would just need a moment to work it out.

The lions hesitated as well. Being circus lions, *stage lions* in a way, old instincts were surfacing. Animal brains were at work, remembering training and punishment, the hammering repetition, the rewards and pain; remembering that humans were masters. And Duma had been the size of a largish buck – their hunger was mostly sated. Feline ears pricked as Kaz continued to wail, amber eyes watched as she deliberately moved closer. Now she was becoming a threat: a scavenger after their meal, a rival invading their territory. They gave warning signals, noises and stances, and one of them, Simba – the large, greenish-yellow matriarch – made a small rush, a mock charge, head weaving, teeth gnashing.

'No.'

It was an old woman who had spoken. Standing up suddenly, and speaking in a quiet, trembling voice. 'No.' The word carried round the auditorium where most people were holding their breath. Everyone knew Kaz – they'd seen her perform. She sang the blues so well she made you long for things you didn't even know about. 'No,' the old woman said again, turning on the spot, arms raised in appeal. Someone out there must be controlling this; someone could stop it. She and the others, they were content for Duma's story to end in blood. But not Kaz. They didn't want this. 'No!' Around her, voices began to echo her protest in a strange manner. 'Nnnn–! Nnnn–!' the crowd murmured, like Felix had once done in a cell, scared to say the full word, the O, to open their throats, to start a howl. A howl would unleash violence.

Their love for Kaz shook Felix awake. 'To the finish' – he'd promised to help Kaz to the finish. He must keep his word. He must stop *this* being the finish. But how? All the routes to the stage were blocked solid. He clambered onto the lighting board, onto the window-ledge, and fell forward onto the audience, trying to walk, trying to crawl across them. 'I'm sorry,' he muttered as he went. 'Excuse me . . . forgive me . . . sorry.' This was familiar; struggling over the top of a crowd, their heads and shoulders forming a strange, sluggish surface, like waves or dunes; his feet sank into it, he struggled with all his might, but made little progress. The journey ahead looked relatively short, yet out of reach. The bright shore, the mirage of light. It stayed over there, bobbing in the distance, rising and falling with his exertions.

Yet there was still hope. The lions weren't attacking. They were baffled by the woman. Why hadn't she retreated, why did she keep kicking at them, running closer? Her wail filled with a kind of ecstasy, rising in pitch. Some of the animals left Duma's remains and trotted off meekly, circus instincts to the fore. Kaz rushed at the

big matriarch, Simba, goading. It snarled, backing away. She
reached for its meal – grabbing, by chance, Duma's hand, which was
intact and came away in hers, offering a greeting from beyond the
grave – and this was, at last, enough provocation. The lioness
charged. Clamping its jaws on Kaz's belly, it shook her like a
puppet.

With a roar of 'NO!' the audience rose to its feet. Felix landed on
the floor in the side aisle, winded, gawping at the shapes above him.
These weren't people – these were giraffes, skyscrapers, forests.
Impassable. He couldn't progress, couldn't get where he was going.
He could only struggle upright, on tiptoe, and watch.

Other people were appearing onstage: Zikki's face, cut and
singed, kept popping, mongoose-like, in and out of the trap; and
Charlie leaned through the doorway at the back, calling Kaz's name
with all his heart, but drowned by the baying audience. Confused by
the noise, maddened by it also, Simba released her prey to rush at
the bars. Kaz stumbled back. Blood – the first clearly visible blood
in the show – sprang from her: a long thick rag of it flowing
through the air, slow and dark, like coffee thrown from a jug. She
looked down, apparently surprised. Her middle was open.

Recoiling in horror, Felix spotted a familiar figure in the dress-
circle box above him. Brak. He'd have a gun. Felix shouted up, but
the man couldn't hear. Leaping at the wall, Felix said to the people
around him, 'Help me, please!' Hands, shoulders, heads . . . a
human ladder . . . it could have been from one of the shows. 'Stop
this, please!' cried Felix, as Brak hauled him into the box. 'You
must have a gun – stop this!'

Onstage Kaz went into a slow, falling run, hugging herself, stuff
slipping round her arms, her feet becoming entangled in her own
loops and whorls, and gradually she went lower and lower, until she
was face down on the floor. The audience bellowed in protest, but
Simba ignored them now, padding back to Kaz, the other lions
following.

'A gun!' Felix shouted at Brak. 'You must have a gun!'

Brak answered calmly. 'Firearms weren't permitted inside the . . .'

'But you'll have one!' Felix screamed, flying at the policeman,
half hitting, half frisking him. 'You'll have one, you'll have one!'

Brak's hands fastened on Felix's arms. 'Calm yourself, hey? – please. There's nothing to be done.'

Felix turned back to the stage. Brak was right. The lions were feeding. Felix covered his mouth with both hands. Big sobs heaved in his belly and throat like vomit. He saw Charlie at the back of the stage, holding his face in the same way, starting to rock like Kaz had done earlier.

'I'm sorry,' Brak said, in a dull, professional tone, patting Felix's shoulder. 'Sorry, hey?'

Felix sank onto his knees, leaning on the front of the box. Down below, the audience were swaying slowly, making a low panting noise. Their sorrow – like their frenzy – was phenomenal. Its scale and power was phenomenal.

Felix shook his head. His 'last go' had succeeded beyond wildest expectations. Here they were: thousands of people packed into the Alex, ready to do anything, love, hate, or both at once, equipped with enough strength to shake the air, lift the roof. He'd dreamed of this. Now what?

Brak seemed to hear his thoughts. 'Jesus-fuck,' he whispered, leaning close. 'You know something? . . . if the new government ever gets round to writing the new constitution' – he gave an indulgent groan – 'and if capital punishment is still on the agenda . . . as it will be . . . then, y'know, it makes one think, hey?' He paused for a moment, testing Felix's compliance, then ventured further. 'I mean, what's happened here today . . . this isn't a million miles from the way it's done elsewhere on the planet . . . as a public event, a public warning, a public spectacle.' He waited again. 'See what I'm saying?'

Felix didn't reply. It was no longer Brak at his side, but a more powerful presence. Its breath caressed his ear, its voice was in tune with his most secret thoughts. Thoughts about how, if he couldn't be famous, he'd be notorious. If he couldn't be an artist, he'd be a criminal. Art and crime, these were just two sides of the same coin. Both were the work of rebels and rainbow-chasers, both drew drunken maps of the world. Making or destroying, it was all part of the cycle. The beauty of blood, the music of sorrow, the elegance of death. And now these strange twins, creativity and violence, now they were together at last, joining hands in Brak's proposal, his plans for – how would one put it? – a regular Big Match at the theatre, an event placed somewhere between sport and drama, with no rules, no rehearsal, no fair play, no suspension of disbelief. Just a pure communion of animal and human forces, not only on the stage, but also among the audience, their appetite and their imagination yanked together, bound tight, fused into one fleshy inseparable knot. It was quite a proposition. To institute something like this could attract a lot of attention. World-wide. It could bring Felix everything he wanted.

'What d'you reckon?' asked Brak.

Felix blinked. At the Long Island clinic he'd joked, 'What if, now that I'm open to colonisation, an unholy ruler comes visiting?' The joke was on him.

'Well?' prompted Brak.

Felix opened his mouth, closed it, swallowed hard, thinking how difficult talking had become since he'd got better.

'Yes?' said Brak.

'No,' Felix replied, quietly, trembling all over. He didn't want this. He'd had *a last go* – he understood the phrase now. 'No,' he told Brak again.

The old war-horse gave a lazy, untroubled shrug. 'Just a thought,' he said, and grinned.

Mopping his face, Felix rose to go – then realised that something was shifting in the auditorium below them. The centre of gravity – Brak's famous phrase – it was shifting, tilting. Kaz's fate had unsettled people. Like a sports crowd, whose team had lost, they needed to appease their feelings. They needed some retribution or release. Instead here was twenty minutes of tedium again – the lions eating, a scrum of haunches, spines, shoulders, not much else to be seen. And even if Felix was in the mood to return to the control panels, no *son et lumière* show was going to do the trick this time. The gathering had been presented with only one clear image of blood – it had stayed in the air for a long moment, like a flag – but it was as though they had tasted it, tasted with their mouths, and they were already drunk on it, they wanted more. Felix remembered Charlie telling him, how, at the Games, the biggest problem was boredom. Monotony. This set in with amazing speed.

Felix and Brak exchanged a look. The day might still be lost.

But luck was on their side – in fact, sewn into Felix's name – for now, onstage, as though fired by a cannon, Zikki shot through the trap, to be instantly followed by another lion, a sixth lion – one which had got lost in the chaotic traffic jam below stage – a lion which hadn't yet been fed.

The audience settled back gleefully.

Zikki picked himself up, looked round, went white. This lion was the runt of the pride. Bullied by the others, always the last to eat, it had suffered most during the last few days, and almost provided a cannibalistic solution to the crisis. With face notched by ugly blackish wounds, and one lame leg, it was now the most dangerous of them all.

Zikki began to run. He scampered this way and that, just managing to outdistance the devilish but enfeebled creature, while shouting commands over his shoulder, trying to remind the animal who was boss. The audience shrieked with pleasure, delighting in the frenetic, comic chase – the lion and the little fella – it was just what they wanted; a spot of light relief.

African Games

forty-one

'Listen!' said Charlie.

He had landed the helicopter on the stretch of overgrown waste-land that used to be the playing-fields of their old school. Even here, on the other side of town, the audience was still audible: big, heavy surges of sound, swinging bells of sound, coming and going, reflecting the action on stage. Clearly the little fella wasn't done for yet.

'Incredible,' commented Felix, as another roar came swelling slowly out of the distance. It was like human thunder.

'No, no, 's not what I meant,' said Charlie urgently, one hand raised like a conductor. '*Now* – listen!'

Nothing. In between the roars. Nothing. The city was strangely still. Lying beneath them in clear, ghostly moonlight.

'Seneca talks about this silence,' whispered Charlie. 'How, on the days of the Games, the city was abandoned to thieves and philosophers. How he loved it on days like this. Just thieves and philosophers.'

'And playwrights,' said Felix.

'Huh?'

'He was a playwright too. So he should have said it was abandoned to thieves, philosophers and playwrights. Must have forgotten. Unless he puts playwriting under the other two categories.'

They turned to one another. Felix was smiling. Smiling and

crying at the same time, like Kaz used to do. Every time he thought of her, a wave of pain went through him, and he tested it, as you might a physical injury, wondering how bad it was, or would get. It was tolerable. Bad, but tolerable. He didn't want it to be worse. He didn't want it to be like Kaz's grief for Zach. He'd always believed he would never know anything like that, never miss anyone that much, and he wanted to prove it now. He loved Kaz – she was one of a tiny group he could call nearest and dearest – but he refused to let her death break his heart. He couldn't afford that. Charlie, on the other hand, seemed inconsolable. His face was a mess of delirium, of swirling emotions and chemicals. When Felix looked at him, he imagined that, as before, he was seeing something from a horror tale . . . a doctor changing into a beast . . . a beautiful man ageing suddenly and terribly . . . turning into an ancient figure with a Belgian accent, whispering 'Devil-up, devil-up . . .'

A giggle rose in Felix's throat. They tasted foul, like bile, these bubbles which kept surfacing – and which he instantly swallowed, lips flickering.

'Thieves and philosophers,' Charlie said again. 'And he talks about how the silence is very conducive to thinking, how you stop noticing the cheers booming from the arena, it just becomes like the sea or the wind in a forest, y'know, it's just sound, 's just *there*, just nature.'

They stood, listening again. Now Charlie said, 'Amazing, 'mazing. Caesar, Julius Caesar, he was assassinated in a theatre.'

'The senate, I thought.'

'No, the senate was being renovated, they'd moved into a theatre for a few months, Rome's only stone theatre. He was assassinated there, in a theatre.'

'Like Lincoln.'

'And Eichmann was *tried* in a theatre. Did I ever . . .'

'Yes, you did.'

'Fucking amazing,' said Charlie, his eyes swivelling, making all sorts of connections. 'Amazing, 'mazing, 'zing, 'zing –' He interrupted himself. 'You feeling sore with me?'

'Pardon?'

'Me. Popo-boy.'

'But it wasn't you.'

'Huh?' Charlie hesitated, flicking his head, trying to clear it, his wet eyes focusing for a moment, as one who, against all expectations, had found something they'd mislaid, something precious: some miraculous thing that could undo the last few hours.

'Didn't Brak say it was Bi Mirza?' said Felix. 'She was arranging it all. So wasn't she Popo-boy? And other people were *doing* it all. So they're Popo-boy. And Brak was in charge at this end, so he's Popo-boy, and –'

'And me?' Charlie asked urgently. 'They were *my* parties. I *allowed* everything.'

'Well,' spluttered Felix, trying to be helpful, 'everyone, then. Everyone was Popo-boy!' He felt giggles rising again.

Charlie came closer. 'What – you too?'

'Well, no, not *me*, but –'

'"Everyone." You just said *everyone*.'

'Yes, but not me.'

'*Everyone* but not *me*.' Charlie sneered. 'That's a new one.'

'Well, I wasn't there, at the previous parties,' said Felix, his voice quavering hysterically. 'So I couldn't –'

'*I* wasn't there, *I* didn't know, it wasn't *me*, sir,' the other chanted, in a ghastly, high-pitched voice, hopping around the school field. 'I'm excused, sir, I've got a note, sir, look, sir, excused for a whole fucking year, sir!'

Felix went still. 'Pardon?'

Charlie stopped also. 'You don't remember?'

'Remember what?'

Charlie studied his friend's face – this was a subject they never discussed – how much did Felix actually recall? 'Straight after Miss Rosewood died. After you found her. You remember finding her?'

Felix nodded impatiently.

'Well . . . straight after that. We had only one coherent conversation. You said, "I want to be excused." I said, "From what?" You said, "From the future, she had the future all planned, and I want to be excused from it now." And that was it. You went walkabout. Stopped washing, stopped wearing clothes, grew your hair, and you kinda . . . you mutilated yourself. D'you honestly not remember?'

Felix didn't answer.

'Huhn? You broke your feet, broke both your feet, I dunno how, with bricks or a hammer, all kinds of stories were going round. You were in plaster for months.'

Felix nodded slowly. So . . . the naked, long-haired boy with crutches . . . so that's who he was. But who, then, was the old man, the legless man?

'I recall being ill for a while, not all of that,' he said quietly, half telling the truth. His memory was of a blissful time, bright and blank, no details, a time of being absolved, let off, safe, free. He thought it was a fever, maybe lasting a few weeks, a month or two. But a year! Oh, to have that amount of peace again.

Charlie shrugged. 'Anyway, you came back. To us, to me.' He hugged Felix tightly, muttering, 'I mustn't get at you, 's not your fault, 'strue, you weren't there, at the farm when those things happened, it was everyone else, Bi Mirza, Brak, blah, blah, and *me*. OK, c'mon, let's go.'

'Where?' Felix asked, as they clambered aboard the helicopter and took off. 'Where are we going?'

'"We turn home, we turn home,"' Charlie recited.

'What's that?'

'Spartacus. Antoninus' song. Well, Tony Curtis just sorta spoke it.'

'*Tony Curtis* . . . ?!' yelped Felix. There was no stopping the giggles this time.

Charlie didn't notice. '"In the" da-di-da . . . how's it go? . . . "blue shadows and purple hills," da-da-da, "we turn home, we turn home."'

'Home, anyhow,' Felix said, from inside his handkerchief. 'Home.' He covered his face. The tears had come as unexpectedly as the giggles; there was no stopping any of it – the drunken mixtures of feelings – it was like the old days, except these didn't come out of a bottle.

'And then away,' added Charlie. 'We turn home, we get Alys, we go away, far away, we three.'

Felix caught his breath, and gradually calmed. He sat back, thinking. He had said no to Brak – Brak's proposal for the future of the theatre – he felt good about saying no, but what now? 'I'm not sure I want to go away,' he said slowly. 'I'm not sure what, or where I . . .'

But Charlie wasn't listening. 'Jus' steer for a sec, huhn?' he said abandoning his controls. Felix stared in alarm at the set in front of him, the co-pilot's set: a thingy like a joystick, another at his side like the handbrake on a car, and pedals down there too. He nervously took hold of the joystick lever, while Charlie rolled up his sleeve, and administered an injection from his magic box.

'Want some?'

'Of course not.'

'Don't have to share a needle,' Charlie mumbled irritably. 'Don't have to catch anything from Popo-boy!'

'Charlie, old chap,' Felix said, trying to adopt a serene tone, in spite of the situation – *he was flying a helicopter!* – but the other continued rapidly: ''s very important in times of stress not to feel any. There will be days an' days of it ahead, weeks 'n' months 'n' years of it, all the whole sad rest of it ahead, so 's very important at first not to feel anything. Am I, am I, like, making sense?'

'Yes, absolutely,' said Felix, knuckles turning white on the joystick.

'This stuff is called Special K,' said Charlie, withdrawing the syringe. 'They used it a lot in –'

'Vietnam, yes, I remember,' said Felix, now watching anxiously as Charlie retook control of the helicopter. Which of the two of them was better equipped for the job? he wondered. The one who'd never flown this machine in his life, or the one who could now fly without a machine at all?

'Gooooood morning, Vietnaaaaaam!' hallooed Charlie, then filled his cheeks with air, making shooting-bombing noises.

Felix gazed on in astonishment. Then he smiled. Then the giggles came again. *Charlie was a doctor – he must know what he's doing – a doctor always knows best!* Rocking forward with laughter, Felix realised his safety belt wasn't fastened. He reached for it. Too late. 'Pgghh! Kshhh!' went Charlie, swivelling his joystick, pumping his pedals. Felix was tipped onto the floor. He struggled upright. Charlie saw a stretch of jungle below and swooped at it – 'Bmmm! Paahhh!' Felix tumbled backwards into the rear of the aircraft. To his surprise, his fall was cushioned. Hands caught him. Two sets of hands.

These belonged to the boy with crutches, and the old legless man.

Felix was fascinated to see them so close. Particularly the boy – now that he understood. How serious the youth looked, adrift in his lost year, the year after his mentor's death . . . unwashed and naked, yet not wild . . . he seemed to be carefully negotiating the perils of his breakdown, journeying through it with a kind of discipline, a kind of curiosity.

Both figures reached out and touched Felix's face now, with such tenderness, such acceptance of who he was and what he wanted from life, that there was no need to ask questions and figure out all the equations . . . *the old man's face was a dark leathery colour – perhaps not white after all – and criss-crossed with small scars, like from broken glass* . . . Felix simply took their hands and wrapped them round his neck, nestling in their arms, infused with their peacefulness. Even Charlie's war games grew dreamier – as the Special K took effect – and the helicopter began swaying from side to side, gently, like a cradle. Felix wanted this feeling to last. He pulled his new companions closer.

All your nearest and dearest, they seemed to be saying, without speaking aloud, repeating this phrase again and again. He wondered if they meant themselves or his small circle of friends. Their tone – unvoiced yet clear – was sometimes venerating, sometimes sorrowful.

All your nearest and dearest

Charlie's mobile rang. Before answering, he told himself, 'OK, hold it together, you're OK,' then managed to conduct a brief and relatively sober conversation. Switching off the phone, he said over his shoulder, 'Tha' was Bi Mirza at the farm. Th' old guy who came with you . . .'

'Oh, that's where he is.'

'Yeah. Uh . . . bit 'f bad news 'm afraid . . .'

'It's all right,' Felix answered steadily. 'I sort of half knew. Was it in his sleep?'

'Yeah, yeah, in 's sleep.' Charlie thought for a moment. 'Who was he?'

Felix stared at the back of his head, the said quietly, 'Tell you later.' He closed his eyes, thinking of Emile, testing the pain. It was tolerable, still tolerable. The old chap had fallen asleep listening to Felix's bedtime stories, the little nonsense stories of his own dreams, and then probably just drifted on. *Sleep well, my dear,* thought Felix, knowing that the figures on either side could hear. He looked at them. *That wasn't a bad way to go.*

They nodded sympathetically. It was strange. He couldn't say why, but their kindness alarmed him.

All your nearest and dearest

'Oh!' cried Charlie suddenly, tilting the helicopter and peering down, his face turning white. 'Oh, oh, Felix, buddy, oh, help me . . .'

Rushing forward, looking over Charlie's shoulder, Felix saw a perplexing image below. He couldn't work it out at all. What was this – this shadowy wooden surface? Viewed as from the steep slope of the theatre gods, Was it the stage? Dimly lit – during a power cut perhaps – just from the wings on one side. Were they back at the theatre? Had they somehow flown *into* the theatre? Was the heli-copter actually inside that vast domed space – hovering in the gilded sky of the auditorium? Felix frowned. If it wasn't the stage, what was it? . . . a wooden floor . . . serving as a kind of table-top . . . a group of animals feasting on it in their usual frenzied way – barely able to swallow fast enough, to eat and breathe at the same time – clambering, swarming over the little figure of Zikki . . .

But there was something wrong. The animals weren't big enough. He'd misjudged the scale. Now that Charlie was dipping the heli-copter, you could see that the animals were too small for lions . . . they were ridiculously small . . . they looked almost like bats . . .

Felix's head jerked back, as images and interpretations finally came together.

It was the sundeck of Charlie's mansion below . . . half lit in a spill from the house . . . the figure wasn't Zikki – you could only glimpse a corner of the little Monet frock, but it was enough – and the animals weren't lions. One of them had been saved by Felix, saved twice at Pembe Cove, saved for *this*. Turning to Charlie, he spoke in a hushed and dry voice. 'You promised she wasn't in danger from them.'

'She wasn't, she wasn't,' wept Charlie. 'Something must've happened, maybe like the lions at the – maybe in the craziness of the weekend – maybe someone just forgot to feed . . .'

Felix swung away from him. The old man and boy were gone. He stared at the space which they'd vacated. She had sat there . . . during the return journey from the farm, wearing a strange, wise look . . . an angel flying through the sky with him. He hugged himself. It was coming now. The pain he promised himself he'd never have, never know, a pain beyond belief. It filled and emptied him. 'Oh, little one,' he whispered, bending double, rocking himself, 'little one, little one, did you know how I loved you . . .?'

The helicopter lurched. Turning back, Felix found that Charlie had lifted his hands off the controls, to cover his head. Poor Charlie, he thought numbly, Charlie must be next. *All my nearest and dearest.* One by one they were going, snuffed out by a Greater Power. And Felix could see Him clearly now – God the Prankster, God the Devil. He was shaped like a mountain. No – it *was* a mountain! A mountain rushing out of the sky towards them. Felix gulped. He wished he'd asked the old man and boy if all his nearest and dearest included himself? But, as Emile might have said, the only one who can answer that question is You.

epilogue

It begins. Darkness, then light, then the flesh of people. They are stripped down to loincloths, the four men and women who will feature in today's event, their wrists and ankles are linked by thin, strong chains, and each is flanked by two guards.

Her nostrils are taut. The smell of the prisoners is spilling down towards her. Their sweat doesn't flow freshly, like the sweat of exercise; it comes from fear; it's bad before it hits the air.

The audience applauds the first sight of the group. Only a quick burst, almost token; they're saving their energy for what's to come.

She twists round to look behind. Her view is of the great tiers of the Alexandra Theatre's auditorium, gigantic slopes packed solid with spectators, inquisitive faces basking in the light from the stage, row after row of them, each mass perched at a giddy angle, each like an avalanche waiting to happen.

A sound brings her round. A large, very elderly man – he could be in his nineties – is tapping the microphone. He has a lazy air, both amiable and arrogant; it's a cowboy's swagger. As he begins reading the charges against the condemned, his accent reveals that he is not local, but from one of the southern African states. He lightens the solemnity of the occasion by adding a joke or two, and seems to regard his job as somewhere between official functionary and ringmaster. He wears some stage makeup, slightly smudged. The audience respond to him warmly; he is a character they know and love.

With the formal procedure over, the prisoners are led off,

waddling in their chains. The old man makes a reference to penguins. The audience laugh. The atmosphere is jittery. The stage stands empty for a moment, but bristling with promise. Drumming starts. Now a cage is lowered. The audience is silent to the point of breathlessness. They explode into life as the first prisoner runs into the space, his chains removed. He is quickly joined, but from the opposite wings, by the first beast, a male lion. Apparently a leopard is to appear today as well, paired with the youngest prisoner. Hyenas are sometimes used also, in pairs, and there's a pack of wild dogs available.

Alys is relieved *they* aren't on the bill today. She has childhood memories of these creatures – pleasant ones – and doesn't wish them spoiled.

As the first fight proceeds – they are called fights because just occasionally the human wins and is granted a reprieve – Alys recalls seeing the *corrida* in Spain. Here, as there, aspects of the ritual remain mysterious to her, while earning huge surges of approval or fury from the audience – they bare their teeth in shrill whistles and ululations, shake their fists in the air, hammer their heels in thunderous rolls of noise.

To her surprise, Alys grows restless quite soon. The reality simply can't live up to its reputation. These spectacles have made the international headlines for two decades now, and the controversy rages on, with new books being published – recent titles include *Civilisation and Cruelty*, and *The Hunger* – documentaries being filmed, debates on television and in places of government. With the exception of those regimes which already practise public execution, the worldwide condemnation has been on a formidable scale, yet the State President, John C. Guwedekko, remains defiant. He arrived on the scene as a rebel and is a rebel still. Never having delivered the promised elections, and still leading a one-party state, he claims the right to invent African solutions to African problems. There's been a drastic reduction of serious crime since this punishment was devised, while as a linked bonus, it had led to a new, soaring tourist industry. Foreigners fly in all the time; adventurous holidaymakers, groups representing animal rights, human rights, movie producers, historians, sociologists, sadists, theatre critics, all sorts of types.

By the third fight, Alys's sense of boredom supersedes all others. Lifting her hands, she discreetly stretches them towards the stage, fitting their silhouette into the picture before her. She remembers making the gesture once before, in this very theatre, long ago. Then it was to try to understand the strange, new magic on display, to grasp it. Today it is simply to remind herself that *she* is here, *she* is seeing this. When she flies home, it is the first thing people will ask, and she will reply, in her languid way, 'Yes, I went to one.' Their next question will be, '*And?*' This will be harder to answer. Her friends are not African. Even though she only spent her first five years here, it has left her with a different relationship to certain things. Gazing at the stage, she's only interested in those chance moments of dignity, even brotherhood, between the man and the animal.

She slips from her seat and exits. Her companion is forced to follow, even though he was enjoying the show. But as her body-guard and the family retainer, old Noah's place is at her side. He has waited for this visit for so long. Over the years she kept promising – but always cancelled at the last moment. The mansion above town is growing dilapidated, but he works hard to staunch the decay, all on his own, and never more so than over the last few weeks, in preparation for today.

This is where they drive now, her luggage from the Swissair flight still in the back of the jeep. At the airport she asked to go straight to the theatre, rather than home – the home she still owns. He was surprised, but she explained that since this afternoon's spectacle was the only one scheduled during her stay, she didn't want to miss it. She puzzles him altogether. He can glimpse a physical resemblance to both her parents – the delicate bones of the one, the blonde curls of the other – but she seems not to have inherited their easy natures. Without meaning to, she sets her features in an expression of sad disdain, a kind of scowl, holding you off.

As they approach the mansion, she suddenly says, 'No. Please go past.'

When the building comes back into view, on a bend of the coast road, all you can see is the sundeck jutting from the cliff edge. She turns away sharply. It is the place she most dreads revisiting. It was from there that she watched the helicopter crash sixteen years ago. She had been playing a favourite game with her cushion-dolls, the Scarecrows, dressing them in her clothes, when her litter of wild-dog pups captured one, and began tearing it to shreds on the sundeck. Calling for help from the servants, she heard her father returning. Then something went wrong. By the time she ran outside, he had lost control of the aircraft.

The accident occurred high on the thickly forested slopes of the Kwatokuu, and rescue work was impossible. The bodies were never recovered; neither her father's, nor that of the other man – the direc- tor of the Alex, apparently, when it was a more conventional playhouse. She remembers him quite well – he had glowering black looks, yet was always kind to her.

After the tragedy, she was taken abroad, fostered and educated in Switzerland, where her father had stockpiled part of his fortune in case they ever had to flee Africa.

She stays silent as they drive. In the absence of instructions, Noah makes for Pembe Cove, the white beach with a lush surround of bush and trees.

It looks vaguely familiar to Alys. She doesn't question Noah, doesn't want to know the details of any childhood visits. It's enough that she feels more peaceful here. At least the sky is blue, the air fresh and clear. That sticky grey-green cloud over town . . . it brings sensations of fever; you feel half awake, half asleep, you doubt your perception of things.

The place looks deserted. Leaving Noah, Alys descends the dune- like slope to the beach. Now she sees that there is one other person present: an old man sitting in the shade of a small bamboo-and- reed shelter. She can see only his back – so sunbaked that it's difficult to define his race – and long yellow-white hair. From the evidence of a meagre scattering of belongings, it looks like he lives here. A local hermit, she decides. He shows no interest in her, per- haps hasn't even noticed her arrival. Or else he's learned to keep to himself, learned that so long as he doesn't trouble people, they won't trouble him.

Alys makes her way over the sand, enjoying the way that each step sinks away, deeply, warmly, and then, with imperceptible delicacy, the surface hardens underfoot, gently, crisply, as you near the ocean.

The hermit is also moving towards the water. He crosses the beach on his hands and rump . . . his legs, she now realises, are just stumps. These leave brushed trails on the sand, as if from a sea-turtle's wings. His difficult progress is made more strenuous by the fact that he seems to be engaged in helping someone else: an invisible presence at his side. He caresses the space here constantly, chatters to it, hears replies, gives smiles and nods. Whoever he's seeing, it's clearly an inseparable companion; a shadow, a child-sized shadow. Alys pictures the old man asleep, still embracing this precious shape.

Reaching the shoreline, he struggles with the small buffeting waves, a task again made harder by his preoccupation with his part-ner's safety. Alys wishes he'd turn round. There's something familiar about his attentiveness, his whispering and fussing; this is familiar in a way that is both vague and intense. She tries to make sense of it, this resemblance to . . . who? Her senses ache from things she can't unravel.

Perhaps everything will become clearer when she summons the courage to enter the mansion above town, but so far she lacks infor-mation and evidence about her early years; the stories, photographs and knick-knacks that normally accompany your growth, displayed by adults from time to time like conjuring tricks, unlocking the dream of childhood, decoding and authenticating that mysterious passage of time, the time when even your memory was soft, unformed.

Alys quickens her step through the sand. She can't say why but it's somehow important to see the old man's face before he plunges through the shoreline waves. She's too late – he's already in the shoal beyond, and now, infused with new dexterity, starts flipping and diving, rejoicing in the warm, glittering, salty freshness around him. Turn towards me, she says in her mind – turn. Still he doesn't. Chatting all the time to the phantom at his side, splashing and play-ing, he makes for a stretch further off, where the depths turn turquoise. Alys frowns. Someone once told her – who was it? – that sea water is the most glorious of the elements, because when you bathe in it, you are connected to every ocean on the planet. The notion strikes Alys as both peaceful and heroic, things that conflict in her mind. But to watch the old chap's pleasure in his afternoon swim is to believe that he's achieved everything he wanted. She envies him. Her own life feels so complicated; it follows loops that seem dangerous one moment, absurd the next; for most of the time it puts a flutter in her belly.

Suddenly he turns. He turns towards the beach. He spots her at last. They're too far apart for her to read his expression – or even clearly discern his features – but he's gone still. They both stay poised. She half lifts one arm, wondering whether to wave, maybe even beckon. She delays too long, and now, with an odd tilt of his head, he resumes his swim. Reaching out as she did at the theatre, Alys puts her hand alongside his distant figure. She wonders why her fingers are trembling.

'Your imagination!' she scolds, in a tiny private voice, a voice from her missing childhood. Then, talking softly, she walks back across the beach.